NORTH EAST of SCOTLAND LIBRARY SERVICE
14 Crown Terrace, Aberdeen

The Heritors

The Heritors

Agnes Short

Constable London

First published in Great Britain 1977
by Constable and Company Ltd
10 Orange Street London WC2H 7EG
Copyright © Agnes Short 1977

ISBN 0 09 461610 8

Set in Intertype Garamond
Printed in Great Britain by The Anchor Press Ltd
and bound by Wm Brendon & Son Ltd
both of Tiptree, Essex

For the present indwellers of the Old Town
and particularly those of Chaplains Court.

The details of Burgh and Session meetings are taken from the *Records of Old Aberdeen I and II* printed for the New Spalding Club by the Aberdeen University Press. I found my characters in the same records: all of them lived in the Old Town at the time of my story and only the Edinburgh group are imaginary. In a few cases I have given names to the nameless: William Montgomery's 'wife', Christian Grant's mother and the many children of the Gardens, Middletons and Baxters. Where the facts are available, I have incorporated them into the lives of the heritors: where they are not, I have supplied them.

William Montgomery, mason, was banished from Old Aberdeen on 5 March 1705 for the second time, after signing an undertaking never to molest or trouble the Sledder family again.

Margery Montgomery, wife of George Cumming, is a name on a tombstone in St Machar's churchyard.

George Cumming is one of the many generations of Cummings – blacksmiths and wrights – who gave their name to Cumming's Wynd.

Adam Urquhart, son of the Mediciner, is an item in the Session accounts for 1705, 'buried in the Cheyne aisle, £6.13.4.'

Christian Grant appears in the Council Minutes for 1720, banished for 'habitually recepting and haunting scandalous persones'.

The College officers and their affairs are as authentic as my sources allow, and the falling of the great tower is described as I found it recorded in William Orem's *Description of Old Aberdeen in the years 1724 and 1725.*

Various places in the Old Town are marked on the map on page 9. Douglas Wynd exists to this day, though Cumming's Wynd and Widow Irvine's Close have long disappeared.

A 'wynd' is a lane or narrow alley: a 'close' is the same, or, as in this case, a blind alley.

Kale was the traditional name for the broth which, with oatmeal, was a staple part of the Scotsman's diet. At its best, kale con-

tained meat and the green vegetable from which it took its name:
at its worst, it could be merely groats and water.

The meaning of the other Scots terms will, I hope, be clear to
the reader through the context in which they appear. They have
been retained as essential to the flavour of Scottish life at the time.

The map is reproduced from Parson Gordon's map of New and
Old Aberdeen, 1661.

ABREDONIA VETUS
The Old towne of Aberdone

The Loch of Old Aberdeen

1. Widow Irvine's Close
2. Chaplains' Court
3. Chaplains' Port
4. Cluny's Port
5. Market Cross
6. Cumming's Forge
7. Douglas Wynd
8. The Chanonry
9. St Machar's Cathedral
10. Principal's House
11. Musician's House
12. Alexander Fraser's houses
13. Mediciner's House
14. Powis Bridge
15. The Spital

Part 1
1688–1689

I

'Highlandmen!'

The cry screamed its warning down the Spital past the weavers'
cottages and the Humanist's house and the ruins of the Snow
Kirk, past the little bridge where the burn crossed the High Street,
past Bartlett's Wynd and College Wynd and Baillie Baxter's tenements to the gates of the Chanonry itself.

The women treading the tubs of clothes, with their skirts looped
up around their waists and their bare legs glistening, broke
instantly into confusion. On the banks of the Powis burn where it
crossed the meadowland from Broome Hill, fires were dowsed or
scattered, sodden linen bundled hastily together, children shooed
and smacked and scooped into frightened arms, tubs spilt or left
full where they stood.

The length of the cobbled High Street doors and windows
slammed, bars fell into place, animals squealed and scurried under
beating sticks into the safety of dwelling-house or byre. The men
in the fields driving the ploughs for the spring planting made for
home if they could; if not, they armed themselves with pikes and
staves and grouped together in attitudes of wary defence. And the
women ran, their skirts still bundled high, their plaids flying, their
children screaming at their sides.

Janet Christie, wife of William Montgomery the mason, found
herself jostled aside as the women fought to gain their homes in
safety before the soldiers reached the town. Someone buffeted her
back, knocking her to her knees against the dyke of the Mediciner's
house and striking the breath from her chest. Someone else trod on
her belly as she lay. She was trying feebly to struggle to her feet
when she saw the full-breasted, leaping figure of Isobel Sledder
bearing down upon her. The woman's bare brown legs exulted
over the turf towards where Janet lay, until, glint-eyed, she leapt
deliberately over Janet's cringing body. Spread legs, hair, the unwashed stench of female loins and a derisive crow of laughter as
the woman bounded away. Janet rolled on to her side and retched
into the grass. The horror filled and held her in draining, terrified

disgust. The Sledder woman was evil: she had spread her evil first over William and now over Janet and their child. There could be no escape.

A cow lumbered, lowing, past. Chickens scattered, squawking. The turf shook with the weight of running feet. Beyond the dyke of Dr Urquhart's house the street was empty. Even the cows had gone, driven hastily into byres and sheds and dwelling-houses and locked inside. There was silence now, but for the steady breathing of the wind in the trees beside the College and the song of a blackbird somewhere close at hand.

And, coming down the Spital, the thud of feet.

'Get up, Janet! Get up!'

Someone was shaking and dragging at her with small, agitated hands.

'The Highlandmen are coming! Get up!'

Janet looked up into Christian Grant's anxious, nine-year-old face and fought against the dizziness which rocked her body to the very centre of her womb.

'Get up! They'll kill us if they find us. And rape us first.'

Janet obeyed the urgency in the child's voice, though the sense of the words escaped her. Somehow she regained her feet and, with the girl tugging at her hand, managed to stagger lumbering and swaying with the weight of her belly towards where the burn crossed the causeway at the bridge.

There was a whoop from the hill to their right and Janet saw a rabble of a dozen unkempt men. One of them had a claymore, another a firelock, others pikes and staves.

'Whores!' came a drunken cry. 'Charge!'

The men broke into a lumbering run down the Spital towards them, roaring obscenities and lust.

'Bastards!' screamed Christian, facing them in brief defiance. Then the child dropped Janet's hand and took to her heels. In a moment she had turned the corner into Widow Irvine's Close and vanished up the forestair to the upper tenement and the slamming safety of her mother's barred door.

There was no one in the length of the town but Janet and the approaching men. On either side of her stretched houses; she knew they held people who could help her, but the doors and windows were barred and would not open to her frantic knocking. There was no escape. Yet she staggered on, clasping her hands across her swollen belly for support as every breath seemed to rip her apart.

Past King's College where the chestnut trees were newly breaking into bud, past the squat square building of the song school and the Musician's house, and on towards the dyke at Bartlett's Wynd where a froth of appleblossom topped the stone. The wind had freshened till the white petals blew like snow across the sky. There was only one more house to pass before she reached the Close and home . . . then she caught her bare foot against a sett and staggered.

'She's winged! We have her!'

Without warning Janet's knees buckled. She sank against the wall of the house and sobbed, raspingly now as each breath tore her body and the men grew closer until she could see the leering, cruel grin of the leader, his filthy, bloodstained plaid and broken teeth.

'Help me, someone!' she screamed. 'Dear God, help me!'

William Montgomery, mason, made his way along the battaline, under the slates of the toofall towards the bell-tower of the great steeple. The two lesser steeples at the western end of St Machar's Cathedral were each one hundred and thirteen feet high from the base to the top of the stang, but Bishop Elphinstone's great four-square structure at the eastern end towered effortlessly above the lesser and dwarfed them. William Montgomery was a big man with the neck and shoulders of an ox, yet he felt its awesome, dominating power as he reached the end of the passageway eighty feet above the nave and opened the wooden door into the tower itself.

The vast, square hollow had a ladder leading upward to a little four-cornered chamber and the bells: Michael Burgerhuyes' bell, the largest, and the new bell, made only two years ago by George Kilgour expressly to be tolled for Sabbaths, solemn meetings and funerals. Above the bells the tower rose so high that it had become a landmark for sailors: it had a stang five ells in length with a cross and a great globe of brass and, above the second cross a brass cock an ell long. Montgomery had seen the dawning sun strike red from the cock's copper breast as he made his way to work that morning in the crisp and windy sunlight.

'How is it?'

The master mason's voice came trailing from far below, clinging to the stone walls and echoing hollowly overhead.

15

'Steady enough,' called Montgomery, but his eyes were troubled and his big-boned frame moved uneasily on the narrow platform. The wind which had been fresh at dawn was strengthening hourly. It gusted through the structure, howling, moaned in the bell-chamber overhead and set the bell-ropes swaying. Montgomery felt the stone quiver under his hand and remembered Alexander Crystal's warnings and Kenneth Fraser's scornful reply.

'The tower has stood well enough for two hundred years. Should it fall just because some interfering hammerman fancies he sees a crack?'

Nevertheless there was a crack – a great slanting gully running from the base almost to the platform where Montgomery stood. The mason moved uneasily towards the ladder, keeping close to the wall and avoiding the centre where an oval vacuity allowed the bell-ropes to pass down to the church floor so that Gauld the beadle could summon the heritors to sermon. A year ago the King's mason had sighted the tower and declared it in need of buttressing. Kenneth Fraser, master mason, had been employed to undertake the work and had hired other masons to help him. William Montgomery was one of them, but he had not been happy since he joined the team at the church. The work was disquieting, though he had not been able to say why. Now, with Crystal's warning fresh in his head, he understood, but the knowledge did not clear his deeper misery. Nothing could do that, except a son. At the thought of his unborn child the man's face brightened. The child would be a boy and strong. He would grow to show the whole Burgh that William Montgomery was as good as his brother – and as good as any heritor in the town. The Sledder woman would know, then, what she had lost.

A bitter blast buffeted his chest as he passed one of the narrow window embrasures which studded the tower at its height. William Montgomery stooped to look outwards and down along the spread echelon of the old town. To the east were the dunes of marram grass, known as Bentihillocks, the Bailiff's Bog and the Links, with the long fringe of sandy shore between the land and the grey German sea. To the west, the hills of Midstocket and Forester, rich in the season with game, and the blue sweep of the Don river. He and his son would fish there together, for the salmon. Immediately beneath and to the south, the tree-studded seclusion of the Chanonry with its dykes and entrance ports, its hospital for old men and its one-time manses, some in lay hands, some in ruins, and beyond Cluny's Port the long shaft of the street. The Royal Burgh would be busy now: there would be cattle in the pastures, men steering the plough, pigs, hens, dogs, women at the burnside washing, children playing in the street. Somewhere, she would be moving about her business, mocking . . . Then his eyes reached the Spital and what he saw sent the warning booming through the bell-tower.

'Highlandmen!'

Small enough at that distance, but there could be no mistaking the grouped black specks or the menace in their progress down the centre of the street.

But already the tiny figures of the indwellers had scattered briefly to flow again in a broken river along the High Street until, in a matter of seconds it seemed to the watcher in the tower, the long double row of houses had sucked the river dry.

Almost dry.

There was one figure left in the long cobbled causeway. The mason could not see who it was. Pray God it was not Janet and his unborn child! He cast about the tower for some way to descend quickly but there were only the bell-ropes, far out of reach in the centre hollow. It would be ten minutes before he reached the place! He turned and thrust his way back through the door to the battaline, bounded the length of the rafters high above the cathedral nave to the south steeple and leapt the stairway, three at a time, to the ground.

'Oh God, help me!'

The first man was not twenty yards away now and breathing heavily. She could smell the foul ale on his breath and the hand which reached towards her was scored with filth. She pressed back against the wall of the house whimpering . . . The plaid which had covered her shoulders fell open to show the blue drugget material stretched tight across her swollen breasts and the hard dome of her belly. The man's step faltered and he swore.

'Look at the belly on her! She's with child, goddamme!'

'She's a woman,' growled another, pushing him aside, 'and young enough. She'll do.'

With the last strength of terror Janet turned and ran, past closed shutters to a door at the end of the wall. She fell against it screaming and beating wildly with her fists as the men roared after her.

But the door opened. There was the flash of light on steel as hands pulled her roughly inside. The door slammed again and she was thrust aside as someone heaved against the timber to hold it firm while someone else dropped the crossbar into place. Firelight. Safety. The comfort of many crowded people. Janet sank to the floor against the wall and closed her eyes.

'Are you all right?' asked someone, a lady, anxiously. Janet nodded without opening her eyes. 'Are you sure the door is barred, George? And the window?'

Janet heard the crash of another beam falling into place across the door and let relief engulf her. There was silence now and the beat of waiting hearts. Then came the voices, deep, harsh, male voices shouting and laughing. There was the noise of heavy feet, thudding fists against barred doors, oaths, the clash of steel. Then from somewhere close at hand the terrified cackle of chickens, more laughter and a whoop of triumph. Someone crashed a fist against the shutter with an obscene invitation. Then the voices passed on and faded gradually into the distance.

The people in the room began to move, murmuring together, reassuring. A child whispered, another demanded loudly, 'Have they gone?' A handsome man of forty-three in a grey coat with a white lace collar, grey breeches, and a full brown wig, took the musket firmly in his hand and opened the door.

'Bar it after me, my dear,' he said. 'I will find out if all is well.'

Janet saw there were five or six children in the room, and two servants, one a girl, one a big woman of thirty or more with black hair and a red face. There was also another woman with a baby in her arms. This woman turned to her.

'You look pale, my dear. Are you sure you are all right? You must take care when your time is near. Isobel, fetch my smelling salts and the phial from my chest. You are Janet Christie, aren't you? Montgomery the mason's wife? I remember when you worked at the Bishop's. I believe you were a very satisfactory girl. I wish there were more like you.' This last with a reproving look in the youngest servant's direction.

'Yes, ma'am.' Janet had recovered enough to feel awed at the realization that she was in Principal Middleton's house and that it must have been the Principal himself who had saved her. 'Thank you, ma'am.' Dutifully she drank the draught which Mrs Middleton prepared for her and as the mixture steadied and strengthened her, she stood up to go.

'No, Janet. You cannot leave until Dr Middleton returns to tell us all is well. Sit there at the fire and rest awhile. Then you can help Margrat to mix the bannocks. Isobel, do not sit idle. The shirt is already cut out. I shall expect it to be sewn by midday and see your plain seam is neat and true. James, attend to your slate. Now, George Cumming' (this to a barefoot, brown-skinned boy of eleven) 'why were you running about the streets instead of working in school? Your father sent you there, I'll be bound.'

'Yes, Mrs Middleton.'

The boy was tall for his age, well-set though thin enough to show the ribs through the homespun shirt. His hair was light brown, bleached pale on the top where the sun caught it, and his eyes were green with a mischievous glint to them even now, in the sober business of apology.

'I am sorry, ma'am.' He cast his eyes downwards, briefly, in submission, then looked swiftly up again, grinning. 'But Mr Couper only knows the Rudiments and the Rule of Three and I mastered them both long ago.'

'It is not for you to criticize,' began Mrs Middleton sharply then, in spite of herself, she laughed. There was something about the boy's cheerful honesty which was irresistible. 'What were you doing instead, may I ask?'

'Rabbiting – only the invaders came and I thought that Elspeth . . .' He stopped too late and Mrs Middleton frowned, but before she could speak, Elspeth scrambled to his defence.

'He saved me, Mama. One of the hens had been laying astray and I was searching for the eggs when I heard the shouting. I was so frightened, but George came and . . .'

'Very well,' interrupted her mother. 'We'll say no more about it this time. But as you are here, George, you may make yourself useful. I cannot abide idleness. The fire needs more peat. After that, as you are so accomplished a scholar as to need no further schooling, you may read to us from the Bible. Elspeth, stop staring and see to your spinning and Margrat, look to the kale before it burns dry. Then there is your father's breakfast to prepare. He will be ready for it when he returns.'

Janet was startled. She had served William his breakfast of ale and broze three hours ago.

'Jean Catto!' Mrs Middleton said sharply to the big woman with the red face, 'get back to your work at once, and as for you, you lazy baggage,' this to the girl, 'if I see you idle again you'll leave this Whitsun and without a character. The idle servant is a sure temptation to the devil.' Mrs Middleton herself opened her gown and began to suckle the baby, while the other children meekly resumed their various occupations.

Isobel, a child of fourteen, took up the homespun linen and bent close over the first seam of what would be her brother George's shirt. George was sixteen and a student at the university though now, as it was vacation, he was on an extended visit to a cousin in Edinburgh. Nine-year-old Elspeth took up the distaff and soon the rhythmic whirr of the spindle filled the room. Little James crouched laboriously over the unformed letters on his slate while one of the servant-girls took up the candlestick she had been polishing and began to rub it vigorously with brick dust and spittle. The other took a huge ladle and tended the pot which hung over the great open fire at one end of the room, while George Cumming fetched fresh peat from a store-room which opened out of the kitchen. Janet took the wooden bowl which Margrat offered her and obediently handed meal and water into it to prepare the bannocks. Margrat, the ten-year-old, watched carefully and when it was time shaped the mixture into flat cakes and set them on the hearthstone to bake. When the work was done, Janet sat on a stool at the fire to watch over them and to look about her while she awaited the master's return so that she might leave.

It was a large, low-ceilinged room with a polished wooden floor and a refectory table of scrubbed deal on which were the wooden platters and spoons the family would use for breakfast, beside a basket of newly gathered eggs and a great pail of milk. There were two wooden benches, and at the head of the table, the master's chair. There were books on a shelf along one wall. Janet could not read the titles, but she knew that they were Latin, like the words which her husband William cut into the gravestones in the church. There was a mirror, too, and a Bible, open on the table. George Cumming had just picked it up to read a passage from it, as instructed, when there was a heavy double knock on the door.

'There is the master!' cried his wife. 'Open the door!'

George Middleton replaced the musket in the rack above the hearth, smiled as his children crowded round him, squealing and demanding. He looked above their heads to where his wife stood anxiously in the background, the baby sleeping now on her shoulder.

'It is all right, my dear. They have gone. I met Alexander

Crystal and a few of the men. It seems they sent them packing over the Brig and northwards, with no more damage than a broken window-pane, three of Widow Irvine's chickens and a keg of brandy – Baillie Baxter's and he can spare it.'

'Who were they? Papists?'

'Riff-raff from the New Town, owing allegiance to no one but themselves. But I am afraid there will be more of them. There's unrest in the air. Presbyterians, Papists, Loyalists, Williamites, everything at sixes and sevens and everywhere the excuse for looting and disorder. There are even people who would defy the Bishop's court! I shall speak to the Bishop tonight. A town guard might not be inappropriate if things go on as they promise to do, especially with the news from London so uncertain.'

'Will they really send for that Dutch William, Papa?' asked Isobel earnestly. She was a solemn-faced child, with dark, intelligent eyes.

'Isobel!' said her mother sharply. 'Do not speak until you are spoken to.'

'No matter, my dear. The child asks an intelligent question and shall be answered. Who knows, Isobel, what the English will do? But we in Scotland must not forget our sovereignty. After all, James may be a Papist but he is, nevertheless, a Stuart.'

'Please, sir, my father says John Graham of Claverhouse will never bow the knee to that Dutchman. If he gathers men, I hope he'll take me.' George Cumming squared his chest with all the arrogance his years could muster.

'George Cumming!' snapped Jean Catto, swinging the ladle at his head. 'And who asked you to speak? I don't know what boys are coming to, speaking to their elders and betters without so much as a by your leave!' She swung the ladle again, but George dodged nimbly out of reach.

Dr Middleton smiled, though briefly, before he said, 'Dundee is a man of courage and integrity. He did splendid work against the Covenanters, and I have no doubt that if his conscience decrees it so, he will fight again for the true king and the Established church. But you are a mere boy. What have you to offer any cause but an unformed body, an untrained spirit and an untaught mind? You must stop playing truant, keep to your lessons and learn all you can. You must serve your apprenticeship until you are as good a blacksmith as your father and your grandfather before him. Then perhaps you will be worthy to serve so great a man.'

'Yes, sir.' The boy lowered his eyes meekly but the excitement remained, and when Elspeth left her spinning to move to his side and put a comforting arm around him, he turned towards her eagerly. As she watched them together, the boy whispering earnestly and the girl listening with wide, adoring eyes, Janet Christie felt a pang of sadness which held more than a little jealousy. She stood up and moved to the door.

'If you will excuse me,' she said, 'I will go now.' There was her precious linen and her tub to retrieve from beside the burn and her husband's kale to prepare. 'Thank you, sir.'

'God bless you,' said George Middleton kindly. 'A good girl, I believe,' he said to his wife when Janet had gone. 'I remember when her father died. He was a worthy man and an expert weaver, though he left her little enough. But she has worked hard and stayed honest. I trust her husband is kind to her.'

Janet found the door of her house open, the chair overturned and ale spilt on the floor, but no worse damage. They had looked to see what they could find, found nothing and moved on. Carefully she began to put the house to rights. She was sweeping the dirt floor with a besom of heather twigs when he came, stooping low under the doorway and blocking out the light. He took her shoulders and looked intently at her: her white face, her breasts, the hard mound of her belly.

'Are you all right? I came as soon as I could.'

'But the work . . .'

'Fraser sent us all home. I am to go back directly if all is well.' His eyes moved over the dimness of the room and back to her face. 'Did they come inside?'

'Yes, but I was not here. I was at the burn, washing, and Dr Middleton took me in.'

The tension left him in relief. He took the besom from her hand and said roughly, 'I'll finish that.'

'But it's woman's work. I can manage . . .'

'I said I'll finish it. You look ill. Lie down.'

William Montgomery strove to keep the irritation from his voice. He had married Janet Christie, as the whole town guessed, for his unborn children's sake. As he looked at the swollen figure on the pallet a sudden, treacherous pain gripped his loins: the bile of humiliation welled in his throat at the memory of that other, bold-bodied, low-laughing, brown woman who had taken him, exalted him, left him drained and worshipping. And thrown him away. For that stiff-necked merchant Sledder with his grey, pock-marked jowls, his puny codpiece and his long, thin shanks. And, of course, his money.

'You're sure you're all right?' he repeated tautly when the floor was clean. When she nodded, he directed his frustration at the struggling fire. Before she left that morning, Janet had turned the peats to keep the fire in, but when he turned them back now he found only smoke and crumbling turfs. The peats would not burn and the smoke stung his eyes. He took more from the stack against the wall. He had cut the peats himself from the common moss with the other indwellers in October last, but he knew, as he had known then, that his march was a poor one. Everything he had was second-rate. It had been the same all his life. His brother John was small, dark and lithe, whereas William was blond and twice his size, but it was John who always prospered, John who excelled in all he did, John who found friends, wealth and position. John's word was listened to and respected, William's always shrugged aside. Three years ago they had made John an honorary burgess of Old Aberdeen on account of that monument to Bishop Scougal which he had put up in the south aisle of the Cathedral – and what had William got from it? Nothing. And he had worked alongside his brother, hewing and shaping every bit as skilfully as John. John Montgomery, they said, was a master mason. His younger brother merely helped. But let them wait. His son would show them. He kicked the crumbling brick of heather roots and humus and coughed as the smoke billowed up into his face. The water in the great iron pot was barely simmering.

'Mind and open the window, Janet, if the fire smokes.'

There was a timber half-leaf in the bottom part of the window, with a small glass pane above. The timber kept out the light, but also the cold. 'But take care. The wind is high today.'

Janet did not answer. She lay bloated and breathing shallow, mouth open, on the straw of the bed.

'Like a landed fish.' Her husband put the thought quickly behind him. The bed had been made by the local carpenter against their wedding eight months ago, four straight wooden posts bound together by narrow side pieces which bore the wooden base. The linen which covered it was homespun and the straw Janet had gathered and strewed herself. They would need more for the lying-in.

In one corner of the room was the linen press which contained William's and Janet's wedding clothes and the single set of fine sheets, the tablecloth and napkins for which Janet herself had spun the yarn. There was the wooden barrel which held the oatmeal, still a quarter full in spite of the long winter, and, beside the hearth, the salt cruse. A pot-shelf, a table and bench, Janet's spinning wheel and three-legged stool, and William's chair made up the rest. On the ceiling hooks hung a few shreds of dried meat, black and leathery after a winter above the peat fire, and the salt-fish barrel was not quite empty. There were sufficient peats, too, against the far wall. William Montgomery nodded in satisfaction. His home was well plenished.

His eyes roved over the small dark room checking whether there was more he should do before he left her. She seemed well, but he must take no risks: his unborn son must not be harmed. The room was square with narrow windows, one on each side of the door, bare stone walls and an earthen floor. Overhead were solid rafters across which stretched the planks which formed the floor of the tenement above. The hard-packed earth of the floor, Montgomery noted with satisfaction, was dry enough in spite of last week's rain. The turfs he had laid between door and fireplace and stamped flat into the mud had baked hard in the warmth of the room. They should hold yet awhile. His mother, he remembered, in their cottage in Rayne, had strewed her floor with bent grass. When summer came and the babe was growing, he would send Janet over to Bentihillocks to cut the bent for his own hearth. They would have a kale yard then, and hens. Perhaps even a cow, by and by, for fresh milk for his sons.

Montgomery stepped outside, avoiding the heaped refuse at the door, and cocked a head towards the tenement above. Steps led up the outside of the building to the room where the Grant woman lived with her brood.

'Christian!'

A girl appeared on the steps overhead. With one brown hand she scraped the hair from her eyes while the other thrust under the ragged homespun skirt and vigorously scratched her buttock. Brown hair tumbled thick and matted about her face, but the bare legs were firm and agile and, in spite of her childishness there was something about the unformed roundness of her hips and the boldness of her clear eyes which proclaimed her already a true daughter of her mother.

'Here's a penny,' said Montgomery, tossing her a coin. 'Fetch me ale from the brew house and I'll give you a sup yourself.'

'I'll take more than a sup from you one day,' retorted the child with a deliberate flick of the hip. 'If you've got it to give.'

As he lunged good-humouredly to cuff her ears she skipped nimbly aside and ran.

'Ask Isobel Johnston what he's got,' cried her mother gleefully from the room overhead. Montgomery strode back inside his house and slammed the door on their laughter. There was a small gasp from the bed. He was at her side in a flash.

'Is it the bairn?'

She shook her head. 'You startled me, that's all.'

She heaved herself slowly off the bed and stood up, moved carefully across the room towards the hearth.

Montgomery felt disappointment as sharp as the ice on the morning pail. And then relief. For after all it was too soon. But he had waited a long time for his son and the waiting was grown hard beyond endurance. Now he watched his wife as a hunter might watch a hare. When she stumbled on the uneven floor anger split his head into fire.

'Take care, woman! That's my son you carry. I will not have my child born halt or maimed for the town to mock me. They mock me enough as it is.' But he spoke the last to himself alone. His wife was not to know his shame under the barbed tongue of Isobel Johnston, John Sledder's wife, who had put it about with gleeful malice that the stonemason, big though he was, had not the tool to spawn a tadpole on a breeding frog.

The thought of frogs brought sudden sweat to his palms. Suppose the woman were to charm him? Or his child in Janet's womb? At that moment the door burst open to let in Christian Grant and the spilling luggie of ale. Montgomery seized it eagerly and drank till the pale foam flecked his lips and his fear was drowned. Then he handed the flagon to Janet.

'Here. It will give you strength. But mind and leave some for the quine.'

'Never mind me,' said Christian cheerfully. 'You take it, Janet. She fell, you know,' the child explained to Montgomery, 'and the Sledder woman jumped on her. Are you all right now?'

Janet nodded, but her eyes were on her husband. He had gone

white and then a fierce, burning red, and the great fists clenched and opened. 'If she has harmed my child . . .' The words were spoken so low that Janet had to strain to hear them, but before she could answer he turned for the door, saying only, 'I'll be back for dinner at twelve.'

Janet looked at him with dumb yearning. 'Not sooner?'

'There is work to be done. And the Bishop himself is coming to view the buttressing.'

'Is it true what Alexander Crystal says?' interrupted the Grant child. 'Is the great tower to fall?'

'Alexander Crystal is a wright, not a mason,' said Montgomery carefully. But he and Crystal had spoken together nevertheless and what they had decided must be told to the Bishop.

'He is a burgess,' began his wife timidly, 'and well thought of. He was a member of the Session, too.'

'Until he took matters into his own hands and nailed up the tradesmen's lofts. I doubt the Minister and Session will forgive him that, although he is an honest man and knows what he is about.'

'Kenneth Fraser does not think so,' said Christian pertly.

There was a call from beyond the Close.

'There's Fraser now,' said Montgomery. 'Mind, Janet, and send if you need me. There'll be a penny for you, Christian, if you stay within call. See you fetch the midwife for her if she tells you.'

'But there is another month yet,' said his wife. 'There is no need.'

'Hear what I say! And you, Christian.'

'I will. But my Ma can bring a child into the world as well as any midwife.'

'You will fetch the midwife,' said Montgomery firmly. 'I will have no risks taken with my son.'

Janet Christie watched the huge blond figure stride across the Close until he turned the corner by Baillie Baxter's tenement and was gone. He did not look back. If only she knew how to make him love her as she loved him. As she had always loved him, ever since the day he came to the town four years ago, to work on the Bishop's monument with his brother. She had been fifteen then, small and slight as she was now, and she had seen him swing a hammer in the churchyard, breaking stone. William Montgomery was a head taller than any man in the town but there was the grace of perfect proportion about him. His hair was burnished gold and

26

thick, and when he swung the hammer it was as though hammer and arm were one. Janet, the pale-skinned, dark-haired, solemn-eyed daughter of her father's old age, had watched him with the same dumb yearning as filled her eyes now. It was a look which Montgomery found irritating, but which she could not help.

She had not been able to help it four years ago when she had first watched him in the churchyard and he ignored her; nor three years ago when the whole town knew what he and Isobel Johnston did together on the night of St Luke's fair and when they paid three dollars to the Treasurer of the Session as penalty and consignation money for their wedding. Nor two years ago when the woman refused him, paid the fine for resiling from her purpose and wedded merchant Sledder instead. She had been there, waiting, when Montgomery had ranged the town for a new mate, driven by God knew what anguish behind his simple strength. He was a slow man, not clever except at the work of his hands, but sensitive to slight and with the uneasiness of someone who feels he might be at a disadvantage he does not understand. Janet's intelligent eyes had seen the vulnerability behind the strength and had loved him the more. But even now she did not know why he had married her. She knew his heart to be a stranger.

'I am here, aren't I!' he said roughly on the one occasion when she had dared to ask him if he loved her. Now, after eight months of marriage she knew she was no closer to him. 'Oh God,' she prayed with sudden desperation. 'Let the child be a boy.' Then at least he would stay.

George Haliburton, Episcopal Bishop of St Machar's, read over the letter in his hand and frowned. Then he read it again, more slowly now, and his face set in its habitual expression of troubled sadness while he prayed silently for strength and guidance.

William Montgomery, passing along the Chanonry from Cluny's Port, looked up at the house and saw the imposing, white-haired figure seated motionless in the window. He wore a black skullcap over flowing, silken hair, and the loose homespun robes which he always wore inside the house in the morning. Montgomery lengthened his already mighty stride and hurried on to the eastern end of the churchyard where the great four-square tower with its two flanking aisles rose high into the May morning. The air was cold and crisp with a gusting wind and he could see every line of stone against the brilliant sky. He could also hear the tell-tale chink of a hammer. Fraser was there before him and would be ready with a reproof. The usual slow frustration welled inside him when he thought of Fraser. Montgomery knew himself to be a better mason. Perhaps Fraser knew it too, for he lost no opportunity to keep Montgomery in his place. Nevertheless, when the Bishop came to inspect the progress of the work, Montgomery would say what must be said.

But the Bishop had forgotten the business of the tower. The letter in his hand was from friends in London and the news it brought confirmed all the growing fears of the latter months. If the royal child whose birth was expected in June should prove to be a son, his informant wrote, then rebellion would be inevitable. The Bishop knew that, remote though Aberdeen might seem to the potentates of London, their Revolution would topple him and his as inevitably as a high wind strips the apples from a tree.

George Haliburton was a man of fifty, though he looked older. He had started ecclesiastical life as minister of Coupar in Angus from where he had moved to the bishopric of Brechin ten years ago. Translated from Brechin to Old Machar in 1682, he had held the seat now for a mere six years. The Bishop sighed, remembering his four surviving children. One of them, John, had only recently become Civilist at the King's College. If his father fell, John would fall too.

His wife Margaret came softly into the room. She was a tall, handsome woman nearing fifty, with white hair drawn back from a face which was serenely unlined in spite of the five buried babes and the tribulations of childbearing and disease. Now, in her plain dark dress and white collar, she looked both ageless and unshakeable.

She laid her hands affectionately on her husband's shoulders, bent to kiss the top of his head and said, 'Come for breakfast, dear. It has been ready these past two hours. There is cream for your broze and the barley cakes are especially fine today. The new girl is a treasure. I hope she does not choose to leave us on Speaking day. I have saved a jar of currant jelly for you,' she added coaxingly as he made no move. 'Please?'

The Bishop did not answer, but allowed his head to rest lightly against his wife's breast. 'What is to become of us?' he sighed.

'Is the news bad?'

'Bad enough. I know there are still plenty who say that there is nothing to swell the Queen's gown but cushions and that she will be brought to bed of some substituted foundling child, but I do not believe it. The pregnancy is true enough and if the son and heir is born next month, they will send for William of Orange and you know what that will mean.'

'Perhaps it will not happen,' she said comfortingly. 'And if it does, God will protect us.'

The Bishop was silent. God, these days, was pressed into support of many causes. First there had been the long drawn-out and harrowing wars of the Covenant and then, when the Protestant religion had begun to shake down into some sort of harmony, back came the Papists to oppress and kill afresh. The new King James II believed himself answerable to none but God and saw his personal mission as the protection of the Catholic faith. To be sure, when the King had suspended all laws against Catholics in last year's Indulgences, he had given Presbyterians equal freedom to worship, but the Episcopalians of the Established church remained dissatisfied and uneasy at the erosion of their strength. Papists were being quietly insinuated into positions of authority and the Established church already felt itself sorely threatened. If James were to have an heir, Catholicism would take over. On the other hand, if William of Orange ousted James, the old Presbyterian system would revive and flourish. Either way it would be the end of the Episcopalian bishopric which had ruled the ancient Burgh since the Reformation – and the end of the Bishop himself.

James II was long-nosed and arrogant. He had no sense of humour and no perception to warn him of the dangers of his course. Yet he was a Stuart, and old loyalties die hard. In the face of the alternative – the Orange king from Holland with his Calvinist kirk – there were plenty who would cling to the house of Stuart.

The Bishop thought of his many friends and acquaintances here in the Old Town: George Middleton, as staunch an Episcopalian as he, James Garden and George Fraser, George Cumming the hammerman, and that big, slow-thinking Montgomery. Surely all loyal to the Established church and the Stuart line? There were others, of course, more sympathetic to the Presbyterians – Urquhart the Mediciner, for one, and that self-righteous and litigious Baillie Baxter. Crystal, too, perhaps.

The Bishop's face creased momentarily with worry. Crystal was an honest man, hardworking and good at his trade. To be sure he had made enemies. He had had his troubles, too, with the courts, the hammermen's as well as the Bishop's own. Yet Crystal was a first-class wright, as were each of his five surviving sons. The family had done valuable work for the church over the years. It was the more worrying that Crystal should have behaved as he did, nailing the loft when no one would listen to him, and daring to tell the master mason his job. Kenneth Fraser had gone fuming to the Trades' Council – and who could blame him? Nevertheless the Bishop recognized an honest man when he saw one, and Crystal had been driven solely by conviction. The structure of the Cathedral building must be strengthened, but what the future of the church itself would be was becoming daily more uncertain.

He thought of the King's increasing favours to the Catholics, and of the asthmatic Dutch Calvinist who had offered to rid them of their tyrant and assume the throne himself. And of his own church, trapped between the two. It was a sad choice, but in the end he knew where his loyalty must lie.

'Come, dear,' urged his wife. 'Things will look brighter on a full stomach. Besides, you have church work to attend to. The masons are back at work on the tower since that rabble moved on, and you know you promised to visit them and inspect their progress.'

'So I did.' The Bishop pushed back his chair and stood up. 'You are quite right, Margaret my dear. I need the fortification of your excellent table.'

He put an affectionate arm around her waist and led her downstairs. In the living-room he found the floor already washed and sanded, the brass candlesticks rubbed up with brick dust, and fresh linen on the table. There were barley cakes and cream, newly churned butter, honey from the hive and his own wooden dish of broze, beside his own, waiting chair. The simple room held warmth and friendliness and above all the comfort of his wife's unceasing care.

'Thank you my dear,' he said with contentment. He knew now that whatever happened God, and Margaret, would sustain him.

When he paid his visit to the Cathedral masons an hour later his mood had brightened to one of cheerful optimism, and he was able to smile at Kenneth Fraser's anger when Montgomery blocked his path and asked to speak with him. Kenneth Fraser was the mason the church had appointed and Kenneth Fraser was of course in charge, yet the Bishop chose to listen to Montgomery, patiently waiting while he sought for the right words to explain his fears.

'The work should be started at a distance of five ells from the walls,' Montgomery said. 'I heard the King's mason say so and I know that is how it must be done. The foundations are weak already and if the work is started close in to the wall, as Kenneth Fraser says, they will be made weaker.'

The Bishop nodded. 'I will discuss the matter with the Sub-principal, Montgomery, and tell him what you say. Thank you for giving me your ideas. Now,' he went on, turning to Kenneth Fraser, 'before you tell me your opinion on the matter, how is the stone supply holding out?'

All the building materials came by sea – the blocks of squared and dressed stone from the quarries in Morayshire, the slates, timbers, beams, even the lime – and must therefore be carefully husbanded.

'Well enough,' growled Kenneth Fraser with a glare in Montgomery's direction. 'Though it is a great pity the English took all that good stone from the Bishop's Palace. But there is some in the Chaplains' if we do run short.'

'Yes, yes, of course. I had forgotten. I will speak to James Garden about it. Now, about the buttresses, please explain to me the system of support which the King's mason recommended.'

'They must be started at a distance of five ells from the wall,' said Montgomery doggedly, but the Bishop waved a silencing hand and turned to Fraser.

'The buttressing must be built from the base outwards,' began Fraser with a glare at Montgomery, 'in order to give the greatest support.' He went on to explain how the stones were to be blocked and packed and all the time Montgomery stood two paces away, listening, every now and then shaking his head in silent contradiction.

Fraser was angry. 'I'll report you to the Deacon of Trades,' he snarled when the Bishop had left.

'The King's mason said so,' repeated Montgomery. 'And I am as good a craftsman as you. Let the Deacon come and see for himself.'

But Kenneth Fraser continued to block the stones for the supporting buttress close into the foundations and ordered Montgomery to do the same, while all morning the wind blew higher and they heard it keening in the bell-tower till the metal sang. When Montgomery laid a hand against the stones of the tower he felt them tremble under his touch. The work was urgent now. If the wind grew much stronger it might well be too late.

Janet Christie stirred meal into the pot for the kale which would be their dinner and handed more meal and salt into a wooden bowl to mix dough for the bannocks. She kneaded water into the meal, shaped flat discs and spread them on the bakestone at the fire. Then she lifted the lid of the kale pot, took a spoon and tested the viscous brew. It was thick and tasteless. She added salt from the wooden cruse and a sprig of the precious thyme which she had collected and dried the previous summer. There was very little left. But it would soon be spring. There would be fresh meat, green leaves and sunshine. William would bring her hare and salmon and there would be nettles for the gathering. She had husbanded their winter provisions well. She could afford to add a little meat to the kale today: the wind was cold and William would be hungry after a morning of trimming and squaring the stone blocks at the church.

Janet took a knife and scraped it sharp on the stone at the door. Then she reached upwards to cut a strip of beef from the leathery hunk on the ceiling hook, and the pain tore at her back and sides.

She sank on to the stool at the hearth while terror gripped her. It could not be the child. It was too soon. The Session would be angry. They would force her to confess to fornication before them all. They would set her in sackcloth at the church door. They would examine her baby and pass judgement. No matter what she said, they would condemn her. But she was innocent and it was too soon. An eight-months child – the worst, the most unlucky. It was that Sledder woman's doing. The Sledder woman had overleapt her and blighted the child in her womb.

Janet crouched at the hearth, her eyes big with terror, until the pain passed, but the fear of the Session stayed with her, and the fear of her husband's rage if his child should come to harm.

But when Montgomery returned late for his midday dinner he was preoccupied and asked no questions. She served him kale and the bannocks, warm from the stone, but she could eat nothing herself although the pain had not come again. But for once her husband noticed nothing. He was concerned only with the buttressing and whether it could be finished in time, for the wind grew stronger every minute.

He took the wooden bowl on to his knee and hurriedly spooned

in the steaming kale, then thrust another of the thick bannocks
into his mouth and stood up to go. The door crashed back on its
hinges and an icy blast lifted the straw on the bed and set the pot
swinging. Smoke gusted upwards in a shower of sparks.

'What a wind! I'll be back early if it blows any stronger.'

Then he was gone, crashing the door shut behind him. Janet
rinsed the wooden bowl with water from the pot and tossed the
slops into the Close, though the wind threatened to blow them back
in her face. She swept the earthen floor, tended the fire and threaded
the spindle with fresh yarn. She had intended to walk to the
Chanonry and see the tower for herself, but the wind was
strengthening and she felt an unwillingness to leave her hearth.
Instead she took her seat on the stool and picked up the spindle.
As she stretched the yarn the pain came again, stronger this time
and tugging at her sides, dragging her remorselessly down into
the earthen floor. Resolutely she gripped the spindle and drew the
yarn taut. The child must *not* be born.

No one noticed exactly when the wind changed its temper; all they
knew was that the afternoon was clear with a freshly buffeting wind,
and that the evening howled with the fury of a hurricane.

Montgomery in the churchyard sensed it first when the tower
above him creaked and he felt the ground shake. Grass thrashed
flat against the stones and the gale tore through the belfry with the
singing glory of wind on bell-metal. There was rain in the wind
now, and a roar from the distant sea. Trees strained and creaked and
straw flew straight in the wind from cow byres and rooftops and
cottage floors. The apple trees were stripped bare of blossom.

Kenneth Fraser called the men to halt work.

'We'll do no more today,' he said, collecting his tools. 'But be
sure and come at five in the morning, if the wind dies.'

Montgomery, however, did not move away. He was standing
close to the tower, head tipped to one side, listening. Then he laid
his huge hand against the stone.

'The tower is cracking,' he said with awe. 'It will fall before the
night is out.'

Fraser blanched. 'Nonsense, man.' But he too listened and felt
the stone shake.

'There are bells up there,' said Montgomery. 'Burgerhuyes' bell
and the new one. They will be riven if they fall.'

'They'll not fall,' but Fraser's voice wavered.

'The aisles will be broken,' went on Montgomery slowly, 'and the trades' loft. The graves will be split and their stones smashed. There is nothing we can do about that. But we can save the bells.'

Fraser looked at him sharply. Everyone knew Montgomery was a slow-thinking man, but he was a good mason. His hands communicated with the stone, and made a concord between them. If he said the tower would fall tonight, perhaps it was because the stones had told him?

'You may be right,' he said nervously. 'But we must take no risks. I will speak with the Subprincipal and see what he advises.'

He hurried away into the Chanonry with his head drawn into his shoulders and the wind lashing the clothes to his body. Subprincipal Fraser was the man in charge. The decision must be his.

As Montgomery stood waiting and listening to the creak of the stones in the great tower a boy joined him.

'Will it fall?'

Montgomery turned to see that young George Cumming had appeared from nowhere, bare-legged and bare-throated as he always was in spite of the snatching wind. The boy's face was earnest and solemn as he repeated, 'Will it fall? You are a mason and know about such things.'

'Aye,' said Montgomery, surprised and flattered by the boy's trust. 'It will fall. I told them so, but no one would listen.'

'I heard and I knew you were right. It stands to reason that a tower as tall as that must be buttressed from a proper distance. It's only logical. And the wind is strong. That is why I came.'

They stood together, side by side, in silent understanding and listened as the wind moaned and the stones creaked. Block upon block of squared stone layered with lime and sand, packed tight and crumbling . . . There were bells up there, valuable bells. When ten minutes had passed and Kenneth Fraser had not returned, Montgomery made up his mind. He turned to the boy.

'The tower will fall tonight. When they come, tell them I am gone aloft to fetch the bells.'

'No,' said George. 'I will come with you. I am not as heavy as you are and I might be useful.'

'Come, then,' Montgomery accepted the boy's help without question. 'But we must hurry.'

Montgomery moved away to the west porch and the entrance to the south steeple. He climbed up to the batta*'ne where he had stood that same morning, along the length of the Cathedral nave, high under the slates of the toofall, until he reached the door into the great steeple itself and felt the tower rock under his feet. George Cumming was beside him.

The bells dipped and swayed, the ropes writhed downwards into the gusty gloom, and the tower clattered with the scrape of stone against stone and the creak of the great oak beams which supported the bells. The bells would have to be lowered to the ground, carefully so as not to crack them, but quickly before the tower fell and buried them. It did not occur to Montgomery or to the Cumming boy that the tower might bury them, too.

It was dusk and still Montgomery had not come home. Janet sat on in the darkness of their one room. She forbore to light a candle although the firelight was too faint for her to see the spindle. She had laid aside her yarn an hour ago when the pain grew too strong. Since then she had walked restlessly up and down, or crouched on the three-legged stool, waiting for the pain to come again and willing it not to come. When it did, she fought against it with all the obstinate strength of fear, and the resulting conflict brought an agony she had not known possible as the child inside her thrust to wrench her loins apart. The sweat stood in beads across her brow and her face had lost all colour hours ago, yet still she would not acknowledge that her time had come. It could not, *must* not come for at least another month.

She moved carefully towards the hearth, one hand on the wall to steady her in case the pain came and she was not prepared. She had handed the oatmeal into the pot of boiling water two hours ago and the porridge had thickened nicely. Now she stirred it and bent to add another peat to the fire. This time the pain that gripped her as she straightened had a different quality: it enveloped body and mind in fire, wrenching downwards till she gasped aloud. When it passed she stood rigid, gripping tight to the back of William's chair, but she was rigid now with terror, not only of the Session and of William's anger, but of the birth itself.

'Oh God,' she gasped. 'Someone help me!'

With her arms crossed tight over her womb as if to keep the child in place, she moved to the door and managed to lift the latch. The moment it was free, the wind snatched the door from her hands and slammed it wide, knocking her back against the house wall.

Wind blasted into the tiny room and peat smoke gusted everywhere in choking clouds of dust. Janet gasped as the wind tore the breath from her throat. She clutched the door-jamb with both hands and shouted 'Christian!' but her voice was lifted and tossed over the battered rooftops to whirl with the straw and heath twigs into the racing clouds. Beyond the Close she saw men running. Someone rushed past her crying, 'The tower is falling!' There were cries everywhere, faint behind the wind but gathering in numbers, and there were many figures, running. No one saw or heard the small, torn figure of the stonemason's wife. The wind lashed the skirts across her bare legs and slashed a swathe of ice across the fire in her loins. With arms outstretched and pleading she staggered forward towards the stream of running figures, but they swept on, heedless, and the Close was empty. The dark shapes of the empty buildings ranged all around her, mocking, and somewhere in the centre of the yard she knew the unprotected mouth of the draw-well lay in wait to swallow the unwary. People had fallen to their deaths there before now.

At the thought of that well, she stopped and shrank back against the wall of the nearest house. Darkness crowded round her and the endless shriek of the wind. As she listened for some sign of human help, the shutters clattered round the Close, doors rattled and slammed, trees lashed, and the endless, lilting moan strengthened and rose to a shriek of vengeance which ripped the sky as the pain seared through her to split her body apart.

Frantic now with terror, she felt her way back along the rough stones of the wall to her own house and the forestair. She clutched at the rail which led upwards to the Grants' tenement and shrieked 'Christian!' But there was no response. Either the Grants did not hear or they had joined the rest of the indwellers and gone to see the tower fall. She cried again and again until she had no more strength and sank, sobbing, on the steps of the forestair as the pain lashed her body with all the venom of the gale. She dared not climb the stairs to Christian's door. She dared not set out on the journey to the church alone. She dared not even make her way across the Close to Baillie Baxter's or the Principal's house. Instead, she clawed her way back to her own door. Somehow she forced it shut behind her, to keep out the wind and the darkness, somehow she unhooked the drugget gown whose skirts were already sodden and stained, then, choking with the smoke and the pain which was forcing her in two, she sank on to the straw pallet in her shift. The fire was out, doused by the invading wind. The small window-pane was only a paler darkness in the black vacuity of the room, but she had not the strength to move to find a candle. The straw was mercifully cold against her burning thighs and the bed hard as she tossed and writhed and fought until the blood-red heat consumed her and she had no more will. Then she screamed.

Christian Grant heard the scream from the room above where she lay huddled on a pallet with her two young brothers and her infant sister. She had heard her mother in labour enough times to recognize childbirth when she heard it and not to be afraid, but as the scream came again through the single layer of boards which separated the Grant establishment from Montgomery's beneath, the child raised herself on one elbow and listened, straining to hear the voice of the midwife or of some other woman, comforting.

But there was nothing. Only the wind in the shutters and the shrieking gale outside. And, close beneath her, the moaning. Christian was wide awake now and troubled. William Montgomery had paid her to stay close to his wife and to fetch the midwife if he was away. Her own mother, she knew, would not be back till the dawn. If she was not in some man's bed, she would be at the Cathedral with everyone else, waiting for the tower to fall. Christian would have been there herself, only she knew better than to disobey her mother who had ordered her to stay indoors and care for the others. Her mother wielded a besom with enough strength to break the back of an ox. Yet when the scream came a third time, she slipped bare feet to the boards, shook the nearest child awake and said, 'I'm going down the stair. I'll be back soon.'

Then she tugged her skimpy shift down over her thighs, pushed the hair from her face and made her way to the door. The wind almost snatched her from the steps as she tugged the door fast again behind her and she was glad of the rail which George Cumming's father had fixed for them only a month ago. She scrambled down the steps to the safety of the ground and pushed open the door to Montgomery's house. Inside, the room was in darkness, even the fire was out, but from the bed came shallow, rapid breathing and a sudden, gasping scream.

Christian slipped quickly inside, pushed the door close and fumbled for the tow candle which she knew was kept on the pot-shelf against the wall. Then she crouched over the remnants of the fire, turning the hot turfs, blowing, searching for the spark of remaining life. At last she found one and the candle sputtered into flame. The pale, pungent light showed her an unrecognizable, sweat-drenched figure on the tumbled bed – and no one else.

'Janet?' cried Christian anxiously. 'Are you . . . ?'

But Janet screamed. When it was over, the child put down the candle near the bed. Then she took a rag, wrung it out in water from the pail and mopped the sweat from the woman's brow.

'I'll fetch help,' she said soothingly. 'Ma is out, but I'll find someone. You'll be all right. Everyone has babies. It's nothing really. My Ma's had ever so many. They come easy enough in the end.' All the time she was talking, with a kindness and wisdom beyond her years, she was bathing Janet's brow and neck and arms with the cooling water.

'Thank you, Christian,' whispered Janet.

'I'll fetch someone to help you now,' said the child. 'I won't be long.'

But the woman's eyes clouded with fear as the pain washed through her, searing and tearing.

'No!' she cried, clutching the child's arm till the nails bit into the flesh. 'Don't leave me. It's too late.'

So Christian stayed. She collected straw and scraps of heath and coaxed the fire back into life. She swung the pot over the flame so there would be hot water, and she hunted out a length of homespun from the chest and laid it near the fireside to warm. Then she went back to Janet and stood at the head of the bed as she had seen the women do for her mother.

'Take my hands,' she said. 'And pull. It is better that way.'

Neither of them noticed when the great crash came and the earth jarred under their feet.

When the Subprincipal arrived at the run with Kenneth Fraser, Alexander Crystal, George Cumming and several others with him, Montgomery was sitting astride the great crossbeam in the belfry securing a rope end to the eye of the first bell. A boy was standing on the narrow platform below him, paying out the rope.

'May the Lord preserve us!' The Subprincipal paled. If the beam snapped or the man lost his hold he would crash a hundred feet to his death. And the boy too.

'It's George,' gasped his father. 'Dear God!'

But Subprincipal Fraser had recovered and detailed the master mason to climb aloft to help Montgomery while the rest of them took the weight of the bell on the ropes. They lowered the newest bell first, George Kilgour's bell ordered by Bishop Haliburton himself and completed two years previously. As soon as it reached the ground, men swarmed to transport it to the safety of the west porch while Montgomery's hands worked steadily on to secure the second, larger bell.

The noise was deafening now. The wind roared everywhere with tearing force, snatching the breath from men's bodies and the clothes from their backs. A tree fell somewhere in the Chanonry and the crash of its falling sent fear racing through the crowd at the foot of the great tower.

'Come down, Montgomery!' ordered Subprincipal Fraser.

There was the crack of breaking stone and a chunk of the bell-chamber fell away to crash splintering on the gravestones a hundred feet below. A cry of fascinated horror surged upward and ebbed on a sigh as the crowd drew back to safety.

'Come down, man!' yelled George Fraser against the roar of the wind. 'Get back all of you!' This to the huddle of men who still clung to the bell rope, straining to take the weight of the larger bell.

'It is ready now!' Montgomery's voice exulted over the wind. 'Lower away!'

As soon as the bell was safely on its downward journey the stonemason jerked backwards across the beam and dropped to the platform of the now roofless tower where George was waiting for him. Kenneth Fraser was nowhere in sight, fled long ago to the safety of the ground, but the door to the battaline was open, crashing rhythmically against the stonework of the tower. Montgomery thrust George out on to the battaline, but he himself stayed in the doorway, his big hands on either side of the door-jamb to brace himself against the wind and his huge shoulders blotting out the night. He watched his bell sway and jerk its way through the darkness towards the ground.

'Look out!' came the cry from a score of voices.

The bell crashed the last twenty feet to the ground with the dumb clang of riven metal and Montgomery closed his eyes at the pain of it. As a craftsman he felt the breaking of that bell like a physical wound – and a personal failure.

'It is broken,' said George in awe. 'I am sorry.'

Montgomery laid a hand briefly on the boy's shoulder, then thrust his way out of the tower and into the full force of the hurricane as it tore across the slates of the Cathedral roof. Somehow they fought their way back along the passage under the toofall towards the south and lesser steeple.

Below them, in the churchyard, men were trundling Michael Burgerhuyes' bell in the same direction while all around the Cathedral the heritors crowded, silent now, waiting, every eye on that creaking, swaying tower of stone which reared four-square and crumbling against a rocking sky.

Montgomery was in the south steeple when the tower fell. The earth shuddered under his feet and all around him the air crashed with the sound of splitting rock and the rumble of stone settling on broken stone.

'You were right,' said George. 'I knew you were.'

At the foot of the steeple they went out through the doorway of the west porch and joined the group of silent men: Subprincipal Fraser, his wig awry and his black meitt-coat white with dust; Kenneth Fraser, master mason, grey-faced and quivering; George Cumming, still white but proud too; Alexander Crystal, Gauld the sexton, awe on their faces. Others quietly joined them: Principal Middleton, James Garden the professor of Divinity, Patrick Urquhart the Mediciner, Baillie Baxter, Dr Keith. Then the Bishop himself.

Gradually the stones settled. Even the wind dropped, as if in casting down the great tower its fury had been spent. Where there had been a towering four-square glory against the sky there was nothing now but a heap of rubble under billowing dust.

'Praise be to God,' said the Bishop in the new silence.

'But the bell is riven!' At the anguished cry everyone turned to look at Montgomery.

'William Montgomery,' explained the Subprincipal to the company, 'was instrumental in saving the bells. He strode the cross beam and tied the ropes himself. He could not have done more.'

'A brave man and I thank him. And you, my young fellow,' added the Bishop vaguely with a nod in George's direction. 'You were right, Montgomery,' he went on. 'You warned me this morning of what might happen.'

'But the bell is riven . . .'

'You did all you could. To God alone be Glory,' said the Bishop. 'See, the words are on the bell itself. If it is God's will, who are we to question it? We must give thanks that no one has been killed.'

40

'The new bell is unharmed,' said Kenneth Fraser nervously. 'It can still be tolled for Sabbaths and for funerals.'

'Aye,' said George Cumming, a burly man of forty. 'You did well young fellow. And you, too, George my lad, though I ought to tan your hide for it. Thanks to you things will not be so much changed after all.'

But many an indweller in that assembled company looked at the heap of rubble, dark against a darker sky, and knew instinctively that nothing would ever be the same again.

'Cheer up, lad,' said Crystal kindly, putting an arm around Montgomery's shoulder. 'At least now the whole town knows that you were right. Come. There's nothing anyone can do till dawn. Walk home with me and share a mug of ale.'

So it was almost morning and the wind dead before William Montgomery opened the door to his home and saw little Christian Grant crouched on a stool in the firelight with a bundle in her arms, crooning. She looked up as he came in and said simply, 'Your child is born.'

He started forward and snatched the bundle from her, holding it wonderingly in his huge hands. Joy flooded through him till he felt his heart would burst.

'Now you're here, I'll fetch Ma,' said Christian. 'We'll make the cakes and caudle for the neighbours, but you must buy the whisky yourself to drink her health. And she must be christened before the fairies take her.'

'*She?*'

'I'm sorry.' The voice was so faint that Montgomery did not at first hear. Then he saw the flat white shape on the bed, the anguished eyes, the outstretched, pleading hand. 'I'm sorry,' she said again. But he did not seem to understand.

'The child is a boy,' he said.

'See for yourself,' shrugged Christian.

Montgomery tore open the swaddling cloth until the child lay naked, hardly covering the width of his hands. He stared for a long moment at the top-heavy head, the fragile neck, the paper-like skin which wrinkled over limbs as brittle as a bird's, at the soft belly with the newly-tied cord and at the fold of female genitals. Then, with an animal roar of despair he flung the child away and strode out of the house.

'William!'

The cry held all the desperate yearning of her loveless life:

a life which was slowly seeping out of her with the blood which soaked the straw to spread in a dark stain across the wooden boards beneath. But William Montgomery did not hear her. As he strode through the Close to the High Street he heard nothing except the rage which churned through his head until he thought his skull would burst.

In the stonemason's house in the Close, Christian Grant gathered up the infant who, after one sharp scream, was crying weakly and jerking futile, aimless limbs. She wrapped it in the linen, cradled it against her flat chest and rocked it gently to the rhythm of her own breathing, crooning lovingly as if it were her own.

'Hush now, little quinie,' she whispered. 'A stonemason's daughter must not fret. He didn't mean it and he'll come back. You'll see. He'll come back to you one day.'

The baby whimpered and nuzzled blindly at the unformed breast.

'Nay there's nothing for you there. You'll have to seek your mother.'

But Janet Christie's eyes were glazed, and though Christian shook and pummelled her and even slapped her cheeks, there was no response.

2

Christian missed her footing in the darkness and stumbled.

'Quiet!' warned George Cumming, son of the blacksmith. 'There's someone there.'

'Not the ghost?' breathed Elspeth Middleton, moving closer and clutching tight to his hand.

'There's no such thing,' whispered Adam Urquhart, but his thin face was pale and his eyes large with apprehension.

Christian hugged her tiny bundle protectively to her chest and muttered a quick prayer. She did not like this expedition, but there had been no question of refusing. Whatever George ordered, Christian obeyed as she had done since they were infants playing in the field below Cumming's yard while their mothers gossiped or trod the clothes together. And when George said they were all going to climb into the roof of the church to see the ghosts, she knew she would go too. But she had insisted on bringing the Montgomery child with her.

'You can't bring that baby,' said George when he saw the dirty scrap of cloth in her arms. 'It'll cry.'

'She's not an "it" and she won't.' Christian could not have explained what she felt for the stonemason's baby. She knew only that the birth had bound them together, like mother and child. And when Janet Montgomery died it was Christian who soothed the screaming infant, Christian who named her Margery, Christian who begged her mother to suckle the child with her own, at least until the father returned and made other arrangements.

'But you'll have to keep her out of my way,' warned Isobel Grant. 'I've enough wailing bairns in the place as it is. I'll feed her when she needs it, till she can take her pap, but don't let me hear her fret, that's all.'

So Christian carried the child on her hip, or in the crook of her arm, wherever she went, until the baby grew as much a part of her as her own limbs. Now she had repeated, 'Margery comes too.'

'But Christian, if she cries she'll give us all away.'

'She won't cry. She never does when I hold her.' This was true.

At first the baby screamed whenever anyone touched her, but Christian had learnt how to hold her in a certain way, with her legs curled against Christian's arm: that way the child was quiet.

'She only cries when she's hungry and she's just been fed. Anyway,' she finished defiantly, 'if she doesn't come, I don't either.'

'Don't be daft, Christian. You know we can't go without you.' But when Christian remained obstinate, George gave in. 'All right, bring her. Only keep her quiet!'

Now, in the shiver of Elspeth Middleton's fear, Christian wished she had not come. She crossed herself surreptitiously and moved closer to Adam on the narrow stair. Behind her James Middleton and the Garden children huddled together whispering and she heard someone squeak with sudden fear. She turned her head quickly, anticipating George's anger.

'Do you want to get us all caught?'

It was dark inside the tower although the evening bell had not yet sounded and William Walker, the town drummer, would not make his round for another hour. Somewhere high above them hung the bell which Margery's father had rescued from the east tower before it fell. Somewhere below them to the east stretched the vast empty nave of the Cathedral, open to the sky now where the tower had stood, the gap only half filled with tumbled stones and newly gaping graves.

'There's bodies,' whispered George to Elspeth as they reached the top of the stone stair and the door on to the battaline. 'When the tower fell it smashed the gravestones in the south aisle and all the graves burst open. Skulls and bones everywhere!'

Elspeth shivered in delicious terror. 'Aren't you scared, Georgie? You are brave!'

Privately, Christian agreed, but the sight of Elspeth's adoring face annoyed her. Why did the girl have to follow George about everywhere he went, clutching at his hand and pretending to be so helpless? Christian herself was frightened, but she would no more dream of saying so than of stripping naked in the middle of the Minister's sermon.

'They're only bones,' shrugged George. 'They can't hurt you.'

An apprehensive silence greeted this remark and George decided it was time to move before he lost his followers to discretion. He pushed open the door and led them into the narrow, gusty loft under the slates. Rafters stretched the length of the nave, making a straight, triangular passageway from the south tower to what had once been the great steeple. Now the passageway was in darkness except where it ended, far ahead of them, in a jagged patch of sky.

They crept silently forward. A rat scurried from under their feet and someone gasped. Cobwebs brushed their faces. James began to cry, soundlessly, with fear. Then they reached the end of the toofall and looked down into the darkness of the heaped stones.

'That's where the bones are,' breathed George, pointing to where the floor of Gavin Dunbar's aisle lay exposed to the darkening sky. Broken flagstones cast solid wedges of shadow across the grey.

There was the click of stone against stone and a flicker of light. Elspeth gasped and clasped a hand across her mouth. John Garden's eyes grew wider as he watched, but he made no sound. The Mediciner's son stared, motionless, his arm around the terrified James, while Christian crouched beside them, the baby clasped to her chest and her lips moving in frantic, forbidden prayers. The light moved slowly across the shadows. They heard a soft, scraping sound.

'Dear Lord preserve us!' breathed Elspeth. The sound came again, louder now. 'Georgie,' she whispered urgently, 'let's go home.'

George turned his head and glared at her: Christian looked at Elspeth with irritation.

'Idiot. I don't know why George lets her come.'

She wriggled defiantly to the edge of the toofall and looked downwards into the broken vault of the south aisle. A dark figure was hunched over a stone in a pale pool of light. Christian drew back.

'There's someone down there,' she mouthed at George.

She leant forward again, fascinated, to see what the apparition would do. Whoever – or whatever – it was was crouching over a flat pan and she heard the rhythmic swish, swish of shifting sands. George joined Christian at the edge.

'It's Gauld,' he whispered excitedly, flapping a hand towards the others to warn them to keep quiet. 'What is he doing?'

'*Gauld!*' John Garden went dead white. 'If he sees us, Mother will kill me.'

'Sh! Do you want him to hear?'

They crouched together watching, fascinated by the softly rhythmic sounds which came regularly now, like the pull of shingle on the shore.

'What's he doing?' mouthed Elspeth, but George put a finger to his lips in warning.

Then Christian felt the baby stir. The little scrap began to twist and fight with surprising strength as wind contorted her stomach. Christian clasped the child's head against her chest in horror. If Margery gave them away, George would never forgive her! She wriggled away from the gaping edge and Gauld, and scurried quickly back towards the south steeple, bending double under the slant of the roof and stumbling on the uneven rafters in her haste. She was almost there when the baby cried: a short, yelping cry which ended on a rasp of wind. There was a moment's silence and then consternation.

'Who's there?' roared a voice from below them.

'Run!' cried George, pushing her towards the steps of the steeple as the others ran squealing past her. Christian found herself jostled aside and because she still held the baby in one arm she waited until the others had piled down the narrow stair before scrambling after them.

'Come back!' roared Gauld from the east end of the church. More voices shouted from somewhere in the Chanonry, squeals and terrified cries. At the foot of the steeple Christian hesitated, clutching the baby tight to her panting chest. She was alone in the dim vault of the west porch. The wide domed door stood open, but where were the others? And Gauld? Then, from close at hand, came the sound of light, running feet.

'Christian, where are you? For God's sake hurry! The others are away!'

She seized George's hand and they ran, bare feet soundless in the dew-soaked grass. They were almost at the stile and safety when a tall figure stepped into the path in front of them and barred the way. Swiftly George ducked to avoid the outstretched hand, but the man was quicker and though George fought and twisted with all his strength he could not escape.

'Run, Christian, before he gets you too!'

Christian hesitated, torn between loyalty and fear. Then she felt the earth thud and looked swiftly behind her to see the squat, square figure of the sexton, Gauld, bearing down upon them. With a squeal of terror she darted off the path into the longer grass of the kirk-yard with Gauld pounding after her.

'Come here, you Papist devil!' he roared, lunging.

At the sound of his voice the girl panicked, stumbled and, under the impact of his grasping hand, fell full length in the grass. There was a sharp, high cry from the baby, another from Christian, and a torrent of triumphant abuse from Gauld.

'Got you, you thieving vagabond. I'll have you branded at the market cross for this, see if I don't, you snivelling little wretch.'

'Leave her alone, you bastard,' cried George. 'If you hurt her I'll kill you!'

'George Cumming, calm yourself!' The voice was firm and authoritative and the boy recognized it instantly.

'Mr Keith, sir,' he gasped, appalled. 'I'm sorry, sir. I thought it was ... I mean ...'

Mr Keith, Minister of the first charge of St Machar's Cathedral, looked down sternly at the boy.

'Do not attempt to run away, George. And help Christian to her feet.'

'Yes, sir.' George moved obediently.

'You varmint!' Gauld was purple-faced from his exertions and his breath rasped in his chest, yet he lunged belatedly at the boy with his free hand while he clutched Christian's arm with the other. 'I'll nail your lugs for you yet. See if I don't.'

'Let them go, Gauld. They will not run away. Well, get up girl. You are not hurt, are you?'

Christian still crouched on one knee in the grass. At his voice she turned her head towards the Minister and her eyes blazed accusation through the tears.

'Murderers!'

The Minister stepped forward and held out a hand.

'Come now, Christian, you are not hurt. You know it is forbidden to play in the kirk and that laws are made to be kept. Stand up and ...' He checked as he saw the baby lying in the grass. 'What is this? Whose child ... ?'

'You've killed her, both of you! You made me fall and it's your fault!' She had lost all fear of the Minister and of Gauld in the new fear which flooded through her. If Margery was dead, she'd never forgive them, never! She felt George's arm, awkward, across her shoulder.

'It's all right, Christian. She's not dead. And if she is, I'll ...'

But the Minister had dropped to his knees and gathered the baby into his hands, murmuring comfortingly, 'You're not hurt, are you my little one?' His hands were big and gentle and Christian remembered that when Mr Keith did the baptisms the infants never

47

cried. He was standing now, with the child in the crook of one arm.

'Christian! George! Come with me.'

Christian hung back. 'Where are we going?'

'To the Bishop.'

'No! Please! I'll take her home to Ma. Ma will know what to do.'

'The Bishop's wife will know better.'

'But we can't go there,' cried George. 'The Bishop . . .'

Mr Keith looked at him sternly. 'You will do as I say. You have transgressed and must face your punishment. While the Bishop's wife does what she can for the child, you can tell me what you were doing in the kirkyard when you should have been at home in bed. Come, Gauld.'

'Thieving varmints,' growled Gauld as he hurried along behind the Minister, George's ear held firmly in one calloused hand, Christian's forearm in the other. 'It'll be the brand for the pair of you if I have my way.'

They were ushered into the kitchen of the Bishop's house by an agitated and scarlet-faced servant. The reason was soon obvious: there was to be company for supper and the kitchen was full of preparations – pickled oysters and smoked beef, a great pot of bacon and pease pottage, and a pair of capons on the spit. The mistress had been instructing the servant-girl how to turn the handle of the spit when they arrived, and the room was thick with the smell of roasting fowls and sputtering fat. When she saw the baby, the Bishop's wife cried out in alarm.

'I fear the child has been crushed, Margaret,' explained John Keith. 'Do what you can for her.' He laid the child gently on the kitchen table among the wooden bowls of milk and meal.

'Poor little thing,' she said, unwrapping the skimpy cloth which had swaddled the infant. She ran competent hands over the bird-like limbs. 'No harm done as far as I can tell. Breathing steady. No bones broken. At least . . .' She took the tiny legs in one hand and examined them. 'No. No bones broken, but I'd like Dr Urquhart to have a look all the same.'

'Oh no, ma'am,' Christian gasped. 'The fee! Ma will kill me.'

'There will be no fee. Dr Urquhart is upstairs at this moment with the Bishop and will examine the child as a personal favour to me.'

'As the Bishop is engaged,' said Gauld, 'shall I take these two straight to the tolbooth?'

48

'The tolbooth is for civil offenders, Gauld.' John Keith was a tall, spare man in his fifties, with iron-grey hair and fine-drawn, sensitive features. He had started his career as a tutor in Lord Fraser's family, and had won his first stipend twenty-six years ago when he had successfully applied for admission to Echt, pleading his own humble condition and the parish's need. Thence he had moved to Birse before coming to Old Machar four years ago, as Minister of the first charge. He was a simple, scholarly man, impatient of hypocrisy and all forms of deceit. Now he looked at Gauld with distaste.

'A child is injured and all you talk of is punishment. Have you no compassion?'

'I'm only doing my job, Mr Keith. There's enough complaints when I don't, God help me. And when I catch a pair of thieving vagabonds defiling God's own house with their wickedness, do you blame me for wanting them brought to justice?'

'They will receive justice,' said the Minister calmly. ' "If any man defile the temple of God, him shall God destroy." '

'Yes, sir, but . . .'

' "For the temple of God is holy, *which temple you are*." Remember, Gauld, and be merciful.' He turned to Margaret. 'Would you ask the Bishop if he could spare me a moment?'

George Cumming blanched, but squared his shoulders bravely. Christian squeezed her fists tight till the nails bit into the flesh. Usually offenders appeared before the Session, the lowest of the ecclesiastical courts, presided over by the Minister and consisting of the Elders and deacons chosen from the most worthy men of the parish. This court met once a week to deal with moral backsliders, those indwellers who had been caught swearing, blaspheming, profaning the Sabbath or who were accused of fornication or adultery. A crime, such as witchcraft or charming, which was too serious for the Session to deal with was referred to the next court, the Presbytery, on which sat twelve or more ministers under the Bishop's appointed moderator. The next court above that was the Synod, presided over by the Bishop himself, and, finally, the General Assembly. Christian felt her legs tremble. Suppose their crime was serious enough to warrant the highest court of all? Mr Keith seemed to think so as he was taking them straight to the Bishop. But Mrs Haliburton was unperturbed.

'There is no point in waiting till the Session meets if we can settle things now, is there?' She smiled encouragement at the children. 'After all, it is not as if it were Sunday, and I trust you did no harm? Go with Mr Keith and face your punishment bravely.'

They found the Bishop in his study where a fire burnt brightly, its glow reflected in the polished wooden floor and panelled walls. The Bishop wore his usual skullcap and simple homespun robe, but his companion was dressed in a neat black coat and breeches, silver-buckled shoes and white lace at the throat. His pale wig was immaculate and tinged with rose from the firelight, but the eyes above the gold-rimmed spectacles were curiously benign and devoid of arrogance.

Dr Patrick Urquhart was a man of learning and considerable personal accomplishments. Not yet forty-seven, he had been physician in the King's College for seventeen years, and two years previously, on January 7, 1686, had caused a considerable stir in academic circles by inaugurating public lessons in medicine. Although his opinions on church matters did not always coincide with the Bishop's, they were firm friends, sharing as they did a taste for good food, good music and good conversation. Now, the room smelt pleasantly of tobacco and brandy.

Dr Keith explained his mission. Dr Urquhart instantly excused himself and went downstairs to the kitchen. When the door closed behind him the Bishop motioned the children to stand in front of his chair.

'So,' he began slowly, fingertips together under the point of his chin. To Christian he seemed as awesome and omnipotent as God himself. 'You are the boy who helped save the bells, I believe?' George nodded. 'Yet you were in the roof of the Cathedral, which is forbidden. Why?'

George looked at the floor and did not answer, but when the Bishop's eyes moved to Christian she mumbled reluctantly under his compelling gaze, 'To see the ghosts.'

'Ghosts? There are no ghosts in the roof.'

'No, sir. They're where the tower fell.'

The Bishop's fingertips tapped together with impatience. He knew that superstition still flourished in the town in spite of all the efforts of the Session. Charms, fortune-telling, Christmas festivities, wedding parties, gambling, even midsummer fires. These last had been forbidden year after year, yet to no avail. Worse, Papist idolatry and mumbo-jumbo were increasing under the open encouragement of King James. In spite of repeated reminders from

50

the pulpit that the heritors were forbidden to bury their dead in the Spital kirkyard of the ruinous Catholic church, there had been trouble there only last week. Some indwellers had actually been seen praying at the graves of their ancestors. And this girl, he remembered, had a mother who was not above suspicion. The Bishop frowned at the reminder of the worry which preoccupied him more and more as the months passed.

'Am I to understand,' he said now, fixing Christian with a stern eye, 'that you believe these poor departed souls are no longer at rest because an act of God has broken open their graves?'

Christian looked at him in silence, mesmerized by the slender white fingers and the whiter, flowing hair.

'They were all good Christians, child,' went on the Bishop impatiently. 'They received Christian burial and are at peace. It is not for you to trespass on forbidden ground in order to prove otherwise. Do you hear, boy?'

George jumped. 'Yes, sir, but I . . .'

The Bishop brushed his words aside. 'You know the punishment. Can you give me any reason why you should not receive the maximum penalty of . . .'

'No!' cried Christian in terror. 'Don't nail his ears! We didn't do any harm, honest, we didn't. And we didn't take anything. He has it all in his pouch.'

'Who?' The Bishop looked baffled, while the blood left Gauld's face. 'All what?'

'I think she means the gold, my lord,' said Mr Keith quietly. 'You see, I did not intrude upon your privacy for a mere prank.'

'*Gold*, Mr Keith?'

'Yes, my lord,' said George. 'It's in the Sexton's pocket.'

'Is this true, Gauld?' said the Bishop.

The man opened and shut his mouth helplessly. Mr Keith crossed the room, slipped a hand into the man's pouch and drew out a ring. Then another. He laid them in the Bishop's outstretched hand, saying only:

'It is as I suspected.'

'Where did you get these rings, Gauld?'

'I . . . my lord . . . I didn't . . .'

'Were you sifting the ashes of the graves?' prompted the Minister.

The Sexton nodded. He seemed to have shrivelled suddenly inside his clothes.

'God hath chosen the weak things of the world to confound the things that are mighty,' said Mr Keith quietly.

'Take them away,' said the Bishop wearily. 'And come back to me. This other matter must be investigated at once, while events are fresh in the mind.'

So Christian and George were bustled downstairs to the kitchen, where they found the baby peacefully sleeping and Dr Urquhart and the Bishop's wife deep in conversation.

'. . . a slight cracking of the thigh-bone,' the Mediciner was saying. 'Already set, unfortunately. Probably sustained at birth or immediately afterwards. Nothing to be done about it now. No other injury that I can see . . . a remarkably tenacious child for one not yet full-term, whatever the gossips might say. Something will have to be done, of course.' Christian lifted her head in sudden fear. 'The child's future will have to be settled – or Montgomery found. I understand the matter is to be discussed at the next meeting of the Session, and after tonight's episode it must be given the earliest and most serious attention.'

The Mediciner moved towards the door on his way back upstairs. 'However, to have survived such a disadvantageous beginning augurs well for the child's spirit. If Margery Montgomery achieves maturity, she promises to be a remarkable woman.'

'And now,' said the Bishop's wife when she had given them each a bowl of broze and a mug of fresh milk, 'you had better take Margery home. Remarkable she may be, but she needs her supper like anybody else.'

George and Christian exchanged glances. 'You mean we can go?'

'Why not?'

'But the kirkyard . . . they said . . .'

'Never mind what they said. Take the baby and run along home before the curfew. William Walker will be on his rounds any minute now.'

Later that night when Christian lay in bed with the infant cradled carefully in her arm, she pondered for a long time on the words she had heard. If Margery's leg was broken, she knew when it had happened and how, but it was not that which filled her with wonder. It was the idea of Margery, not yet three weeks old, growing up into a remarkable woman. Then she remembered the Session. 'Please God,' she prayed, 'don't let them take her away.'

'What is to be done about the Montgomery child?' John Keith, with the memory of the baby fresh in his mind, looked expectantly at the assembled company.

The Session was holding its weekly meeting under the direction of the Minister of the first charge. Among the elders present were Principal Middleton, Subprincipal George Fraser, Dr Patrick Urquhart, and Baillie Baxter. The schoolmaster, Alexander Couper, was acting as Session clerk and for once the Bishop himself had chosen to attend. After a morning's discussion, the Consistory chamber in the north steeple of St Machar's had grown airless and stale. But the business of the Sexton had at last been dealt with, and the matter of fines for the parents of George Cumming and Christian Grant settled.

It had been agreed unanimously to drop all idea of finding out the other children involved – too many of those present had reason to doubt the rectitude of their own offspring, especially when an expedition led by that Cumming boy was involved. But the Session knew it could safely leave the matter of chastisement to the parents.

'Poor Christian,' reflected John Keith. 'She will certainly get her full share of punishment. But she is a good girl at heart and it is best that she be taught early to follow the right path. The matter of this baby must be settled quickly, though, before Christian goes any further astray.' As Urquhart and Middleton were both present, the Minister had some hopes of success: the Mediciner had seen the baby himself and was both enlightened and compassionate; the Principal had the highest reputation as a humanist, philosopher and divine and was known to be a kindly man. William Baxter, however, looked up, frowning.

'One moment, if you please!'

He held out an imperious hand to the schoolmaster who had been entering the proceedings in a leather-bound volume with careful, close-packed script. Now he laid the quill aside, dusted the page with fine sand from the shaker and blew away the excess. Then he handed the ledger to Baxter.

'Thank you, Mr Couper. Before we proceed to any other matter,' and here he directed a reproving look at the Minister, 'we must approve the minutes of the Session in the regrettable case of the Sexton.'

John Keith suppressed a sigh of impatience. He found the Baillie invariably irritating. William Baxter was not yet thirty-five, yet he had the manner of a man twice his age. There was something in the pompous set of head on thin neck, the colourless eyebrows and the dry, yellowish skin which, together with his dusty black clothes and disapproving expression gave him the air of one who is always right, yet whom nothing pleases.

'Hypocrite,' thought the Minister and reproved himself quickly for lack of charity.

Baillie Baxter was an advocate in the New Town, but as a life-long indweller in Old Aberdeen he was a frequent member of the Session as well as of the Burgh Court. The Court, however, was presided over by the Provost, James Scougal, who until last year had held the Chair of Civil Law in the University and who kept a firm check on the Baillie's aspirations. In the Session there was no such curb. Now the advocate glared at them sternly above his gold-rimmed spectacles and cleared his throat.

' "May 27th, 1688. William Gauld, bellman, being convened before the Session for a barbarous and inhuman act of sifting the ashes of the dead out of a covetous design of searching for rings which he supposed might have been amongst the ashes the said William making a judicial confession of the premises, the Session considering the great scandal and offence it had given did enjoin the said William Gauld to appear before the Congregation and make an acknowledgement of his fault . . ." '

'I am still not convinced that public confession is necessary,' interrupted Middleton. 'It brings the office into disrepute.'

'Of course it is necessary,' snapped Baxter. 'The sinner must confess his faults. Besides, it was put to the vote and carried over-whelmingly.'

'It is necessary,' said the Minister wearily as the Bishop made no comment. In truth, the Bishop was lost in his own thoughts, thoughts which seemed to him of more importance than the punish-ment of a covetous Sexton. The royal child's birth was imminent and the future of the church – and country – in the balance.

' ". . . and also at the Bishop's order was suspended from his office," ' resumed the Baillie, ' "during his Lord's pleasure." Are we all agreed that this is a fit record of the morning's proceedings?'

'Yes, yes, of course, Baxter,' said George Fraser with impatience. 'It is all settled. Now is there anything else? Because I have several pressing affairs to attend to.'

'Not the rebuilding of the east wall, by any chance?' said Urquhart, exchanging a wink with Principal Middleton.

'There are masons to be hired,' blustered George Fraser, 'and work to be directed. All sorts of arrangements to be made. It is not as simple as selling ale,' he finished with heavy meaning. The schoolmaster looked uncomfortable while Baillie Baxter busied himself ostentatiously with his books.

'You seem to thrive on it, anyway,' said Urquhart with studied innocence.

'It's all very well to sneer,' retorted Fraser angrily. 'But the nave cannot be left open to the skies indefinitely, for the starlings to fly in and out as they please. The work must be put in hand as soon as we can hire the work force, but the men ask so much these days, and what can one do, with the Lodge behind them every time? Kenneth Fraser says they want 1s 4d a day now, and how I'm to find the money out of what the church allowed me I just don't know. What we really need is men who will do the work of two.'

'Then you'd better find Montgomery,' said Middleton calmly. 'He's a good mason and a good worker – which is more than can be said for Kenneth Fraser. I suppose you've put him in charge again?'

'And what's wrong with that?' demanded George Fraser. 'He knows his workmen. He's a good overseer.'

'But a bad mason.'

'He passed his "sey" to the trade's satisfaction. He knows his job.'

'And the buttressing?' said the Principal quietly.

'An act of God, nothing more. Everyone knows it was the storm that toppled the tower.'

'And everyone knows you and Kenneth Fraser are hand-in-glove over the men's wages,' said Urquhart cheerfully. 'How much do you plan to make between you this time?'

John Keith suppressed a smile. What Urquhart said was common knowledge, though no one else dared say it as bluntly as the Mediciner. The Minister liked Dr Urquhart, though sometimes he had the uneasy suspicion that the man was laughing at them all from some superior standpoint of his own. Moreover, the Minister suspected that behind the Mediciner's outward conformity in church matters ran a definite vein of scepticism. But he was undoubtedly a brilliant scholar, far more so than Fraser who was opening and shutting his mouth in futile indignation. Before George Fraser could find an answer, the Bishop raised a hand in warning.

'Enough. We are not here to air our private disputes. Mr Keith has raised a question which demands your attention, namely the problem of the Montgomery child. You all know the care of the parish poor is one of the first duties of the Session, likewise the maintenance of orphans and foundlings. Mr Keith, be good enough to refresh our memories on this particular case.'

'Certainly, my lord. The mother, you will recall, was Janet Christie, indweller of the town, and an orphan with no living relatives. She died in childbed and was buried by the good offices of the hammermen's trade.'

'That was Crystal's doing,' said Dr Urquhart. 'A kindly man.'

'But he'd no need to let them use the trade's mort cloth,' said Baxter. 'The free one would have been sufficient, especially as the woman was undoubtedly a backslider.'

'It was not proved.'

'God struck her down in her wickedness, as He punishes all who fornicate and commit abominations.'

'Nonsense!' said Urquhart sharply. 'The woman died of a postnatal haemorrhage – a common enough occurrence. And as for fornication, I had occasion to inspect the child myself only the other day and found every sign of an eight-months delivery.'

'So you say, but ...'

'The Doctor is right,' interrupted John Keith. 'You would do well to remember, Baillie, that God also punishes slanderers and the bearers of false witness.'

'Please let us proceed,' said the Bishop testily. 'Surely the trades can sort out the business of the mort cloths for themselves?'

'To return to the Montgomery child,' resumed the Minister. 'The father left the town on the morning of the child's birth and has not been seen or heard of since.'

'On the contrary, as I believe I mentioned to you at the time,' interrupted Baxter, 'I heard a report in the New Town that the man had been seen on the road to Dundee. As you know, my work as an advocate puts me in a position to receive information which might otherwise not be forthcoming and on Tuesday of last week as I was ...'

'Yes, yes,' interrupted the Bishop with growing irritation. 'Get on with it.'

'As I was saying, my lord, I had occasion to speak with a seafaring gentleman who told me he had spoken to a man answering

56

Montgomery's description and who had made inquiries as to mason's work available in the south. My informant is under the impression the man intended to make for Dundee or possibly Edinburgh.'

'Masons are a nomadic race,' mused Dr Urquhart. 'Since that valiant band of British masons made the trek to the Byzantine Empire to aid in the building of Constantinople, they have moved across the globe to wherever there are stones to be fashioned or monuments to be built. No doubt our William has felt the urge to raise a castle or a church to the glory of God, and has gone to find a patron.'

'I doubt he will have much luck in Dundee,' said Middleton drily. 'I hear Claverhouse has other things on his mind than the peaceful building of churches.'

'That,' said Baillie Baxter, 'is as may be. The fact remains that Montgomery has left the town without paying his wife's funeral expenses and without making arrangements for his child's maintenance.'

'Come now, Baxter,' protested Urquhart, 'be fair. He had no reason to think his wife would die. He left in the disappointment of finding he had fathered a daughter and not a son – a natural enough disappointment and one which I am sure we have all shared.' His face was impassive: only his eyes betrayed him as they met the Principal's above his spectacles. The whole town knew of Baillie Baxter's cold rages on the birth of each of his four daughters.

'True,' said Middleton solemnly. 'Especially as the man is not so well equipped as others might be to provide a dowry.'

'Nevertheless,' snapped the advocate, 'his child is virtually an orphan and dependent upon the town for her maintenance. Is it to be the poor fund? Or adoption?'

'I would like to make a suggestion,' said Mr Keith quickly. This was the moment he had been waiting for. 'In view of the great affection shown to the infant by the Grant family, I would suggest that Montgomery's effects be impounded and the money obtained thereby be given in wages to Isobel Grant to care for the Montgomery child until such time as the father might be found and brought home again.'

'An excellent idea,' said Urquhart, smiling.

'I cannot agree.' Baillie Baxter was still smarting under the Doctor's jibe. 'The Grant woman is a known Papist. How can we condone the handing over of a helpless infant to idolatry in this manner?'

'The woman is a faithful and diligent attender at the kirk,' said Mr Keith. 'She brings up her children in the fear of the Lord.'

'So she does,' agreed George Fraser and added piously, 'Slanderous tongues will always wag, whether with cause or none.'

'Aye,' sneered Baxter. 'It shows *great* fear of the Lord to play in the roof of the Lord's own house.'

'The children were instruments of the Lord's will,' said the Minister, 'through whom a greater wickedness was detected. And at least none of her family has been found guilty of breaking the Sabbath.'

There was a short silence after this remark. George Fraser looked uneasy. It was only a month since his brother John who lived with him *in familia* had been caught fishing in the Don during afternoon sermon, and at least one of the Urquhart children had been with him. Even Baillie Baxter looked wary. His own wife was not above reproach in the matter of church attendance, especially when she was with child and took odd fancies to disobey him.

It was the Mediciner who broke the silence. 'The woman is suckling the child. Who else is there who would do it? You know the reputation Montgomery had in the town.'

This was true, reflected the Minister sadly. He had felt sorry for the stonemason, but the man had gone out of his way to alienate affection, with the result that he had had few friends. Only Alexander Crystal had come forward to help at Janet's funeral, and Crystal had said at the time that he could do nothing for the babe. His own wife had died not six months ago, leaving him with an infant on his hands as well as half a dozen older children. Elizabeth, his daughter, did her best, but she was only seven and could not cope with another baby. Crystal had been genuinely regretful and had himself suggested Isobel Grant.

'She is a kindly woman at heart,' said the Minister now. 'The arrangement need only be for a few months while messages are sent to find out Montgomery. When the child is weaned it will be easier. There may be offers of adoption for her then. She seems a healthy child and will make a good servant if properly trained. When the time comes, we can discuss the matter afresh.'

In the end the Minister's proposal was agreed to, with the proviso that the church keep a good eye on the Grant household to ensure that the child was brought up in the true faith. The matter of payment was to be arranged with the town Treasurer.

'Then that's settled,' said the Mediciner cheerfully. 'Any news from London?'

'Much the same,' said the Bishop. 'But the birth is expected imminently.'

'If it is a birth,' said Baillie Baxter.

'Of course it's a birth, man,' snapped Fraser. 'The evidence would satisfy the most sceptical.'

'Nevertheless,' persisted Baxter, 'I have heard it said that . . .'

'You have heard it said indeed! And by whom? Tell me that!' When Baxter made no answer, Fraser went on, 'The truth is an heir at this moment will be, to say the least, *inconvenient* to a certain faction I could name. Is that not so?'

'I don't deny it would be inconvenient,' said Baxter, 'but there'll be no heir.'

'Come now, gentlemen,' said Urquhart mildly, 'you can hardly expect the poor Queen not to produce when her time comes, merely to avoid inconvenience.'

'I simply wished to point out,' said Baxter to the room at large, 'that even if the pregnancy is a true one, who is to say the child will live? The Queen's offspring have not been conspicuously healthy so far. The last son and heir she bore the King lived, if I recall correctly, a mere five days.'

'Then let us all pray that the new child may be strong and healthy,' said the Bishop. 'Nevertheless, when the child is born, I fear things will move fast.'

'They say in the New Town that preparations are already in hand in Holland,' said Baxter. 'There is constant talk of invasion. Informed opinion says there will be large levies of troops before very long.'

'Informed opinion is probably right,' agreed Middleton, 'in which case it might be necessary to form a town guard.'

'I have already had thoughts on the matter,' said the Baillie. 'There will be unrest of all kinds and until matters are settled one way or another, the Old Town is sure to suffer if we omit to make adequate preparations for its defence. The town must be quartered, measuring northwards from the market cross to . . . But perhaps you would care to accompany me home to discuss it further? When the Session business, of course, is finished?'

'I think we can declare it finished now,' said the Bishop, rising.

'You will deliver the sermon on Sunday, Mr Keith, reproving Gauld for his misdemeanours. He has undertaken to attend and make public confession, so an address on transgression and repentance might be in order. I leave the choice of text to you.'

'Yes, my lord. And the Montgomery child?'

'Make the usual arrangements, Mr Couper.' The Session clerk nodded. 'And perhaps you would call on Mrs Grant, Mr Keith, and tell her of our decision?'

'Certainly. I'll go at once.'

'Then I think that settles matters to everyone's satisfaction. And now, when I have said the blessing, perhaps you could spare me a moment Dr Urquhart? I have a new brandy on which I would like your opinion.'

The Elders dispersed, the Bishop and the Mediciner to the pleasures of brandy and tobacco, the Baillie and the Principal to similar pleasures, although disguised under the name of town business – for whatever faults the advocate may have had, no one could criticize his cellar – the Subprincipal to find out Kenneth Fraser and discuss the financial intricacies of the Cathedral rebuilding, and the rest about their various businesses. Mr Keith was the last to leave. As he turned the key in the door of the Consistory chamber, he had a moment's doubt.

'I hope we have done the right thing for the child.'

Still, there was no alternative and the thing was done. He strode out through the west porch and turned his steps towards the High Street and Widow Irvine's Close.

'You get that brat out of here and take the others with you!'

'Yes, Ma,' sighed Christian. She tucked Margery, five months old now and heavy, into the fold of her hip, smacked her brothers quickly about the ears and pushed them out of the door.

'And keep out of trouble!' Isobel Grant stood, plump arms akimbo and watched them safely down the forestair to the Close. Then she turned quickly and closed the door behind her.

Christian wondered what it was to be today. The cards, perhaps? Or the potions? But she knew better than to speculate too closely or to mention the matter to anyone, not even George.

'Come on,' she said irritably as one of the boys dawdled, dabbling bare feet in a puddle, 'or we'll be too late to see the soldiers.'

The two boys skipped ahead only to collide with a pair of plaid-wrapped women turning into the Close. A flashing hand, a squeal and the boys were scurrying for safety, but the women came straight on towards her and Christian saw with surprise that it was the Sledder woman and Baillie Baxter's wife. Both were muffled in plaids which covered their hair and half their faces, but Christian knew them well enough. When they had passed, she waited a careful moment and then looked back over her shoulder. It was as she thought. The women were mounting the forestair to the Grants' room and, as she watched, the door opened and they vanished quickly inside.

'Oh well, Margery,' the girl said philosophically, 'that means we'll have to stay out till the curfew. When we've seen the soldiers, we'll go to the wood and look for raspberries.'

On the grass beside the College, the town guard was being put through its paces by a man from Edinburgh who had come specially to drill the men and train them in the use of firearms. Christian liked to watch, as did most of the town's children, though she had little idea what it was all about.

In June the King's son had been born. He had been christened James Francis Edward, and against all Baillie Baxter's pessimistic prophecies, continued to thrive. Mr Keith had announced the royal birth from the pulpit and there had been bells and a special feast day with a public bonfire and wine. They said it had cost nearly nine pounds, paid for out of town funds. Yet it was strange because the Minister seemed sad and so did the Bishop and Dr Middleton. Christian thought people were always glad when a son was born. Her mother had lit a candle to the blue painted lady she kept behind a brick in the fireplace, and had made them all kneel in thanksgiving. But other people had been angry. Then the Minister had told them, only last Sunday, that there might be an invasion and that the King needed four more soldiers from the town. The heritors had to contribute four pounds each to fee them. Her mother had been furious about it, but she would have to pay all the same, and as a result there would be no money to spend at the fair.

The four soldiers had been duly fee'd and had gone to the King. Now there were these other men as well, ordinary men who were to be trained to defend the town against anyone who attacked it. William Walker had made the announcement at ten o'clock on Saturday, at the market cross.

'The town shall be divided into four equal quarters. The said guard and watch will enter with their overseers into that part where it shall begin, on Monday next at ten at night and shall continue till five in the morning as long as it be found necessary.'

George Cumming had listened enthralled and Christian even then had been jealous. She knew she could shoulder a pike or a musket every bit as well as any boy. But when she said so, George laughed at her. 'You? It's men's work. Anyway, you're always trailing that baby everywhere.'

She looked at Margery with defensive pride. The infant had thrived, especially since the youngest Grant child had died of the croup in June and Margery had had double the milk. But Christian knew she would not get it much longer. The child that died had been eighteen months old and her mother was tired of nursing and impatient for Margery to be weaned. She seemed as infected as the men by the martial preparations and was restless and irritable. It was time, thought Christian, that her father came back. Her father was a soldier, in the King's army, and it was two years since he had been home.

But in spite of her jealousy, Christian liked to watch the guard at their daily drill and the boys marching on the fringes of the company, sloping staves on their shoulders instead of the muskets and the firelocks which the men had. They were marching now on the grass beside the College.

She saw Alexander Crystal and George's father, even William Walker the town drummer, though as an ex-militia man himself he hardly needed training. Then she saw George. He was marching in time with the men, just as if he belonged. She called out to him and he turned and glared. Then he ignored her, stepping out more briskly and standing as tall as many of his seniors.

'Isn't he splendid?' breathed a voice at her elbow and she saw Elspeth Middleton, shining-eyed and worshipping, with a basket of eggs forgotten on her arm.

'Who?' said Christian brutally.

'George of course. His father thinks they will let him take his place with the real guard soon.'

'He's out of step,' said Christian cruelly. 'And I think it's stupid to pretend you're a man when you're not.' With that she turned her back and walked away. Her brothers had disappeared, but she knew she could rely on them to keep out of trouble and not to go home till William Walker beat the drum.

Christian crossed the street to the Mediciner's house and followed the dyke which bordered his land until she reached the open fields and struck right along the track past Broome hill to the old loch.

The loch was dry now, drained and dyked long ago to make fertile land and rouped yearly by the town to whoever would pay the rent. The corn was already harvested and rabbits hopped lazily over the golden stripes of stubble and earth. The sun was warm overhead and as she passed under the wall of Cluny's garden Christian could hear bees droning heavily from the other side of the dyke and the deep-throated purring of doves. A thrush chattered angrily till she passed. Sir Alexander Gordon of Cluny had the best garden in the town : not a kale yard like other people had, but a pleasure garden laid out in patterns of little hedges and flowering plants and trees. The garden reached back from the Chanonry right to the boundary of the loch. Christian knew it well, for she and George had climbed the wall often enough and once, when they knew Sir Alexander was away, they had dropped to the grass inside and walked in wonder along the neat avenues of fruit trees and scented herbs.

George Cumming's yard was on the south side of Cluny's Wynd, but Christian knew that today it would be empty. Besides, she told Margery indignantly, even if George had been there, working with his father at the furnace or the bellows, she would not have looked.

She turned her back on Cluny's Wynd and followed the path westward to the wooded hummocks of the Kettle hills. For where the Don wound its way through the ravine behind the church there were still trees – the poor stunted relics of the great forests which had once covered the land and which were too old or too twisted to have been of any use for roof beams or timber or even common staves. These trees, birch and ash and a sycamore or two, clung tenaciously to the slopes of the river valley, among the heath and broom and the long, coarse grass.

The woods were pleasant that afternoon, the turf warm under her bare feet and soft with new-fallen leaves. Below her in the valley the river flowed gently over stone and from her right came the distant, grumbling drone of voices. That would be the hospital. Christian glimpsed its spire through the trees. The old men must be quarrelling again. That reminded her of Gauld the Sexton. They said he would never get a pension and a white coat and a place in the hospital now. Christian still shuddered at the memory of that night in the kirk, but at least it had given her Margery, and for good. They said Montgomery would come back one day, but Christian did not believe it. Why should he come back, with no wife and no son?

The girl moved slowly on, searching for the pale-toothed leaves of the wild raspberry and lifting the prickled fronds to pick the berries which hung in scarlet clusters underneath. She had woven a shallow basket out of twigs and lined it with leaves, and by the time the sun had moved round to the west so that the shadows lay long across the grass, she had heaped the basket full. Satisfied at last, Christian lay on her back on the turf and stared upwards into the filigree of branches and turning leaves while the sun warmed and soothed her and everywhere the birds sang. Beside her the baby gurgled and waved her plump limbs quietly in the sunlight. Christian listened to her with contentment, every now and then feeding her one of the succulent berries. She ate none herself, knowing that Mrs Haliburton would give her a penny for them, perhaps two, and Christian desperately wanted something to spend at St Luke's fair.

All sorts of people came to the fair. There would be stalls and sideshows, sweetmeats and ribbons, beggars, pedlars, acrobats, tinkers, sellers of broadsheets and songsheets and pictures: Christian's eyes grew dreamy at the thought of it. Then from nowhere a shadow of unease slid across her mind. All sorts of people came to the town at fair time. Suppose Montgomery were to come back after all and demand his child?

She stood up, scooped Margery close on to her hip and picked up the basket. It was then that she heard the voices – soft, confiding voices and a girl's laughter. Christian stood motionless in the dappled shade of the beech trees, till the muted browns of her hair and dress and skin merged into the shadows of evening as a fawn melts into bracken. Then she saw them, hands linked and heads close, talking. The girl laughed softly with a sound like birdsong. Christian watched, tense and white-faced, until they were out of sight.

Mrs Haliburton, as Christian had guessed she would be, was delighted when the child knocked on the kitchen door and offered her wares.

'See,' she said triumphantly to the servant-girl who had been beating barley at the knocking-stone for the evening cakes. 'The Bishop's favourite dish. We will serve them tonight with a handful of meal toasted brown on the griddle and a bowl of beaten cream. Here is a penny for you, Christian.' Then with a smile at Margery she added, 'And another for the stonemason's child.'

On her way back along the Chanonry, Christian met Mrs Middleton looking both angry and worried.

'You, child!' she called to Christian as the girl tried unsuccessfully to avoid her under Cluny's Port. 'Have you seen Elspeth anywhere?'

Christian hesitated. It was a basic rule for survival never to give information to anyone, but why should she protect people who ignored her, or treated her as nothing?

Before she might change her mind she said, 'Yes. I saw her in the woods.' And added recklessly, 'With George Cumming.'

Immediately the words were spoken she felt like Judas himself.

Elspeth did not go to the fair. She was confined to the house for persistent and wilful disobedience until such time as arrangements could be made for her to go to Edinburgh, to an aunt.

'Margrat is to come too,' she explained. 'We are to share our cousins' governess and learn to speak French and play the spinet. But I don't want to go,' she finished unsteadily.

Christian, who was delivering freshly laundered clothes at the house, felt sick with guilt. 'I'm sorry, Elspeth,' she mumbled awkwardly. 'We will miss you.'

'But I will come back,' cried Elspeth eagerly. 'In the summer I will be back. You won't forget me, will you? And you will tell George I . . .'

But Christian's face had closed.

'Oh, it's not fair! I wish I was dead!' Elspeth flung her head on her arms and burst into tears. The sound of her sobbing followed Christian far into the High Street.

3

'Well, don't look so miserable, child. Anyone would think you had been sent to purgatory instead of Edinburgh. Surely you are not still moping for the country?'

'No, Aunt Cunningham,' Elspeth dropped a dutiful curtsey.

'Then try to cultivate a pleasant and open countenance. Head up! Back straight! I want to look at you.'

Elspeth fixed her eyes on a bright gold nectarine in the far corner of the ceiling and bit her lip to keep it from trembling. The Cunninghams occupied a comfortable flat on the third floor of a six-storey 'land' in the Lawnmarket, a position which afforded a perfect view of the gentlefolk, noblemen, merchants and townsmen who thronged the thoroughfare below or passed on business of varying importance between the Castle and Holyrood a mile away at the foot of the hill.

The street was no longer than the High Street at home, but whereas the Old Town street was flanked by a single row of one or two-storey thatched buildings, with the fields visible everywhere against miles of unbroken sky, this street was cramped and claustrophobic with six, seven and eight-storey buildings leaning towards each other over layers of timbered galleries, and buttressed on either side by wynds and closes as packed with houses as the main street, and as densely populated. Twenty times as many people were crammed into the royal mile of Edinburgh as dwelt in the Old Town street. And their buildings, to Elspeth at least, seemed twenty times as high. From a small window on the turnpike stair of Advocate Cunningham's house, it was possible to glimpse a green triangle of hillside, but from ground level one saw only rooftops and broken scraps of sky. Margrat found the bright crowds of the city exciting, but today the noise drifting up from the Lawnmarket reminded Elspeth of market day at home. She blinked to keep back the rising tears and concentrated harder on that nectarine.

Aunt Cunningham's ceiling was beamed, like the ceiling at

home, but someone had painted it all over with luscious, tropical-coloured fruits: purple grapes, golden apricots, brilliant scarlet strawberries and raspberries and plums. It was as crowded with colourful life as the street three storeys below, and the high polish of floorboards and panelled walls reflected and threw back the colours in a rainbow blur over her aunt's spinet and clothes press and large oak settle. Her uncle had gone as usual to the Club to hear the latest intelligence from London and abroad, but she knew it was too soon to look for letters from home. They had not been in Edinburgh a week.

'Yellow damask, I think,' her aunt was saying, 'with blue stomacher and petticoats. She must have a long-sleeved shift – that one is too short – with two, no three layers of lace cuffs, and cross-lacing on the bodice. And stays, of course, for them both.' Aunt Cunningham turned her attention to Margrat. 'I am glad to see that you at least look cheerful.'

'Oh yes, Aunt Cunningham. And please,' ventured Margrat with unusual daring, 'please may we walk about and see the grand ladies and gentlemen when our lessons are done?'

Aunt Cunningham frowned. 'We shall see, child.' But she was not displeased at Margrat's eagerness. 'Purple I think for this one,' she told the dressmaker. 'In a stiff brocade. Her hair is dark and will look well. And scarlet petticoats with an *echelle* of pink ribbons on the bodice. They will both need caps of course and I shall expect you to dress their hair, Ford, as you do for Lilias and Susanna.'

Jean Ford, the governess, a vacuous-faced woman of thirty with pale brown hair and freckles, flushed pink with excitement. 'Oh, madam, I have been waiting to tell you. Yesterday when I was escorting Miss Lilias to her singing lesson we saw the Countess of Crawford stepping into a sedan in the Canongate and her hair was dressed high in front in the newest French style – *fontange* I believe they call it. If madam would give her permission, I am sure the Countess's maid would teach me how to dress madam's hair in the same style. Jean Irving, as madam knows, is a relation of mine by marriage.'

'Thank you, Ford,' said Aunt Cunningham with satisfaction. 'Lady Erskine mentioned the *fontange* to me at her "four hours" only yesterday, when Lady Eglinton appeared with a new style of headdress. Her maid is notoriously incompetent and the style was merely . . . unusual. However . . .' She paused thoughtfully. 'I hear there is an excellent place for linen caps in the West Bow and I believe the Lady Anne Crawford has a dancing lesson this afternoon. We will walk there together and call afterwards at the dancing master's to make arrangements. Elspeth and Margrat must begin dancing lessons as soon as they can be suitably clad.'

'Oh Elspeth, isn't it exciting?' whispered Margrat when her Aunt and the dressmaker had left and the four girls had resumed their morning studies.

Miss Ford rapped warningly on the spinet where Lilias was painstakingly picking out the notes of a new piece by Mr Purcell. 'No talking, girls. Except in French.'

Behind the raised pages of their French readers the sisters exchanged glances. Beside them in the windowseat Susanna was making urgent faces and pointing downwards to the street, where a young man dressed entirely in sky-blue brocade, with a wide plumed hat and a sash from which swung a light dress-sword, was threading his way carefully on red cork heels through the crowds.

'*Voici le* turkey-cock!' hissed Susanna. She and Margrat broke into helpless if silent giggles, and even Elspeth managed a smile.

They saw the young man at close quarters later that day as they walked behind Aunt Cunningham to the West Bow. He had another young man with him this time, a cheerful-faced youth in a plain grey short coat and breeches. Both men bowed to the little procession led by Aunt Cunningham in her full finery of beauty-patch, half-mask and muff, with her eldest daughter similarly clad beside her. The 'turkey-cock's' eyes were openly admiring and Lilias Cunningham blushed, but it was Elspeth who held his companion's attention and when he caught her eye as she looked up from a hasty curtsey, he smiled. When the men had passed, gallantly stepping into the fouler regions of mid-street to allow the ladies free passage under the protective galleries, Margrat and Susanna dissolved once more into helpless giggles.

'Hush, girls,' said Miss Ford reprovingly. 'Don't you know that was James Baird, son to Alexander Baird the merchant, and his younger brother Hugh? They have the splendid mansion house next to the Earl of Moray's in the Canongate. Mr James has just returned from a tour of France, but if events go on as they threaten to do, it is said he may well go back again before the year is out. I hear the Earl of Balcarres talks of retiring to the Continent if the Orange King gains power and if he does go, they say he will take many with him. Don't dawdle, child!' she called to Margrat who was lingering in front of a periwigmaker's, 'and watch where you put your feet!'

In the West Bow, Aunt Cunningham dismissed Miss Ford and the younger girls. 'I will keep Lilias with me to choose the bonnets. You may escort Susanna and our guests as far as Whitehorse Close in the Canongate,' she told the governess. 'Then return to me here. I know their father would wish them to learn something of the history of our royal city.'

'History!' snorted Susanna. 'All Ford knows about is who had dinner with whom and whether the latest moppet has arrived from London. Just look at Lilias,' she added wickedly. 'Flouncing and prancing like a barnyard hen just because a young man bowed to her. Come on Margrat, race you to the Cross!'

The two bounded away, ignoring Miss Ford's protests, and while the governess hurried after them, as fast as her cumbersome skirts and the cobbles would allow, Elspeth followed more slowly, trying not to wrinkle her nose against the reek of the ill-cleansed and ill-ventilated street. Pigs rooted in the street as they did at home, but here they found the gutters clogged with refuse, and Elspeth had early realized the importance of the brown paper which her aunt gave orders to be burnt each evening at the first warning cry of *Gardez l'eau*. But there was so much to see that Elspeth soon forgot the malodorous filth underfoot and ignored it like a native of the town.

She passed bookbinders, goldsmiths, saddlers and sievewrights, lingered at the litsters and periwigmakers, admired the many coloured phials at the chirurgeon's booth. Sedan chairs swayed past them at the jog and through their tiny windows she glimpsed the masked and beauty-spotted faces of ladies on their way to musical gatherings or social evenings at the great mansions off the Canongate. Once a coach rumbled past them, blocking the road and forcing them under the overhanging piazzas of a ten-storey 'land' in the High Street. Here there were open booths displaying all kinds of wares, and when they reached the wider spaces near St Giles' they found market stalls heaped with all kinds of woollen cloths, linen and ribbons, pots and platters and spoons.

They had passed St Giles and were almost at the end of the High Street when Elspeth saw the familiar sign – a hammer surmounted by an imperial crown – above a narrow booth squeezed between a candlemaker and a weaver in a passageway off the main street. The booth contained a forge and bellows, and the flaming mouth of a stone furnace. A young apprentice stood, bare to the waist, his skin glistening with sweat as he hammered at the molten metal. Elspeth stopped.

'What are you making?' she asked curiously.

The lad glanced up and said 'Trencher.' Then as the girl still lingered he added, 'For the Lord Provost.'

Elspeth watched him in silence for a while, then ventured, 'I am from Aberdeen. I have a friend who . . .' But a hand seized her arm and another boxed her smartly round the ears.

'You are not in the country now, Miss Elspeth, to run about when and where you choose. You are in the city, to learn city ways and to be a lady!' Miss Ford was red-faced with indignation and exertion. 'We have been searching the length of the High Street for you, you tiresome child! Now walk smartly or we will not reach Moray House before it is time to turn back.'

'Miss Ford says this is the way Queen Mary rode,' chattered Margrat excitedly, 'and King James after her and our own King James on his visit to Edinburgh, though he was only Duke of York then. I wish he would come again while we are here.'

'So do we all,' sighed Miss Ford. 'There were such grand balls and masques and entertainments when the royal party was here. However, I am thankful to say there are still families who keep up the old ways.'

They were almost at the Canongate now. The houses on either side seemed taller and grander the closer they drew to Holyrood, and through open archways they glimpsed the Closes which contained the mansions of dukes and earls, barons, rich merchants, and Lords of Session. Ahead of them, at the foot of the dipping street, lay Holyrood and beyond it Elspeth saw green fields and hills. But she was not permitted to linger.

'This is the best part of town,' Miss Ford was saying. 'Over there is the Earl of Moray's town house. They say that is the very balcony where the Marquis of Argyll stood to watch Montrose dragged on a hurdle to the Tolbooth. And next we have . . . There! Did you see that sedan? That was Lady Eglinton I am sure. They say she is to give a grand dinner for the Lord Lyon next week and will serve *three* courses *and* a dessert, with fifteen dishes in the first course alone! There are to be musical diversions, too. Lady Grisell is to sing a song of her own composition and Lady Margaret Crawford will play a piece by Mr Purcell never heard before in the city. And they say . . . But there is Lady Grisell herself! The tall lady in the green silk. Curtsey girls! She is looking this way.'

'Aren't you glad we came, Elspeth?' whispered Margrat as they curled up together in their truckle bed that night. 'And doesn't home seem *dull*? I hope Papa lets us stay for years and years!'

Elspeth did not answer, but she lay awake a long time listening to the wind in the chimneys and once, high overhead, the call of wild geese, flying . . .

The fair came and went, but the usual excitement was lacking. For one thing, Christian found to her surprise that she missed Elspeth. For another, George had changed. He seemed to have grown older overnight. He no longer went fishing or snaring rabbits with the other boys, but was always and voluntarily busy in his father's smithy.

'I am learning to fashion a claymore,' he explained to Christian. 'When I have mastered it, I shall make another, for my "sey".'

Christian knew better than to ask why the first one would not do. A 'sey' must be made entirely by the candidate, under strict supervision: some trades went so far as to lock the aspiring member and his implements into a chosen room until the task was done. Then the finished article – teapot or tankard or whatever it might be – was presented to the Deacon of the trade for judgement. Christian knew the hammermen were strict. They had been known to refuse a 'sey' as inferior, and the stigma of such a failure was difficult to outlive. Not merely for reasons of pride, but because a man who failed to qualify was forbidden to practise the work of the trade. But George would not fail. He had been working at his father's side all his life and had the natural, inborn skill of his father and grandfather and great-grandfather before. She could see it in the ease with which he turned the red-hot metal on the anvil, beating and shaping it as the glow faded and the sparks flew.

Watching him, Christian felt excluded. George was moving into a man's world where she could not follow. Even his choice of 'sey' excluded her, as a teapot or a set of filigree toasting forks would not have done. Those she might have imagined were made for her. For Christian was changing, too. Her breasts were swelling, for one thing, and for another her mother had decided it was time she went into service.

'I'll keep my ears open, Christian,' she said. 'I hear the girl at the Gardens' is a lazy baggage and Baxter's wench is no better.

Though I wouldn't have you go there unless he paid through the nose. We'll see what offers at the Whitsun hiring fair. Meantime you can help me with the wash.'

But the most disturbing change was deep in the girl herself. She had odd longings and waves of desolation which she could not cope with and did not understand.

'What will you do with the claymore?' she asked George now. But he had turned back to the anvil and the bright sparks sputtered from his hammer to dance like fireflies across the dim interior of the shed. It was open on one side to the causeway of Cluny's Wynd and through the huge doorway one could see, close across the Wynd, the dyke of Sir Alexander's garden with its trailing roses and its apple trees. Margery gurgled and stretched out a hand towards the scarlet fruit.

'You can't have those Margery,' said Christian. 'They're for the rich folk,' and added illogically, 'in *Edinburgh*. Do you mind, George, that time last summer when we climbed the wall and nearly got caught?'

But George was absorbed and did not hear. Christian stood a moment watching in the heat from the furnace, but as he continued to ignore her, she hitched Margery higher on her hip and left. It was always the same now. When he was not in the forge, he was drilling with the guard. Christian wandered back down Cluny's Wynd to the market cross, and was almost glad when her mother called her to tramp clothes for the Garden family.

'It's easier with two,' said Isobel Grant. 'I'll be finished that much sooner and be paid the same.'

Together they collected the linen from the Gardens' lodging and carried the tub to the well at the foot of the Brae, close under the Chaplains' Port, which still stood intact, though the Reformation had destroyed for ever the close-kept security of the Cathedral precincts with their four entrance gates and enclosing walls. Isobel Grant, with a furtive glance over her shoulder, crossed herself quickly and dipped a knee to the defaced figure of the Virgin above the gateway. Christian saw her mother's lips move swiftly in the familiar words, before she tossed her head, laughing, rolled up her sleeves to expose strong forearms and set to to fill the tub from the well. Then she added the soap which she and Christian had made from the ashes of bracken mixed with lime and water, and had boiled with tallow and salt until the scum rose. The scum was carefully lifted off and cooled to form the soap. Sometimes Isobel Grant had not the patience for the long process of soap-making and used only the lye, but not this time, for Mrs Garden was particular about her linen and Isobel had a shrewd eye on the Gardens' household as a possible sinecure for Christian.

Now Christian dumped the baby on the grass and climbed into the tub with her mother. Hands on each other's shoulders and skirts looped up to the waist, they trod the linen together till their legs were blue with the cold and the water flew in icy sprays across the grass. As their legs pounded in rhythm, up and down, up and down, in the thick suds, Christian felt her melancholy slough away and when her mother's voice lifted suddenly in a wild, exuberant song, the girl joined in with delight. For the first time in her life, she felt at one with her mother.

The crisp air of late October brought high colour to their cheeks and overhead the sky was pale and clear as ice. The trees behind the Chaplains' Court were gold and bronze and gleaming, and the grass at the well-side was already brittle with autumn. As Margery crawled across the dying turf, the drugget garment rucked up around her waist to show firm bare buttocks and sturdy legs. The child was miraculously healthy. Others had the croup or the flux or the whooping-cough, but Margery seemed to lead a charmed life. She was quiet, too, and contented. Only one thing worried Christian: the left leg, the one Mrs Haliburton had pointed out to the Mediciner, was shorter than the other and bent.

'No matter,' said Isobel Grant when her daughter mentioned it. 'If she's crippled, we'll ask for a beggar's token for her. She'll do well enough.'

Christian did not answer, but her lips set tight. Margery would *not* wear the lead *fleur-de-lis* of the registered town beggar. Margery was not going to join the leprous and the maimed and shuffle through the Burgh with a begging bowl. Besides, the child was bright. She crawled early and would surely walk at twelve months. And the leg might grow.

So Christian watched the baby over her mother's shoulder as they tramped and sang, and she felt happiness bubble inside her like a pot of clear water on a high fire. They were still tramping half an hour later when Baillie Baxter turned into the Chanonry from the High Street with several members of the Session. With a wicked glance over her shoulder, Isobel Grant laughed and kicked her legs higher. And Christian did the same, outdoing her mother in deliberate provocation. And when Isobel broke into the words of a satirical ballad which enjoyed much favour among the Stuart king's supporters, Christian joined her.

Good people come buy
    The fruit that I cry
That now is in season tho' Winter is nigh
Twill do you all good
    And sweeten your blood
I'm sure it will please you when once understood
    Tis an Orange . . .

'Disgraceful!' fumed Baillie Baxter, averting his eyes. 'This business of public washing must be stopped. It is positively immoral.'

'I'll tread your shift for you, Baillie,' cried Isobel with a wink at Christian. 'I've got the thighs for it. Look!'

'And for you she'll do it free!' called Christian gleefully as she saw the Baillie blush.

'That Grant woman is a disgrace to the town,' stormed Baxter as he strode up the Chanonry to the Cathedral. 'And her daughter is as bad. And did you see the Montgomery child, stark naked in the grass? I said all along it was a mistake to leave the infant with that family.'

'Is there any news of Montgomery?' asked John Keith. They were in the Consistory house now, for the weekly meeting of the kirk Session.

'None,' snapped Baxter. 'And not likely to be.'

'Why do you say that?'

'It's obvious. The man's run away.'

'What about the masons?' asked the Minister of George Fraser. 'You have had six of them working on the church for weeks. Surely one of them has heard something?'

But it seemed they had not. 'The man's disappeared,' said Fraser. 'Unless he's got caught up in the troubles. I hear Claverhouse is not taking developments without protest.'

'That Dutchman is having his setbacks too, I'm glad to say,' said Middleton. 'It must have been a blow to his ego as well as to his prospects to have his expedition defeated by a mere storm.'

'The hand of God,' said the Bishop drily. He rarely missed a meeting of the Session now that time was running out so fast. The Scottish bishops, including Haliburton, had only that month declared their loyalty to King James and by that declaration he knew that he had sealed his fate. The foiling of William of Orange's first invasion attempt had given them no more than a reprieve.

'Montgomery will come back one day,' said Urquhart. 'And so will the Dutchman. He is not the sort to give up, and there are too many people depending on him for their own political fortunes to allow him to do so, even if he wanted to. He'll be back within the month, or I'll eat my wig.'

'And if he does come back and is successful,' said the Bishop quietly, 'there will be changes.'

There was silence in the Session chamber. Everyone knew the implication of the Bishop's words and everyone knew that it was the Bishop himself who would suffer more than any of them. For him there could be no compromise, no outward conformity with inward reservations, no silent self-preservation. The Consistory house had seen many changes in the hundred and more years since Bishop Gavin Dunbar had built it. It would no doubt see many more and survive. The indwellers had had good training in such things. Both Presbyterians and Catholics had learnt to practise their faiths in secret while conforming publicly to the established church of the day. Episcopalians could learn to do the same. All churches needed congregations. But the Presbyterian church did not need – or allow – bishops. When King James went, Bishop Haliburton must go too.

'About the washing,' said Baxter briskly; 'it must be forbidden.'

'Come, come,' said Dr Urquhart. 'Cleanliness is next to godliness. You cannot *forbid* washing. Besides, many women earn an honest living that way.'

'Then they must do it in the proper place, preferably in their own houses behind closed doors.'

'With all that water to carry?'

'In a properly run household with diligent servants there would be no problem.'

'Perhaps not. If, like you, they had a well at the door.'

'Washing has always been done in the stream, at Powis or the High Street or wherever is convenient. I see no harm in it,' said Middleton. 'It is an honest enough occupation.'

'Perhaps,' snapped Baxter. 'When it is not used as the excuse for flagrant immorality. Besides,' he finished triumphantly, 'the washing water fouls the burn.'

'This is not a fit matter for the Session,' said the Bishop with asperity. 'It is purely a town matter and would be more properly discussed by the Council. As so many of you gentlemen belong to both bodies, there should be no difficulty in carrying your discussions over to the next meeting of the Burgh Court. Meanwhile, I would be grateful if you could turn your attention to the business of this meeting, namely the arrangements for the service to mark the opening of the new term. I assume, Principal, that in your establishment at least, business will be as usual?'

And as usual at the beginning of November, the Bishop led the academic procession from the College to the Cathedral porch. Also as usual, the Bishop was followed by the Principal and Subprincipal, the Professors and the Regents, each in his black gown, each at the head of his particular group of red-gowned students. There were seventy students that year and the procession reached from the gate of King's to the market cross on its solemn journey to the Cathedral of St Machar's which, with the passing of winter, was to become a simple parish kirk.

Bishop Haliburton had a premonition that he was leading the procession for the last time, and his fears were justified. In November William landed in Tor Bay. James Thomson, Treasurer of the Council, was commissioned to buy the town more arms so that the heritors might the better protect themselves if it should prove necessary. George Fraser took charge of them: nine firelock guns, ten halberts, two swords and two banderls. Together with the two militia muskets, two pikes and two more swords which the town already possessed, this made quite an armoury. The guard was drilled carefully in the use of the new arms and every heritor in the town was ordered to provide himself with a weapon of some sort, be it only a stave.

But in December James II prudently left England to join his wife and infant son in France. By then the King's cause in Scotland was lost.

The news of the Stuart king's flight precipitated a movement which removed some two hundred episcopalian ministers from their seats. And in the Royal Burgh of Old Aberdeen, Bishop Haliburton prepared to leave. When Episcopacy was abolished by the Estates the following April, he quietly removed his household to his mansion house near Coupar Angus where eventually, though not for twenty-six years, he died.

Many in the old town were sorry to see him go. Christian felt unexpected tears spring as she watched the cart pass along the High Street towards the Spital. Mrs Haliburton saw her standing at the entrance to Widow Irvine's Close and beckoned. Obediently Christian trotted along beside the conveyance as it rattled over the setts. Mrs Haliburton sat with a servant-girl amid a mound of bundled luggage, while the Bishop rode ahead of them beside his son John. For John Haliburton, one-time Regent and Civilist in the college, was also leaving. Christian held on to the wooden side of the cart with one hand while she clasped Margery jogging on her hip with the other.

'Goodbye, Christian,' said Mrs Haliburton, giving her a penny. 'You are a good girl. Take care of the stonemason's child.'

At the Powis burn beyond the college Christian let go of the cart and watched it blur into the distance and out of sight.

That was in April. For in February William and Mary had accepted the throne of England and in March they had summoned a Convention of the Estates. William prudently reinforced his new position by three regiments of Hugh MacKay of Scourie's army and a band of Highlanders under the new Earl of Argyll. Their only opposition was a troup of fifty horsemen gathered by Claverhouse. A month later Claverhouse raised James' standard outside Dundee, but with such disappointing results that he went north again to lure the MacDonalds of Keppoch away from their harrying of Inverness by an offer of close on three thousand Scots pounds. Then he set off down the Great Glen, collecting Donalds, Camerons, Stewarts and Macleans until at last he had an army fit to confront the Earl of Argyll, newly returned from the hurried coronation in London and with a commission to support the new King in Scotland.

News of the gathering armies filtered slowly into the town. Baillie Baxter brought regular and pompous reports from the New Town. Principal Middleton had letters from Edinburgh and there were the wildly exaggerated and differing word-of-mouth reports of pedlars, beggars and travellers from both north and south. Meanwhile, with the removal of the Bishop, the balance of power within the town was subtly shifting.

The Provost was busy about his own business which kept him for long periods out of town, but the other nineteen members of the town council, the baillies, the deacon, the convener of trades and the town officers, busied themselves assiduously with consolidating the internal everyday running of the Burgh. The

Minister, left in sole charge of the parish by the removal of the Bishop, was equally assiduous in maintaining kirk discipline and good order, while in the heart of the town the University continued in healthy independence, like the kernel in a nut.

And in the Council Baillie Baxter, at last, had his way over the washing.

'Hear ye! Hear ye!' William Walker beat a summoning roll on the drum.

'Go and see what way they've thought up to get our money this time,' said Isobel Grant to Christian. 'It'll be that Baxter man's idea, whatever it is, the old misery.'

So Christian took Margery and joined the other indwellers at the market cross.

'Hear ye! Hear ye! It is ordained by the Provost and baillies that no person nor persons within the old town of Aberdeen or Chanonry wash any clothes or anything else at any part of the Chanonry from the head to the foot, but only at the back, next to the loch and that they set their fire and washing vessels there and throw out their foul water on the south side of the entry of the said channel so that no part of the said foul water may fall in the said channel. Likewise, that no person wash at any part of the Powis burn above the bridge unless they set their fires, wash and throw out their foul water at some distance from the burn where the foul water may not fall or come thereto. Likewise no person may tramp and wash in tubs upon any part of the High Street from the one end of the town to the other, under the penalty of forty shillings Scots to the officers who are hereby impowered to impound their clothes and washing tubs until the fine is paid and that for each transgression *toties quoties*.'

Christian listened with growing anger and dismay. Now she and her mother would have to trek the distance to the loch or find some spot below the Powis bridge – or do their wash in the Close with what water they could get from the draw-well. But if all the tenants of Widow Irvine's Close used the well for washing, it would soon be dry.

'A pox on the man!' shrieked Isobel in fury. 'The snivelling, whey-faced, spavinned warlock!'

'Hush Ma!' cried Christian in terror. 'Someone will hear!' Women had been pilloried for less.

'Let them hear! And the devil take his skin for windows! But I'll get him!' A gleeful look swept the anger as suddenly away.

'Listen, Christian, I want you to do something for me. You know the Baxter woman is not yet with child, in spite of all his plunging and his sweating and his lechery? And her daughter weaned a good six months?'

Christian nodded. She knew also that her mother had sold the woman potions, so far, apparently, to no effect.

'And you know the Baillie wants a son and that his wife would do anything to get him one and escape a beating?'

Again Christian nodded, this time with sympathy.

'Well, listen carefully and do exactly what I say.'

As Christian listened her face brightened with excitement and not a little fear. Quickly she folded her thumb against the palm of her hand and closed her fingers over it for protection. 'But suppose they tell?'

'They won't. They need me too much to give me away and besides . . . they're afraid.'

Christian did not need to ask why. She was a little afraid herself when she saw her mother casting fortunes and mixing herbs.

'Now away you go. And don't let anyone see you.'

It was cool under the trees. Below the hill, the river shimmered in the pale midsummer darkness and in the clearing between the stunted birch trees the figures were more than mere outlines. When the fire flamed and the red light danced, faces leapt clean and clear.

Christian saw the Sledder woman and Isobel Baxter, Kenneth Fraser's new wife and Jean Catto, with two of the servants from the Chaplains'. There were more women, too, all with quaintly fashioned oatcakes in their hands, all dancing slowly round the fire. As the flames flickered and darted higher, the dance grew faster, plaids were cast aside, skirts lifted, bare legs pranced. The night air was warm and the smoke from the burning turf crept sweetly acrid into the nostrils. Sparks danced under the shadowed leaves. And the dance grew faster.

'This to thee! Protect my hearth.' The woman flung a knob of oatcake over her shoulder.

'This to thee, O fox! Spare my fowls.'

'This to thee, O hoody crow . . .'

'This to thee . . .'

A shrouded figure stepped from the shadows of the trees and held up an imperious hand.

'When the owl has three times hoo-ed, When the cat has three times mewed,' she intoned, and spilt a libation of caudle into the earth. 'When the moon is come and gone, Fill her with a bonny son.'

One of the women stepped forward to the fire, cast off her gown and stood naked. The light of the fire licked over her body, smudging it with red. Slowly she began to dip and twist in the firelight while the circle of women closed around her, arms linked and hips swaying as they chanted, 'When the owl has three times hoo-ed, When the cat has three times mewed, When the moon is come and gone, Fill her with a bonny son.'

Hips thrust in the leaping shadows to the rhythm of the words, faster and faster until the voices merged, suddenly, into the driving chant of '*Fill* her, *fill* her, *fill* her, *fill* . . .'

Christian watching from the bushes felt a thrill shiver through her body. Her breasts tingled and there was a disturbing ache deep in her loins. She would have liked to cast off her own dress and join them, to feel the hot fire in the folds of her body, thrusting . . . But again the dark figure raised a hand and Christian knew it was time. Quietly she edged back into the cooler darkness of grass and heath. Then she was on her feet and darting swiftly down the hillside to the stile.

She found Baillie Baxter at the change-house, with the schoolmaster.

'Please sir,' she panted. 'There is a fire in the wood. And dancing!'

'Where, child?' demanded the Baillie, rising purposefully to his feet.

'Over behind the loch, near the river.'

'Crystal! Cumming! All of you, follow me! We'll catch them this time! We'll bring them to justice!'

The matter of the midsummer fires had long been a thorn in the flesh of the Session. Over and over they had been forbidden and year after year, somewhere and secretly, fires were lit, caudle spilt and the old rites carried out. Baillie Baxter had almost caught the culprits last year, but by the time he reached the place the ashes were cooling and the dancers gone. This time he set out at the run, a handful of men at his heels, up the High Street, left into Cluny's Wynd and across the field to the river. At a safe distance, Christian followed until she stood in the lee of Cluny's dyke. A figure joined her.

80

'Well, Christian? Did you do as I said?'

'Yes, Ma. He's on his way in a flaming rage, with some of the men.'

'That will be sport!'

'But the others, Ma? What will happen to them?'

'They'll run. If they want to. Don't you worry, Christian, they've done it often enough before. Why, I mind last year when . . .' She stopped as a figure came speeding silently across the grass from the loch, skirts lifted, hair streaming and bare feet flashing.

'Run,' cried Jean Catto as she sped past. 'They're after us.'

Isobel Grant seized her daughter's hand and pulled her into the shadow of Cumming's forge. They crouched in a corner behind the anvil and waited until the figures had passed – several running women and, some way behind, the men.

'They'll not try too hard to catch them,' said Isobel with satisfaction. 'At least,' she giggled, 'not unless it's in the woods. It's only the Baillie who's after blood. I'd like to see his face when he corners her!'

'Suppose she gets away, Ma? Like the others?'

Isobel laughed softly. 'Without these?' She produced a bundle of clothing from under her plaid. 'She'll be dodging in the trees as naked as the day she was born. I wonder who'll catch her?' she added wistfully. 'If he's even half a man, she'll get her son before the night's out.' After a minute she added, 'You go on home, Christian, and see to the bairns. I'll be along later.'

But it was morning before Isobel Grant came home and when she did there was a lingering scent of excitement about her and a new contentment which the girl found strangely disturbing.

'I'll not have it,' roared the Baillie. 'No wife of mine shall kneel on the stool of repentance in full view of the town. I'll not be shamed!'

'I would ask you to remember, Baillie,' said the Minister sternly, 'that the meeting of the kirk Session is not a place for unseemly shouting.'

'I am not shouting, sir!'

'With respect, Baillie, if you do not lower your voice, I shall be compelled to ask you to remove yourself until such time as you are calm and collected.'

'I am perfectly calm! I was never more collected! I see my way as clear as in a glass! No wife of mine shall disgrace me in public!'

'But you said yourself, Baillie,' said Urquhart solemnly, 'that sinners must make public repentance.'

'And make a mockery of one of the town baillies? A respected member of the kirk session? It is difficult enough to hold authority nowadays without having my position deliberately undermined. Public servants must be protected from public shame!'

'I recall that you had no such objection to Gauld making public confession,' reminded Middleton. 'And he also held a position of authority in the church.'

'That was different. He paid for his own sins. But I tell you here and now that I will not be made a public laughing-stock. If you persist in demanding public confession from my wife, I will disown her.'

'Come now, Baxter,' protested Mr Keith. 'You cannot disown your wife merely for dancing at a midsummer fire. She must repent, of course, before the congregation, and she must make retribution, but she cannot be disowned.'

'Especially,' put in Urquhart with studied lack of expression, 'when, through whatever misguided motives, she was only doing so for your . . . increase.'

'Besides,' said George Fraser, 'the whole town knows she was brought home naked by Alexander Crystal.'

'Almost naked,' corrected Urquhart. 'I understand he gallantly stripped and lent her his shirt.'

'If you had cornered her yourself, of course,' said Fraser, 'you could have dealt with her in private and no more said about it. But once such a thing is public knowledge, public justice must be done.'

The Baillie's complexion had passed from pink to purple to chalk-white and his hands on the table-top trembled. He was remembering his wife's face when he had chastised her. She had laughed at him – actually laughed in his face – and her eyes had shone with an excitement he had not seen there before, not even on the night of their first union. And when he beat her, the look had not left her face, merely retreated like an inner and indestructible joy.

'I will disown her,' he repeated woodenly. 'If she is not permitted to make reparation here, privately, before the Session, I will publicly disown her. I will not be shamed!'

'What's done is done,' murmured someone, but Mr Keith lifted a hand in reproof.

'It is not a matter for levity,' he said sternly. 'Pagan superstition must be rooted out and destroyed whether it be found in the houses of the great or of the lowly. But I am inclined to agree with the Baillie that private confession might be expedient. Not, I hasten to impress upon you, because the Baillie is a man of influence, but because nothing must be done which might weaken the position of the church. King William is already established in England. It is only a matter of time before he is accepted here in Scotland, and when that day comes, he must find our church united, ready and worthy to accept him. There may be those among us who regret the passing of the old Episcopalian church,' and here his eyes met those of Principal Middleton, 'nevertheless, we must all pull together to build in its place a stronger, purer, *Presbyterian* one.'

There was a moment's silence at this timely reminder. They were all aware that the new Parliament would abolish prelacy and establish Presbyterianism as the true kirk. Episcopalian services were already forbidden in many parts of the country, bishops excluded and the new kirk in power. In the Burgh it made little outward difference. The Burgh remained at heart Episcopalian, yet too many people knew what would be their likely fate if they were seen openly to fall out of step. Besides, they told any nagging conscience, Christ remained Christ whether St Machar's was dubbed a cathedral or a mere parish kirk.

'I heard news of Claverhouse today,' said Urquhart quietly. 'He has rallied an army at Dalcomera and is moving down the Great Glen towards Killiecrankie. The meeting with Argyll cannot be far away.'

'We must strengthen our defences,' said George Fraser. 'I suggest a rota of twenty-four men from nine at night till five.'

'And every fencible man in the town to provide himself with a weapon.'

'Gentlemen, gentlemen,' reminded Mr Keith. 'You are not at a Council meeting now. Please proceed with the disciplinary action to be taken against the laird of Balgownie's servant-girl. A shocking case, but a first offence and both her master and her mother have interceded for her.'

'About that guard,' whispered Fraser to Middleton. 'I'll draw up the statutes for Saturday, then Walker can cry them at the cross.

The sooner we get things in motion, the better, if the clans are on the move again.'

'. . . Likewise it is enacted and ordained by the baillies and the Council,' boomed Walker, 'that every fencible man within the town shall provide for and have a firelock and sword or sword and partizan or sword and halbert against this day eight days, that is by the twenty-ninth of the month, under the penalty of twelve pounds scots money. Hear ye! Hear ye!'

That was on July 22. Five days later at the pass of Killiecrankie, Claverhouse's army, although outnumbered two to one, routed the Williamites till they fled in panic through the pass in a wave of blood and broken heads. A thousand spades, the victors sang, would not level the graves of the enemy. But one spade on their own side dug a grave that was to be the grave of their cause. For Claverhouse himself was killed, and with his death the heart went out of the Jacobite army. After an ineffectual attempt to capture Dunkeld, the clans prudently dispersed and drifted home to their glens.

Most of them struck inland through the lands of Mar and Invercauld and northwards to Inverness. Other bands took the coast road and passed sporadically down the Spital and through the Old Town, over the Brig o' Balgownie and northwards into Banff. Detachments of the King's men followed, harrying.

And Montgomery came back.

Christian heard her mother retching over the pail and propped herself on one elbow to call, 'Are you all right, Ma?'

The boys were already at school and Christian had lain down again with Margery for an extra few minutes. She was often tired these days with a strange and dragging melancholy. On other days she felt so full of energy that she ran and laughed aloud. Yesterday had been like that until she met George Cumming in Cluny's Wynd.

'Come to the sands, George?' she invited. 'And look for crabs?'

But he shook his head. 'I have to work on the new door for the Council house.' He had grown three inches in the last year and his voice had deepened. She followed him to the door of the forge where his father was already at work.

84

'Hello, Christian,' called Cumming and added, 'how's your mother?'

Christian was surprised. 'Well. Why?'

'Just asking. And the little one?'

Christian looked down at Margery, walking now in her own lopsided way but still silent. 'She's well.' She and the child stood in the doorway and watched as George shovelled more turf into the fire and heated the strip of metal till it gleamed. The muscles of the boy's bare shoulders swelled under a film of sweat as he began to beat out the metal for the lock and banding. Christian watched, mesmerized by the movement of his body. When he caught her eye she looked quickly away and, to her embarrassment, blushed.

'I'll go then,' she mumbled, pulling Margery after her.

He stopped, resting the hammer on the earthen floor between his feet. 'Have you been to the Middletons' lately?'

Christian nodded. Isobel Grant often helped out at the Middleton household when they held a washing week. Christian, George knew, was her mother's messenger.

'I mean,' he went on awkwardly, 'is there any news of George and ... and the others? Are they coming back?'

'I don't know,' she snapped and left, tugging Margery impatiently after her. All the brightness had gone out of her day. That had been yesterday and the melancholy was still with her now as she watched her mother straighten at last.

'Are you all right, Ma?' she repeated. 'You're not ill?'

Isobel Grant shook her head. 'No lass. I fear it's a bairn.' Her face was suddenly old. 'Mother of God,' she went on, 'what am I to do? They'll get me this time, Christian, and I haven't the strength ...' Christian was dismayed to see tears in her mother's eyes.

'It's all right, Ma,' she said awkwardly, pulling an arm around her mother's shoulders. 'Perhaps Dad will come home.'

'If he does, he'll beat the life out of me. No, lass. I'm done for this time.'

Christian knew what she meant. There would be endless questions till the father was found, and then the punishment. If she refused to tell, it would not help. They had been known to question a woman in the worst pangs of childbirth and with the fear of death in her eyes in order to get at the truth. And when she told, there would be the punishment ...

'Perhaps no one will find out,' said Christian, but she knew it was a futile hope. Once, a girl had managed to conceal her pregnancy and the birth too, only to be caught burying her new-born, strangled child in the fields. Another had left her baby at the Minister's gate and slipped home again, but the Elders had searched the town, feeling every woman's breasts until they found those newly swollen with milk. Christian felt the sweat run at the idea of all those hands, feeling . . . Other women had fled the town rather than face the Session. One poor servant-girl had even drowned herself in the pool at the Brig. Christian shivered at the thought of it. She did not know which would be the worst: the cold, black water in her eyes and ears and mouth – or the Minister's wrath as the victim knelt in sackcloth on the stool of repentance to be scourged by the tongues of the righteous. But surely her mother would never kneel? As if in answer, Mrs Grant stood up.

'But they'll not see me beaten.' She tossed her head defiantly and smoothed the grimy drugget over her already thickening waist. 'Remember that, Christian. Never let them beat you. Never let them see you down.'

At that moment, thought Christian, her mother looked indomitable.

'Well, what are you staring at, girl? I've that Sledder woman coming this morning and not a drop in the place. Fetch me ale and then get yourself and the brat out of here.'

'But the money, Ma. They'll not let me have it without.'

'Curse that skinflint of a dominie! But I must have ale . . . Away to the Council house and fetch Margery's poor money, before they lock up.'

'But Ma, suppose they won't give it to me? You know what happened last time.'

'Last time they said Montgomery would be back. Well he's not, is he?'

'No, but . . .'

'Then get to the Council and ask for more!' She swung an arm but Christian dodged expertly out of range.

'Ma,' she called from the doorway, 'suppose Montgomery does come back, what'll we do?'

Her mother laughed. 'We'll give him a sup!'

The Treasurer leafed irritably through his accounts. Ever since the Provost had demitted to go to the Bar and left them to their own devices, the baillies had run riot with the funds. Now they wanted to vote money for a new suit of clothes for the town drummer.

'It's only five years since the last suit,' he grumbled.

'Six,' corrected Baillie Baxter. 'In '83.'

'There is still no necessity to fit the man out like a lord at the town's expense. Meitt-coat, breeches, stockings, even a pair of double-soled shoes! You'll give him ideas above his station!'

'He has been useful to us,' said Subprincipal Fraser, 'in exercising the guard and serving with the watch. It's the least we can do. Besides, what will Major Guthrie and his men think of us if we can't even clothe our drummer with decency?'

'If we do, they'll think we've money to burn. They take enough as it is without provoking them further.'

'It's a question of civic dignity,' protested Fraser.

'Bunk! It's a question of money. And you don't have to balance the books!'

'You always managed before,' said Fraser.

Thomson bristled. 'That was when there were no soldiers.'

'Then turn it to the town's profit, man. That's what I would do.'

'Aye. Or to your own,' observed Dr Urquhart.

'What?' demanded Fraser angrily. 'Say that again!'

'I was merely remarking, my dear Fraser, that some people find profit-making easier than others.'

George Fraser reddened. 'I am tired of these veiled accusations,' he blustered. 'The kirk Session gave me two thousand marks to organize the repair work on our church. It took six masons to complete the job and they have to be paid.'

'Twenty Scots shillings a day?' said Urquhart drily. 'For six weeks?'

'And no stone to buy,' said Baxter.

'The lime was a large item,' protested Fraser. 'Transport costs, shipping . . . and ale for the masons, of course.'

'Not so large as to cost, say, two thousand marks?'

But the Treasurer had been making rapid calculations. 'Total expenses could not have exceeded half that sum.'

'So Mr Treasurer,' remarked Urquhart blandly, 'if our drummer is to be a credit to the Royal Burgh he could be decked in ermine and cloth of gold out of the tower . . . *savings?*'

'I protest,' shouted Fraser, scarlet to the ears. 'I'll bring actions for slander! The kirk Session is perfectly satisfield.'

'Or will be,' said Middleton coolly, 'when we receive the magnificent new Bible you have promised us.'

'Come now, gentlemen,' interposed Dr Urquhart as Fraser leapt angrily to his feet. 'Let us not resort to violence. I propose that as there is no more business to settle we leave the Treasurer to his accounts and adjourn to the change-house for refreshment and a cooling of the tempers. Will you join me, Principal?'

'Delighted. And in return I will give you the latest news from Edinburgh. I had letters only yesterday.'

They moved away down the High Street, talking, and the other Councillors followed. Christian waited till only the Treasurer remained, then she raised a hand and knocked on the open door.

'Well?' demanded Thomson.

Christian swallowed. 'I've come for Ma's money,' she said. 'For the stonemason's child.'

'Is that her?' asked the man, looking with distaste at the dark-eyed infant who stood unsteadily on bowed legs, clutching at Christian's skirts for support. Her hair was matted and dirty and one leg was bent at an unnatural angle, but her eyes were intelligent and she looked healthy enough. No sign of the itch, anyway.

'How long is this to go on,' grumbled Thomson, unlocking the strong-box. He began to count out a careful amount. 'I heard the man was coming home to support his own brat, but he's taking long enough about it.'

Christian snatched up the money and hurried out into the street before the Treasurer could change his mind.

She heard the voices from the High Street, women's voices shouting, and a man's. The ale tankard slopped in her hand as she dragged Margery impatiently after her into the Close.

Her mother leant over the forestair, the Sledder woman beside her, both shouting abuse at a stranger who stood below them at the door of Montgomery's house. The man was tall, but stooped with weariness. His hair was matted and his clothing unkempt. Even from the distance of the Close Christian could see the vicious wound which slashed his cheek from brow to chin. His shirt was in tatters and his breeches thick with mud. Or blood. A leather bundle was propped against the closed door of Montgomery's dwelling, and when Christian saw it she paled.

'Wait!' she warned Margery, pulling the child back. They stood together warily under the wall of Baillie Baxter's tenement and waited.

'You killed her!' she heard Montgomery roar. 'You evil carlin!'

'Liar! You killed her yourself,' shrieked the Sledder woman. 'Your puny female child killed her. If it *was* your child!'

'Slanderous, evil-tongued witch!'

By now the Close was filling rapidly as people appeared from open doorways or hurried in from the High Street and the neighbouring wynds.

'What's this? What's this?' demanded a voice of authority and Baillie Baxter pushed his way through the crowd past Christian and into the Close.

'The woman's a witch!' roared Montgomery. 'First she put the evil eye on me and then on my wife and child.'

'This is a serious charge,' warned Baxter. 'Take care you do no slander. You, woman,' he demanded, turning to Mrs Sledder, 'what have you to say?'

'I'll slit his other cheek for him, the lying warlock!'

Montgomery staggered and put a hand to the lintel for support. The blood sprang again from the wound on his cheek and trickled in dark rivers down his face and neck.

'That's a bitter wound, man,' called someone in sympathy. 'Where did you get it?'

'Killiecrankie . . .'

'The English . . .'

'A sword from one of Argyll's men . . .'

The words ran through the crowd in deep-throated sympathy: many stories had come to them via travellers and the soldiers themselves of what had passed between the two armies at Killiecrankie. Montgomery, they said, had been engaged in mason's work for Claverhouse and had been pressed into the ranks with the others. There were many Jacobite sympathizers still in the Old Town, and they looked on Montgomery with kindness. But the stonemason had gathered new strength.

'She trod on my wife's belly,' he shouted. 'She trampled her!'

'Aye, she did right enough.'

'Pushed her in the dirt and overleapt her.'

'Killed her, too, like enough with her so near her time.'

'Witch . . .'

The Sledder woman cowered back into the doorway of the Grant tenement. Isobel Grant looked frightened, too. And with reason, thought Christian. If her mother's activities were discovered, she would be branded, scourged, excommunicated, banished . . . the child's imagination ran wild as all the known punishments snowballed into some vast and terrifying torture chamber. She had seen a woman scourged, once. They beat her with sticks from the market cross to the Spital and when at last she staggered across the town boundary she had been spattered from head to foot with blood and moaning terribly. Christian had seen her pitch on to her face in the dirt beside the road, but in the morning she had gone. That woman had stolen a salmon from the sacrist at the college. What would they do to her mother if they found out about the cards and the mixtures and the other things?

'Oh Ma!' she prayed, clutching Margery's hand tight. 'Holy Mother of God, help us all!'

But Baillie Baxter was speaking. 'Your wife died in child-bed as many women do. It was God's will.'

'The devil's will! That woman's will! She cursed my wife and killed my child!'

'Nonsense, man,' said Baxter briskly. 'The child is not dead. And it is time you came home and supported her. The town has done it long enough. Christian! Bring Margery Montgomery over here!'

Christian was as white as her mother and her hand in Margery's trembled, but there was no way out. Slowly she walked forward with the ale tankard in one hand and the child in the other. Margery limped trustingly beside her with that strange, dipping motion she had developed to counteract her shortened leg. As they advanced over the trampled mud of the yard, the crowd parted to let them through and Christian tipped her chin and straightened her back in unconscious imitation of her mother.

Montgomery watched them with wild, incredulous eyes as they moved towards him: the frightened, newly-adolescent girl with her swelling breasts, her brown skin and her too-tight, homespun clothes: and the child, ragged and half-naked, but with its mother's dark eyes and clear skin. And a twisted leg.

The pieces snapped suddenly together and he roared aloud.

'The devil take the Sledder woman for his own! See how she has marked my child! Witch!'

He leapt for the stairway, but half a dozen men seized him and held him back. He struggled, but even his strength was not enough now. His face was a mask of blood and dirt through which the eyes blazed with the brilliance of madness. The Sledder woman paled. The voices in the Close were strengthening now as people remembered.

'Aye, she cursed the bairn right enough.'

'Mind poor Janet's funeral when the Sledder woman said the bairn was uncommon strong? And didna' bless her!'

'The evil eye, surely!'

'The uncanny eye . . .'

The Sledder woman clutched at the rail of the forestair and shouted above the babel of voices, 'Liars, all of you! It's her you want!' She spun round on Isobel Grant and spat the accusation in her face. 'She's your witch!'

She flung herself on Isobel, slashing with filthy nails, screaming abuse. Isobel fought back, clawing at the woman's face, shrieking, tugging out great gobbets of hair. Locked together, they crashed against the rail and the forestair rocked.

'Whore!'

'Harlot!'

'Witch!'

Then someone threw a pail of slops over them and they fell apart, gasping. The Sledder woman recovered first. She scrambled, streaming, to her feet and bounded down the stairs. At the bottom she turned and hurled her accusation from the safety of the yard.

'Ask her who lit the midsummer fire! Ask her who casts fortunes and reads dreams! Ask her who brews mixtures and recites charms, and under Montgomery's own roof!'

'Silence, woman!' ordered Baillie Baxter. 'Or I'll throw you in the tolbooth for brawling.'

'Then you'll throw her too and for more than brawling, the adulterous witch! Ask her about the child in your wife's belly! Ask her about the bastard child in her own! Ask her and you'll see who's the witch!'

Baxter flinched. In the tenement above, Isobel Grant pulled herself to her feet by the door lintel and stood grey-faced and swaying as she clutched at it for support. Below her, Montgomery swung his head from side to side searching till he found the right face.

'She-devil!' he gasped and spat the blood from his mouth. 'Whore and daughter of a whore! See what you have done to my child!'

As she saw her mother stagger, the fear burst inside Christian's head and she flung the ale full into Montgomery's face.

'You did it,' she cried. 'I saw you with my own eyes.' She turned to confront the sea of faces: untrustworthy faces, lusting for blood. 'My mother is innocent,' she cried. 'Margery was born whole and untainted. I delivered her myself and I know. She had no blemish until he took her and hurled her across the room because she was not a boy. Ask Dr Urquhart in the College. Ask the Minister himself. They will tell you it is so. Ma didn't do it. Her own father did. He maimed her with his own hands!'

There was silence as they looked from girl to man to woman and back. They had heard the truth in her words, and all eyes turned to Montgomery who had heard and understood as clearly as any of them. The anger and the violence drained out of him. He stood white-faced, quivering, while the blood slowly dripped from his cheek to the dust of the yard and his eyes burned with an unknown light. The men who had been holding Montgomery loosed their grip and fell back in silence so that the man stood facing Christian and his child across an empty square.

'Give me my daughter.' The voice was no more than a whisper. When Christian made no move he spoke again, and this time his voice could be heard from the Spital to the Brig. 'Give me my child!'

Christian flinched and dropped Margery's hand.

'Come here, Margery.' The stonemason held out his hand and the child took it. The indwellers watched in silence as the huge, broken man and his lame daughter slowly crossed the yard to the door of his dwelling. They passed inside together and the door closed behind them.

With a cry of anguish Christian flung her hands across her face and ran blindly from the Close.

In her aunt's flat in the Lawnmarket, Elspeth was crying too. She had just been told that she and Margrat were not to go home after all that year.

'What on earth are you crying for?' asked Margrat in astonishment. 'Surely you don't *want* to go back to those hens and that everlasting spinning?'

The door opened and Miss Ford hurried in. She was pink with agitation.

'Elspeth, you tiresome child! Your stomacher is still unlaced and you know you are to accompany your aunt today on her afternoon calls. The sedan is waiting already and what Lady Eglinton will think if you arrive with your cap awry and your ribbons undone, I do not know!'

'It's all right,' said Margrat soothingly. 'I will do them for her. You go on down and we'll follow in a moment. Stand still, Elspeth!' she snapped when the governess had gone. 'You'll make us late and you know I want to be there before anyone else arrives. Have you forgotten Lady Eglinton is going to serve *tea*? They say it is terribly expensive. How you can be so calm about it, Elspeth, I just don't know. I am so excited! I have never even seen tea and today I will actually taste some! Do you suppose it tastes at all like ale? Or like goat's milk, perhaps? Or brandy? There, I think that will do. You look quite presentable and really very pretty. Oh, Elspeth,' she added anxiously as they hurried down the common stair to join the others, 'do you think Lady Eglinton will ask me to sing? I have learnt a ballad especially, but I know I shall be nervous with all those grand ladies listening . . .'

'Don't be a goose, Margrat. You know you have a lovely voice, and if you are a little nervous, they will only like you the more.'

'I hope so. I do so want to do well. Oh Elspeth, I don't know how you can even *think* of home when Edinburgh is such an exciting place!'

'The affair will have to be investigated. Serious charges have been made.'

The Session was meeting in the Consistory house to discuss the business of Isobel Grant.

'Nevertheless, Minister,' pointed out Urquhart, 'the accusation was made with malice and in the heat of the moment. Everyone knows the woman who made it was, shall we say, under stress?'

'She's a troublemaker,' said Fraser. 'Always has been.'

'The Sledder woman must be punished, of course,' said the Minister, 'for brawling and swearing and striving with her neighbours, and so must Isobel Grant. But the charming and the witchcraft are more serious charges. If false, we have a mere case of slander: if true . . . it is a matter for the Presbytery.' The Minister paused to let the implication sink in. 'We have not had a case of charming in the Burgh for how long?'

'Seven or eight years,' said Middleton. 'Before your time, Minister.'

'A most interesting case,' observed Urquhart. 'The woman used no physic, merely a stocking. She chanted gibberish and invoked the aid of Father, Son and Holy Ghost.'

'This woman Grant has Popish leanings I believe,' said Fraser.

'We'll have her up before the Session and find out,' said Mr Keith. He sounded tired. Since the Bishop's departure he had found the burden of parish affairs onerous and depressing to the spirit. This latest instance of godless superstition was particularly disturbing because the Minister had liked the Grant child. He remembered vividly the night he had caught her in the kirkyard with the Cumming boy and Montgomery's babe. The girl had seemed goodhearted and honest. What would become of her if her mother was condemned? Who would have her in his house with the suspicion of witchcraft about her? Nevertheless, justice must be done.

'The woman must be tried,' he repeated, 'and if she is found guilty of half the sins of which she is accused, she must be severely punished, very severely indeed.'

But Isobel Grant did not appear before the Session. Returning late one night from a riotous evening with Major Guthrie's men, she fell into the unprotected draw-well in the Close and broke her neck.

The Session moved in and took charge. Isobel's two sons were indentured as servants and Christian herself was bound, for a year in the first instance, as kitchen-maid to the Garden family. The Professor of Divinity was a kindly, godfearing man. He knew no ill of the girl, he said, and the charges against her mother had not been proved. Moreover the mother and daughter had done washing for the household on numerous occasions and had been found satisfactory. Christian would be paid £8 Scots a year, with two pairs of shoes. She went to live in Dr Garden's lodgings in the Chaplains' Court, where she slept with the other servant in the kitchen. The tenement above the Montgomery house was empty. There was no one to see or hear how things were between the stonemason and his child.

94

Part 2
1694—1698

William Walker stood to attention at the top of the Spital and awaited the signal. It was an unseasonal morning in early May. Hoar frost prickled on the thatched roofs, sparkled from the brass globe on the King's College crown, glinted from a thousand crusts on the puddles in the causewayed road. The chimneys were dead now as the indwellers slept in their wynds and their closes and one or two of them, gentlemen these, in their solid brick-built houses. There were no lights from the tiny windows, no sounds from the street except softly, from the east, the rhythmic sigh of the sea and from the trees around the College the awakening murmur of birds.

William Walker adjusted the front of the long meitt-coat, pulling the creases straight and scrubbing at the grease until his barrel chest swelled the purple cloth into dignified rotundity. He flicked imaginary dust from the frayed lace collar and stamped the square-toed, double-soled shoes once, firmly, on the frozen turf. It was almost time.

Expectantly he looked down the length of the High Street, past the ruins of the Spital kirk, past the Humanist's house and the Mediciner's house with, between them, the forbidden graveyard of the Snow kirk, past the Powis burn where it crossed the road at the College garden, past the crowned dome of the College itself, with the grammar school and the Musician's house close beside, past Douglas Wynd and Wrights and Coopers Wynd and the brewery, past the Close where that dour and dangerous Montgomery lived and on to Alexander Crystal's house.

Here his eyes narrowed briefly with remembered injury. It was seven years since Crystal had reported Walker to the baillies for dereliction of duty, but Walker had not forgiven or forgotten. And when Crystal had lost his place as Deacon of the hammermen on account of his working this long time in the country, Walker had been delighted. No matter that the whole town knew Crystal had gone in search of work in order to feed his large and motherless family. No matter that with meal the price it was and yet another poor crop threatened, any man who was able would have done the same.

'Sacked,' thought Walker gleefully. 'And if he does not come back soon, he'll find all the work taken and serve him right.'

Yet food was certainly short and what there was, expensive, with little enough money to be had at the end of a hard winter. And whatever else you might say about Crystal, there were times when he talked sense. He had been right about the tower all those years ago and now he was right again. Crystal had warned the town only last year to lay in better stocks of meal, but with so many demands on the town's resources, particularly the new King's constant requests for soldiers, there had been neither time nor money to consider such a precaution.

Now, after the dreary, rain-drenched summer of the previous year and the long, hard winter which had followed, things were no more promising. With little seed for planting and the ground still locked in frost, the coming season threatened to be just as bleak. There would be empty bellies enough by the autumn. Except of course for those who always prospered.

The drummer's eyes flickered over the square block of Baillie Baxter's tenement. Rain or frost, good harvest or bad, Baillie Baxter flourished. With lawsuits enough in the New Town, land to farm, houses to let, and free stock well over five hundred marks, with the profits from the change-house he had run with the music master, until the Council forbade it, and which he now ran alone, with a guaranteed outlet for his ales through Council meetings and Council business, with a wife, seven healthy children and four servants, nothing could stop the man. Baillie of the Council, Elder of the Session, member of the commission to inspect the common moss, to deal with market regulations, to discuss the rebuilding of the school, the repair of the Powis bridge, the disposal of the church's stones . . . the man had a finger in every pie.

Except possibly one.

The drummer grinned. There were some who said it was prudence rather than necessity which kept Alexander Crystal out of town. There was no denying that the eldest Baxter boy had eyes as blue as Crystal's and hair as blond, and folks still remembered that business of the midsummer fire. But the second Baxter boy was fair, too. Perhaps Crystal had been right to keep out of the way for a while. People talked, and Baillie Baxter had a temper.

'Serve the Baillie right,' growled Walker approvingly. 'He

98

should look to his own kale-yard before rooting up his neighbour's.'

The drummer's eyes moved on, past the market cross and Cluny's
Port to the Chanonry itself, above which the great tower had
soared until that day in May six years ago, when the wind had
blown up out of nowhere to destroy it. Now there was only sky
where the tower had been, and the two small steeples at the
western end. Gauld the sexton was gone, too, carried off by the
fever a year past, and Mr Keith the Minister, dead this six weeks
and the church doors closed ever since. With no Minister and no
sermon to keep them right, was it any wonder the town was going
to the dogs?

A movement caught his eye. A leather-clad shape was walking
across the yard in Widow Irvine's Close. The mason's unusual
size was detectable even at this distance: William Montgomery,
come from the parish of Rayne not twelve years ago this Michael-
mas and lording it like a life-long indweller! How dare he rise
before the summons!

The figure was bending now over the draw-well, mended and
safely fenced in by a stone parapet since Isobel Grant had fallen
to her death there five years before.

'And good riddance,' reflected Walker. Though they said she
was with child and her husband not seen in the town for years.
There was nothing Walker liked better than a good fornication
case, except perhaps a case of flagrant adultery, with the perpetrators in sackcloth at the church door. But the Grant woman had
cheated them all by killing herself. And Montgomery had got back
his child.

Walker watched the stonemason resentfully. He was drawing
water now, with the child standing beside him, watching.

'Women's work,' growled the drummer. 'That's what she's
brought him to, the bow-legged little witch.'

But it was almost five o'clock. He knew the moment to the last
second. His fingers flexed over the drumsticks and his breath hung
in an expectant cloud before his face. Moisture beaded the grey
bristle of his moustache and the deep scars and furrows of his skin.
As the first faint boom of the bell in the south steeple floated over
the sleeping town, William Walker struck an answering thunder-
roll from the stretched hide of his drum. Then he stepped smartly
forward down the incline of the Spital on the first solemn stretch of
his morning round.

The child dropped a handful of meal into the pot and stirred it carefully with the long-handled spoon. She replaced the lid and swung the pot back on its chain until it hung from the sway over the centre of the meagre fire. Montgomery watched her without speaking until she had completed the operation. Then he nodded, once.

'Good. Mind and keep back from the flame. And the steam.'

'I will, Father.'

Margery Montgomery limped across the earthen floor and picked up a broom, a bundle of furze twigs bound to a short length of wood. Her father had made the broom for her, measuring the handle length to suit her small stature. Carefully, she began to sweep. In silence the father watched.

The child was pale but clear-skinned and healthy. Her dark hair was matted and unkempt, for neither father nor daughter had the knowledge to keep it otherwise. In the early days when the in-dwellers had still felt sympathy for the wounded, wifeless father, there had been tentative offers of help. But the few well-meaning neighbours who had dared to speak to Montgomery on the sub-ject of his daughter's care had been so violently repulsed that no one had repeated the offer: and somehow the pair survived, the man gaunt and angry and indomitable, the child tenacious and devoted. Somehow he clothed her in shreds of homespun and coarse linen. Somehow he fed her and himself on what messes of meal and broth he could contrive, until now, as the child grew older, he was teaching her to care for him as he had done for her. Margery was solemn, intelligent and willing. She watched what he showed her and, what was of far more use, she watched the women in the Close. When her father was at home she knew better than to speak to any of the indwellers and incur his anger, but when he was away, engaged on mason's work or fishing in the estuary for salmon, she watched the women as they trod the linen or beat the barley on the knocking-stone or kneaded dough, and she re-membered and went home and did the same. Already she could make better kale than her father. Secretly she planned to find out how to make the bannocks so that they did not taste of smoked leather and, one day, how to brew ale.

Christian would teach her as she had taught her to walk and to speak, but Christian worked at the Gardens' house and could not get away more than one afternoon in a month, and then she usually walked out with one of the local boys or attended a secret dance in someone's barn. But Margery met Christian sometimes all the same – at the well or at the market or, when the flesher's bell rang, buy-in meat. The Montgomerys, of course, did not buy the meat, but Professor Garden's family still did, in company with the other Professors and the richer gentry, and Margery liked to watch as the flesher cut lumps of beef or mutton from the haunch on his hook, and to listen to his bell. And Christian always had a word for Margery. The old relationship had faded long ago, but they were still friends although Margery no longer knew the reason for it. She was not aware that they had once been as close as mother and child : she knew only that Christian was her friend and would help her. One day she might even teach her to spin and to sew a plain seam.

Meanwhile Margery ate what her father prepared, helped when she was able, and did her best to please him.

It was a strange relationship. Something had snapped inside Montgomery's head when he had seen his crippled daughter stretch out a hand to the father she had never seen. He no longer hated her for being female, but cared for her with a devotion he had never given his wife. She in her turn loved and trusted him with the whole of her small, untaught being and did not question that he was the greatest man in the town. Within the larger confines of the Burgh they lived in a closed world of their own. But they did no harm : the Burgh tolerated them and left them alone.

For a while, Montgomery had worked on the great house which Alexander Fraser, Professor of Greek in the College, was building at Powis, across the High Street from King's, until he came up against Kenneth Fraser, quarrelled with dangerous violence and strode off the building site, refusing ever to return. Professor Fraser was angry. He had heard of Montgomery's skill and wished to have him fashion the stone crest above the gate, but even his personal request had no success. Montgomery was adamant. He would not work on the same building as the master mason, and as there was no question of dismissing Kenneth Fraser and his gang, Montgomery was proudly the loser.

Principal Middleton found work for the mason about the College and the church. Baillie Baxter employed him to repair the wall of his tenements and to build a dyke. Other small jobs came his way and he survived, for Montgomery was a good mason and worked with the strength and the skill of two. But there were days when he did nothing but crouch at the fireside and moan, and on those days even Margery left him quietly alone.

For William Montgomery had aged in the years since Killie-crankie. He was only thirty-two, but his face was drawn and furrowed by deep lines of pain and the scar which slashed his face the length of one side was purple and in places nearly half an inch across. The eye on that side of his face was glazed, and the severe headaches which attacked him frequently and without warning had given a constant tension to his brow so that the lines were deep-bedded and permanent. He was still tall and broad-built, but he stood with a stoop and when he moved he carried his head at an angle so that he might make the most of his good eye. The result was an advancing sideways movement which the indwellers found unnerving. Children scattered when he approached and grown women crossed the street to the other side. Since Alexander Crystal had left the town, the mason spoke to no one except the Cumming boy – and his own daughter.

He spoke to her now.

'The frost is hard, Margery. It will be another bad summer.'

'Yes, Father.'

'Winter will come again before the crops can ripen,' he went on slowly, thinking out each step. 'We will need meal and there will be none. There will be no barley for the ale and no hay for the cow. It is God's curse on the Presbyterians and on all who bow the knee to the Orange king.'

'Yes, Father,' said Margery dutifully, shaking the straw bedding and laying it flat. She knew her father had been at a battle and that his army had won and then later, at another battle, had lost. She knew that there had been a different king called James and that her father had fought for that king, not the one they had now. But she also knew by instinct that neither she nor her father must mention the other king to anyone. She herself would never do so, but sometimes her father had strange and violent moods when he might do anything. She looked at him anxiously, remembering the time when he had suddenly shouted 'Curse the woman for a witch!' and had hit her. Afterwards he had cried. Margery had not cried, though the blow had blackened her eye and drawn blood where her teeth had split her lip. She bore the scar still. But when he spoke again it was to say, 'I will go fishing. You shall come.'

'Yes, Father.' Margery banked the fire and put the remains of the morning bannock into her apron. She knew from experience that a fishing excursion could last the day.

'We are early. That is good. If we are to catch fish enough to dry and store away for the hard times we must be there at the river before the others.'

But they were not the first after all. In the curve of the river below the Brig where the sandbanks humped against the surf and the sea-birds screamed, a boy stood thigh deep in the racing channel, a birch rod taut in his two hands and braced against his chest.

'It's George!' cried Margery, running ahead. Her father did not stop her. George Cumming was the only heritor Montgomery spoke to voluntarily. For the mason remembered the night of the high wind and how he and the boy had climbed the bell-tower together. A bond had been formed between them then and, for the mason, it was a bond that could not be broken.

'Have you caught anything, George?' called Margery, standing ankle-deep in the shallows.

'Not yet. Hey! Don't come out any further,' he warned as she gathered up her skimpy dress in one hand and waded deeper. 'The current is too strong.'

Margery stopped, her skirt around her waist now and the water lapping the tops of her bare thighs. The child wore nothing under the dress and her skin was purple with cold. 'But I want to see,' she said.

'Go back!' ordered George angrily. As she turned and limped obediently shorewards, George watched her irritably lest that limp of hers should betray her and tip her under water. 'Damn Montgomery! Why can't he look after her properly?' When she reached the shallows, Margery stopped, turned round and stood still, watching him. George drew in his line, rebaited the empty hook and flung it far into midstream.

The stonemason joined them. He and George lifted a hand in greeting, then Montgomery moved slowly along the sandbank, choosing his place. Here the bent grass rattled in the shore winds, sand blew in stinging gusts against the face and the ground was dry and shifting. He baited his hook and he too cast the line far out into the main current. Then, like George, he stood immobile, impervious to the cold and intent only on the swirling grey surface of the water and what might lie beneath.

Margery watched them both for a little longer, then limped away from the shore to where the bent grass grew in sparse, tenacious clumps on the sandy hillocks. Carefully she began to gather the grass, snapping off each stalk at ground level and laying the stalks evenly, in neat bundles.

George Cumming watched her. He could not have explained the fascination the girl had for him, but whenever he saw the dark-haired, solemn-eyed child with her dipping gait he could not take his eyes away from her. He remembered her as an infant in the roof of the kirk the night they had watched Gauld sift the ashes. He remembered her motionless in the grass when they thought she was dead. He remembered her naked and fragile as a new-hatched chick in the middle of the Bishop's kitchen table. He remembered her clamped to Christian's hip. She had been no more than a nuisance then, but since her father took her back and the two of them shut themselves away from the town, she had changed for him. George found her at the same time irritating, appealing and vulnerable.

George Cumming was almost a man now, seventeen years of age and as strongly built as his father. In June, Cumming senior was to be made a Burgess of the town and George knew that he too would be a Burgess one day. He felt it in the power of his arm, knew it in the strength of his hammer on the anvil. Yet a part of him rebelled against the fore-ordained pattern and filled him with restlessness. Nothing and no one seemed to hold his interest for long.

'You'd best marry,' his father told him, 'and settle down before you get some girl into trouble. Marry an honest, hard-working lass like Elizabeth Crystal and leave that Papist Grant girl alone.'

'What's wrong with Christian?'

'She's bad, like her mother before her. I've seen plenty of her kind, warm and willing and then one day you'll find she's trapped you and you'll have to marry her.'

'I'm not ready to marry,' said George defensively and felt the familiar panic which the idea always brought. Marriage meant shackles and commitment, mouths to feed, children to bury, tears and hard work. George was not afraid of work, but he had an in-grown fear of marriage. He had been out with every girl in the town at some time or another, but he had committed himself to none, not even to Christian. Christian was a part of his life and always had been, now more so than ever with her soft laugh and willing body, but he did not mean to marry her and he had told her so, though he suspected she had not believed him.

But he had meant it. He felt the power in him to be anything he chose, to achieve great deeds, to travel the world, to fight to win . . . and his woman would be gentle – as gentle as Elspeth

Middleton – and beautiful and adoring, content only to follow in his wake . . . He watched the water now with unseeing eyes as his mind followed the familiar track.

There was a stir in the water. George drew in the rod sharply, but not sharply enough. The fish escaped him and he cursed, his dream shattered. The morning had been wasted. His father would be angry. And angrier still if he was late. He must leave for the forge, whether he had caught anything or not. He reeled in the line and began to wade slowly towards the shore.

'Any luck?' he called to Montgomery. The man shook his head. 'Nor me. I reckon someone up river has taken them all already. These days everyone grabs what he can get. Will you be here to-morrow?'

'Aye.'

'I thought you might. Take care. The Session is up in arms again about the Sabbath observance.'

'But the church is shut. How are we to attend service?'

'No matter. Everyone is to stay meekly at home until such time as the church may be open again.'

'I shall fish tomorrow nevertheless,' said the mason doggedly.

'Then watch out. It is hard enough to find work as it is, without losing your money in fines to the town's purse. Don't say I didn't warn you.'

'I'll remember.'

'By the way,' went on the boy, 'I hear Lord Whitehill has feued four stances for building houses at the end of his yard, next the Chaplains' Port. There'll be work for someone there.'

The stonemason looked up for the first time and swung his head round until the good eye was on George. 'Who has leased them?'

'Baillie Knight has one, they say, and Baillie Thompson another. Who has the other two I do not know. But there will be houses to be built for someone.'

'Kenneth Fraser,' grunted Montgomery. 'He will get the work as he always does.'

'He is busy enough at Powis. They say Alexander Fraser means to build a second house when the first is finished, and then a row of several more. You should try for it, man. You are a better mason than Fraser and the whole town knows it. Put yourself forward.'

But Montgomery shook his head. 'If they want me, they must ask. I'll not go begging.'

George shrugged. He knew it was no good arguing. The stonemason had never been known to ask anything of anyone. 'As you like,' he said. 'But I thought I'd mention it, with the times getting harder, and the child to feed.'

'Thank you. I'll remember.' The stonemason turned back to his fishing and George went on his way whistling. He might yet be at the Chaplains' in time to see Christian at the pump.

Christian Grant tucked up her sleeves and emptied the brimming pail into the tub. She had been with the Garden family for five years now and was firmly established. She was pert and occasionally hot-tempered, but she was loyal and honest and she worked hard. Mrs Garden had recognized her worth long ago and no longer complained over the occasional burnt porridge or torn shift. Christian kept a friendly kitchen and liked to gossip, but as long as the family did not suffer, Mrs Garden was prepared to tolerate it. Servants were hard enough to come by and good ones hard to keep on the wages they could afford to pay. So Christian stayed, making up for any lack of particular skill by honest hard work. She had nursed the youngest three children from birth. She had scrubbed and cuffed them and the other six with the easy familiarity of long and close living together. Agnes Garden and two of her sisters were away in Edinburgh now, with an aunt, but John was at the University, at King's College in the Old Town. He was fifteen, the same age as Christian, and she had boxed his ears on several occasions when he came upon her alone in the kitchen and made the most of the opportunity. But she never boxed his ears till after he had kissed her, and then not hard.

For Christian had all the cheerful sensuality of her mother, though without her mother's easy affections. Christian liked men as her mother had, liked their attentions and their admirations and the liberties they took, but there was one man who really mattered to her and one day, she vowed, he too would know it.

Now, as she hauled vigorously to draw the water for the morning wash her eyes were on the road from the Brig.

'Well, Christian?' He took the bucket from her and tipped it high. The water spurted out of the tub and across her bare ankles so that she squealed and laughed and bundled her skirts higher.

'So that's the way to lift them, is it?' He scooped a handful of water and dashed it against her knees.

'George!' she protested, laughing. 'Stop it! It's cold!'

'Then how about this?' He put a swift arm round her waist and kissed her.

'Warmer.' She twisted away and backed around the washtub till it was between them. 'But I'm still shivering.'

He lunged after her, but she skipped nimbly out of reach, teasing. 'You'll be late for the forge! Daddy will spank you!'

'Come here, you little bitch.'

'Catch me! If you can!' She dodged behind the well, then darted across the road to the old Port with George close behind her. Under the gate and back again she ran, skirts high and hair streaming, until she fell against the wall of the archway, panting and laughing, full breasts heaving.

'Got you!' George put his hands against the wall on either side of her head, imprisoning her. They were both breathless and excited. He could smell the warmth of her flesh. He bent to kiss her lips and this time she made no attempt to escape.

'Disgraceful!'

They sprang guiltily apart to see Baillie Baxter bearing down upon them from the direction of the church.

'George Cumming! You should be at the forge with your father, not indulging in lewdness and debauchery in the street. And as for you, Christian Grant, wait till Professor Garden hears about this. And in the morning, too!'

'Why is it worse in the morning?' whispered Christian, and George snorted.

'I was on my way home, Mr Baxter,' he said solemnly, 'but I was ... diverted.'

'Disgraceful,' repeated the Baillie, fuming. 'I don't know what the town is coming to. I shall speak to the Session about it this very day.'

He strode angrily away under the gateway and turned right, into the High Street. George followed him, grinning.

'See you Thursday,' called Christian. 'Don't forget.' She too was smiling as she looped her skirts firmly and stepped into the tub. The sound of her singing followed George as far as Cluny's Wynd and his father's forge.

'Lang may his lady, look frae' the castle doon,' sang Lady Grisell Baillie, 'Ere she see the Earl of Moray come soundin' through the toon ...'

Lady Grisell curtseyed her acknowledgement of the applause and resumed her seat. The drawing-room of Lord Crossrig's Edinburgh apartment was crowded. The advocate's musical supper-parties were always a success and even Aunt Cunningham for whom music, except when the necessary accompaniment to dancing, held little interest laid aside her fan the better to applaud Lady Grisell's performance.

'She sings beautifully,' sighed Elspeth in admiration.

'And with unusual enjoyment for a follower of the true kirk,' said her companion with a smile. Hugh Baird, still shabby, open-faced and cheerful, had changed little in the five years since Elspeth had first seen him, but Elspeth herself had changed a great deal. Or so her aunt was pleased to believe.

'Is she not a credit to me?' she murmured to her neighbour, the Countess of Crawford. 'I remember how she was when she first came: brown-skinned and sullen and quite unmanageable, running about the streets like the country wench she was.'

The Countess raised her half-mask and studied Elspeth critically before replying, 'She is certainly greatly improved. That dress is most fashionable and her hair is very becoming. She has quite the air of a lady.'

'Thank you. You do me honour, madam, to say so.' Aunt Cunningham felt sufficiently flattered to add confidentially, 'But it was not always easy. Once, though you may not credit it, she and her sister and, I regret to say, my own Susanna, were actually caught riding a *pig* in the West Bow! The governess could do nothing with them.'

'And is Miss Ford still with you?'

'Gracious yes. She is not intelligent, I know, but she is an expert at dressing hair and she turned Susanna's green brocade most competently only last week. The girls are with her now. They have a slight chill, nothing more, but I thought it best . . .'

'Naturally. Very wise, with the tales one hears . . .'

There was a pause – illness was rife in Edinburgh that year – before Aunt Cunningham resumed, 'Yes. Elspeth is certainly much improved.'

Both women regarded Elspeth in speculative silence.

'The Baird boy seems . . . assiduous. Is there anything . . . ?' The question hung tantalizingly between them before Aunt Cunningham shook her head with unnecessary vigour.

'Nothing at all. He is, as you know, a fourth son, with no means and no prospects. Ah! I see your daughter Helen is to play for us next. How delightful that will be. She is such an accomplished performer. I well remember that evening at Lord Panmure's when she entertained us so elegantly with Mr Burnett's galliard and that beautiful pavan.'

The harpsichord stood at the end of the long drawing-room where the stiff-backed chairs and settles had been ranged against the walls to give more space for the many guests. The fine plaster ceiling and ancient tapestries gave an air of particular distinction to the gathering that evening, and when the candles had been lit in their gilded sconces the hundred tiny flames prickled like a myriad stars in the polished wood of chair-back and floor, and in the silks of the ladies' gowns.

Elspeth, with her hair raised high against a tower of white lace and ribbons in the fashionable *fontange* style, and her lemon satin gown looped up and back to fall in a shimmering train behind her, looked not an inch out of place. The cascade of embroidered flounces on her skirt was the style dictated by the latest fashion 'moppet' from London, and her white satin gloves and embroidered slippers were impeccable. Hugh Baird looked at her with open admiration.

'No, the kirk does not approve of levity,' he said. 'And I doubt the kirk would approve of you tonight, Miss Middleton.'

'And why not? In what have I offended?'

'In looking as you do.'

'And how is that an offence?'

'Temptation is always an offence, and when you look as ravishingly beautiful as you do tonight, you tempt me to dream of forbidden pleasures . . .'

'We were talking of *song*, Mr Baird,' interrupted Elspeth, blushing in spite of herself. 'You said the kirk would not approve of Lady Grisell's singing, but I believe you are too severe. If we are sufficiently solemn on one day of the week, the kirk allows us freely to sing on the other six.'

'Freely? Does that not depend on the choice of song?'

'You can hardly cavil at Lady Grisell's choice. I have rarely heard a song so moving and so sad.'

'Are not all our Scottish ballads sad? Inevitably so, when so much of our country's history is of death and,' his eyes were eloquent, 'the yearning for those we love.'

'Inevitably?' said Elspeth lightly. 'Oh dear. I hope not. I grow so tired of everlasting groans.'

'Miss Middleton, I beg you, do not tease me so! You know my sentiments, and yet you refuse to listen.'

'Did I tease you, Mr Baird? Then I am sorry.' Elspeth looked sweetly contrite. 'I will listen to you immediately and with the greatest attention. What will you say?'

'Damnation!' cried Hugh in exasperation. 'Life is so abominably unfair! There is James, happily married to your cousin Lilias, with a place in the family business and an assured income, and here am I...'

'Yes?' Elspeth looked up at him mischievously over the lace of her fan. 'Here are you, strong, healthy, *reasonably* intelligent – or so you tell me – and poor. Is that what you were going to say?'

'But what can I do? I am trained for nothing. Look at your uncle. Look at our host. Both successful and prosperous advocates. And I am fit for nothing but a tutorship in one of their children's families! How can a poor tutor ever support a wife?'

'But Mr Baird,' reminded Elspeth with wide-eyed innocence, 'you have no wife.'

'Elspeth Middleton you are infuriating! And utterly and absolutely adorable.' He dropped to one knee beside her chair and when he spoke again it was with eager seriousness. 'Miss Middleton . . . Elspeth . . .' he hesitated. 'Say you will wait for me until . . .'

'Hush!' Elspeth tapped him reprovingly with her folded fan. 'Lady Helen is about to play. I believe it is to be a new piece by Mr Corelli and I am most anxious to hear it.'

Poor Hugh had no alternative but to rise to his feet again, though not yet defeated. 'Have you heard of William Paterson?' he asked, when the music was over and the company had adjourned to the dining-room for oysters, neats' tongues, woodcock and smoked beef.

'Is he also a musician?' asked Elspeth. She took a sip from the claret glass and handed it back.

Hugh smiled. 'I think not, though he is certainly a man of invention and ingenuity. He drew up a plan for a bank,' he explained. 'It is said the English government mean to adopt the plan and to establish a Bank of England on the very pattern he laid down, but Mr Paterson is a Scotsman and has plans for the prosperity of his homeland, too.'

'And do these plans include the advancement of the fortunes of moderately intelligent fourth sons?'

'You may laugh, Miss Middleton, but Mr Paterson is a genius. I know it and in a very few years Scotland will know it too. You are, of course, aware that the English have the monopoly of foreign trade, and that for the purposes of commerce the Scots are classed as aliens?'

Elspeth nodded. 'I have heard my uncle talk of it.'

'William Paterson has a scheme to establish a Scottish trading company which will carry goods abroad and establish colonies wherever the land is free and the natives willing. Imagine it! A whole new world of commerce opened up for Scotland! If anything comes of the plan, my father is sure to buy an interest. The ships will need crews and the colonies, settlers. There will be an opening for everyone – even for a fourth son with nothing but health and vigour and, perhaps, a wife?' He reached to take her hand, but Aunt Cunningham was a swift and practised chaperone. She had divined the situation across the barrier of a loaded supper-table and a score of chattering guests.

'What are you talking of, Elspeth?' she inquired brightly, materializing apparently from nowhere between them.

'Mr Baird was telling me of a certain Mr Paterson,' said Elspeth meekly. 'Apparently Mr Paterson plans to found a colony especially for young Scotsmen of health and vigour and restricted means.' Her eyes were solemn over her spread fan, but Hugh coloured to the ears.

'Really?' Aunt Cunningham raised an eyebrow while her eyes darted quickly from one to the other. 'No doubt the subject is of more interest to Mr Baird than it can *ever* be to you.'

She took Elspeth's arm and drew her firmly away. 'Come and meet your hostess, my dear. Lady Crossrig has been telling me of her preparations for removing the family into Berwickshire, as usual, for the summer months. Elspeth and her sister are to go to the country, too, Lady Crossrig,' she continued, when she had successfully steered Elspeth away from that undesirable Baird boy and into the safer haven of their hostess and daughters; 'we will miss them dreadfully, of course, but life is so peaceful in the country, is it not? And so refreshingly simple after a busy season in town.'

'Scolding! Swearing! Drunkenness! Lewdness in broad daylight in the streets and the children running wild! The town is not fit for decent folks to live in.' Baillie Baxter struck the table so hard that the Session clerk jumped nervously, and sprayed a mist of ink across the page. 'Something must be done!'

'The people need a minister,' said Middleton. 'It is six weeks since John Keith died and Francis Ross . . .'

'We'll not have Francis Ross,' interrupted Cumming the blacksmith. 'We want a true Presbyterian minister, not a peely-wally convert.'

In the years since he had stood with the other heritors and seen the Cathedral tower fall, George Cumming had changed. He had always been an obedient and faithful member of the kirk and had kept his family likewise, with a strict though cheerful discipline; but lately his rectitude had hardened to an uncompromising and humourless zeal. Folks said the change dated from a certain midsummer night when he had gone with Baillie Baxter's men to root out the perpetrators of the heathen fire: he had not captured the culprits and he had been a long time coming home. Others said it was a mercy for him that the Grant woman had died, or Cumming himself might have had a spell on the stool of repentance. No one could prove it, of course, and if the girl Christian knew anything, she kept it to herself. As it was, they said Cumming was trying to blind the Session to past folly by an excess of present virtue. Whatever the reason, time and age had turned Cumming into an inflexible bigot.

'Francis Ross or no,' said Urquhart, 'if you don't make up your minds soon you'll have lost your congregation. They will all have gone cheerfully to the devil, and with the church doors locked you can hardly blame them.'

'And whose fault is that?' demanded Baxter. 'We choose our minister by proper order in the Session, and then Cumming here defies the Session decision. He'd be better employed keeping that son of his in order.'

'You leave my son out of it. He's a better man than yours will ever be. If he *is* your son.'

Baxter went white. His mouth opened and shut like a fish before he managed, 'I'll sue you for that.'

'Take no notice,' said Middleton calmly. 'The man is incensed. He does not know what he is saying.'

'I know fine what I'm saying and I'm saying the Session is wrong!'

'The Session is the elected representative of the town in all kirk matters,' reminded Middleton, 'and must be obeyed. Even by its own elders.'

'Fiddlesticks! Things have changed, Dr Middleton, though we all know where *your* sympathies lie. But your old order is gone and good riddance. We have a new order now, with a new king, a new kirk, and by God we need a new Session!'

It was Dr Garden, Professor of Divinity, a soft-spoken, godly man and Christian Grant's employer, who answered him, gently enough. 'We have all seen these changes, Cumming, and have accepted them.'

'Then why haven't you signed the Confession of Faith like everyone else? Or are you following in your brother's footsteps?'

Dr Garden's brother George, until recently minister in St Nicholas Church in the New Town, had been deprived of his benefice for refusing to pray for William and Mary and for refusing to submit to the conditions required of him by the Privy Council.

'My brother would have subscribed to the Confession if he could, and so would I, but you must allow me to obey my own conscience. As it is the majority of us have signed, and acknowledged the Presbyterian Government of the church.'

'Aye, they signed right enough. With "mental reservations"!'

'And would you have it otherwise? Would you have an honest man swear to something he has not had the time to consider and examine from every possible angle?'

'It's well enough for you and your professors in the College to talk of *examining* and *considering*. But we townsmen know what we want – a minister who believes wholeheartedly in the Presbyterian kirk, not a minister with "mental reservations"!'

'You may want what you choose,' retorted Dr Middleton, 'but as long as the Session is the ruling body of the kirk, the Session decides. Not, as you seem to think, according to the whim of one member, but according to the sober decision of the whole.'

'Whim? I'll give you whim!' roared Cumming, pushing back his chair and rising threateningly to his feet. Dr Middleton looked at him calmly. 'Recollect where you are.'

'Since when has Baillie Baxter's roof been holy?'

'You are at the meeting of the kirk Session nevertheless, and owe the company respect.'

'Dr Middleton is right, Cumming,' said Baxter reprovingly.

113

'These things must be settled through the proper channels. You had no right to disrupt the service as you did when a properly elected preacher was officiating. It is not legal.'

'Legal or not,' shouted Cumming, 'we demand an honest, Presbyterian minister, not a boot-licking Episcopalian convert. And by God there'll be no service in that kirk till we get one.' The blacksmith's red fist crashed on the table-top beside Baxter's thin white one.

'That is all very well, Cumming,' sighed Principal Middleton, 'but you put the Session in an awkward position. Mr Ross was elected by a large majority of the heritors, as you very well know, and until . . .'

'*I* put the Session in an awkward position?' interrupted Cumming. 'And what about you? You lock the door of the church and won't give up the key. You disobey the Privy Council and deny access to God's house.'

'The door will only be unlocked when we are assured the Minister will be heard and the service conducted without discord. We cannot and will not have a repetition of the disgraceful brawling you instigated on the last occasion.'

'Then remove the cause of it! Give us a decent, Presbyterian minister and soon, because I'll smash the door down with my bare fists, I warn you, if the church stays locked much longer – and if your Francis Ross so much as sets foot inside to preach to us, I'll smash his teeth down his throat!'

'Come, come, man! You may not do violence to one of God's ministers, especially in God's own house.'

'I'll do violence to who I please and where I please,' roared the blacksmith, 'and I'll crack the pate of anyone who tries to stop me!'

'Gentlemen, gentlemen,' protested Baillie Baxter. 'We have enough discord in the town already without adding to it here.'

'Well said, Baillie,' applauded Urquhart. 'The matter of the minister will settle itself in time. Meanwhile, let us have another mug of your excellent ale and get back to the point of the meeting. I have several practical suggestions to make for improving town discipline.'

'Suggestions? Empty yap! That's all you College people ever do. Yap! Yap! Yap! Why don't you get off your fat arse for once and *act*?' Cumming seized his mug of ale, drained it in fury and slammed out of the house.

'Well, well,' said Urquhart. 'I fear our friend is overheated.'

'Overweening would be more appropriate,' said Middleton.

'No, do not underestimate him. The blacksmith has quite a following among the heritors. Many feel as he does.'

'Perhaps, but he would do well to temper his zeal with a little common politeness. He has changed since the Revolution,' went on Middleton thoughtfully, 'as many people have. I recall when he was a sober, humble, godfearing man, obeying his minister and his baillies and content to let them guide him. Now he has grown arrogant enough to pose as some sort of leader in the town.'

'He would do better to attend to his forge and that errant son of his,' snapped Baxter, 'and leave church affairs to those more qualified to understand them.'

'Errant son?' said Urquhart. 'What has George been up to now?'

'He was kissing that servant of yours, Garden, beside the drawwell in the broad light of day.'

'That is better, I think,' said Garden with a soft smile, 'than surreptitiously, in the dark.'

'There is not much wrong with the Cumming boy,' said Urquhart, 'that time will not correct. He is an intelligent, high-spirited lad and was always inclined to be irreverent. Age will sober him.'

'He is a promising hammerman,' said Garden.

'So he is,' agreed Baxter grudgingly. 'Only the other day my wife ...'

'Yes, yes,' interrupted Middleton. 'No one doubts his skill. But at present he could be a disruptive influence among the young people of the town.'

'You mean among the girls?' said Urquhart. 'I hear it is a new one every market day. But there is no need to fear on George's behalf. The lad will turn out right in the end.'

The Principal did not answer. In truth he was not concerned for the boy: it was George's possible influence on his daughter Elspeth which was the cause of his anxiety. For Elspeth was to come home in the summer, this time for good or until such time as she might marry, and the Principal could not help remembering her childhood adoration of the Cumming boy. Now he answered the Mediciner carefully.

'I do not fear for him, Urquhart, but I remember the influence he has always had over his contemporaries. He is a natural leader, though so far he has chosen to avoid responsibility. But if he should choose to lead his followers along a misguided trail . . .'

'His father will never let him,' said Baxter decidedly. 'And when we get our minister – whom we sorely need – and the church is opened again, young George will be made to toe the line.'

'I am not so sure, Baxter,' said the Principal. 'There is an undercurrent of rebellion in the boy and I doubt that Cumming will find the obedience he expects. I have heard George talk of the army, as all boys do at some time or another. But "what would be the point of fighting the King's battles in a foreign land," he said, "especially a foreign king who is no better than a usurper?" That from the son of as staunch a Williamite as you could hope to find!'

'There are many left in the town who secretly support James Stuart,' said Baxter, 'but I would not have thought young George was one.'

'The glamour of a lost cause, perhaps?' suggested Urquhart. 'Or the simpler pleasure of annoying his father?'

'Just so long as the boy does no harm,' said the Baillie dourly.

'Don't be alarmist, Baxter. What harm could he do that we cannot prevent? Those measures I mentioned for combating lawlessness,' went on Urquhart. 'I thought we might begin by . . .'

'This said day it was enacted and ordained by the baillie with consent of the Council that the whole inhabitants within the town shall be bound and obliged not only for themselves but for their wives, servants and children that the Sabbath day shall nowise in time coming be profaned by scolding, drinking, raging and playing publicly on the streets or elsewhere. But on the contrary that they shall Christianly keep within their families and nowise so abuse the Sabbath or suffer the same to be profaned by any under their charge and that under the pain of twenty pounds Scots money *toties quoties* to be paid to the treasurer for the behoof of the town and poor in terror to others to commit such trespass and all parents to be liable for their children, wives, servants and others within their respective families.'

Margery Montgomery listened with the other heritors as William Walker read out the proclamation at the market cross. She listened till the final roll of the drum and went on her way, unperturbed. She knew her father obeyed no law but his own. He had been fishing last Sunday, unchecked, and he would go again if he wished to, whatever law the Council chose to make about it.

She found Montgomery in the kirkyard, hewing an inscription on a plain stone slab. She stood and watched him in silence as he chipped and hammered at the figures of the date, 1694. Margery had seen her father carve the figures often enough to recognize them now. She knew letters of the alphabet, too, and one or two whole words like 'husband of' and 'died'. There had been many deaths that year. But at last the man finished, laid aside his hammer and looked up.

'Well?'

'Baillie Knight says would you look at the stance he leased on Lord Whitehill's land and tell him whether you could build him a house there, Father.'

'Can he not ask me himself?'

'Oh yes. He says if you will meet him there this evening he will talk to you about it. Please, Father? He was very kind.'

Montgomery straightened slowly until he stood upright and Margery saw that his face was drawn with pain. 'I have the headache, child. I cannot go today.'

'Please, Father. The meal is almost gone and we have nothing more.'

Montgomery looked down at her with his good eye, glazed now as the other one was, and shook his head slowly.

'The pain is bad, Margery. Soon I will not be able to see.'

'I will lead you, Father. Please try! You know you need the work, and all he wants is for you to meet him there and say you will do it.'

'I cannot . . .'

'I wish you would let me fetch a surgeon, Father.'

'And have him cover me with leeches and charge ten shillings for it? And then the headache would not go. No one can cure it. But tomorrow the pain will have eased. Tell him I will come tomorrow.'

'Tomorrow may be too late. I heard him say that Kenneth Fraser wanted the work for himself.'

'Then Kenneth Fraser can have it.'

'No, Father. Please. The Baillie wants *you*. He said so. He said you are the best mason in the town and he would be honoured to have you build his house. But he is afraid you may not come.'

'Why?' Montgomery was instantly on guard. 'What has he heard against me?'

'Nothing, Father, nothing. It is just that you are sometimes stern and you frighten people.'

'Do I frighten you?'

'No, Father. You know you don't.' She took his hand and pulled him gently down beside her on the stone. 'Sit a while and rest and perhaps the pain will go away. Shall I ask Dr Urquhart for a physic for you?' she added anxiously. 'Or I could make you one myself. Mrs Middleton, I know, has a receipt and I am sure she would teach it to me if I asked her.'

'No. I want no one's physic. I want . . .' He stopped and sank his head in his hands and Margery heard only the low, aching moan.

'Oh Father,' she pleaded. 'Tell me what I can do to help you? Please.'

'Nothing,' he said roughly. 'Nothing at all.'

'Shall I fetch water from the well? Shall I bathe your forehead?'

He shook his head, once. His eyes were shut now and his face grey.

'But Father, surely there is something I can do,' persisted the child. 'Please let me help.' She reached out to touch him.

'No!' He struck her angrily on the side of the head and she fell to the ground, gasping. 'Oh God!' He clutched his head in his hands. 'Just leave me alone!'

Slowly Margery picked herself up from the grass and sat quietly beside him until the sun was low in the sky and the air cold. At last she touched him lightly on the arm. 'Come, Father. It is time to go.'

Obediently he let her lead him out of the kirkyard, past the Provost's house and the ruins of the Bishop's palace, and down the Brae to the Chaplains' Court.

The Chaplains' Court had once been a massive structure of four towers at the four corners of a courtyard with a stone archway leading from the Brae to the inner court. Now all that remained was the three-storied west tower, a stretch of crumbling building two storeys high, and the gateway with the little gatehouse chamber above it and Bishop Dunbar's crest still undamaged on the wall. Through the arched gateway they could see the ruins of what had once been the chambers for twenty chaplains from the Cathedral and, after the Reformation, a song-school for the church. Now what was not completely ruinous was in lay hands, except for the west tower where Professor Garden and his family lived. Margery looked up at the window as they passed, in case Christian might be there.

At the draw-well they stopped.

'Baillie Knight said to meet him here,' said Margery anxiously. 'That is the land,' she added quickly as Montgomery showed signs of moving on. She pointed to a gateway in the wall opposite. 'And there is the Baillie himself! Oh, Father, please tell him you will do it.'

'I hear Montgomery is building Baillie Knight's house single-handed,' said Baillie Baxter.

The Session was meeting again, this time in its old place, the Consistory chamber of St Machar's church. In June another order had come from the Privy Council ordering the heritors to hand the keys to Professor Alexander Fraser, baillie in Old Aberdeen, so that he might unlock the church. This time George Cumming had agreed not to disrupt proceedings, the keys had been handed over and on July 1 the door had been unlocked. A temporary minister had been found and services resumed, though not without some rebelliousness and disorder from dissenting heritors. This dis-order was in part the reason for the kirk Session's convening, though that did not exclude the preliminary exchange of Burgh gossip.

'Is he now?' said Urquhart. 'That is quite an undertaking.' Montgomery interested him, as any man with an unusual medical problem did. He would have liked to examine the man's head wound, open up his skull and look inside, but that of course was impossible. Instead, he observed him closely, noting the rhythm of the mason's headaches and their effect. There was potential violence there, the Mediciner was sure of it, though whether from hereditary causes or from some oppressive inner growth as a result of that wound sustained at Killiecrankie, he could not say. But he would have laid ten gold sovereigns against any man that one day the mason's control would snap and he would run berserk.

'Possessed of the devil,' he murmured now. 'That's what they call it in the Bible.'

'What's that?' demanded Baxter suspiciously. 'Who is possessed?'

'No one,' said the Mediciner hastily. 'I was merely thinking aloud. Tell me about this house which is to be built. Is it small?'

'Of modest size, I believe,' said Baxter. 'Two rooms with a second storey for a bedroom, and I am told he plans to roof the place with slate instead of turf and to lay a brick floor.'

'That will cost him quite a bit of money.'

'Aye. But if Montgomery manages it alone, Baillie Knight will have a bargain.'

'He'll manage it,' said Urquhart. 'Montgomery is the living example of what one man can achieve when he has no one else on whom to shift the burden.'

Kenneth Fraser bristled. 'And a fly-by-night, ramshackle sort of building it is, with the walls piled stone on stone before the mortar is dry. The thing will fall flat in the first high wind, you will see.'

'Do you think so? It looked strong enough to me. Stronger, if anything, than Alexander Fraser's new place at Powis. How is it progressing, by the way?' This deliberately to Kenneth Fraser who was in charge of the building of it.

'Well enough, well enough. But the walls are real walls, three feet thick and solid. It will be a grand place when it is finished.'

'And when will that be?' asked Baxter. 'You have been working on it long enough.'

'It will be done before the winter,' said Kenneth Fraser stiffly. 'If weather permits.'

'Do not mention weather to me,' said Principal Middleton. 'I have not known a worse summer. My barley is mildewed and my oats no better. The pasture is waterlogged and trampled to a quagmire by the beasts. It'll be a poor harvest and a lean winter, I fear.'

'God is punishing a wicked people,' said George Cumming piously.

'Poor God is held responsible for everything these days,' said Urquhart wryly. 'Personally I think a better drainage system might work wonders. I will show you my plan, Middleton, for draining my lower meadow by a system of channels, if you are interested. Walk home with me after the Session and we will study it together over a brandy. I have a new consignment just up from London which I warmly recommend.'

'Delighted,' began Middleton, but the blacksmith glowered.

'There are more important matters to discuss than the Mediciner's cellar,' he interrupted rudely. 'The Sledder woman's child died this morning.'

'I'm not surprised,' sighed Urquhart. 'An obstinate and stupid woman, given to dabbling with herbal mixtures she cannot begin to understand.'

'But the child died,' repeated Cumming angrily. 'That's six already this week. And Walker found two vagrants dead in the ditch above the Spital. Not ours, for they wore no badges, but the town will have to bury them just the same.'

'See to it,' said Middleton, waving a hand at the Session clerk. 'There is money enough in the funds.'

'It's not the money we have to worry about,' said Cumming. 'However much the Mediciner may sneer, it is clear that God is visiting his displeasure upon us. Remember how he destroyed Sodom and Gomorrah? Remember the plague on the Eygptians when the first-born were wiped out? God forbid that we should have another visitation of the plague, here in the Old Town, but if we did it would be justly deserved.'

'If we did,' said Urquhart, 'it would be the result of dirt and ignorance as much as anything else.'

'It is all very well for you to mock,' said Kenneth Fraser nervously, 'but I have lost children enough already one way or another and I need someone to follow on.'

'Aye,' agreed Cumming soberly. 'My George is fully trained now. It would be a crying waste if he were to go before he could teach his own son the family trade.'

'I read a new receipt the other day,' said Baillie Baxter. 'In the course of business in the New Town I met with a gentleman from London who insisted on pressing a copy upon me. As I recall it is compounded of saltpetre, flower of brimstone, saffron and cochineal. I have already instructed my wife to prepare some for the family's use, but anyone who is interested may apply to me to see it. It is reputed to be most efficacious.'

'Dr Butler of Cambridge has a different receipt,' said Urquhart. 'Wood sorrel, sugar and mithridate, well crushed and beaten. I dare say one is as good – or as bad – as another. But in my opinion no physic is of the slightest use unless it is combined with scrupulous cleanliness of both house and person. Nastiness and dirt encourage every disease, be it plague, fever, or the flux. But the poor have more to fear than disease this year. There is little enough food as it is, and there will be less when winter comes. I fear the Burgh may lose as many through starvation as through disease, and disease is always rife among the poorly fed.'

There was a moment's silence as each man followed his own thoughts. Death was a normal part of life and to be expected. There had always been death, especially in infancy and childbirth, but the blacksmith was right. The death rate was rising unusually high, and a poor summer would do nothing to check the trend. Most of those present had lost children in infancy and accepted it, but to lose a grown child was something different and more painful. The blacksmith thought of his eldest boy, George, who though often rebellious and erring was a fine lad and a fine hammerman. Middleton thought of his daughters, so sweet and gentle and loving; Baxter of his sons, young still but healthy and full of promise. Which of these children would death carry off next? Or would death come not only to the children, but to the parents too?

When Middleton spoke again it was with a quiet seriousness which echoed the fear in every man's heart. 'We were called here today to discuss the question of disruption in the church. You all know what happened last Sunday when certain rebellious members of the congregation took the opportunity to interrupt the service and impede the Minister in the course of his duties.'

'I told you all along,' said Cumming, 'We demand a minister of the true kirk. That preacher you found for us for Sunday was one of your "mental reservation" men. We'll not have him.'

Middleton sighed. The situation was delicate and difficult enough without the hammerman using his influence to stir up trouble in the trades' lofts. The Presbyterian faction was strong and vociferous, but Middleton knew there was still a solid body of heritors who supported the old order, though they had the prudence not to declare the fact in public. Already meeting-houses were quietly being established for the secret celebration of communion according to the rites of the Episcopalian church just as, before the Revolution, the Presbyterians had met in secret for their own services, and before that, the Catholics. Time would sort everything out one way or another. Time usually did. Meanwhile it was important that the life of the Burgh should continue smoothly and without disruption. Middleton and those who thought as he did would not tolerate a fanatic as minister. Cumming and his faction would not apparently accept a moderate. A compromise must be found, and soon, before Burgh discipline broke down completely.

So Middleton suppressed the anger which the blacksmith's words had aroused and spoke in careful, measured tones which invited his listeners' co-operation. 'In the light of the grave situation which faces us, I am sure you will agree with me that it is time for individuals to put aside their differences and unite to form a Christian and Godly community.'

There were murmurs of approval in which Cumming joined.

'Now that we have a functioning church, we must have a *full* congregation in regular attendance. I know the gentlemen present are all zealous in ensuring their households' obedience to the kirk, but there are still many others who are not and must be made to comply for the good of all.'

'Montgomery for one,' said Kenneth Fraser sourly. 'I doubt that child of his has been inside a church for many a year.'

'An interesting child,' said Urquhart. 'By rights she should have died at birth, or certainly in the first twenty-four hours. Instead she has survived cold, injury, dirt, neglect, and to my knowledge has never had a day's illness in the whole of her miserable life. She must live on the most primitive of diets and in the most squalid conditions, yet her eyes are bright and her skin clear. She defies all the laws of medicine.'

'She's a dirty little cripple,' said Kenneth Fraser, 'and a heathen like her father.'

'Not a cripple,' said the Mediciner. 'Not in the real sense of the word. She suffered a fracture of the femur soon after birth, but it seems to have healed with no more permanent damage than a shortened leg, on which she moves as quickly and as competently as many a normal child.'

'I'll grant you she walks well enough,' agreed Cumming, 'and my George says she has taught herself to read a word or two, but she limps. No man will ever want her for a wife.'

'Then when the time comes she must be found suitable employment,' said Middleton calmly. 'In the meantime, someone must persuade Montgomery to bring her to church, if only to save himself a twenty-pound fine. Who is in charge of Widow Irvine's quarter of the town?'

'Baillie Knight,' said Baxter.

'Good. Then when we have drawn up the proclamation officially, in Council, Walker shall cry it at the cross. Each magistrate shall be responsible for obedience in his quarter of the town and let us hope we fill the kirk on Sunday.'

'Will your daughters be with you by then?' asked Urquhart, as he and the Principal walked together along the Chanonry towards Cluny's Port and the High Street. The Mediciner had a soft spot for Elspeth and would have been happy for one of his sons to claim her.

'God willing,' said Middleton quietly. 'They are travelling northwards by way of Stirling and should be here by Saturday.' He sighed. 'I hope I have done the right thing to summon them back at this time.'

'The whole country is in the same straits,' said Urquhart. 'Edinburgh is as beset by troubles as we are. At least here they will enjoy the comfort and care of their own home.'

'Nevertheless, I have misgivings.'

'None, I hope that a glass of cognac will not help to allay. Ah, here we are at Powis already. See what a grand place Alexander Fraser has planned for himself.'

They stood a moment at the edge of the road where the burn crossed the causeway under a little bridge. Behind them was the crowned dome of King's College, in front of them across the grass the half-finished structure of Professor Fraser's house. Men were working on the floorboards of the upper storey, hammering and sawing. One of them was singing.

'They seem a cheerful, companionable bunch,' said Middleton as they moved on to the gate of the Mediciner's house next door. 'I wonder,' he added, 'how Montgomery will manage alone?'

Christian Grant stood in the archway under the bishop's crest, three cushions pendant at the corners, in a bordure, and watched Montgomery. The man was mixing lime and sand on a slab of stone. Margery was nowhere in sight. He must have sent the child on some errand, unless she was preparing food for him at home. The walls of the house were already three feet high and Christian knew that George Cumming had promised to make the roof-beams and the doors the moment Montgomery was ready. If the man worked at the same speed, that would not be long. He was at work on the site every day before Walker's morning drum, and stopped only when it was too dark to see. Margery brought him food and helped him when he would let her, and when he would not she watched in silence noting all he did until, inevitably, he sent her away. Once Christian had called the child into the Gardens' kitchen to help her make soap, but her father had been angry and forbidden the child to go again. Nevertheless Christian persevered. She had a soft spot still for the child she had nursed, and was sorry for her. She meant to help her if she could, especially now that fortune had brought Montgomery to Christian's own doorstep.

'Would you like some ale?' called Christian now. 'It's hot work in the sun.'

Montgomery looked up and stared until his eyes focused on the plump, cheerful figure in the archway.

'No.' He turned back to the lime and stirred again doggedly while the sweat stood on his brow.

Christian shrugged. Then she disappeared under the arch to reappear almost immediately with a flagon of ale in her hand. She crossed the Brae with it held in front of her and put the flagon down on the top of the unfinished wall beside the mason.

'There you are,' she said. 'That'll put the strength back into your arm. You're sweating like a pig.'

Montgomery turned angrily. 'I said "no"! I want charity from no one.'

'Don't be a fool, man, take it. For old times' sake. You gave me ale enough when we lived up the stair from your place.'

The mason looked at her warily, remembering the pert, dark-eyed child with the bare legs who had run errands for him and who had delivered his child. But this girl was full-breasted and bold. A woman, now, like her mother.

'Go on,' she urged, picking up the flagon and holding it towards him. 'It's good. Look.' She put her lips to the brim and drank, her eyes dancing at him over the sparkling foam. 'There. It's not poison.' She lowered the flagon and ran her tongue slowly across her lips, watching him. Then she held out the flagon again. 'Go on.'

He hesitated, wanting to refuse yet unable to frame the words. Her eyes were laughing at him now, her lips were moist and parted, and she was not afraid. Montgomery felt a stirring deep inside him, something he had not felt for more than six years.

'Go on,' she urged. 'Take it.'

He snatched the flagon, drained it and thrust it back into her hands. Then he scooped up the limestone mixture on the flat, three-cornered trowel and slapped it on to the masonry, spreading and packing with demonic speed.

Christian laughed, bunched up her skirts to show strong brown knees and deliberately leapt the wall in front of him. Then she sauntered back across the Brae to the archway and disappeared. Montgomery's hand on the trowel trembled and the sweat ran twice as thick as he heaved stone after stone into place, working without pause and faster than before, until the sun set and he could no longer see; but even in the blank darkness of the road home the image of the plump-breasted, laughing girl stayed with him, taunting and reminding.

And in the shadow of the Chanonry that he had left behind him, Christian stood under the entrance to the Chaplains' Court, waiting. The curfew drum had sounded long ago, the alehouses had closed their doors and the indwellers were safe at home. Christian herself should have been curled in the blanket under the table in the kitchen, snatching what sleep she could before the lighting of the morning fires for the household, and the endless carrying of water.

Instead she stood bright-eyed and excited, waiting for George. When he came, he did not speak, merely slipped an arm around her waist, kissed the tip of her ear and drew her close. Together they moved silently out of the archway and across the Brae to the private shadows of Montgomery's half-finished house.

'George,' she murmured dreamily, her face against the warm skin of his chest. 'We could live here, you and I.'

She felt him stiffen, but he made no answer.

'Baillie Knight will not live here himself, surely? He will rent the house to tenants. We could have it.'

George sat up abruptly. 'We don't need a house. You are well enough where you are, well paid and well treated, and so am I. Why change?'

Christian was quiet. She saw how it was with him, but one day, surely, he would be ready to marry and she could wait.

'George?' she murmured, her hand caressing his cheek. 'I must go home. Kiss me goodnight . . .'

'I'll not go,' said Montgomery. He stood feet planted apart, one hand on the unfinished wall of Baillie Knight's house and the other holding the trowel. 'I'll have no Presbyterian minister telling me what to do.'

'I understand how you feel,' said Christian. 'My Ma used to say the same about Mr Keith, but only in private. Do as they tell you, Christian, she used to say, and laugh at them behind their back.' When Montgomery said nothing she went on, 'If you don't do what they want, they'll take your money from you and anything else they can lay their hands on. So don't let them. It costs you nothing to sit in a pew for an hour or two and it saves trouble.'

'I'll not go,' repeated the mason. 'Not to a church with no bishop and the wrong king. They'll tell me nothing but lies.'

'Then don't listen. Do as I do. I sit in the pew with the rest of them and think my own thoughts. You'll beat them that way, see?

If you go to church at the proper time and stay quiet, they can't touch you. That's what my Ma always said and she was right. So be sensible, for Margery's sake?'

Montgomery did not answer.

'Baillie Knight asked you himself, didn't he?' said Christian persuasively. 'He came all the way across town just to see you.' She ran a finger up his arm. 'Please, William?'

Montgomery flinched, then quivered violently.

Christian laughed. 'Don't you like me to touch you?' She had a bloom about her today which sent Montgomery's blood churning through his head. She smelt of life and sweat and warm flesh, and he could not speak.

'Then I'll save it for those who do,' she said pertly. 'But you must go to the kirk on Sunday and you must take Margery. It's best.' She picked up the empty flagon and moved away from him towards the gap in the masonry where the door was to be. At the wall she called back to him over her shoulder. 'Mind now and go! I'll be looking out for you.'

The church of St Machar's was full that Sunday. The beadle at the door checked each indweller's face as they passed in under the great west porch, and there were few missing. Church wardens had already checked the town wynds and closes, flushed out the clutch of lads playing penny-stone and kits and rounded up the bowls contingent from the Snow kirkyard. One had even beaten the banks of the Don for fishermen. No one was to escape the kirk's net.

Margery stood at the back of the church with her father, beside Bishop Scougal's monument in the south aisle. She knew her father had built the monument with his brother, and while she waited for the service to begin her eyes strayed repeatedly to the effigy of the bishop with the figure of a young man on either side. If she tipped her head right back she could see the armorial bearings, the mitre and crozier, which crowned the monument. The colours were bright, though already faded in places, blue and scarlet and gold. But it was a wonder the monument was undamaged, when others in the church had been smashed and mutilated. Margery was glad her father's work was whole.

Montgomery also found comfort in the closeness of his own work. He put out a hand and felt the stone under his fingers, and the tension eased out of him. It had cost him all the strength of his being to walk the High Street with Margery limping at his side and to know that every indweller in the town was watching them, whispering and pointing. Now he closed his eyes and let the stone speak through his hand, calming and soothing . . .

Christian Grant sat at the front of the church in the Gardens' family pew with Professor Garden, his lady and six of their children. Nevertheless she managed to take good note of her neighbours in the adjoining pews, the Urquharts, the George Frasers, the Alexander Frasers, the Baxters. The Middleton pew was still empty, but there was plenty of time. Christian's eyes moved on to the trades' lofts, searching . . . The tailors' loft, the shoemakers', the weavers' and fleshers', the hammermen's . . . All were full, and in the body of the church there was constant movement as people wove through the crowd exchanging greetings, searching out friends. A dog barked and was chased outside. Another lifted a leg against one of the pillars. In the Cheyne aisle two men slumped against the wall, miraculously asleep on their feet. There was a constant babble of noise in the well of the church, but above the level of heads, under the splendid heraldic ceiling with its triple row of armorial shields, the noise was smoothed and diluted to a serene, continuous drone, as of a single note on an organ.

Christian looked around the familiar kirk which she had known since childhood, and was happy. In her mother's time she had been at the back of the church with the rest of them, moving between the massive pillars, whispering and gossiping. She turned in her pew now, searching for faces she knew. Her employers were engaged in reading their prayer-books and she was able to nod and smile to her friends, unreproved. Then her eyes turned again to the trades' loft. George must be there. Surely even he would not dare to stay away? Then she saw him and the familiar gladness gripped her heart. He looked handsomer than ever this morning, with his bright hair and green eyes, in a clean shirt and with his face scrubbed gleaming. She strained to catch his eye, but his head was turned towards the west porch and he did not see.

'Christian!' Mrs Garden's voice was stern. 'Remember where you are!'

Obediently Christian folded her hands in her lap and looked straight ahead of her at the two great pillars one on either side of the communion table, with behind it the bricked-up arch that had once led into St John's aisle and Dunbar aisle and the great tower.

Christian remembered the night the tower fell as vividly as if it had been yesterday – Margery had been born that night – and she remembered the night they had seen Gauld in the ruins beyond that bricked-up arch, searching the ashes for rings. George had been there, as he always was, leading them.

With a surreptitious glance to make sure Mrs Garden was not watching, Christian twisted in her seat to try once more to catch George's eye, but his head was still turned to the west porch. As she watched, willing him to look at her, a change came over him. He grew suddenly alert and eager and there was a glow about him as though an inner light had been lit. Christian turned further in her seat to see what it was that had so excited him. Dr Middleton was walking up the centre aisle with his lady on his arm and behind him walked his daughters, Isobel, Margrat – and Elspeth.

Elspeth was beautiful. She was small and slender with pale skin and soft, fair hair. As she walked down the centre of the church behind her father in his solid black gown and periwig, she had the fragile beauty of a wood anemone or a winter aconite. For the first time in her life Christian felt her own hands large and awkward and she pulled her skirts down lower to cover the firm brown flesh of her calves.

The Middletons took their places in the family pew. The Minister raised a hand to still the talking and the service began. But Christian could not listen. She looked mesmerized at Elspeth, and from Elspeth to George. His face was rapt. And from the demure downward tilt of Elspeth's profile and the way her hands played endlessly with the ribbons of her bodice, Christian suspected that she was quite aware of George's eyes upon her.

Jealousy welled inside her like a spated river. She remembered George's hands on her breasts, the way he had kissed her, pleading, caressing, persuading . . . Then she looked at his face as he sat with his father and brothers in the hammermen's loft and saw that, in spite of that exquisite closeness, for him she did not exist. He had eyes only for Elspeth. Christian's full lips trembled, but only for a moment, before they set in determination. Elspeth should not have him. George needed a real woman, strong and tough as he was, not a peely city lass who looked as if she'd melt away in the first rain.

The service was longer than usual that morning. The Minister had much to say on the subject of Sabbath day observance, the dire penalties which would follow disobedience and the need to live a sober, Christian life obedient to the strict teaching of the kirk.

Montgomery heard none of it. His hand was on the pillar of Scougal's monument and his eyes were closed. He was thinking of the house he was building. He had been lucky to find plenty of stones ready worked and shaped among the abandoned buildings of the Chanonry. Baillie Knight had negotiated only last week for more from the north tower of the Chaplains', long in ruins. Lime for the mortar had been more difficult, but again Baillie Knight had secured a sufficiency from a ship newly berthed in the New Town harbour. But the house was to have two storeys and must be roofed with slates. So far there was no word of the slates, though Montgomery had made it plain to his employer that he must supply all materials himself – except for the timber, which George had undertaken to find.

Timber, as always, was scarce. The beams of the prebends' little houses in the Chanonry had been taken away years ago and put to good use in many an indweller's house. There were no trees left standing fit to cut and use. Any of sufficient girth had been taken before Montgomery came to the town. Every stave and beam of The Bishop's Palace had gone in Cromwell's time, and if ever a house fell into disuse the beams were the first to disappear. Besides, Alexander Fraser had scoured the neighbourhood for material for his own house too recently for there to be anything left for Montgomery. However there were trees on Speyside, and fir and oak wood was shipped to Scottish ports from Norway. There would be a timber market, as usual, at St Luke's fair, and if necessary Montgomery would have to wait till then. But George Cumming had undertaken to find timber and to do the carpentry and ironwork for the Baillie's house. George himself had chosen the blacksmith's trade, but many of his brothers were wrights and he himself could turn his hand as competently to wood as to metal. Between them, they could undertake any carpentry and metalwork required. Doors, hinges, windows, nails, the iron sway for the fire . . . George had given his word and would not fail him. George's father, he knew, was hostile, but he would work nevertheless with his son.

A son . . . Montgomery felt the familiar pain building up inside his head until he thought his skull would crack. *He* should have had a son. Unaware of the Minister's voice still droning its warnings, unaware of the indwellers snoring, sleeping, whispering, listening, unaware of the dogs and the children and the irate beadle who saw him just too late, Montgomery pushed his way through the throng to the west porch and out into the gusty morning. Across the kirk-yard, over the stile and down the Brae to the Baillie's stance he strode, with Margery limping and falling and scrambling anxiously after him.

'What is it, Father?' she said. 'Are you ill?'

They were at the site now. He turned to look at her, his good eye glazed with pain. He was trembling and tense with some terrible struggle she did not understand.

'Tell me,' she pleaded, 'and I will help.'

He sank down on to the grass at the foot of the wall and leant his head against the cool stone. His eyes were closed and when he spoke she could hardly hear him. 'Go home, before I . . .'

The child looked at him with troubled eyes, waiting for him to speak until something in the closed face and clenching fists warned her not to stay. She turned and limped obediently away.

2

The day of St Luke's fair dawned cold, the sky overcast. There was a thin skin of ice on the puddles in Widow Irvine's Close and the trees at the College tossed and lashed in the wind. Bright leaves whirled high over gusting chimneys and in the High Street women tucked their skirts close and children rubbed one bare leg against the other to ward off the cold. But Margery Montgomery did not mind the wind or the frost against her bare feet. She was too excited at the prospect of going to the fair with her father, and spending the whole day there if she chose.

As they left the house and pulled the door shut behind them, a babble of noise swelled across the Close from the High Street. Shouting, laughing, the squealing of pigs, hens, dogs, children. The steady click of hooves on setts where those indwellers who owned horses were already patrolling as the Council had ordered them to do, on pain of a £10 fine. Each trade had provided two armed men to assist the horsemen in keeping order at the market, and the baillies themselves would be in attendance in the Council House to dispense instant justice if required. For there would be crowds of strangers milling through the town during the time of the fair, beggars, buyers, stallholders, pedlars, anyone who had goods to sell, money to spend or time to kill.

The High Street was lined with stalls on both sides from the market cross to the College. The horse market was beyond Cumming's Wynd at the loch, with the sheep market near by, the cloth market at the cross itself, the fish market lower down the street at Beverley's Wynd: every trade and every merchant had his allotted place, while the baillies kept a strict eye on the weights and measures, checking them against the town's own weights and the town's own branded pecks in the weigh-house. The cries of the vendors vied with each other in growing competition as the day progressed.

Margery was enthralled. The street was packed. Beggars rattled their bowls, whining, clutching at a passing arm. Pedlars gabbled incessant sales talk. Women in their best clothes, carefully shaken out of wooden presses for the occasion, picked over apples, medlars, pears; fingered ribbons and lengths of homespun cloth dyed garish shades of orange and green and purple. Men lounged in open doorways and laughed and drank ale. For the duration of the fair illness and poverty and poor crops were to be forgotten, marked only in the leanness of the animals for sale and in the hollow cheeks of the poor. The air was cold and clear and alive with a thousand different scents and smells: cinnamon, camphor, apples, fish, lavender, cheese, skins, dung, sweat. Children shouted and sang. Someone played a fiddle, endlessly skirling. Near the market cross a group of girls giggled and whispered, waiting to be hired, while near at hand a shoemaker squatted beside a pile of shoes of every shape and size, from little worsted boots for babies to leather-thonged shoes for the head of the house.

A pig scurried through the crowd, knocking into people's legs, squealing. A skinny country lad in a dirty shirt ran gleefully after it, laying about him wholesale with a switch. Margery's face glowed with delight as she clutched tight to her father's hand and followed in his wake through the pressing crowds. But Montgomery looked at nothing and no one. He made his way unseeing past sweetmeats, salt fish, pickles and spoons, till he reached the cross and branched left for Cluny's Wynd.

Here, in the space between Cluny's Port and the Wynd was the timber market and here among the piles of fir wood and oak, they found George Cumming. He was deep in conversation with a man from the New Town who had roof-beams for sale.

'Six should do,' said George as Montgomery joined him. 'I've picked out these six as the most suitable – well-seasoned wood, straight and strong and each of the proper length. Then we'll need crossbeams and timber for the stair. Tell me what you think of this batch here.'

The two men moved away to a pile of smaller wood and began to examine it piece by piece, bending, smelling, smoothing it under their hands.

Margery stood patiently waiting and savouring the scent of resin and woodshavings and broken bark. The air was still cold in spite of the sun, and the sky thick with racing clouds, white and blue and grey; and over the wall of Cluny's garden she could see the tips of the withering apple trees tossing in the wind. Behind her Kenneth Fraser was bargaining with a timber merchant from Dundee, two of the Crystal boys were arguing goodnaturedly with a Speyside forester, and the entire Cumming family seemed to have taken up permanent positions in the centre of the timber market, talking and arguing and exchanging gossip and professional lore. But George Cumming and her father were still bargaining. They were in no hurry. It might be afternoon or evening before the deal was completed, but the child was content to wait. After her father, George was the most important man in her life.

It was almost evening and several flagons of ale later before the purchase was eventually made, the timber marked and paid for and the team of Cummings pressed into conveying it to Cumming's yard. It took two men to carry each of the six roof-beams.

'We'll keep it here till we need it,' said George.

'Why did you cut numbers into the beams, George?' asked Margery when they were piled one on another against the end wall.

'So I don't lose any, of course.'

'But you can count to six, George, without numbers to tell you so.'

George laughed. 'And can you?'

'Of course. I think the numbers are to show which order the beams are to lie in my Father's roof.'

'You should have been a boy,' laughed George, 'then I could have taught you how to choose a roof-beam, too, but it is no work for a girl. Here is a penny for you, Margery. Go and spend it and enjoy yourself. You have waited patiently for a long time.'

Margery looked at him with worshipping eyes. She rarely had money of her own to spend. 'Thank you, George.' She clutched the coin tight but made no move to leave.

'Well, go on,' urged George. 'What are you waiting for? Go and spend it, quick, before I change my mind.'

The child looked uncertainly at her father.

'You can go, Margery,' he said. 'Spend your money and then go home.'

'But your supper, Father.'

'I will go to see the house, first. The wind is strong and I must see if the mortar holds. You buy what takes your fancy and go home. I will come later.'

Margery hesitated, searching his face anxiously for signs of pain or strain. Then, reassured by a smile and a nod from George, she turned and limped away.

George watched her go. 'That's a bright lass you have there,

Montgomery. If she'd been a boy, you could have taught her anything.'

Montgomery did not answer. He was already moving away towards the High Street and his half-built house. George shrugged
and turned in the opposite direction, whistling. He had an appointment of his own to keep.

'Have you seen George?'

Reluctantly Margery looked away from the juggler she had been
watching for the last twenty minutes, and shook her head. She had
bought gingerbread with her penny, had eaten it ravenously and
spent an hour or more wandering, unnoticed and unchecked, the
length and breadth of the High Street. She had listened to the
balladmonger singing as he offered song sheets for sale, the quack
doctor's chatter as he peddled phials of plague water and mithridate and cures for the itch and the dropsy and the flux, the cries of
fleshers and fishmongers and ale-merchants as they vied with each
other for custom. She had watched the acrobat and the dwarf and
the sheep with six legs, she had seen two beggerwomen whipped
for begging without licences and she had seen the Deacon chase a
gang of boys from the mealmarket, beating them about the head
with a stave. Finally she had wriggled to the front of a knot of
people and found the juggler who could keep not only wooden
balls but mugs and spoons and knives flying in an unbroken arc
from hand to hand. She watched enthralled until Christian grabbed her shoulder and shook her hard.

'Have you seen him?' she demanded.

Christian looked unusually agitated. Her cheeks were flushed
and her thick hair dishevelled. She had been hurrying this way and
that searching for half an hour or more, till the sweat had spread
under her arms and stained the clean linen of her best dress, yellow, tight-bodiced and low-cut so that her plump breasts rose half
out of the cloth. Sweat runnelled in the pink cleft between.

'He said he would meet me,' she said worriedly. 'He promised.'

They had been together only last week in Baillie Knight's unfinished house. He had stayed with her till the dew stood thick in
the grass and the first bird sang, and they had not really quarrelled,
had they? Her heart quickened at the memory. He had seemed
cooler than usual, as if his thoughts were elsewhere, and she had
wanted to bring him close. But she had not meant to mention the

135

house again. When she did, he had not answered, but his face had closed against her. He had taken her back to the Gardens' kitchen and had not kissed her good-bye. She had not seen him since, but it was not a quarrel, surely? St Luke's fair was a holiday for everyone, and he had promised. Christian was torn between anger and dread.

Beside her, Margery stood politely waiting. To Christian her passivity was unendurable.

'Are you sure?' she demanded, shaking her roughly. 'You must have seen him some time. I thought he and your father . . .'

'Yes,' gasped Margery, white with pain as Christian's nails dug into the bones of her shoulder and found the tender muscle beneath. 'They bought wood together in the timber market. But that was a long time ago. My father went to see the house he is building, but I think George went the other way.'

'Which way? The High Street? Or the loch?'

The memory of another autumn day washed through her with icy clarity – she and Margery, a baby then, gathering berries in the birch wood by the river. And later, when the basket was full, she had seen someone else in the woods, on a certain sheltered path.

'It was the loch, wasn't it?' she demanded.

'I think so.'

Christian loosed her hold on the girl and pushed back through the crowd while Margery, rubbing her aching shoulder, returned to the juggler and his miraculously flying cups. Christian pushed her way through the throng until she collided with James Middleton, eleven years old now and a friend of John Garden. Christian knew him well.

'Where's Elspeth—' she demanded, clutching him tight by one ear.

'Don't know,' he retorted, squirming and twisting, but she held on tight.

'Where?' Her fingers dug into the flesh.

'I don't know,' he repeated. 'Ow! You're hurting me. Ow! She went that way, past the cross to Cluny's Wynd. But I haven't seen her, honest. Not for hours!'

Christian loosed his ear, cuffed him and hurried away. The tiny seed of fear had grown now to a huge, thrusting plant which threatened to blind and choke her. Cluny's Wynd . . . the Loch path . . . the birk woods by the river . . . She looped up her skirts and ran.

On the edge of the trees she stopped and listened. It was very still. The leaves lay thick on the ground but overhead the branches still glanced with brown and red and gold. A single leaf fell, turning, past her cheek, its edges curled and dead. The wind had dropped. It was cold and damp and drear. Christian shivered. Resolutely she moved in under the trees and stopped to listen again . . . the ripples of the river, moving, the sudden flurry of a blackbird pecking in the leaves for food, and the distant murmur of the fair.

Then a different murmur, close at hand and intimate.

Christian stood rigid, her fists clenched against her thighs and her heart thumping as she strained to hear the sound again. It came, and the blood drained from her cheeks. She took a step forward; carefully her bare feet sought and found the silence in the spongy turf. Another step. Another. Until she stood at the edge of a shallow incline, looking down through a scattering of stunted trees to the river bank. There were rushes here and grass through which the grey water combed freely; brambles, dying to black-toothed, tangled ropes, bracken curled and dying too; and, in a thick-leafed hollow by a shadowed stone, what seemed to Christian's blurring vision a writhing figure with two heads. Her eyes took in the flung-back skirts, the white, raised thigh, the plunging legs before she turned and fled, stumbling, blundering back through the trees, her eyes blind with tears and the blood pounding so loud in her ears that she did not hear the noise of her own crashing flight. Past the old men's little hospital, past the kirkyard, past Lord Whitehill's and the Bishop's garden, to the foot of the Brae and home. But at the Chaplains' she heard voices and laughter, and veered away from the arched entrance and on to the doorway of Baillie Knight's house, stumbled unseeing into the darkness of the building – and choked on the scream as she was caught, pinioned, and crushed till the blood sang in her head.

Then the grip loosed, so suddenly that Christian fell to the ground, sobbing and gasping and too frightened to move.

'I am sorry,' said Montgomery. 'I thought you were one of Fraser's lads come to spoil my work.'

Christian began to laugh, but the laughter changed unexpectedly to tears, great tearing sobs which shook her body from head to toe. She turned her face to the damp grass and let the jealousy and the pain flow through her unchecked. Montgomery stood uncertainly in the shadows, watching. His eyes, unlike hers, were used to the half-light. It was evening now and cold, and the clouds which had masked the sun fitfully for most of the day had thickened and lowered to bring darkness sooner than usual. Christian's yellow dress showed pale against the ground, and where her skirt had risen, her bare legs were pale too, spread and helpless. He bent on one knee beside her and put out a trembling hand to touch her shoulder.

'What is it?' he asked awkwardly. 'Why do you cry?'

At the touch of his hand on her flesh, Christian's sobs stopped abruptly. She rolled over on to her back, flung her arms around his neck and tried to pull him down upon her with a desperation he did not understand.

'Kiss me,' she ordered. 'And damn him to hell!'

Puzzled and wary, Montgomery held back while the long-smouldering fire roared in his head till he thought his skull would burst. Then she was kissing him and the fire broke free to rage unchecked. He did not hear her terrified 'No!' He did not feel her nails in his face or her futile, beating fists and when she tried to scream his great hand closed over her mouth.

'I'm sorry, darling,' whispered George. 'Forgive me. I never meant to . . . but you were so beautiful . . .' Already his head was clearing, and with clarity came the appalling realization of what he had done. 'Oh God, Elspeth, you should have stopped me!'

'Darling Georgie,' she murmured, kissing his throat, his ear, his cheek. 'I didn't want to stop you. I liked it. And I love you.'

'Oh God!' He rolled over now, face down on the rough grass while the full horror washed over him. Suppose she were to be . . .

'Georgie, darling,' she was saying now. 'My own love. My dearest. Don't worry, Father will come round to it in the end. I know he will.' She stroked his head, caressing.

'Come . . . round to it?' He dared not look at her.

'Oh, I know he wants me to marry one of the Cluny Gordons, but I can get round him. I always do in the end. Besides,' she blushed with a charming mixture of modesty and knowledge, 'if there is a child, he will have to agree.'

'A child?' George kept his head averted so that she might not see the terror in his face. 'But we don't want a child.'

'Don't worry, darling.' She put an arm around him now, cradling his head, crooning to him lovingly. 'Georgie, my love. I adore you. I always have. All those years in Edinburgh I could hardly bear it without you, except that I knew you would be here, waiting for me, when I came back. And you were.' She laid her cheek against his head. 'Georgie? Love me again? Now?'

'No!' George sat up abruptly. 'You must go home. Your father . . .' He choked on the thought.

'Tomorrow, Georgie? I can slip away after supper and meet you? Oh darling, I do love you.' She twined her arms around his neck and kissed him, but he twisted his head away nervously, saying, 'You must go back. They might have missed you.'

'Darling Georgie, don't worry. And I'm so happy.' An idea occurred to her. 'I was all right, wasn't I!'

George gulped. 'Yes, of course you were. It's just . . . Oh God, what am I going to do?' Panic washed over him and left him gasping.

Elspeth laughed, a soft, loving little laugh which froze the blood in his veins. 'Georgie, you're so sweet. But there's no need to be frightened. Don't worry about Father. After all, your father is a Burgess and a master craftsman. Papa will be angry, of course, at first, but he will come round to the idea, you will see.'

George could stand no more. He stood up and pulled her to her feet.

'Tidy yourself, Elspeth,' he managed. 'Put your dress to rights. I will take you as far as the stile, but I think it would be best if no one saw us together just yet.'

'If you wish it, Georgie.' Elspeth brushed at the leaves and bracken in the creases of her skirt. Her eyes were lowered and her cheeks flushed. George saw the glint of a tear against her cheek. Guilt made him irritable and rougher than he meant to be.

'It's no good crying, for God's sake. It's too late for that.'

'I'm sorry,' gulped Elspeth. She flung her arms around his neck and clung to him. 'I love you,' she sobbed piteously. 'Don't send me away. Please? Walk home with me, Georgie? Show them I am yours now, for always?'

George's face was tense above the soft tumbling hair. He held her and stroked her and murmured some sort of comfort until she was quiet, then he took her hand and said firmly, 'Not yet. I must speak to my father first. He would be angry and slighted if he heard from some idle gossip before he heard from me. Dry your eyes, Elspeth and smile for me? That's better. Now we must go, or you will be missed. Are you ready?' She nodded. 'Then I will walk with you as far as Cluny's Port. We will go by the back dyke and the loch, but at the gate you must go on alone. There will be people still. You will be safe enough. I promised to meet a man at the Baillie's change-house,' he lied, 'to talk about a piece of work he wants me to do. It is urgent and there will be an outcry if I am not there.'

'I am sorry, Georgie. You should have told me. If it is your work, of course you must go. And I understand about your father,' she added meekly. 'I will not speak until you say I may, and I will walk home alone.'

Nevertheless George walked with her as far as Cluny's Port. It was the least he could do.

The High Street was lit now with tapers and lanterns and flambeaux, which cast an eerie warmth across the faces of the crowds who still clustered around the booths or stood together gossiping while their children played and squabbled and slept.

'Good-bye, Georgie. Till tomorrow.' Her eyes were soft and adoring as she stood on tiptoe to kiss his lips. 'I love you.' Then she was gone.

George watched until Elspeth's small figure was safely swallowed into the crowd, then he made his way by the back dyke and a convenient wall to Baillie Baxter's change-house near the College. He had a great need for ale and masculine company and free, uncomplicated talk of work and war.

The change-house was packed and reeking. It was a dark and airless place at the best of times, down three steps to a bare-walled, dirt-floored room with one small window which, as it admitted neither light nor air, served no apparent purpose. At the moment the place was crammed thick with men and the stench of ale and sweat and burning tallow. At a table in one corner, Baillie Baxter himself was entertaining three members of the guard to ale. Not of course from his own pocket: you could be sure every drop would be charged to the Town Treasurer's accounts. At another table half a dozen dragoons were singing lustily, their arms round each other's shoulders. Ale dripped from the swimming table-top in a steady trickle to the dirt floor. A group of officers watched them indulgently from across the room where they were drinking whisky with George Fraser, Subprincipal of the College, and Dr Urquhart the Mediciner. At the sight of these two, George blanched and would have fled, but there was no sign of the Principal – or, thank God, of George's own father. George had banked on his going as he always did to the ale-house at the cross.

George paid for his drink and pushed his way to a place near the door where he could keep a weather eye open for the approach of anyone he might prefer to avoid. God, he'd been a fool! The terror of it washed over him afresh. At best, she would expect him to marry her. Elspeth, so docile and undemanding, was just like the others after all. That would mean trouble enough, but if there should be a child . . . He gulped hastily at the cooling ale. Her father, his father, the Session – they would all attack him and threaten him and sit in judgement, and then if they made him marry her there would be the child and he would be trapped. He downed the first luggie and ordered a second. As that, too, spread its warmth through his veins, the panic receded. Perhaps there would be no child after all. If not, there would be no hurry to marry. He loved her, of course, but he was not ready to settle down. There were things he wanted to do. He must be free. His own master. Not tied to a hearth and a meal-pot and a screaming child. One day, yes. But not yet. He could put her off somehow, surely? She would wait for him. She loved him, she was gentle and beautiful and he knew she would be faithful. He liked the idea of her waiting for him, lovely and adoring, till he chose to take the final step. Yes. That was the solution. He would ask her to wait. As the panic loosed its hold, George began to relax and listen to the conversation around him.

'It will be a joint English and Scots venture I understand?' Baillie Baxter had left the guard well plenished and had joined Dr Urquhart and the officers.

'Just so long as that blackguard Dalrymple has no hand in it.' Urquhart drained his mug and called for another.

Sir John Dalrymple, Master of Stair and at one time the King's Secretary of State for Scotland, was a notable supporter of the idea of a Treaty of Union between the two countries, an idea which had been rejected by the Convention of Estates five years before but which continued to gain support, except of course among the Jacobites of whom there were still plenty in the Old Town, though they had the sense and the caution not to flaunt the fact. Dr Urquhart was not one of these. He had signed the Oath of Obedience cheerfully and without reservation. He saw the advantages of one king and one parliament, and was farsighted enough to see the benefits of a firm political union granting equal rights and privileges to both parties. But he could not forgive Dalrymple the massacre at Glencoe, which no one disputed had been of his planning and on his orders. It had been a bloody and ignoble affair from start to finish and had done nothing to advance the cause of civilized co-operation between the two countries. Although more than two years had passed, the stink of treachery still hung in the air. Since that time the Highlanders had given no more trouble. Scotland was passive, submissive and still waiting for fulfilment of the promises held out to her by the Orange King, while the crops dwindled, the seasons grew more hostile and the people were called on to fee more and more soldiers for the King's wars.

'If Dalrymple has a hand in it,' repeated Urquhart emphatically, 'the venture is bound to be corrupt.'

George Fraser glanced uneasily at Major Guthrie, head of the garrison quartered in the Old Town, but the Major registered no sort of annoyance or unease.

'You can rest assured on that point,' said Fraser. 'It is not political union yet, merely a practical arrangement to pool resources. The idea is very much in the planning stage still. My informant, a most reliable fellow in London, tells me it is the idea of a group of Scots merchants there.'

'Then why bring the English into it?' asked Baxter.

'The more capital they can collect, the more chance the project has of succeeding. A joint venture would be to everyone's advantage. Well? Are you interested?'

'I might be,' said Baxter cautiously. 'Tell me more.'

'The idea is to establish a Trading Company in Africa and the Indies.'

'After Nova Scotia?' demanded Urquhart. 'And New England? Look what disasters they were.'

'I grant you those ventures were ill-advised, but their lesson will be a useful one. The new merchant company is to be built on sound business lines and not launched until there is solid, country-wide backing. Your money will be safe enough.'

'Are they sure Africa is the best place?' said the Major dubiously.

'It seems so at present, though plans are not rigid as yet. There have been other suggestions. There is a lot of work yet to be done. We'll need ships, men, finance . . .'

'What sort of return will there be on investment?' asked Baxter. 'I might be interested if the rewards are big enough.'

'Unlimited, if all goes as planned. We'll need a great deal of capital of course to provide ships and cargo. We'll need warehouses and goods for trading . . .'

'That's a lot of money to sink in what seems to me no better than a gamble,' said Baxter.

'It is a gamble, I grant you, but a gamble with a very great chance of success. And if it does come off, we will be made for life.'

'. . . Oriental spices . . . gold . . . rare silks . . . jade . . .' George Cumming listened entranced, the ale mug forgotten in his hand.

'It sounds too much of a risk to me.' Major Guthrie's voice interrupted his reverie. 'Any young man seeking travel and excitement would do better to take the King's shilling and ship to Flanders. No waiting about for years until some stranger in London makes up his mind. He can go now if he wants. My man is signing on recruits at this very minute at the market cross.'

'But this trading venture,' persisted Baxter. 'I am interested. And there might be others in the town who would be prepared to risk a moderate outlay in the hope of large returns. Alexander Fraser for instance, or Dr Middleton.'

At the name the old panic forced up through the haze of wellbeing which ale and company had induced, and George's mouth went dry. His hand trembled as he raised the luggie.

'I doubt that Middleton has a penny to spare,' said George Fraser. 'You forget he still has to provide dowries for those daughters of his.'

'Aye,' agreed the Mediciner. 'I doubt there'll be much money left for speculation when he has found husbands for those three. Isobel seems content enough as she is, but Elspeth is ripe for marriage, anyone can see that. She is a beautiful girl and ready. He'll have trouble there if he doesn't find a husband for her soon.'

George crashed down the empty mug on the nearest bench, shouldered his way out of the doorway and collided with his own father.

'Steady,' growled Cumming, gripping his son by the forearm and wrenching him back. 'I've been looking for you! What's this I hear about you and the Middleton girl?'

'What?' blustered George. 'I don't know what you mean.'

'Oh yes you do. You were seen at the back dyke together. Now I'm warning you, lad . . .' He raised a great fist threateningly.

'Oh yes?' Ale and panic made George reckless. 'And who are you to talk? I've heard a thing or two that you wouldn't want repeated in the kirk Session. A midsummer fire? The birk woods?'

Cumming swung at George who ducked and then crashed his fist hard into his father's face. With a roar of fury, Cumming fell on the boy. They locked together, heaving and grunting. For Cumming, his parental authority was at stake, for George his manhood, and neither would give way. As they staggered this way and that over the uneven setts, a crowd gathered from nowhere and closed in around them, cheering encouragement, welcoming this additional entertainment at the tail end of the fair. They were well-matched in size and in determination, and it promised to be a lengthy contest. Cumming's lip was split and bleeding, George's left cheek was swelling rapidly and his nose ran blood, but neither showed any sign of giving in.

'George!'

The voice of authority penetrated the red haze of rage and pain, and from years of habit the boy checked in obedience. As his grip slackened, Cumming knocked him sideways with the flat of his huge hand. George sprawled on the cobbles, humiliated.

'George Cumming! How dare you strike your father in the public street.' Baillie Baxter's sallow face was flushed with righteousness. 'Get up and beg his pardon this instant, or I will call the guard and have you arrested for brawling.'

Slowly George pulled himself to his feet. He looked from father to Baillie and back then said clearly and with careful enunciation, 'The devil take you both to hell.'

He turned and thrust his way quickly into the dark turbulence of the crowd which closed instantly behind him. Baillie Baxter opened his mouth to call the guard, but Cumming laid a hand on his arm.

'Leave it to me, Baillie,' he said ominously. Then he, too, was gone.

The street was dark now, the tapers dying one by one as the indwellers dispersed to their homes. But though he searched every close and wynd and dyke from the Spital to the Brig, the blacksmith did not find his son.

'I will see the Session clerk tomorrow,' said Montgomery. 'We must be wed.'

Christian did not reply. She smoothed the shreds of her dress, plucking automatically at the laces and pulling them straight. Her lips were bruised and swollen and her whole body ached. She pulled herself slowly to her feet and her knees gave under her so that she clutched at the unfinished wall for support. When she had summoned her strength she moved unsteadily away from him towards the vacant doorway and the street.

'Christian! Where are you going?'

'Home!'

She did not turn her head but moved onwards, more quickly now. He lumbered after her, calling, 'Christian! You came to me. Now we must be wed.' He reached out to touch her arm and she whirled on him.

'Bastard!' she spat. 'I'd rather wed the devil!'

It was later that night – much later – that she heard a tapping at the great barred door into the yard.

'Christian?'

At the sound of the familiar voice Christian's face set hard and obstinate. Her mind was dull with a misery as chill and all-enveloping as the autumn haar from the sea.

'Christian! It's me! George. I must see you.'

Christian had been lying on the flagstones near the hearth, with her head against the meal tub and behind her the great oak table where the wooden bowls were already set for the morning porridge. Now she stood up, slowly for her limbs were still aching, and with great care lest the mistress should hear. She glanced anxiously upwards to where two massive beams supported the floor-boards of the room where Professor Garden and his wife and two of the youngest children lay sleeping. If the mistress heard her, there'd be trouble.

Christian slid back the bolt and eased the door open an inch. 'What is it?' she hissed. 'Hurry up before they hear.'

'Can I come in, Christian?' he said, pleading. 'Please?'

'No.'

'What's the matter?' he asked with concern. 'What have you done to your face?' His own face was shielded by the darkness of the courtyard and Christian did not see the bruised and blackening eye.

'Nothing.'

'Then let me in. Please.' He put out a hand to touch her cheek. 'I must see you.'

'No.' She moved to close the door, but he put a foot in the gap and a shoulder against the wood and forced it open again.

'Listen Christian, I don't know what's got into you, but I'm in trouble. You must help me. We've always been friends, haven't we?' She did not answer. 'Please listen. My father's after my blood, never mind why, and I'm leaving.'

Christian gasped and caught her breath.

'I don't know how long I'll be away, but I want you to do something for me.'

'What?' she said coldly, but her voice trembled and her face was dead white in the half-light of the yard.

'See Elspeth for me. Explain what has happened. Tell her . . .'

Christian leant all her weight against the door, forced it shut and slammed home the great iron bolt.

'Please Christian? Tell her I love her. Tell her I'll come back.' The voice was urgent, caution forgotten.

There was a sound from upstairs, a voice calling 'Who's there?' Christian heard a step on the flagstones outside, then silence. She went to the foot of the spiral stair which led upwards from one corner of the kitchen.

'It's nothing, madam,' she called. 'Some vagabond from the fair. But the door is barred and he is gone.'

He is gone.

The three words tolled like a burial bell in her aching head. Slowly Christian moved to the hearth. She took one of the fire-irons from its nail and turned back the peats to let in the air and bring the fire to life. She swung the iron pot to the centre of the flame and stood watching until the fire took hold and the water in the cauldron began to sing quietly against the metal. It was too early. The morning drum had not sounded and outside no one was astir. But Christian knew she would not sleep again. George had gone and without George there was nothing.

'George Cumming has gone for a soldier.' William Walker had it from one of the dragoons in Major Guthrie's troop. 'Signed on for two years to fight the King's wars in Flanders.'

Montgomery could not believe it. 'He is contracted to me,' he said. 'To build my house.'

'Not now he's not,' said the drummer with satisfaction. 'He's contracted to King William and you'll have to wait your turn.' Walker moved on down the street towards the Brig, beating his drum and calling his news at every door.

'George Cumming has gone for a soldier, two years to the

Flanders wars. Five o'clock and time to rise. George Cumming has gone to the wars . . .'

Montgomery marched to Cumming's yard and demanded that the father complete the son's contract.

'He's no son of mine,' growled Cumming senior. 'You can take your timber and your roof-beams, but you'll find someone else to do the work for I'll not touch it and nor will my sons.'

So Montgomery took his wood, slowly, piece by piece and alone, even the beams which had needed two men to move them from the market. But when the wood was stacked in the roofless house there was nothing he could do except wait and hope that some wandering wright would come seeking work. He sought out Christian at the Chaplains', but the kitchen maid told him she was upstairs with the mistress and could not come. Montgomery was puzzled, but obstinate. 'She came to me,' he muttered. 'She must wed me.'

He sent Margery several times, but Christian still would not meet him.

'She is busy,' explained Margery. 'She has the washing week and the mistress is brewing ale.'

Nevertheless and without consulting Christian, Montgomery paid a visit to the Session clerk and handed over the fee.

'I hear Montgomery is to be married again,' said Cumming senior. 'I had it from the Session clerk this morning.'

Urquhart was surprised, as much by the satisfaction in Cumming's voice as by the news. 'Who is the girl?'

'Christian Grant.' Cumming's satisfaction was explained.

'But I thought she and your George . . .' began Baxter.

'He's no George of mine,' thundered the blacksmith. 'And he may go to the devil.' So, he might as well have added, may she. It was well known that Cumming had disapproved of George's association with 'that Papist bitch the Grant girl'. He was obviously delighted that she had found her just deserts.

'Christian Grant,' said Middleton thoughtfully. 'I hope she knows what she is doing.'

'She knows,' said Baxter grimly. He had not forgiven Christian for being her mother's daughter. 'I only hope he does.'

'They'll be well matched,' growled Cumming.

'At least she will have charge of that child,' said Urquhart.

'Really a most satisfactory arrangement for them all. It might make the man human again.'

'Human? He's a villainous heathen devil,' said Kenneth Fraser. 'And he'll not get his house built, neither. Not if I can help it.'

'I hear Alexander Crystal was seen in Rynie,' said Urquhart blandly. 'I understood he was heading for home.'

Kenneth Fraser was silent. If anyone was likely to help Montgomery it would be Alexander Crystal.

'How is the Powis building?' asked Middleton quickly. 'I hear you have run into difficulties over the crossbeams.'

'No difficulty at all,' snapped the master mason. 'Three of the beams are too short and it is merely a question of replacement.'

'A pity the measurements were not properly taken until the timber market was over,' remarked Urquhart. 'You'll have to go to the New Town now. Or Dundee. There'll be transport costs, of course.'

The mason glared.

'Why not do a deal with Montgomery?' suggested Baxter. 'You use his beams in return for helping him finish his house? He can't use them himself till he gets help anyway, and by that time you can get timber from the harbour.'

'I'll do no deal with Montgomery,' said Fraser and added ominously, 'He has no need of those beams. And he'll get none of my men to help him. He'll not finish his house now.'

'Baillie Knight will not be pleased to come back and find his contract unfulfilled,' said Baxter. Baillie Knight was in Edinburgh on family business.

'*If* he comes back,' said Urquhart. 'I hear the fever is rife.'

'So it is everywhere this winter,' said Baxter. 'If not the fever, then the flux or the coughing sickness.'

'Or plain starvation,' said Urquhart. 'There was a man found at the top of the Spital only yesterday, not an ounce of flesh on his bones and a gobbet of grass in his mouth.'

'But not an indweller,' said Kenneth Fraser piously. 'We have not yet come to such straits that we feed our poor on grass.'

'It might come to that if the crops fail again next year,' said Middleton. 'Barley is scarce enough already, and at the price of meal who can afford to feed a family, let alone the public poor?'

The Principal had aged during the summer. His cheeks were drawn and his forehead bore a perpetual line of strain. Now, with November upon them and the dead heart of winter promising only hunger and poverty and disease, even the opening of the new session at the College could not banish the worry from his mind.

As usual, the Principal had led the red-gowned students – seventy-four of them this year – in procession to the kirk, though still they had no settled minister. The Principal himself had given the address and the Session clerk had read the passages from the Scriptures. Everything had proceeded as usual, yet the Principal was uneasy. Ever since Bishop Haliburton's departure with the accession of the new King, he had felt the same disquiet. He was still the Principal and titular head of the College, yet the Orange King in London was not sympathetic to those who had carried over from the old order to the new. In spite of the signatures to the Confession of Faith acknowledging the Presbyterian Government of the church, Middleton knew that he and most of his colleagues were regarded with suspicion. Sometimes in the dark hours he knew with certainty that he would fall. They would watch him and wait, and one day they would find a pretext and he would be removed. Meanwhile he must endeavour to rule the College as he always had, with honour, circumspection and humane judgement. Yet at the same time he must ignore the cavern which yawned wider and wider at his feet. If he took one false step in any direction, he would fall. He and his fellow professors were on sufferance only. It was a situation which both irked and oppressed him. Now, with the added worry at home, the strain was beginning to tell.

'Sixteen more dead this week,' Cumming was saying. 'The Session clerk was entering them up when I saw him. "A bairn in the kirkyard, six shillings and eightpence" all down the page. And not all bairns at that.'

'Aye. It'll be a hard winter,' agreed Kenneth Fraser.

'Yes, yes,' said Baxter. 'There is little we can do about the weather, but we can at least put our town in order and make sure there is no waste of money or resources. The bent, for instance. In spite of regulations, far too much grass is being cut from the Links, with the result that the sand is slipping badly and the grass itself will be lost if something is not done.'

'There was rioting on the moss last week,' put in Kenneth Fraser. 'The Sledder woman and another came to blows over who was cutting whose peat. The marches must be redefined.'

'It is time the road beyond the Brig was cleared again.'

'There is muck in many of the wynds. The stench is over-powering.'

'Beggars are insinuating themselves into the town without licences or badges. And so many of them that they are hard to dislodge.'

But at last the week's affairs were settled and the Council dispersed. The Principal and the Mediciner left the Council chamber together.

'How is Elspeth?' asked the Mediciner quietly as they walked down the High Street towards the College. His own son Adam had been ailing now for some months, and he knew the anxiety of a helpless parent in the face of his child's suffering.

'No better. She is pale and listless, yet she has no fever and she says she feels no pain. I do not understand it. She cannot eat, I fear she does not sleep and she sits for hours staring out of the window. We have tried blood-letting and all manner of electuaries, but to no effect. Even when her mother makes her spin, she does so only by instinct and completely without thought. She is fading before my eyes, and yet she assures me there is nothing wrong.'

'Is she missing Edinburgh, perhaps?' suggested Urquhart. 'Or a young man?'

'I wondered about that, but when I asked her if there was someone in Edinburgh she denied it. I only half-believed her until I suggested sending her back to her aunt, when she protested so vehemently that I believed her fully. No, Urquhart, if there is any cause it lies here, in the Old Town, but she will not speak of it. When I beg her to tell me she closes in upon herself and assures me there is nothing to tell.'

'She is not . . .' Urquhart hesitated. He had heard a rumour, yet he did not want to offend his old friend. 'Not . . . in trouble?'

Middleton was too worried to take offence. 'No, no. I thought of that, too, but my wife assures me the girl's month comes regularly as it should. Yet . . . would you look at her? As a friend? If something is not done soon I fear . . . You see she is grown to look so frail.'

Urquhart put an arm around his shoulder. 'I will see her. Though I doubt that it will do any good.'

'Why not now?' They had reached the Principal's house and Middleton stood with a hand on the latch. 'Come in and take a dram.'

'Why not?'

Middleton opened the door and stood aside to let the Mediciner enter. The heavy door closed behind them.

Christian Grant watched from across the street. She had been sent by her mistress to deliver yarn to a weaver in the Spital and was on her way home when she saw the tall figure of the Principal approaching. She slipped into Douglas Wynd and waited till the door of the Principal's house closed.

Christian had a horror of meeting Dr Middleton or any of his family. She had not seen Elspeth since the day of St Luke's fair. She had heard that Elspeth was ill and still she had not sought her out. George's message drummed in her brain, bruising and stabbing her with every word.

'I will not tell her,' vowed Christian. 'He should not have asked me and I will not do it.' She turned determinedly away.

Elspeth had been weeping now for a long time, though she had learnt to do so noiselessly and only when alone. In company she sat silent and withdrawn, while her heart bled quietly for the man who had left her. In private she let the tears flow unchecked.

'Why?' she moaned over and over. 'What did I do wrong? Was it because I let him take me?' Even the memory of their loving had ceased to be a comfort to her. There was to be no child and George had gone. 'Georgie, I love you. I will never love anyone but you. Georgie come back to me.'

So her mind endlessly reiterated the same phrases, until the eyes she turned on her family became vague and mindless and her strength failed.

'What is troubling, you Elspeth? If it is something you cannot tell your parents, I promise to keep your secret. Try to tell me. It will ease the burden.'

'Thank you, Dr Urquhart,' said Elspeth politely. 'You are very kind. But nothing troubles me. I am quite well.'

The Mediciner retired defeated. All he could suggest was nourishing food and a tot of brandy night and morning. But Elspeth could not eat and the brandy burnt her throat. The Mediciner's prescription was useless, but it was not his fault. Elspeth knew there was only one man who could cure her, and he was far away.

'When will George come back?' asked Margery. She was helping Christian in the kitchen of the Chaplains'. Christian had given her

rags, a dish of sand and the brass candlesticks from the upstairs
dining-room, and the child had been dutifully polishing for half
an hour. Her father, as always, was guarding the shell of Baillie
Knight's house at the foot of the Brae. Since George's departure
he had grown wary and suspicious, and only returned to the house
in the Close to sleep. Consequently Margery spent many hours with
Christian in the Gardens' kitchen and her father made no objection.
Nor did Mrs Garden. Margery was quiet and self-effacing, helpful
and always polite. The mistress tolerated her, and had begun to
value her unpaid assistance to the extent of sending her occasionally
on messages or allowing her to nurse one of the children.

'It is a fine thing for you,' Christian told her on one such occasion.
'When you're older and need a situation, they might take you here
— or at least recommend you to someone. With that leg of yours,
you'll need all the influence you can get.'

Margery looked surprised, then nodded obediently in agreement.
She never considered her leg an impediment and it always surprised
her when people drew attention to it, as Christian did now, and
as the town children sometimes did, calling after her in the
street 'Hopping Maggie', 'One-leg' or just plain 'Cripple'. But
George never drew attention to her leg. He accepted her as she
was.

'When will George be back?' she asked again. Christian's face
took on a blank, closed look which was new to Margery and which
made her uneasy.

'How should I know?'

'But George is your friend,' persisted the child. 'Did he not tell
you when he said good-bye? William Walker says he is gone for
two whole years, but William Walker was not George's friend as
you were. He cannot know. And two years is too long. When will
he be back?'

'Stop chattering,' snapped Christian. 'And that brass is *green*.'

'I'm rubbing as hard as I can,' apologized Margery, and added,
'I wish he would come back. George is my friend, too, and I miss
him.'

Christian did not reply. She felt the familiar panic rise inside
her and the familiar pain. If George were here, he would help her.
George would know what to do. But George was not here. First he
had betrayed her with that peely Middleton girl and now he had
left her when she needed him more than ever before. He would not
come back, or not until it was too late. And even if he did, that

treacherous voice reminded her, who was to say he would come back to her? The picture of the two-headed creature in the woods swept searingly across her mind and she bit her lip hard against the pain.

'I wish he would come,' repeated Margery wistfully.

'For God's sake be quiet!' shouted Christian and rushed outside as she felt the vomit rise.

When she came back to the kitchen, a long time later, the candlesticks were bright as lamplight in the centre of the table and Margery sat meekly on the little stool at the hearth, her hands folded in her lap. The pot simmered quietly, the fire glowed and the hearthstone was neatly swept. Christian's weary eyes took in every detail. She sank to the floor beside Margery, put her arms around the child and cradled her head against her breast. 'I'm sorry, love,' she murmured. 'It's not your fault. But I'm so worried and I don't know what to do.'

'What are you worried about, Christian?'

'Everything.'

The man I love and who does not love me. The man I want who has gone and the man I don't want who wants me. The sickness. The dizziness. The burning pain in my breasts. My breasts are big now and red-veined. They will give me away soon. The bruises still yellow on my thighs. The child growing, unwanted, inside me. But most of all, Baillie Baxter and the Session. Even Ma was afraid of that and I am not as brave as she was. Cheat them, she said. Don't let them get you down. If George came back perhaps he would . . . ? But no, the idea was madness. He would not come back and if he did it would certainly not be to marry her with someone else's child inside her.

'I am worried . . .' she began slowly, then fear and despair engulfed her and she said in a rush, 'Your father wants to marry me.'

Margery gave a cry of delight. 'But Christian that would be lovely! Why are you worried about it?'

'Because . . .'

Because he is huge and maimed and tormented and he frightens me. Because he is not George.

'Don't you want to marry him? I know he likes you. Please Christian? Then you could come and live with us. I would like that.'

Christian's mind was numbed now with anguish. Suddenly recklessness took over. Deliberately, as if challenging fate to arrange it otherwise, she chose the road to self-destruction.

'If you want it, Margery, then I will. Tell your father . . .' she choked on the words, but the memory now deliberately conjured of that scene in the woods strengthened her resolve. 'Tell him I will marry him. But,' she added maliciously, 'he must see Professor Garden about it himself.'

However, she underestimated Montgomery. He had not her horror of the kirk Session, and when Christian's employer refused to allow her to marry before the expiry of her contracted term which would be at Whitsun next, Montgomery told him that the matter would not wait if the child was to be born in wedlock. For though Christian had not yet told him so Montgomery had no doubt there was to be a child. The Professor was shaken, concerned that a servant in his care should have transgressed, and was left with no choice but to mend matters as far as he was able. Christian was to be married at once, but was to stay in their service until the next Quarter-day which would be Candlemas, in two months' time. After that, she could go to her husband's house in Widow Irvine's Close.

Generously, Mrs Garden offered to give Christian a 'penny' wedding, but the girl refused. If it had been George who was to be her husband she would have been delighted for Mrs Garden to fill her house with her friends, to dine and dance the night away and finally to take up a collection for the bride and groom. As it was, Christian wanted only to get the business finished as quickly as possible and with the minimum of fuss. Montgomery had no friends and relatives in the Old Town and Christian wanted no one to witness her travesty of a wedding.

Later on the same day that William Montgomery married Christian Grant with only his crippled daughter to see it, the kirk bells rang for a different and more sombre reason.

'Item,' wrote the Session clerk in his careful script. 'Elspeth Middleton, lawful daughter to Geo. Middleton in the College, buried in the Dunbar aisle aged fifteen years and the bells rung. . . £20.'

Christian wept when she heard. It was too late now for her to deliver George's message. That was one more sin upon her conscience. And it was too late for Christian herself if George should come back. From that day Christian's heart grew harder and her bearing more defiant. And she refused to go to bed with her husband.

'You've bedded me already,' she told him. 'You'll not touch me now till the child is born.'

Montgomery submitted. He had secured a wife and his child would be born in wedlock. The idea of the child took hold of him and grew until that promise of a son blotted out all other thoughts. Christian was fifteen and healthy. He would have liked to bed her, but she did not want it. He could make her, of course, but his child was too precious to him to be put at risk. So Christian resumed her place on the kitchen flagstones in the Chaplains' Court and Montgomery and his daughter returned to the Close.

That night of her wedding when she should have been happy in her husband's bed, Christian wept on the hearthstone, alone; for herself, for George who was lost to her, and for Elspeth whom she had wronged and who had died without the knowledge of his love.

Many more were to die in the dark months that followed. The fever, which had carried off Elspeth Middleton in the short passage of two days, raged the length of the town finding out others equally weak and unresisting, until the death roll mounted beyond the hundred mark. Parents lost entire families in a matter of days, men were widowed, children orphaned, and those who survived the fever faced months of near-starvation before the spring. Even the houses of the gentry did not escape, neither in the servants' hall nor above. The Urquharts lost a child, the Gardens two, the George Frasers two and the youngest Middleton child followed Elspeth to the kirkyard. Kenneth Fraser lost three children in as many days, several of the Cummings died and both Christian's brothers. Merchant Sledder lost three of his four children, in spite of sending to the New Town for the doctor with his leeches and his boluses and in spite of the other, different remedies which his wife procured in secret and at night. Not a family in the old Town escaped bereavement. Except Montgomery.

Folk looked at him askance and crossed the street to the other side. They talked of the evil eye and remembered long-forgotten things. Someone threw a stone at Margery and called her a witch. For Margery survived the fever as she had survived everything else, though her dark eyes sank deeper into their sockets and the skin hung empty on her brittle bones. Montgomery also endured, keeping constant guard over the shell of his house even when his skin burned, his body shook and his good eye glittered with the fever.

And it was on a night at the height of his fever that the men came.

At Candlemas Christian's time at the Gardens was finished and she moved into Montgomery's house in Widow Irvine's Close. She was thick at the waist now, but pregnancy suited her and she was glowing with health. She had been well fed at the Gardens', she had escaped the fever and she had still a bloom about her which three weeks in Montgomery's house had not yet dulled.

'I'll not share your bed,' she announced on the day she arrived. So Margery joined Christian in the wooden bed which had been her mother's bridal, birthing and death bed, and Montgomery took Margery's place in the inglenook beside the hearth.

But not for long. One day he found the planks gone from his building site and from that moment he made his home in the unfinished house. Baillie Knight was still in Edinburgh, the roof-beams were still unused and the work was no further on, but one day George Cumming would come back and fulfil his contract – or someone else would arrive to do the job. Meanwhile no man should tamper with his building or take away what was lawfully his.

So Montgomery abandoned his daily trips in search of fish or rabbit or hare, and took up his position on guard in the house at the foot of the Brae. No one knew what he did there, but Margery took him his broze, and ale when there was ale, carrying the wooden vessels the length of the High Street, past the market cross and down the cobbled causeway to the old Chaplains' Port.

Then one night in early March the men came. They came in the darkness, long after the ringing of the curfew bell, but Montgomery heard them. He took a stave in his hands and crouched in the shadow of the chimney-well, while his skin burned and his head split with the blazing fever. There were six of them and they came silently through the empty doorway and across the trodden turf to where the roof-beams lay stacked against the far wall. Montgomery waited, while his hands shook on the wooden shaft and his good eye gleamed. He did not move until the first man stooped and cupped his arms around the topmost beam.

Then with an animal bellow of rage he leapt towards them, and the stave cut through the group of men as a scythe through corn. Two men fell senseless, another screamed with the agony of a splintered thigh. The rest fled. Montgomery hurled the stave aside and heaved the bodies one by one through the doorway into the street; the third man fell with the scream of a man on the rack. Then there was silence.

Montgomery returned to his seat and waited quietly for the morning and Margery's broze. The men did not trouble him again. And the next week Alexander Crystal came back. He was emaciated and much aged, but when he heard about Montgomery's house and George Cumming's disappearance, he went straight to the Chaplains' Brae.

'I have come to do George Cumming's work,' he told Montgomery. 'I am a wright, he a blacksmith, but we are both hammermen. I will complete his contract for the honour of the trade. Besides, it is wright's work and my family is hungry. I have a new wife and I need the money.'

'There will be no money,' said Montgomery, 'till Baillie Knight returns.'

'No matter. There is no money anywhere without work and I can wait.'

The men spoke no more about the matter, but from that day work was resumed on the house. Christian did her best to provide food for the two men and Margery was sent further and further afield to forage for gulls' eggs, shellfish, seaweed and nettles, anything that could be turned into food. And they cut bent on the Links, to sell for fuel and for bedding and to burn in place of tallow to give light. Until one day at the end of March they were caught.

Christian was five months pregnant now and beginning to feel it. The weight made her quarrelsome. When they arrived on the Links that morning they found others there before them. The wind was cold and blowing straight from the sea. The sea itself was grey and lashed all over with speckles of white. On the shore the surf pounded and sucked while the spray soared high to be flung inland and dashed against their faces with the stinging sand. The bent grass rattled and sang in the wind. Christian pulled her plaid tighter, took the knife in her hand and stooped to cut the first clump. Margery followed, cutting and bundling the stiff grasses until her hands were lacerated to a mesh of cuts and her bare legs were slashed and blue with cold. They had collected two armfuls when they topped a small rise and came across a group of women also cutting bent. The Sledder woman saw them first.

'Get off my hill, you heathen witch,' she screamed. 'And take that crippled she-devil with you!'

'Your hill?' taunted Christian. She thrust her armful of grasses into Margery's hands and took up battle stance, hands on her thickened hips and chin tilted. 'You cross-eyed thieving whore! The devil break your neck!'

With a screech of rage the Sledder woman launched herself at the slope which rose from where she stood to the hillock where Christian towered above her, taunting. The woman's feet slipped and scrabbled in the sand as she clawed at tufts of grass to pull her upwards. Christian threw back her head and laughed, a full-blooded, exultant laugh which set the Sledder woman screaming anew.

'Shut your mouth, you stinking evil carlin – or I'll cleave you from the pate to the chin!'

She found her footing and lurched suddenly upwards. Light flashed from the blade in her hand.

'Try it,' crowed Christian, brandishing her own knife. 'And by the Lord's wounds I'll feed your innards to the fishes!'

'Witch!'

'Whore!'

'Daughter of a whore!'

The two circled each other now in the sand while the women closed in around them, calling encouragement. Margery stood silently watching, over the bundle of bent grass in her arms. Her eyes in their sunken sockets were huge.

The Sledder woman lunged and a gasp rose from the watchers.

'I'll rip your belly yet,' she cried. 'And spill your bastard in the dirt.'

'Begetter of pigs,' screamed Christian. 'I'll split you to the chops, you dung-faced witch!'

'Stink-arse!'

'Whore's tit!'

The two women hurled abuse at each other in a hysterical crescendo of fury. Then the sand shook with the thud of hooves as a rider came galloping across the Links in a swirl of sand and flying stones. The women scattered at his approach, scooping up children and bundles and running for home, but the two contestants had eyes and ears only for each other. They were in full voice when the town officer reached them, pulled his horse to a stop and leant from his saddle to lay about their shoulders with his stave. He held it in his left hand, for his right was bandaged and his forehead bore a fresh scar.

'Away home the pair of you,' he shouted. 'It'll be the Court house for you all. Flyting and brawling and stealing the bent. I have your names and those of your friends, so you can tell them to save their legs and their breath. I'll know the lot of you again and you'll not escape.'

The women instantly united and whirled round on him, shoulder to shoulder in defiance.

'You're brave enough when it's women you're fighting, Kenneth Fraser,' taunted Isobel Sledder. 'But when it's a man you take a dozen friends – and make them go first!'

'And if that man has a blinded eye,' added Christian, 'you wait till it's dark in case he sees you coming with the other one!'

'Enough of your lying lip!' roared the master mason. 'Or I'll break your heads for you. Now get on home before I drag you by the heels behind my horse.'

'Grand words,' taunted Christian.

'From a little runt,' added Isobel Sledder. They linked arms and walked away together, laughing.

Margery waited until the officer had ridden out of sight, then retrieved her bundles from the dip where she had hidden them at his approach and ran limping after the women.

On Saturday they appeared before the baillies in the Court house and were each fined four pounds Scots, and on Sunday their names and those of all the women caught that morning on the Links were read aloud in the kirk by the Session clerk, as a warning against scolding and raging and cutting the bent.

Montgomery stood in his usual place by the Scougal monument, with Christian on one side and Margery on the other. At the name of Isobel Sledder he blanched and Margery saw him tremble from head to foot. His lips moved over and over in some rapid and private incantation, then he took his woman by the forearm and before the beadle could stop him thrust her roughly outside. Margery followed

'The Sledder woman!' he said, his voice hoarse with rage. 'You did not tell me it was the Sledder woman.'

'What difference does it make?'

'What difference? When the woman blighted Janet and my child in her womb? She will do the same to this one if you let her.'

'Nonsense. She'll not touch me. I know a trick worth two of hers.

My mother taught me. And if she so much as tries, she'll know it. But she won't try. She was afraid of Ma and she's afraid of me.'

'But she said she'd slit your belly, Christian,' protested Margery. 'With her knife.'

'And did she do it?' Christian laughed. 'Words, that's all. She'll not touch me.'

'She had better not.' Montgomery was quivering violently now, his big hands clenching and unclenching and his blank eye twitching. Margery laid a hand on his arm.

'It's all right, Father,' she said anxiously. 'Christian is well and the babe unharmed.'

'You'll not go to the Links again,' warned Montgomery. 'Send Margery if you must, but you will not go. Do you hear me?'

'I hear you,' sighed Christian. 'But you could have saved your breath. We'll none of us go now, not unless we've ten pounds to spare. They've made a new law.'

'. . . no person nor persons within the town nor freedom thereof presume nor take upon hand in any time coming to shear, pluck, take away or reset the bent from the Links and Bentihillocks under pain of ten pounds Scots . . .' The voice of the Session clerk came faintly to them from the west porch.

'You will not go anyway,' growled Montgomery. 'You will stay at home and wait for my son.'

But when the child was born it was a puny thing, a daughter, and lived only three days.

Montgomery looked at the tiny body for a long time in silence, then he turned and pushed his way out of the house. They heard the noise the length of the High Street as he thundered at the Sledders' door, shouting and cursing. Eventually the town guard removed him and escorted him home, but it took six men to hold him.

When they had gone, he put Margery out of doors and bedded Christian there and then. The child heard her screams from the Close and her father's voice roaring 'You will give me a son!'

Montgomery finished his house and Baillie Knight was pleased. He had come back from Edinburgh sombre and depressed both by the state of his country's politics and the emptiness of his country's barns. It was another disastrous year of harvest, when rain and wind lashed what standing corn there was to a grainless midden of mud and straw. But the sight of the new house pleased and cheered him. The house was strong and well made and the Baillie could find no fault. He put in his tenant and Montgomery was well rewarded. When he had paid Alexander Crystal his share there was enough to buy meal for the winter, even at the high price the merchants demanded in that autumn of general dearth.

'Something must be done,' said the Principal. 'The poor are dying in the streets and our parish is not alone. Reports come from all over the country of parishes losing a quarter, a third, even half their members through disease and starvation.'

'I tried to buy oats yesterday in the New Town,' said Urquhart, 'and could find none under £10 the boll: twice what it cost last year. Who but the King himself could afford to buy at that price?'

'It is the duty of Session and heritors alike to maintain the poor within the parish,' reminded Middleton. 'And the town has funds. Would it not be possible for kirk and Council to co-operate and buy meal for the Burgh in order to sell it cheaply to those who could not otherwise afford to buy? If everyone were to contribute...'

'*Everyone?*' George Cumming interrupted. 'And is *everyone* to buy the meal cheaply, rich and poor? We all give to the poor fund already. Are the trades to give still more while others sit back and count the pickings?' He glared at Fraser who lowered his eyes. Fraser had a warehouse in the New Town packed to the roof with grain, though he believed no one knew it.

'This is no time for personal differences,' reminded Middleton sternly. 'In the absence of a minister, we Elders must unite to ensure the spiritual and physical health of our parish.' It was more than eighteen months since Dr Keith had died and they had still been unable to find a permanent replacement. 'We must do what we can to help *everyone* survive the coming winter.'

'I will make inquiries,' said George Fraser. 'When we have figures to work on, we can move.'

'Good. Bring the figures to the Burgh Council on Saturday and we will go over them. Now to the next item. James Thomson, you are the Elder responsible for discipline in the east side of town, from the cross to College Bounds and the Spital?' Thomson nodded. 'Then why have you put in no report about the Montgomery child?'

Thomson looked down at the minute book in front of him and made great play with the sander. 'The child is dead,' he said.

'We know that,' said George Fraser impatiently. 'We also know, as does the whole town, that the child was the result of pre-nuptial fornication. Since when did that cease to be a sin?'

Thomson was silent.

'The pair live in your part of the town,' resumed Middleton. 'What have you done about it?'

'I visited the house,' said Thomson hesitantly, 'and . . .'

'And?'

'Both man and wife were . . . unco-operative.' In fact, Christian had shrieked obscenities at him through a storm of hysterical tears and Montgomery had raised a fist in a way which had sent Thomson hurrying from the Close. 'They are hardened sinners,' he went on hurriedly. 'If you were to order them to the stool of repentance, they would not come or come only to mock, and if you excommunicate them they will not know the difference. Montgomery speaks to no one as it is and no one speaks to him. As for the girl . . . we all know her origins.'

'She was a good servant,' said Professor Garden mildly. So far he had taken no part in the discussion, being absorbed as often these days in his private thoughts. Today they were unusually sombre.

It was some time now since his colleagues had signed the Oath of Allegiance, with their own reservations to be sure, but they *had* signed. He alone had held out and was lucky, he knew, to have been allowed to continue so long in his post. He had gained a temporary reprieve by claiming exemption from the Visitation on the grounds that the Chair of Divinity came under ecclesiastical rather than university discipline, and that he could only be 'visited' or dismissed by the Synod that had appointed him. When the Commission demanded nevertheless that he subscribe to the Confession of Faith, take the Oath of Allegiance to William and Mary and submit to the government of the Presbyterian Church, he steadfastly refused to yield and submitted an appeal to the Visitation Committee in Edinburgh. The matter was still in abeyance, but he knew it could not remain so much longer. Only the unusual clemency and mildness of the government had allowed him to continue so long. Today a letter from his old friend George Haliburton, one-time Bishop of St Machar's and now in enforced retirement in Coupar Angus, had reminded him that unless he signed the Oath at the next Visitation of Aberdeen, the Professor of Divinity was doomed. Such individual stands of conscience could not be tolerated in a gentleman with responsibilities for teaching divinity to susceptible students. George Haliburton approved of his friend's integrity, applauded his honesty in publicly maintaining his beliefs, and warned him that the inevitable result of such a course was dismissal.

Professor Garden was grateful for the warning which only confirmed what he had suspected for some time. His house in the Chaplains' was the hereditary lodging of the Professor of Divinity. The time had come to look about him for alternative accommodation against the day when he should be dismissed. Alexander Fraser was building two large houses, and there was talk of several more. One of those might be suitable. But with a wife and nine children he must choose carefully and soon. It was a pity that the Grant girl had left them. She had proved irreplaceable, and his wife talked endlessly of what they might offer her to persuade her to come back.

'She was a good servant,' he repeated now. 'And I hear she is not happy.'

'That is beside the point,' said George Fraser irritably. He was trying to decided whether it would be wise to sell some of his own store of meal to the Burgh – at a good price of course, but at the risk of considerable public hostility – or to try to sell it elsewhere at the risk of swindle or theft. He was a canny businessman and meant to make a good profit. At the same time it was only three years since he had presented the magnificent gold-tooled Bible to the church. The gold lettering impressed on the boards read only *Donus Mri Georgii Fraser Sub Primarii Ecclesiae Cathedralis Aberdonensi 1692* but everyone knew it represented conscience-money for the profit he had made out of the Cathedral repairs. Was it safe to risk reopening that sore? But Cumming was speaking.

'She does not deserve to be happy. Her mother was a Papist and a whore. The girl is the same. She should be scourged out of town.'

'Scourging is a civil punishment,' said Fraser. 'And for theft. We are dealing with a moral offence against the teachings of the church. Such sins must be publicly punished.'

'People are beginning to say the kirk pays too much attention to sin,' said Thomson, 'and not enough to filling empty stomachs. They tell me they would be better churchgoers if they were better fed.'

'I think,' said Middleton slowly, 'that it might be best to shelve the matter for a while. Record the sin in the minute book with the others. We have quite a list now, I believe. Read the culprits' names from the pulpit but reserve the punishment for a later date, when we have an established minister to lead us and when the in-dwellers have sufficient meal to let their minds appreciate higher things than the appetites of the stomach.'

'A good point,' agreed Thomson quickly. He did not relish the idea of a return visit to Widow Irvine's Close. 'After all, they are married now and the child is dead.'

'That reminds me,' said Middleton. 'As you know we have been ordered to take a census of the inhabitants to assess the poll tax. May I ask you all to consider both the matter and the manner of execution and give your opinion at the next meeting? Now, if there is no other pressing business, you must excuse me. I have an appointment at the College.'

In fact the appointment was at Baillie Baxter's change-house on the opposite side of the street.

'Well, Baxter?'

The two men were seated at a table in a corner, each with a glass of brandy from the advocate's still well-stocked cellar. 'What de-velopments?'

'George Fraser is still hesitating. I suspect he has other, more immediately profitable uses for his money, though so far I have no proof. However, as to the trading venture we spoke of. As you know our Scots parliament has officially authorized the establish-ment of a company trading to Africa and the Indies. So far so good. Now our agents in London are trying to enlist the support of the Hanseatic towns.'

'And the place for the colony? Has that been decided?'

'Not yet, though we have several suggestions. But the venture will go ahead. It must. It is our only hope of recovery with Scot-land in such a miserable state. I see no other way.'

'And the capital? What sort of return can we expect?'

'Unlimited.'

'Who in the town will give support?'

'Everyone,' said Baxter decidedly. 'The Burgh itself should buy a share in such a patriotic and profitable undertaking.'

Middleton was dubious. 'I would not put it to the Council yet,' he said. 'We have too many other calls upon our resources. In the spring, perhaps, when things are brighter.'

'But the matter cannot wait indefinitely. We need a firm com-mitment, now.'

'It will not do. George Cumming was bitter enough in the Session this morning when I suggested the collective purchase of meal. The man is obstinate and he has many followers in the town.'

'He has grown even more hard and unreasonable,' agreed Baxter, 'since that boy of his left.'

Middleton was quiet. His face betrayed new lines of sadness. He was remembering Elspeth and her tragic end. On that last day when the fever raged, she had cried 'Georgie' in her delirium and died weeping. The memory troubled him with the suspicion that there had been more than he knew of between his sweet daughter and the Cumming boy.

'Any news of young George?' asked Professor Garden of the blacksmith as they left the Session chamber.

'None. And not likely to be. He'll not show his face here again.'

'Come now, he has gone to fight for King and Country. Where is the disgrace in that?' James Garden knew Cumming's sympathies lay fair and square with the Orange King. 'After all, it is not as if he has gone to join some highland rebel of the King's lost cause.'

Cumming merely grunted, but later, in the ale-house at the cross, he reflected aloud that some of those professors in the College had best watch their step.

' "The King's lost cause", Professor Garden said. As if James Stuart was still the king. He and the rest of them had best watch out, that's all.'

But in one thing Professor Garden had been right. At least his George was fighting for the proper King. If the boy did come back, perhaps there would be a place for him in Cumming's yard after all.

3

The summer of 1698 was as miserable as its predecessors. Year after year of rain and cold, of lingering winters and drab, unfruitful summers had brought dearth, and with it near-starvation, to the Old Town as to the rest of the north-east.

The census had been duly taken in the summer of 1696, since when it had been easy to chart the diminishing numbers of indwellers in the Old Town. Yet somehow the town survived. New lives replaced the old and when the new lives, too, were snuffed out yet more new lives replaced them. The men foraged and hunted and fished and tilled the unfruitful land with all the strength of their emaciated limbs; the women contrived and endured and bore children; the children sickened, the old folk died; the timeless pattern of renewal continued. And that summer of 1698 Montgomery worked like three men to find food for his wife, his daughter and his unborn child. For Christian was pregnant again at last.

It was October, the week after St Luke's fair, when George Cumming returned. Margery saw him walking down the Spital towards her as she watched the men repairing the little Powis bridge with stones from the kirkyard. They were the same stones, though she did not know it, which had fallen with the great tower on the night she was born.

The bridge across the High Street where the burn flowed eastward from the Powis grounds had fallen into disrepair, and now that Alexander Fraser's houses were finished and the man himself was in residence, he had agitated in the Council for the refurbishing of the bridge which was almost at the gate of his new property. Kenneth Fraser's men were in charge of the work, though Kenneth Fraser himself had not been the same man since that night three years ago when he had come home bleeding from a gash in the head and with his right arm loose in his sleeve. Nothing had been said about that night: but afterwards Montgomery was left unmolested and his building untouched, and Fraser was still a master mason with men at his command to do the work he could no longer do himself.

Margery stood at the corner of the College garden watching. She had been sent by Christian to the Middletons to ask if there was washing to be done, and as she had been unsuccessful the girl had lingered at the bridge in spite of the chill wind and threatening sky, before returning to Christian with the sombre news.

For Christian had changed since her marriage. She rarely laughed now and was often ill-tempered and defiant. There was a hardness about her which Margery had learnt to accept and which in part she understood, but on those days when Christian turned on Montgomery and taunted him till they came to blows the child took care to stay out of the house. Her father rarely struck her now. When the headaches came it was Christian who attracted his blows, deliberately as it seemed to Margery, but Christian fought back as Margery never could and Christian ruled the house. Today Margery had been sent to find work. When she went home without it, Christian would have a ready hand with which to show her displeasure.

Margery was ten years old now and growing. Though she would always be small, like her mother, she had a feminine roundness about her which her mother had never had. Her limp was as pronounced as ever, but she found it no handicap, moving as nimbly with her one good leg as others did with two. Her skin was clear and her eyes dark and lively, her hair thick and brown and beautiful. When she smiled there was an elfin quality about her which her crooked limb made magical rather than grotesque.

She was a quiet girl, self-contained and solitary – from necessity as much as choice, for the Burgh children shunned her company, either as a result of parental orders or because they knew Montgomery would chase them if he saw them speaking to his daughter.

'You leave that scum alone,' he told her. 'They're villains all of them. Keep away.'

When Margery walked with Christian she was tolerated by the women Christian met, and when Christian had the women to her house, as her mother had done, Margery was often set to keep watch and warn them of Montgomery's approach. But the girl had no other companion, except her father, and no friend since George Cumming had left the town.

Now as she saw the familiar figure striding down the hill from the Spital she ran dipping like a sea-bird towards him, crying 'George!' with ingenuous delight.

He dropped his bundle, took her by the waist and swung her high.

'Margery! I do believe you've grown! Not much, I grant you, but an inch or two.'

'I am ten now,' she said, 'and will grow more before I am a woman. But you are grown enormous! Where have you been?' He picked up his bundle again, she took his hand and ran beside him, limping to keep up with his soldier's stride.

'I have been to the wars in Flanders and now I am come home.'

'For good?'

'Maybe,' said George lightly. 'Who can tell? What is happening here?' he asked as they reached the little bridge. He called a greeting to the men who looked up in surprise, then bombarded him with questions until he raised a hand in protest. 'Later,' he said, laughing. 'I'll tell you everything over a mug of ale. To-night, at the ale-house at the cross?'

'It's good to be back, Margery,' he went on as they moved away. 'But what is this grand mansion here? Don't tell me Kenneth Fraser actually built it after all? And a second one beside it! And both of them still standing.' He stopped and looked momentarily embarrassed. 'I hope your father managed without me. I left in such a hurry, I had no time to explain, but . . . but I knew your father would be able to do the work. Nothing could stop him. He wasn't angry, was he?'

'No,' said Margery earnestly. 'He was not angry. He was puzzled, I think, and wounded inside. You see, he thought you were his friend.'

George looked shamefaced. 'I am sorry.' Then he looked down at her and his green eyes were twinkling with irrepressible good spirits. 'That was a long time ago, Margery. I was a boy then and thoughtless. He will forgive me now that I am come home. You forgive me, don't you?' He put a finger under her chin, tipped her face upwards and smiled. 'Please?'

She nodded, blushing happily.

'Then so will he. We will go and see him now, shall we, and you will see I'm right. But first, how is Elspeth?'

'Oh George, didn't you know? Elspeth died.'

George stood still, his face washed grey with shock. 'Died? When? How?'

'I think it was soon after you left. She caught the fever and she died. Many people died.'

'Was she . . . ? Did she . . . ?' George did not know what to ask. The image of the pink and white and loving girl, which he had carried with him across the German sea and back again, had withered in that moment and crumbled to dust. He felt empty without it and too shocked yet to feel pain.

'Poor Elspeth,' he whispered. Margery took his hand and squeezed it with what comfort she could give.

'She is in heaven, George, and happy.'

George did not answer. He was remembering that evening in the woods on the day of St Luke's fair and his shameful flight. Somehow he had managed to forget the cause of his departure: he had left to fight the King's wars and expected to be welcomed home with glory. Now the news of Elspeth's death was like a pail of icy water in his face. She had loved him and he had left her, without a word. He had hurt her and abandoned her and she would never again look up at him with those soft, adoring eyes and call him 'Georgie'. But how would her father look at him? They were passing the Principal's house now. If she had told . . . George hurried past the house, his head averted, while the tears stood in his eyes.

'Margery,' he began hesitantly when they were past the house with its too-painful associations, 'did Elspeth say . . . ?' But the girl could not tell him. No one could now except perhaps Christian. He brushed the tears angrily away. 'How is Christian?' Christian, he knew, would be loyal to him whatever he did, whatever anyone said. Christian and he were one.

'You will see her in a moment. We are almost home. Come.' She tugged at his hand. 'Hurry up! You are too slow.'

They turned into the Close and there was the familiar house with Montgomery's door at ground level and, on the side wall, the forestair leading to the tenement above. George put a hand on the stair rail and leapt the steps two at a time. Margery giggled.

'Come down, silly. That's George Crystal's house now. Alexander Crystal's son. Christian is here.' She opened her own door and called eagerly, 'Christian! See who I have brought home!'

Christian looked up irritably from the hearth and pushed a small pot quickly out of sight behind a pile of peats. 'Well? Who is it?' she snapped. 'Don't just stand there.'

'It's me!' George pushed past Margery then stopped in the doorway, staring in horror. 'Christian!'

Christian was seven months pregnant, grey-faced and haggard. Her hair hung in colourless wisps from beneath a dirty cotton kerchief. She had aged much since her marriage and looked nearer forty than nineteen. Now, after the first unguarded start of joy, her face closed in hostility.

'You've come back then.' She stared at him accusingly.

'Christian, what's happened to you?' She looked old and tired and angry. Then his eyes rested on her stomach. She was large this time and carried the child high. Isobel Sledder said it was a good sign and meant a boy. 'Who . . .?'

'My husband, of course.'

George looked blankly uncomprehending. 'You're not *married*?'

'And why not? Or did you think I'd wait, like her, till you chose to come back? Well I didn't, did I, and neither did she.' She turned away from him to hide the tears which rose out of nowhere to choke her. 'You should never have come,' she said angrily. 'It's all your fault.'

George stood silent and appalled. Christian married! Christian who had been his from as far back as he could remember. Christian, as timeless and reliable as the rock under his feet. He realized that, just as she said, he had expected Christian to wait for him. Even now he did not understand.

'Who?' he demanded again. His voice had an edge of jealousy which Christian was quick to recognize.

'What business is that of yours?' George had no answer. 'Well come in if you're going to. The ale is poor stuff and thin as water, but I've no doubt you'll take some all the same. You always took what you wanted and I don't suppose you've changed.'

George stooped meekly under the lintel and entered the small, low-ceilinged room. Margery made him sit in her father's chair while Christian poured the ale.

'It isn't *Montgomery*?' he gasped as the implication hit him.

'And why not?'

'But you *couldn't*! He's not sane. He's . . .' He was suddenly aware of Margery's eyes and stopped.

'He asked me, which is more than you ever did – or would have, even if I'd waited.' She looked him straight in the eye, defying him to contradict. Her eyes were hard and challenging and George lowered his. 'Or had you forgotten *her?*'

This remark snapped George out of his confusion. 'Tell me, Christian, what did she say when you gave her my message?'

Christian turned her back and busied herself at the fire. 'Nothing.'

'Are you sure? She must have said *something*, Christian. Did she cry? Or ask where I'd gone?'

Christian turned on him then. 'She said nothing because I didn't tell her.'

'Holy Mother of God!' George gripped the arms of the chair and his whole frame shook. 'Then she died believing I had abandoned her!'

'Well you had, hadn't you?' said Christian cruelly. 'You walked out on her like you walked out on the rest of us. You never did think of anyone but yourself, so why should I?'

'But I asked you.' George clenched his teeth against the rising anger. 'And you promised.'

'I did not. I said nothing at all. You thought I promised because you thought I'd do whatever you asked me to – even take a message to your whore!'

George shot out of his chair and seized her by the shoulders. 'You bitch!' He shook her till her feet slid from under her and she would have fallen had not Margery intervened.

'Leave her alone, George!' she cried. 'You'll hurt the baby.'

George loosed his grip then and slumped into the chair. He held his head in his hands and groaned as the anger drained out of him and grief took its place: grief for his sweet, dead love, and, worse than the grief, the terrible torture of remorse.

'I am sorry, Christian. You are right. I should not have gone away as I did. I should not have asked you to do what I was too cowardly to do myself. Everything was my fault. And if Elspeth died hating me, that was my fault too. And if you hate me, Christian, it is only what I deserve.'

'I don't hate you.' Christian's voice trembled and there were tears again in her eyes. 'I could never hate you, George. Don't you know that? Oh, why did you go away?' She burst into tears.

Margery ran to her in consternation. Christian never cried! The girl put her arms about her, comforting and turned on George. 'Look how you have upset her. You should not do that. Christian is not well these days. She tires easily and must be humoured.'

But Christian had already recovered. She brushed the tears from her eyes, straightened her dress and pushed Margery impatiently away. When she turned to George the hard, brittle mask was back in place.

'You had better go,' she said. 'My man will not be pleased to find you here. You had best go before he returns.'

But it was too late. The door opened and Montgomery came in, stooping low under the lintel, his head turned sideways so that at first he did not see the visitor in his own chair. Then George stood up. Montgomery's head swung round till the good eye focused on the straight young figure. He looked hard and for a long time in silence. When he spoke it was in little more than a whisper.

'Leave my house.'

'But Montgomery, I have come specially to see you, to apologize for leaving as I did. I had no choice, you see, with the recruiting officer here in the town and in a hurry. I had to go. I know it left you in a difficult spot and I am sorry. Truly I am.' He offered a tentative smile and held out a hand. 'Let us shake and be friends. I have come to make peace between us and to offer myself, free, for any work you might have needing to be done.'

'Leave my house!' The voice was stronger now as Montgomery took a step towards him. His good eye was blazing, the other glazed as milk above the purple scar, and his great hands clenched and trembled. 'I have no need of those who break their word.'

'But Father,' cried Margery, 'George has said he's sorry and he wants to be your friend. Let him stay.'

'I said, leave my house! Will you go, or must I throw you?'

'I will go. But I am sorry you take it so hard. I had hoped to . . .'

'Out!' roared Montgomery. 'You traitorous, lying devil. And do not come back! If you set one foot across my threshold I'll break your neck!'

Quietly, George left. Montgomery slammed the door and rammed down the bar to fasten it tight, and then turned to face his wife and daughter.

'If either of you speaks to him again, I'll thrash the life out of you. Do you hear?'

'We hear,' said Christian resignedly. 'Sit down and I'll bring your kale.'

But Margery did not answer him. She crouched on her stool at the hearth, her eyes on the meagre flame, while her thoughts strayed after George who was her friend and who had at last come home.

Deacon Cumming was at work in the forge when his son strode down Cluny's Wynd, whistling.

'You've come back, then.' He swung the hammer, crash, on the glowing metal, twisting it deftly to shape. Sparks flashed as the metals met.

'Yes,' said George. He swung his bag down off his shoulder and slung it against the wall. 'What's that you're fashioning?'

'New bit for the branks. You staying?'

'I might.'

Cumming put down his hammer and stood squarely, his fists loose at his side. 'You *might*?' he repeated ominously. 'And where were you planning to live?'

George met his father's eyes without flinching. 'Here.'

'I see. And whose house is it?'

'Yours.' When his father looked mollified, George added with a grin, 'And mine.'

'I owe you one,' said his father menacingly. He took a step towards George and flexed his fists. 'Don't think I've forgotten.'

'Come on, Dad. That was years ago, when I was a lad. I'm a grown man now. I've fought for the King – and your King at that. And if you strike me, I'll strike you back.' He smiled as he said it, but the older man knew he meant it.

The two looked at each other for a long moment. Then the blacksmith shrugged, and turned away. 'You can stay,' he said, picking up his hammer and resuming work. 'But you'll earn your keep. And you'll not make trouble. It might be your house, too, but I'm the head of it and I'll have you remember that or you're out!'

George sat alone at a table in Baillie Baxter's and stared morosely into his ale. He could not face another evening in the ale-house at the cross with his father and his father's friends. His father irritated him. As for his father's friends, they would ask him for the hundredth time to tell them about Flanders and the wars and he was bored with the whole story. He was bored with everything. Bored and restless . . . till a word from a neighbouring table caught and held his attention.

'Gentlemen, I give you Darien,' said George Fraser, raising his glass. 'The door of the seas, the key of the universe.'

Solemnly the four men drank. George Fraser, Baillie Baxter, Dr Urquhart and Dr Middleton had joined the Darien venture for different reasons. George Fraser's was the simplest: he was in it purely for profit. He was pleased that the profit was to come to Scotland, but he would have pledged just as much of his money had it been a purely English venture, or that of a corporation of Hottentots. Baxter's motive for profit was equally strong, but tempered with a political caution which left him carefully uncommitted. If the venture were a success, he could swing to the side of patriotism: if not, he would still be able to support Union with a clear conscience. Urquhart was a wholehearted and outspoken Unionist already and supported the venture, uncharacteristically, out of sentiment. Middleton alone felt that his future rose or fell with the Trading Company of Scotland. If the venture succeeded, Scotland would be rich again, and financial and political stability went hand in hand. A rich Scotland could afford to reject the Act of Union. A rich Scotland could stand alone. But if the venture were to fail, there would be nothing left for his country but the Union with England, and once that Act of Union was signed, Middleton knew his days were numbered. The English king would do what he had longed to do all along and replace King James' men with his own.

Already James Garden had been removed, and you could not have wished for a more devout and religious man. He had gone peaceably and without protest, removing his cumbersome family to the lesser of Alexander Fraser's two new houses at Powis, where he continued to live quietly and contentedly under the crown of King's College, a perpetual reminder of what he had lost. So unfairly lost as it seemed to Middleton: good men should not be made the pawns of politics, yet many a good man had been sacrificed to the monster of reform which ate its way without discrimination through church and college and state. There was no escape, least of all for those in public office, in the public eye. There would be Commissions of Inquiry and Reports and a show of legality, but the result would be inevitable. The Darien venture was his one hope. The Darien venture must succeed, for Scotland's future and for his own.

'Any news?' asked Middleton now.

'Not yet,' said Baxter. 'There has hardly been time. The ships only left Leith in July, and must navigate the Atlantic ocean be-fore they make a landfall. They might be making that landfall at this very minute, gentlemen. Trade may have already begun! But we must allow them time to send news of the venture back by the same route they travelled, and Darien is a long way distant.'

'I still think Africa might have been a better choice,' said Urquhart. He had held out almost to the end against investing in the project, but when England and the Hanseatic towns pulled out and left Scotland alone, patriotism had triumphed over prudence. With men and women, burghs and whole corporations up and down Scotland pledging their enthusiastic support to the collective tune of £400,000, Urquhart could no longer hold back. His money, too, had gone into the venture and helped to stock the five laden ships which had set out so bravely to a land which not one of the subscribers had seen, not even William Paterson himself who had planned the venture. Darien was unknown, a mere name on a map.

'No, no,' said Baxter. 'Africa was quite unsuitable. Darien is far better. It is on the isthmus of Panama and will cut the time and cost of trade to the East by half. China and Japan will be freely open to us. As our leader said, trade will beget trade, and money will beget money. Believe me, gentlemen, not one of us will regret giving our support to such a splendid undertaking. And it is pure Scottish.'

'Aye,' agreed George Fraser. 'Every town in Scotland has sent its products. Stockings, plaids, leather work and gridirons, linen and pipes and periwigs. A piece of Scotland herself has gone out with those ships.'

'And think what they will bring back,' said Baxter, already counting the profits he would make on his own investment. 'Spices, silks, jade . . .'

'Are you sure there is a market for Aberdeen stockings in Darien?' said Urquhart dryly. 'Or for Musselburgh serge? I be-lieve the climate is somewhat hotter than our own.'

'Don't be ridiculous, man,' said George Fraser. 'No one suggests the goods are to supply the natives of Darien. They are for trade with the East. They wear stockings in China, certainly in the mountain regions.'

'Then no doubt they make their own,' snapped the Mediciner with rare ill-humour. Already he was regretting his own commit-ment. The crops had failed yet again that summer, before the country had had time to recover from the previous year's poor harvest and the universal disaster of the year before that. Urquhart would need every penny he had if he were to buy meal at the current rate, yet somehow his large family must be fed. This Darien business was all very well, but the profits would not come for years, if they came at all, and Urquhart needed money now.

Middleton also was untouched by the enthusiastic plans of George Fraser and Baillie Baxter, who were already discussing the stocking and manning of the next ships to sail westward to Darien. He was thinking of all those men, young and enthusiastic as his own sons, who had sailed with golden plans for the colony they were to build on the peninsula no one had seen. It was to be a new El Dorado, with none of the political turmoil and domestic famine of their homeland. But what land would they find at the end of that sea-journey? If they survived to see it? Two of his own nephews from Edinburgh had gone with the expedition, and many of his friends had sent their sons.

'We plan to equip another four ships,' Baxter was saying. 'We'll need men and goods, of course, as well as the ships themselves. We will need ministers and teachers, farmers, fishermen, masons, tailors, wrights. We'll need advocates and doctors and shoemakers and fleshers. The colony must be firmly established on a working basis right from the start. I tell you, gentlemen, if my sons were older I'd send them on the next ship.'

George Cumming drained his ale and called for another, but he did not move away from his place near the Baillie's table, in spite of the proximity of Elspeth's father. For Principal Middleton had met him soberly enough, with cordiality and with no hint that he knew of anything against him. When George had ventured to offer his true sympathy on Elspeth's death, the response was the same: sorrow, but no blame. George had breathed a little easier from that day, and now he felt no guilt as he listened to the conversation among the men at the Baillie's table. The talk of adventure and far places was physic to his soul.

'I'm bored, Margery.'

George skimmed a stone across the grey surface of the river and watched it jump once, twice, before it disappeared into the racing depths. He had been home a month, and already the confines of the Burgh irked and irritated him. Elspeth was dead – his heart still contracted at the thought of her – and Christian married. The other girls he had dallied with were dead or married too. He had not the energy or the interest to pursue the younger ones. There was little work at the yard to occupy him – money was too tight that year – and he found himself with long hours on his hands and nothing to do. So he took to walking aimlessly beside the river, with Margery Montgomery.

She seemed to have forgotten her father's warnings, or she ignored them, and limped at his side for hours, listening or prompting him with questions. He enjoyed the captive audience and made the most of it. It was, he felt, the only time when he was free.

For at home his father blustered and boasted and needled him unceasingly, demonstrating on every possible occasion that he was head of his own house. In public he welcomed George and commended him on his service to the Protestant King. In private he lost no opportunity to remind George that he was a grown man and should have a home of his own, but that as long as he lived under his father's roof he would give him the obedience and deference that was his due. George bristled and endured while the pressure built up inside him.

'Do you miss the fighting?' asked Margery now. She sat on the river bank, her knees under her chin and her hands clasped about her ankles. Her eyes over the ragged cloth were huge in sockets which hunger had made hollow and pronounced. But there was the same lively intelligence about her which George remembered from the years before he left, and he talked to her as to an equal.

'No, not the fighting. That was disgusting. Brutal and ugly, with the fear rising in your gullet like vomit and the screams. No, it's not the fighting I miss. It's the company.'

'The other soldiers?'

'Aye, and the local people too. And the girls. You meet all sorts in an army. This group I was with for instance. There was one man who'd been right round the world. The tales he told us! Of black men and pygmies and horrible monsters. He'd been to the Ivory Coast, he said, and to Mandalay. There was another man who'd been to the Americas and back. The world is so big, Margery, and full of sights you and I could never dream of.'

'Would you like to see them, George?'

'Who wouldn't?'

'I don't think I would,' she said seriously. 'At least, I might if I knew that I could come home again safe and find it just as I had left it. But I would not like to lose the places and the people that I know.'

George looked at her indulgently and laughed. 'You are a quaint one, Margery.' He flung himself down on to the turf beside her. 'And you should not be talking to me at all. Your father will break your neck. Or was it mine he was to break?'

'It was yours, George. And you'd best keep away from him or he might do it. But he will not hurt me. At least, I do not think so. I am useful to him, you see. I understand his needs before he has spoken and I help him. Sometimes when the headaches come I do his work for him. I carved a name on a headstone only last week when his head hurt so badly that he could not see.'

George looked at her in astonishment. '*You* did?'

'Yes. Why not? I have watched him often enough and I can do it. I can lay setts, too. Father has done that lately as there is little mason's work to be had. And when the Burgh causewayed Douglas Wynd, my father laid the setts and I helped him. I like to help him. I would like to build a monument like Bishop Scougal's in the kirk, with shields and figures and little dogs, but there are no new monuments now and the old ones are broken. The only monuments are names and dates in flat stone.'

'And can you read and write enough for that?'

'Oh yes. It is not difficult.'

'You are a remarkable girl.' From the depths of his memory flashed a picture of himself and Christian and a baby, naked on the Bishop's kitchen table, and the Mediciner saying if the child reached maturity she would be a remarkable woman. He glanced quickly sideways and saw the woman already under the child's exterior. She would be a beautiful woman, too, with an underlying serenity which some man some day would give his soul for. Montgomery should take better care of her. There were too many beggars and pedlars roving the countryside these days, as well as bands of starving peasants in search of food.

'You've no business to be out alone at this time,' he said with sudden irritation. 'It will be dark in an hour.'

'Christian sent me out,' said Margery.

Christian was entertaining the Sledder woman and the Baxter woman and a few others to a secret session such as those her mother had held. Phials of strange liquids would change hands. Fortunes would be cast and perhaps tomorrow there would be a marrow-bone to add to the kale, or a strip of salt fish. Montgomery was gone to the hills of Forester after rabbit and would not be back till dark. Christian was safe enough from discovery and Margery would not tell.

'I am supposed to gather slaters for her – you know, the little woodlice under the stones – but I shall say the apothecary's boy was there before me. I would rather walk with you. Besides, she is busy and does not want me in the house.'

'Busy or not,' said George, climbing to his feet, 'you are going home. If I have to take you myself.'

'Only as far as the Brig,' she said anxiously. 'Father must not know that we have been together. I do not want him to hate you any more than he does already.'

'Does he hate me?' George found the idea disturbing.

'Oh yes. You see you were his friend and you betrayed him. Then you fought for the wrong King. Father was at Killiecrankie, you remember, and it was King William's men who took his eye. He thinks you have gone over to the enemy and joined the side he fought against. If he meets you with me he will kill you. He is very strong.'

'Then I had better leave you,' said George lightly. 'But see you hurry home. There are evil men about these days.'

'They will not hurt me,' she said with the innocent confidence of childhood. 'Why should they?'

'Nevertheless, take care.'

As he watched the small, limping figure hurry up the cobbled road from the Brig, his heart twisted inside him with an emotion he could not explain. Instead he turned on his heel and followed the bank of the river as it wound inland towards Grandholm and the waulk-mill at Balgownie. The wind took and tossed the dead leaves in his face as he moved under the grey skeletons of the birks.

Montgomery struck the rabbit once, hard, on the back of the skull. Then he laid down the stave and bent on one knee to loose the snare which had tightened round the animal's hind leg. The body was limp and warm and twitching with departing life. It lay in his palms like a newborn child. He could have closed his fingers over it and crushed it to pulp. He stood looking down at the creature for a long time, remembering. Margery, his daughter, had lain in his hands once, like this rabbit, small and helpless and fluttering. He did not remember his rage or that these same hands had flung her across the room. She was grown now, dark-eyed like her mother, but independent and strong as her mother had never been. Margery needed no one. He thought of her with dour pride. They would not humble her, however hard they tried. As they had not humbled him. And would not. And when his son was born, the boy would stand beside him, strong and proud, and they would not humble him either. Together they would defy the world. Margery would be there with them. But not Christian. Her place was with the pots and the tubs and the women. The thought of Christian troubled him. She scorned and tormented him, deliberately and with malice, until he could not endure it and struck her. Then she taunted him with it afterwards and the whole ugly pattern rolled round again. But she was his wife and this time she would give him a son.

He took the rabbit by the feet and turned for home. It was early still, but he was weary and his head was beginning to ache. Besides, if he went home now there would be time to skin and gut the creature before the light failed. The skin could be pegged out to dry and the flesh in the pot cooking before the fire died. Christian would be pleased. Few things pleased her these days, but with a healthy kale pot and soon a baby son, everything would change.

He left the sparse dead trees behind him and strode fast for home, with his stave in one hand and the rabbit swinging from the other. The air was damp and cold, and when he reached the Chanonry the haar was blowing in from the sea. There was the tang of fish and seaweed in his nostrils. A beaded greyness clung to the turf-roofed houses and the humped cobbles of the street. Widow Irvine's Close had filled with mist. It swirled towards him to blur his second eye as he skirted the low wall of the draw-well and made for his own door.

But at the door he stopped. There were voices inside. Chanting, female voices which rose and fell like the tide. He pushed open the door. Christian stood at the fireside stirring a small pot of thick green liquid, her swollen belly casting grotesque shadows across the walls and over the women who squatted in a circle at her feet. There was some sort of sign scratched into the dirt of the floor, and after the first startled moment Christian stepped forward and swiftly scrubbed out the pattern with her bare feet. The other women scrambled to their feet, bundling plaids about themselves and pulling them tight across their faces. They herded together,

whispering nervously as Montgomery stood squarely in the doorway, barring their escape.

'You are home early,' said Christian, pushing the pot behind
her back. 'I see you found us food.'

Montgomery flung the rabbit across the room to land at her feet.
Then he took the stave in both hands.

'Who are these women?' he said with ominous quiet.

'Friends,' retorted Christian with returning defiance. 'Surely I
may invite friends to share my ale with me now and then? And to
wait with me,' she added with inspiration, 'until my time is come.'
She folded her hands across her swollen belly and looked him full
in the face. 'You would not want me to be alone and without help
when your son is born, would you?'

Montgomery did not answer. His eyes moved watchfully over the
huddled women. Their faces were hidden in the gloom of twilight
and folded plaid, but there was one he would have recognized anywhere.

'You!' He leapt forward and raised his stave. 'Get out of my
house!' He swung the stick and would have struck the woman had
not Christian seized his arm. He wrenched away to throw her off,
but she screamed, 'The child! Mind the child!' and he checked.
In that moment the women ducked and ran, pushing and gasping
and tripping over one another to escape through that single door
and into the safety of the Close. Margery met them at the corner by
Baillie Baxter's tenements; a group of terrified women, running.
She looked after them in astonishment until the mist closed over
their hurrying figures and only their footsteps lingered, echoing.
Margery shrugged and continued on her way.

'That woman!' roared Montgomery. 'You have had that woman
here again. Do you want to kill my child?'

Christian laughed in his face. 'That woman? She can do nothing.
She is harmless, and stupid. They're fools, all of them. I tell them
anything that comes into my head and they pay me. See! You have
spent the whole day hunting and caught one skinny rabbit. I have
spent one hour in my own house and caught that.' She waved a
hand towards an assortment of objects on the edge of the pot-shelf:
a twist of wool, several pennies, a candle, and a scrap of meat
smoked black and tough as leather over someone else's fire.

'Witch's payment,' roared Montgomery. He swept them to the
floor and ground them under his heel. 'You tangle with the devil
when you meddle with such things. I know, and believe me, she

knows too. And if you have let her harm another child of mine, she's not the only one I'll strangle with my own hands.'

In spite of her bravado, Christian flinched and folded her thumb in the palm of her hand in the old, childhood gesture of protection. 'It's all right, I tell you,' she said. 'I am the one in charge, not her. She buys my mixtures. She believes the tales I tell her. She'll not harm me. She dare not.'

'You meddle with what you do not understand, woman. You tamper with evil!'

'Nonsense. I tell them what they want to hear and sell them harmless mixtures of this and that. There is no witchcraft. It is a game I play to win their money, that is all.'

Margery, who had stood in the doorway watching and listening unnoticed, stepped over the threshold and crossed to the hearth. She picked up the corpse of the rabbit, drew a knife from the turf of the floor where Christian had thrust it for safety, and began to skin the animal, working from the hind legs upwards as she had seen her father do. She kept her eyes downcast. She preferred not to look on her father's anger or on Christian's lies.

For they were lies and Margery knew it. Christian more than half believed in the incantations and the rigmarole, and wholly believed in the mixtures of wild herbs and mosses and the squeezed juice of insects which she made up from the receipts her mother had taught her. There was a brisk and open trade in apothecaries' elixirs in those days of hunger and disease, but there was an equally strong and secret trade in the primitive potions which women such as Christian brewed. Margery knew that Christian herself had been taking a particular blue mixture for a son from the moment she knew she was pregnant, and another red one for an easy birth. Margery had helped to gather the herbs herself. So she slit the skin and peeled it back over the sinews and the still-warm flesh, and she kept her eyes on her work.

Montgomery's anger escaped like the snort of a bull as he slumped into his chair. Christian retrieved the skein of wool and the pennies and dusted them clean on her skirt. The candle was crushed to a mess of wax and dirt, but Christian picked up the meat between finger and thumb, sloshed it in the water pail and impaled it on a nail above the hearth. It would keep until the fresh meat was finished and would come to no harm. Without a word she drew a mug of ale and handed it to her husband. He took it and drank in silence, then his head fell back against the wooden chair and his eyes closed against the pain. Christian picked up the stocking she was making for a merchant in the New Town, settled herself on her stool and began to knit. The only sounds in the room were the click of her needles and the scrape of Margery's knife blade on the stretched skin.

The church was full that bleak December Sabbath. There was snow in the kirkyard and the sky behind the south steeple was grey and threatening. The black bones of the trees glistened with frost and inside the church the stone struck cold underfoot. People huddled close for warmth and when they spoke their breath puffed out in little clouds about their faces. Christian pulled her plaid tighter, rubbed her purple chapped hands and stamped her feet. She was restless and impatient to be home again, but it was Christian who had insisted they come early to church in time to hear the new schoolmaster, William Christie, read the scriptures. For since Montgomery had found her with the women, Christian had grown nervous. Montgomery had mentioned witchcraft. He would not repeat it of course, not about his own wife, but suppose someone else did and it came to the ears of the Session? The Baxter woman, for instance, in one of her silly moods, or Alexander Crystal's young wife? So Christian made a point of going ostentatiously and early to church, and took Margery and Montgomery with her. They stood together at the back, near the west porch, Montgomery dour and silent, his face closed, Margery bright-eyed and eager, taking in everything she saw about her, yet at the same time standing calm and still.

Christian on the other hand fidgeted constantly, shifting weight from one foot to the other, clasping her stomach, breathing heavily. Her eyes flitted from one part of the kirk to another, picking out a face here, a coat there, yet registering nothing deeper than the surface of her mind. Underneath she had only one thought which filled and choked her like the full-term child in her womb. For the child would be born any day now and it must be a boy. She glanced sideways at her husband and looked quickly away. If it was not a boy, there was no saying what he might do to her. Well, let him try. She'd had enough. Husband or not, she'd leave him if he knocked her about any more. She'd leave him and go back into service. Or sell ale to students. Or keep a change-house. Anything. And if he tried to bed her, she'd slit his throat. She set her jaw in determination and clenched her fists at her sides, but her hands trembled. Underneath the bravado she knew she was afraid.

Margery looked about her with contentment. She liked the kirk. She liked the packed bodies, warm as a byre of cows. She liked the colours: the red splash of the students' gowns against the black of the Regents' and the Professors', the oranges and scarlets and purples of the Professors' ladies in their private pews, the infinite shades of browns and greys and greens of the indwellers in their homespun coarse cloth and their linen and their knitted stockings. And the pale haze of the gentlemen's wigs, like flecks of foam on a grey sea. She had watched them all come in: Dr Middleton the Principal, Professor George Fraser the Subprincipal, Dr Urquhart the Mediciner, Alexander Fraser the Professor of Greek, with the Civilist and the Regents whose names she did not know. And Dr Garden, one-time Professor of Divinity in the College, though he had not come in with the students. He sat with his family in his private pew. She saw Baillie Baxter in his pew, his wife and children and servants crammed in around him. She saw the trades' lofts of the five trades of the Old Town, the tailors, the weavers, the shoemakers, the fleshers and the hammermen. And she saw George. He looked dissatisfied and restless, but when he caught her eye he smiled. She raised a hand and waved. Christian started in apprehension that her husband might have seen, but William Montgomery saw and heard nothing. He stood motionless, his eye on the magnificent oak ceiling with the rows of bright-painted armorial coats, and even when William Christie, Precentor and Session clerk, took up the Bible which George Fraser had gifted and read aloud the scriptures, the mason did not move.

The sermon began. A dog wandered down the south aisle, sniffing, and yelped as someone landed a careful kick. Somewhere someone coughed incessantly with the dry cough of disease. That would be the Urquhart boy. A child's voice whined, complaining, and stopped abruptly under the sharp slap of a chiding hand. At the back of the kirk, friends chatted and neighbours exchanged the week's news in voices they did not bother to subdue. The beadles moved among the indwellers, rebuking and chiding. Montgomery heard and saw nothing but the dream of his son at his side.

'William Christie is a sanctimonious prig,' said Middleton when the service was over. 'And devoid of humour.'

'He will do well,' replied James Garden. 'He is the man the times require. Remember his election and how his competitors were eliminated one by one – this man for inefficiency, that man because he kept a public inn, another because he was known to be disaffected to the government? But our Mr Christie is not disaffected. He knows exactly where his allegiance must lie if he is to keep his post and prosper. It does not do these days to hold unfashionable opinions. I know it to my cost.' He smiled, but without rancour. 'Come home with me, my dear friend, and take a dram. We will talk about old times.'

Middleton looked about him. They were standing in the kirkyard outside the west porch. The snow was trampled and packed to a brown crust over the frozen earth. People grouped and parted, moving their several ways. Baillie Baxter stood talking to George Fraser – exchanging business tips, no doubt. Urquhart had already left. Middleton saw him striding down the Chanonry towards Cluny's Port, with his wife and his eight children hurrying behind. The Mediciner was brisk and erect in spite of his fifty-six years, and they had trouble keeping up with him. George Cumming senior was talking loudly to a group of tradesmen, boasting or stirring up some local trouble. Middleton knew that every one of them would note his departure with the man whose Episcopalian sympathies had lost him his post. If Middleton had had the calculated sense and the cold cunning of a man like William Christie, he would not have walked the same street with James Garden, let alone drunk his dram. But James Garden was his friend and an honest man and George Middleton bent his principles for no one. He took the ex-professor's arm and smiled.

'Thank you, James. A splendid idea.' They left the kirkyard together in full view of the assembled town.

'That man Middleton's asking for trouble,' growled Cumming the blacksmith. 'He'll not last long, and a good riddance. It's time we cleared the town of everyone who is not of the true kirk.'

'A man's entitled to his own beliefs,' argued George, his son. 'And if he harms no one, why harm him?'

'Because his beliefs are wrong, that's why.'

'He is a professor in the university. He reads learned books and studies the writings of better men than we are. Who are we to say he is wrong?' George had begun his argument purely for the sake of contradicting his father, whose dogmatic statements never failed to irritate the boy, but now he began to see the truth in his own argument. 'Suppose,' he added recklessly, 'it is you who is wrong?'

185

Cumming swelled with outrage. 'How dare you defy your own father? I'll tan your hide for you, you impudent, lazy gowk!' He lunged for George, who twisted neatly aside and out of reach.

'Really Father,' he said with mock gentility. 'Brawling in the kirkyard on the Sabbath day! And you an Elder of the kirk Session!'

Cumming let out a roar then and swung at George, but the boy had had enough. All the frustration of the past weeks boiled up inside him and he turned on his father with blazing rage.

'Touch me and I'll smash your face in!' The fury in his voice stopped Cumming in mid-stroke. 'Hypocrite! You shout and bluster and swear and tell everyone how to live their lives and if anyone dares to criticize or contradict you, you hit them! And as for sin, you spend your day prying into other people's, but I'll bet there's not one sin in the book you haven't committed yourself!'

Cumming went for him then, seizing George in his great arms and grappling with him till the veins stood out on his temples. They fell to the ground and rolled, grunting and swearing in the slush. Those of the townspeople who had not left for home gathered in a protective circle round the pair, shielding them from anyone of authority who might be watching and at the same time ensuring that they had a ring-side view of the fight.

'George!' a child's voice ordered. 'Stop it at once!'

When the men took no notice, Margery pushed forward through the press and seized George by the arm, tugging at him.

'Stop it, both of you,' she cried again. 'Someone help me, please, before they kill each other!'

They moved then. Alexander Crystal and his son George, and several other men. They thrust Margery aside, pulled the combatants to their feet and forced them apart.

'You'll pay for this,' panted Cumming. 'Wait till we get home, my lad, and I'll squeeze the life out of you with my bare hands till you scream to me for mercy.'

George looked at him coolly, then deliberately spat into the snow at his father's feet. He shook off George Crystal's hands and strode from the kirkyard. Margery ran after him, limping and slipping in the snow, calling 'George! Wait for me!' He did not turn his head, but when she caught up with him and clutched his hand he did not withdraw it and he slackened his pace a fraction to accommodate her lameness.

'George,' she panted. 'Where are you going?'

'Away.' He glared straight ahead of him down the High Street to the Spital.

'But where to? Will you come back? What will you do? Please tell me, George. I thought you were my friend.'

'I'll go south,' he relented. 'Possibly to Leith. I need adventure, Margery. I need to see the world.'

'But you will come back, George, won't you?'

He looked down at her earnest, innocent face and when he saw the tears brimming he said more gently, 'Yes, Margery. I will come back, I promise you.'

'When, George? Will it be soon?'

'Who knows? But I promise you I will come back. One day.'

They had reached the bridge now at the College Bounds and Margery stopped. She stood at the bridge watching as George climbed the hill to the Spital, his figure dark and clear-cut against the snow of the street. At the brow of the hill he turned and raised a hand before he dipped out of sight. Margery made her way slowly back along the High Street. There was ice in the puddles at the side of the road and the branches of the trees at Powis had each a tiny layer of snow. Bird prints patterned the white square of the College garden and as she passed Principal Middleton's house a puff of wind showered her with powdered snow.

When she reached the entrance to the Close her steps faltered. Her father had been in the kirkyard. He had seen what she did and would be angry. But when she reached the door of her house and pushed it open, Montgomery called only 'Margery? Is that you? Run for the women, quickly. Christian's time is come.'

Christian was in labour for two days. When at last the child was born, it was a boy and it was born dead.

Montgomery would not believe it. He took the tiny body and wrapped it in the scrap of linen which Margery had hung beside the hearth. He cradled the child in his arms, rocking it. He squatted on his haunches near the fire and held the bundle near the heat to warm the ice-blue limbs. He poured whisky from the bottle he had bought to celebrate his son's birth and spooned it carefully through the unresponsive lips. Finally he opened his shirt and held the child against his chest, crooning.

The women whispered nervously together while they did what they could to make Christian comfortable, then one by one they slipped quietly out of the house. Christian closed her eyes and turned her face to the wall. She was drained even of fear.

Margery stood quietly waiting and watching while her father rocked slowly to and fro in the glow from the fire as he crooned a lullaby to his dead son. But at last he stopped singing and was still. He cupped the body in his hands then and looked at it in silence for a long time. Margery saw tears in his eyes. She took the bundle gently from his unresisting hands. Without a word she laid it in the shadows at the foot of the bed. Slowly Montgomery stood up. He took his mason's hammer from its place by the pot-shelf, picked up the whisky bottle and moved for the door. Something in the quiet purpose of his movements made Margery start after him in fear.

'Where are you going, Father?'

'To do what must be done.' His cheeks were wet with tears.

'But there is nothing to be done. We will bury him tomorrow, Father, not today. We must see the beadle and the clerk and pay the fee.'

Montgomery brushed her aside. 'There is evil in this town, Margery. I have known it for a long time. Witchcraft and evil. No son of mine will live until the evil is destroyed.'

She hung on to his arm, pleading. 'Stay, Father. Wait till tomorrow, when it is light.' But he shook her off.

'It must be done, Margery, and now.'

When he had gone, she heard a faint voice from the bed.

'Bar the door, Margery, and when he comes back, for God's sake do not let him in.'

'But we cannot do that, Christian. This is his house.'

'Bar the door. Do as I say. The man is possessed!'

Obediently Margery lifted the heavy beam and dropped it into place across the closed door. But Montgomery did not come back.

The Sledders lived in a two-storey house near the cross. The walls were timber-faced and the roof of turf, but it was strongly built and substantial. It would last a generation, perhaps two. Montgomery swung his hammer and with one blow smashed the upper panel of the great front door. He swung the hammer again and splintered the remainder. Then he tore at the splitting planks with his bare hands. He heaped the broken pieces in a hasty pile and poured the whisky over them, like a libation.

There were cries from above. Casements opened in the street and someone lit a lamp. Impervious, Montgomery picked up his hammer and smashed the door lintel to shreds. Then he stepped inside. He took a taper from a pot beside the Sledders' hearth, lit it at the fire and set it to the heap of wood across the doorway. As the flames crackled and rose he stepped past them to the street and cried triumphantly, 'Burn the witch! Burn her in her bed!'

There were screams from overhead and from the neighbouring houses as doors burst open and the terrified indwellers gushed into the street with pails and jugs to douse the fire, and besoms to beat it out, lest the flames should take hold and burn the town to the ground. Montgomery fought like ten men to keep them back.

'The witch must burn!' he roared. 'My fire must burn her!' He laid about him with the hammer like a madman. Women and children screamed and the town guard needed many reinforcements before they dared to take him. Even then it took a dozen men, turn by turn, to disarm him, to drag him to the kirk and to imprison him in the south steeple for safety, and the two men told to guard him refused to stay unless two more were sent to keep them company.

In the morning Margery visited her father. He was bright-eyed and unrepentant.

'They are fools, Margery. They suffer a witch to live among them, daily cursing them with the evil eye, and they lock up the one man brave enough to beard her in her den.'

'Will you take ale, Father?' asked Margery, offering him a mug.

'Thank you. You were always a good girl.' He looked at her, then. 'You should have been the boy. I wronged you once, but you have been a good daughter to me.' He added sadly, 'If you had been a man, we would have done great things together.'

'Yes, Father.' She laid a hand on his arm. 'You will have to go before the court tomorrow. Be calm and quiet and all might still be well.'

But when Montgomery appeared before the Burgh Court and was asked the reason for his violent behaviour, he replied only, 'The Sledder woman is a witch.'

The Council's verdict was inevitable. William Montgomery, mason, of Widow Irvine's Close, was banished from the Old Town for life, on pain of branding and scourging should he ever dare to return.

Christian laughed when she heard the news. It was a hard and brittle laugh which held no mirth. Margery said simply, 'I will go with you.'

Her father refused. 'The town may turn me out if it must, but it will not dispossess my wife and daughter. You must stay, Margery, and beat them. You must have a son.'

'But I am a child, Father. I cannot.'

'You will grow. And when you are a woman you must bear a son and name him William. One day they will learn that mine is not a name to scorn.'

Christian kept to her house on the day he left, but Margery was there to see him go. He walked, a solitary figure, through the double ranks of indwellers at two of the afternoon on a bleak December day. The crowd stood silent as he passed. There had been talk of scourging him, as thieves were scourged, but the idea had been abandoned. Montgomery was a strong man and the memory of his violence at the Sledders' house was too fresh in their minds. No one would admit it, but they were a little afraid. So the huge, maimed mason walked alone and untouched between the silent, staring ranks, the tools of his trade slung over one shoulder and a staff in his hand. Down the High Street, past the Principal's house and the College, past Fraser's new houses at Powis and the Mediciner's, over the little bridge and so to the Spital.

Through the tears Margery watched him pass over the horizon and out of sight. He did not look back.

Part 3

1699—1705

The *Hope of Bo'ness* rode at anchor in the bay. The ship looked deserted, its sails furled, its yards frayed and rotting in the torpid heat. There was mould already on the log-book in the captain's cabin, mosquitoes whined in a steady cloud over the empty ale barrels and maggots swelled on the reeking scraps of salt beef. Below decks the rats grew bold in the foul detritus of a three months' voyage and the boards of the deck were splitting under the heat. The few men left aboard had stripped to their ragged breeches although it was mid-December. The stench of swampland and jungle hung over the emerald sea – motionless but for the glaucous heave where it met the shore in a curl of green bubbles.

'Lower away!' George Cumming guided the barrel into the stern of the jolly-boat. His companion loosed the rope and together they pulled for the shore.

The bay was deceptively beautiful: a swath of calm water against a hill of trees. But the land of the promontory was swampland, marshy and unwholesome and vilely infested with crabs. The woods were too dense to penetrate except by means of the rare footpaths of the native Indians, and the nearest fertile soil was three or four miles inland where the Indians had their plantations. Besides that, for much of the year the steady onshore winds made it hazardous for ships to put to sea: a point of some consideration now when many of those who had newly arrived from Scotland were already talking of returning home.

'How long will your supplies last?' asked Hugh Baird, pausing to take breath. The least exertion in this humid heat was enough to drench a man in sweat. His brown-tanned skin was salt-encrusted and pitted all over with the festering scabs of mosquito bites.

'Six months they estimated at the court yesterday, but only on sharp allowance. Each man a half-pound of bread, the same of beef, and a third part of a gill of brandy a day.'

'It is not brandy I long for,' said Hugh, 'but a draught of clear Scottish water, ice-cold and fresh from a mountain burn.'

'Aye, and the wind in one's face – a cold sea wind to freeze the ears and catch the breath in the throat.'

The two rested on their oars while the water heaved gently beneath them and the wood burned under their hands. The sun's glare had already closed their eyes to protective slits and both men wore wide-brimmed hats roughly fashioned from banana leaves.

'If help does not arrive soon,' said Hugh, 'I fear you will have to leave as those before you left.'

'But you stayed.'

When the *Hope of Bo'ness* had put into Caledonia Bay on the first day of December in the expectation of a joyous welcome from the settlers, they had found the colony deserted and their countrymen gone. The settlers' huts were in ruins, the fort destroyed and the place overrun with mangroves. Only a small ship from New England, under Captain Drummond, and another from Jamaica rode in the bay, to take in fresh water – providentially, for the new arrivals were thus able to buy a few much-needed provisions – but ashore no more than a handful of the original settlers remained. The two sloops still lingered awaiting the final decision of the new arrivals, to whom they had already given an account of the disaster, an account confirmed by Hugh Baird.

The colony had been finally deserted on June 20, 1699, a full two months before the *Hope* had put to sea. The combination of sickness, want, the threat of Spanish attacks and the complete lack of any news from home had demoralized and finally defeated the settlers.

'There was squabbling, too,' said Hugh, grimly. 'And worse. The Councillors fought among themselves, some tried to capture the ships and steal the stores. There was much drunkenness and obscenity and lewd living. One ship was burnt to water level on account of a common whore, and ship and provisions were all lost. Others put to sea and made for Jamaica where it is rumoured they sold their men for sugar and brandy. The food rotted, the men fell sick, and finally, when the greater number had died, the poor remainder lost all courage and put to sea.'

'But you stayed,' repeated George.

'Aye.' Hugh Baird's face had grown haggard under the repeated onslaughts of swamp fever, but his eyes were still clear and honest. 'At home I loved a girl and she died.' He smiled sadly at the memory of Elspeth and those long-past Edinburgh days. 'I came to build a new life in a new land and I mean to do so. I have made a clearing beyond the fort and planted maize. When I have cleared more land I shall plant banana trees and breadfruit and make a stockade for fowls. After that, a house.'

George Cumming looked at him in silence. Hugh Baird was older than he was by three years or more, yet he had about him the eager innocence of a child. And a child's unquestioning faith.

He'll need it, thought George. I doubt he has ever had to scrape a living by his own hand. 'Have you experience of building?' he asked.

'None. My companions and I were ill-equipped. I see that now. Enthusiasm is not enough. We should have brought particular skills. A wright or a mason is worth ten ordinary men here. I trust your expedition comes better supplied, for I dearly need to learn.'

To such simple optimism George could find no answer but to say, 'I am a hammerman, as you know, and will teach you what I can and gladly, though this is a bitter land to choose in which to learn. Tell me,' he said as he pulled again at the oars, 'is it always as hot as this?'

'*Hic perpetuum ver, hic formosissimus annus.* I could be grateful enough for perpetual spring if it brought me an abundance of crops without a similar abundance of pests to devour them. And the heart grows satiated with beauty when the beauty is putrescent and conceals so much decay.'

They had reached the shore now and a green snake which had been coiled, basking, on a rock slid soundlessly into the water and disappeared. George shuddered with involuntary dread, but stepped into the water nevertheless to pull the boat ashore. A thousand tiny, darting fish netted the shallows with quicksilver, and the sand under his bare feet burned. From the swamp beyond came the steady drone of flies and the harsh, monotonous rasp of a cricket. They were the only sounds in the heat-weighted air.

From the bay the hills rose almost vertically, their slopes dense with trees far bigger than anything George had ever seen. They made the birks at home seem no more than marram grass. Here and there the thick chain-mail of leaves flashed scarlet with some tropical blossom and once, from far inland, came a high-pitched whoop which crescendoed to a scream and stopped as suddenly as it had begun.

'Monkeys,' said Hugh. 'Little devils. They stole my shirt only last week and a peck of meal. They make tough eating, too, if you are lucky enough to catch one.'

'Lucky?' George dropped to one knee to heave the barrel of nails on to his shoulder, and the sand erupted into a hundred volcanoes as a hundred tiny crabs scrabbled for safety.

'You'll think yourself well feasted on a single one of those little creatures before the week is out,' said Hugh cheerfully. He took the second barrel on to his shoulder and staggered under its weight. 'But let's get this load safely locked up in the store before someone thinks it is food and a riot breaks out.'

George was silent as the two men made their way along the rough pathway at the fringe of the trees which served to shield them from the worst of the sun's glare. They passed the sweat-drenched, staggering figures of the half-dozen men who had been detailed to fill the water casks of the *Hope of Bo'ness* at the river, for the use of those officers who lived on board. But the other ships had taken on water too, the *Little Hope*, the *Hamilton*, and the *Rising Sun*. There was rumour in the air and a mutinous unease. Provisions were short and the food bad. The first settlers had gone and it was rumoured that there was to be a tally taken of all those who were sick, unfit or unskilled for work. It was said they were to be shipped to Jamaica, but below decks and in the sweaty shade of the makeshift palmetto huts in the compound there was wary talk of slavery and the quick profits to be made from selling men.

George saw suspicion in the eyes of every man they met and resolved to keep his own eyes open and his hand on his knife. There were men here who would kill for a hunk of bread.

By the time they reached the roughly-repaired warehouse inside the fort and deposited their load, George was ready to drop with exhaustion.

'You'll get used to it,' said Hugh encouragingly. 'Scarcely one Scotsman in twenty can live here and survive, but the twenty-first man has a chance. It's a question of expectation. I expect nothing, so I rejoice at any fortune that comes my way — a fish, a turkey's egg, and I am happy. Others look for El Dorado and when they find their gold is merely sand, they run amok with fury. But you are tired. Before you go back to your work, let me show you my small plantation. We will sit and talk for a while in the cool shade.'

George hesitated. As one of the few skilled men in the expedition, he was much in need to direct the repair work in the fort and the construction of the new settlers' huts. Already he had detailed work parties to cut trees for the shoring-up and reinforcement of the gun emplacements, and while some men cleared and deepened the ditch which protected the fort on the inward side of the promontory, others were already repairing and strengthening the stockade at George's direction. Nails and tools were in short supply and must be carefully husbanded by someone who knew his work. Then there were the huts to be built and a warehouse for stores. George's skill was valued as it had never been before, and he found himself suddenly overseer, expert, teacher and master tradesman. He was as important a member of the settlement as the Councillors themselves and he took his new responsibility seriously.

'Well,' he began now, 'I really ought to be . . .'

'Please,' interrupted Hugh. 'I would like your opinion of my shelter – whether I should build on to it as it is or start afresh – and I will introduce you to Andreas.'

'Andreas? Who is he?'

'One of the Indian leaders and my friend.'

They had not been long at Hugh's hut, a primitive affair with a hammock on the Indian model and little else, when Andreas appeared. Andreas was a small, copper-coloured man with brown eyes as dark and darting as a bird's. 'Goddam you for a son of a bitch,' he said cheerfully when Hugh introduced him to George Cumming. This was the most coherent sentence he uttered, for the rest of the conversation consisted of a rapid hotch-potch of English, Spanish and his own incomprehensible tongue. Hugh, however, listened gravely and when Andreas had finished, bowed his thanks and offered his guest tobacco. Later, when the Indian had left, Hugh explained.

'He says the Spaniards at Carthegena have exact information as to our numbers and munitions. They are gathering men and ships to attack us by land and sea. They intend to dislodge us from the promontory and this time to drive us out for good.'

' "This time"? Have they attacked before?'

'Oh yes. In February, I think it was, some three months after we arrived. A small land party of Spanish scouts was routed by our men with no trouble. That was a mere skirmish, but Andreas says the Spanish retreated only to regroup and strengthen and to gather ships.'

'And what is your opinion? Is he right?'

'The Indians are our friends. Unhappily they are also friends to the Spaniards. But in this instance I think we would do well to heed the warning.'

'Then I must go.' George moved out of the shade of the hut and flinched as the heat hit him. 'The huts must wait. I will put every able-bodied man I can find on to strengthening the stockade.'

'I will come with you,' said Hugh. 'I may be unskilled, but I am able-bodied, thank God, and I can learn.'

Hugh's hut was not on the promontory, a flat sandy stretch of land which the first settlers had christened New Edinburgh, but a little way inland, close to the river and to one of the Indian paths which made progress through the massed trees and tangled mangrove a little easier as the two men made their way back towards the fort.

Monkeys clattered in the branches at their approach and the green gloom flashed with the rainbow brilliance of a parakeet. Once George almost trod upon the pebbled back of an iguana. The stone eyes looked up at him with unblinking malignancy.

'Christ!' George brushed the sweat from his face with a hand which trembled. 'Are those things dangerous?'

'Oh no. The lizards and land-turtles are harmless enough, but take care you do not cross one of the wild hogs which roam the forest, unless you are well-armed and a skilled shot. But it is the spiders you must really watch for, and the scorpions. They can give a venomous bite.'

'I wonder you dare walk abroad, barefoot and unprotected as you do.'

'One grows accustomed to such things,' said Hugh. 'The Indians survive and so can we, if we do as they do and keep our senses alert.'

'That might be hard for some people,' said George grimly as they emerged from the trees to find the ditch abandoned and the members of the party whose job it was to clear the weeds stretched inert in the shade.

'Get up you idle bastards!' he roared. 'Or I'll ship you to Jamaica in chains!'

The men rose resentfully to their feet and moved back to the ditch, but there was something in their silence which made George and Hugh Baird exchange glances.

'There will be trouble,' said George Cumming that evening, when he made his report to the Councillors who were meeting in the best preserved of the gentlemen's huts inside the fort.

The Reverend Archibald Stobo, who had travelled with George on the *Hope of Bo'ness*, nodded gravely. 'They looked for peace, but no good came; and for a time of health and comfort, but behold trouble.'

'We must send away all surplus men immediately,' said Councillor Byres, a blunt, square-built man with wiry black hair and a quick temper. 'I have told you till I am blue in the face! There is not enough food.'

'The Spaniards are arming to attack,' reminded Captain Drummond. 'We will need all the men we can get to strengthen our defences.' Thomas Drummond was the brother of Robert Drummond who had captained the *Caledonia* on the ill-fated first expedition, but the misfortunes of his brother's venture had merely strengthened his own faith in the future of the settlement.

'What good are men if they are starving?' retorted Byres.

'I have told you, gentlemen,' said Drummond. 'Provisions can be had in abundance from New York.'

'And while we wait for the ship to return, the belly-ache will carry off half our men and the Spaniards the rest.'

'Nonsense,' said Drummond briskly. 'If the Spaniards attack us by land they will be in no condition to fight anyone after a march through such heat and jungle as they will encounter. And we can beat off any attack by sea once our fortifications are complete and our guns in place.'

'And when will that be?' demanded Byres. 'We'd do better to pack up and leave tomorrow than to depend on your empty "onces" and "whens".'

'Give me one hundred and fifty men and provisions for three weeks, and I'll drive back the Spaniards for you myself.'

'One hundred and fifty men? And who will be left to build the fort? The work goes slowly enough as it is!'

'Come, come,' said the Reverend Stobo mildly. 'Our friend George Cumming is doing his best. No man can do more. But you must excuse me. I have letters to write home before the sloop leaves for Jamaica and tomorrow, who knows, the wind may be fair?'

'Aye!' snapped Byres. 'We'd best all write our letters while we're still alive to do it.'

'Where is your faith, Byres?' chided Stobo. 'God will protect all good Christian souls.'

'Then He will have his work cut out,' retorted Byres. 'If the swamp fever does not kill us, the Spaniards will.'

A drum sounded from the darkness of the compound.

'The curfew, gentlemen,' said Captain Drummond, downing his ration of brandy. 'All those who sleep aboard, back to your ships. Tomorrow there is much work to be done.'

'Aye,' thought George wearily, as he shook the ants from his hammock and settled down for the night. 'There's work enough to be done before those Spaniards come. But I'll do it and I'll make the bastards work! Because if we don't finish that building in time . . .'

A mosquito whined at his ear and he lashed out fruitlessly. Through the slatted roof of the hut the sky was hot with stars. The sweat runnelled along his breastbone and in the folds of knee and elbow and armpit. A thousand crickets trilled from the swampland of the coast, and somewhere a toc-toc bird drummed its monotonous rhythm in time with his throbbing head. Cramp gripped his stomach and his palms were wet, while the skin on his forehead burned. George clenched his teeth with determination.

'I swear to God I'll build that stockade before the Spaniards come, if it's the last thing I do.'

Somewhere in the camp a man cried out in the delirium of fever and from the night forest came an answering shriek. A macaw? A gibbon? The endless clatter of the crickets swelled until his head spun round with the noise of it : until the noise blurred into the sound of voices and laughter and his body glowed with the remembered warmth of an ale-house at home.

'Curfew!' Christian banged on the cooking-pot with a wooden ladle. 'Come on lads, drink up!'

John Garden raised a luggie, still brimming with ale. 'Your health, Christian, and your beautiful eyes. Not to mention other, warmer, parts of the anatomy!' There was a roar of approval from the students who packed the little room from wall to wall.

'Get on home with you!'

Christian smacked him playfully round the ears. He put an arm round her waist and pulled her down on to his knee, laughing. Christian was laughing, too, and when she put up her face and kissed him, deliberately, on the lips, Margery looked quickly away. She busied herself with collecting the wooden bickers, the small, half-pint ale-cups and the luggies. As she squeezed her way between the crowded wooden benches and ale-stained tables, no one molested her.

She was no longer a child now and her breasts were well grown, but there was an aloofness in the clear, intelligent eyes which made those students who dared to touch her lower their own eyes in confusion as she drew away, and talk boastfully to their neighbours to cover their embarrassment.

The youngest students were no more than fourteen, others were as old as Christian or older. At first they had come in ones and twos, warily. Then Christian persuaded her childhood friends, James Middleton and John Garden and the Urquhart boys, to come and to bring their friends. John had taken his degree some years ago, but still lingered on in the College as did Adam Urquhart and James Middleton, though neither of these showed any sign of taking a degree. They came and brought others with them, and Christian kept such a free and cheerful ale-house that they came again and again. Besides, the ale was good, and Christian made sure it was brewed according to the Burgh regulations.

'They'll not get me for selling under-strength liquor,' she told Margery. 'Or for selling drink after hours. So as soon as the curfew rings, you collect the luggies, empty or full, and leave the lads to me. And if they won't go, you fetch the Baillie. Baillie Knight. He lives the farthest away. There's no need to hurry,' she added with a wink. 'And don't go till I tell you.'

Almost two years had passed since Montgomery's banishment and in that time Christian had recovered much of her old bloom. She was plump and bright-eyed and confident, and the old bond had grown again between the two girls.

'I delivered you into the world,' she told Margery affectionately, 'and I always thought of you as my child, even in those days after your father took you back. Now that I've lost my own two babies and am not likely to have more, you are the only daughter I have.'

But since the opening of the ale-house Margery had noticed a reserve on Christian's part. Often when Christian sent her in search of the Baillie, the girl returned to find Christian flushed and dishevelled and the students gone. Once the door had been barred from the inside, and she and Baillie Knight had waited five minutes before Christian opened it. That time there had been only one student left, apparently in a drunken sleep, though he had walked well enough under the encouragement of the Baillie's tongue.

'His friends were battering at the door,' explained Christian earnestly, 'so I dropped the bar across to keep them out. He was dead to the world and harmless enough.'

But there were two red patches on her cheeks all the same and her eyes were unnaturally bright. And on more than one occasion Margery was sent outside to the forestair and told to go to bed.

For when George Crystal moved out to one of Alexander Fraser's new houses, a row of six at right angles to the High Street, Christian had leased her own old room above Montgomery's so that she and Margery could sleep there and make over the ground floor entirely to the sale of ale. Besides, there were days when the women came to her as they had come to her mother. Christian had persuaded Alexander Crystal to make benches and tables for her and had negotiated with Merchant Sledder for barley to brew her own ale. She had even hired one of Kenneth Fraser's men to lay stone slabs on the floor and had scrubbed them herself.

'It's the students I'm after,' she explained to Margery. 'Baillie Baxter has the monopoly of the businessmen and merchants, and the ale-house at the cross has the trades. The students have to make their own way as best they can. We are close to the College here and they'll not have far to go home when the curfew rings. We should do well.'

And she had, though not without some public disapproval.

'They can disapprove to their miserable hearts' content,' she told Margery, 'but there's nothing they can do to me as long as I stay within the law.'

'Out!' she called again, pushing John Garden away and climbing to her feet. 'Do you want me to be fined and the ale-house closed?'

'Come along, lads,' called Adam Urquhart, a thin, serious boy with bright, dark eyes and his father's intelligence. He coughed quickly in a dry spasm which curled his chest, and called again, 'Out, all of you, before you get the lady into trouble.'

There were grumbles and ribald remarks but the boys prepared to leave nevertheless. For in spite of his cough and his skeletal build, Adam Urquhart spoke with the authority of a natural leader to whom it did not occur that he might be disobeyed.

Margery held open the heavy wooden door and the cold winter air sliced through the fetid heat of the room. The students filed past her into the night. As they emerged into the cold of the Close, they huddled inside their thick red gowns and dispersed in twos and threes in the direction of the High Street. The light of the ale-house lay in a wavering block across the yard as the candles guttered in the sudden air. At last only Adam and the Garden boy were left.

'You are right to be careful, Christian,' said Adam. 'The new Minister is a rigid, inflexible man. Since the heritors gave him the right hand of fellowship, there has been no stopping him. He knows himself upright and honest and will tolerate no backsliding in others. My father says he has taken home the Book of Discipline to check every sin and its punishment since Dr Keith died five years ago.'

Christian paled at his words. 'Surely he will not bother with things that happened so long ago?' She was remembering the birth of her first child, seven months after her marriage. Somewhere there was sure to be a mention of that.

'Mr Thomas Thomson is a dedicated man,' said Adam with something of his father's sarcasm. He coughed again quickly.

'What Adams means,' said John Garden with careful if blurred enunciation, 'is that he is a strait-laced, narrow-minded, Calvinist bigot with sin on the brain. You don't think Deacon Cumming would allow him in the kirk otherwise, do you? He's probably signed a contract with the devil to send him twenty souls a week in return for his own immunity.'

'John! You must not say such things,' warned Adam. 'Your father has had enough trouble as it is, without you courting more.'

'The kirk can go to the devil,' said John Garden with the cheerful if incoherent bravado which several luggies of Christian's ale had induced. 'And if ever you want to be put in touch with an honest, Christian minister, let me know.'

'I'd better take him home,' said Adam quickly, 'before he becomes indiscreet. And you won't say anything, will you?'

'Of course not.' Christian was too worried about her own position to notice the reference which Adam had been quick to see. He knew there were houses where Episcopalians met secretly to celebrate their own Communion, and no doubt Dr Garden's house was one of them, but it did not do to say so and certainly not to voice the matter in public.

'Goodnight then, Christian.' Adam took John Garden by the arm and helped him to his feet. 'And goodnight Margery,' he added as he steered his companion safely through the door.

'Goodnight and Godspeed,' called Margery, smiling. She liked Adam. He was the only student who looked at her clearly, as a person. Behind the conventional jollity, his eyes were serious and he spoke to her without the brittle, meaningless raillery of the others. On the rare occasions when they talked together, it had been as equals. She felt the same affinity with Adam as she had felt with George Cumming, though Adam was a gentleman and she merely a tradesman's daughter. Besides, no one could begin to replace George in her heart.

George had been gone almost two years now and still no word of him. Margery closed the door and bolted it. Then she poured water from the kettle into the wooden tub and sluiced the ale mugs quickly before setting them to drain on the nearest table. Christian watched her for a long time without speaking. When at last she broke the silence, her voice was lifeless and dejected.

'They'll get me sooner or later.'

Margery looked up in surprise. 'Who will?'

'The Session. The Elders of the kirk. They nearly got Ma but she escaped by dying before they could clap her in the branks. And they'll get me one day.' She slumped on to the stool by the hearth and held her head in her hands. 'I wish I had a man.'

'But Father . . .' began Margery uncertainly. She missed her father deeply, but she knew it irritated Christian to hear him mentioned.

'Him?' Christian laughed derisively. 'He's gone to the devil and good riddance to him, but as long as he's alive he's my husband and I can't take another.'

Margery lowered her eyes to the water tub and said nothing.

'That's what finished Ma, too,' said Christian absent-mindedly reaching for a wooden mug which still held ale and draining it. 'Her man left her and disappeared off the face of the earth, except that whenever she was beginning to think he was dead he'd come breezing back again, swearing and knocking her about and staking his claim so she could never take a good man of her own. I wonder where he is now, the old devil?' She refilled her mug and drank reflectively. 'It's the same with me, Margery. Until someone sends me his head on a platter, I'm married to the great gowk, and in the eyes of the kirk if I so much as look at another man it's adultery. But I'm young and lusty and sometimes I have such a longing in me . . .'

Margery rinsed out the last mug and put it with the others. She began to scrub the ale-splashed tables and put the benches straight. Christian watched her idly and sipped her ale.

'You're a good girl,' she said. 'You always were. They'll not get you like they'll get me. We must find you a job.'

'But I have a job, helping you.'

'You're not right for it, Margery. I've seen the look in your eye when they take liberties. You're cold and aloof. You make them uneasy.'

'I'm sorry.' But Margery knew it was true.

'Besides, you're a woman now and soon you'll be beautiful. I don't want one of those students taking you in his cups and spoiling you. That's not to be the way of it for my Margery. You are to do remarkable things. You'll marry well and be respectable. One of the Sledder boys, perhaps, or even Baillie Baxter's William. Then when you are well set up and prosperous, you can give your stepmother a home in her old age.'

'Oh yes, Christian! You know I will.' Margery threw her arms round Christian and kissed her. 'But I'll not marry for a long time yet, if at all.' She was remembering George who had promised one day to come back. 'I am happy to stay here and help you as long as you need me.'

'No. You have been here long enough. We'll find a good position for you at the Whitsun hiring, with the Gardens or the Middletons or the Alexander Frasers. No, not the Gardens. John Garden is too hard to handle. Besides, the Gardens are out of favour and it might be bad for trade. The Urquhart household would be better, or even Baillie Baxter's. You leave it to me.'

'But who will help you here?' Margery did not protest at the suggestion. In truth it was what she had hoped for, but been too loyal to suggest for herself. She found the ale-house tedious and irksome, and the noisy jollity jarred on her nerves. She longed for the quietness of a domestic life where she could learn as well as work. In a gentleman's house she would be able to learn many things, even perhaps to read properly and to write, as well as to sew and to cook more elaborate dishes than the incessant bannocks and kale on which she and Christian lived. She remembered the warm contentment of the Garden kitchen in the Chaplains' when she had been allowed to help Christian, and she yearned for such a kitchen for herself. She would gladly be indentured for whatever sum Christian thought fit, if she could be certain that Christian herself would not suffer.

'Don't you worry about me,' said Christian cheerfully. 'Whitsun is six months away yet and by that time I'll be well set up here and flourishing. You'll see. I will manage and if I can't, I'll easily find a girl to help me out now and again, and you can give me a hand yourself on your free day.'

So it was settled and all that remained was to wait for the Whitsun hiring fair.

'Though there's no harm in asking about,' said Christian, 'and letting it be known you're available. You may be lame but you're a good girl. Both the Gardens and the Middletons can give you a character.'

'What is to be done about Christian Grant?' Mr Thomas Thomson looked sternly over gold-rimmed spectacles at the assembled elders. He was a thin-faced, ascetic man nearing seventy and had come by a succession of moves through Kirkudbrightshire, Carstairs and Forres to Turriff in Aberdeenshire and finally to the church of Old Machar, where already he was wielding his cleansing besom as vigorously as even Deacon Cumming could wish.

'I have studied the Book of Discipline with particular care,' he said now, 'and have noted many misdemeanours which are still uncorrected.'

'Not entirely uncorrected,' said George Middleton mildly. 'The culprits were rebuked at the time. It was only official punishment which was deferred.'

'*Only?*' said Mr Thomson severely. 'Punishment is the essential counterpart to sin. How can you expect the weak-minded to resist temptation without the threat of punishment to keep them on the narrow path?'

There was no reply to this and the Minister went on, 'The record is disgraceful. All kinds of uncleanness and scandalous conduct remain unpunished. We must make an example of these offenders as a salutary warning to the rest.'

'That might be difficult in Christian Grant's case,' pointed out Dr Urquhart. 'Her husband is banished and Christian insists he overpowered her against her will. In Montgomery's absence it will be difficult to prove otherwise.'

'Did she agree to swear to this?'

'Yes, Minister. She vowed she would swear on the great Bible that it was none of her wishing and I, for one, believe her.'

'Tell me more about this woman. She keeps an ale-house I am told. Is it well conducted?'

'I believe so, Minister. On several occasions the Baillie has been sent for if the students do not remove on the stroke of eight o'clock. It is clear the woman means to keep herself and her customers strictly within the law.'

'She has a daughter, has she not?'

'A stepdaughter,' corrected Baxter. 'The daughter of her husband by a previous marriage. A lame child of twelve, at one time in the town's care.' Briefly he outlined Margery's background.

'A fatherless girl of that age is in moral danger if she spends her life in an ale-house frequented by young men,' said the Minister. 'This orphaned child is clearly in need of our help.'

'I believe we decided some years ago in this very place that when the time came, Margery Montgomery should be found a suitable position in service,' reminded Middleton. 'I for one know nothing but good of the girl.'

'I'd think twice before I had her in my house,' said Cumming. 'You forget there was talk of witchcraft, and the Grant girl's mother was a Papist. Montgomery himself was an out-and-out rebel to the last, a blatant Episcopalian and a Jacobite, too.'

There was a moment's silence. Many of the gentlemen present held Jacobite sympathies still, though they were careful to conceal them, and more than one of them adhered in secret to the old, Episcopalian church.

'I know nothing against the girl,' repeated Middleton. 'She works hard and attends the kirk.'

'She is a good girl,' agreed Urquhart. 'I would take her into my house without a qualm, except that I am already supplied with servants of long standing who are not likely to leave.'

'You are lucky,' said Baxter. 'Or easy to please. Most servants these days are idle good-for-nothing baggages, not fit to be given house-room.'

'And would you give house-room to the Montgomery girl?' asked the Minister quietly.

Baillie Baxter paused before saying carefully, 'I know no harm of her. She could be given the chance to prove her worth, in a lowly capacity, for a limited time.'

'Is that the general opinion?' asked the Minister of the company. 'Then it seems, Cumming, that you are uncharitably prejudiced. At the next hiring fair I shall see to it myself that there is no such bias against the girl. As for her stepmother . . .' The Minister deliberated, drumming thin fingers on the wood of the Session room table. 'I will bow to your judgement in this particular case and accept the woman's word that she was forced against her will. However, the next fornication case must be settled publicly. Both parties must appear before the congregation and swear on the Holy Book.'

'Is that really necessary after all these years?' protested Middleton. 'The girl is married now and it can do no good to anyone to resurrect old indiscretions.'

'Tolerance of sin is no better than sin itself.'

'Nevertheless there is a case for forgiveness,' began Urquhart.

'Most certainly. *After* confession and punishment. I will see Bartlat and the girl myself, in private, and try once more to obtain confession from whichever one is lying. If neither will give in, there will be no help for it but to require the man to take the solemn oath.' He held up a warning hand to still any protest. 'Now Mr Treasurer, if you would be good enough to read your accounts?'

'A stern but not, I think, a heartless man,' said Urquhart as he and Middleton strolled home together along the Chanonry.

'He certainly put Cumming in his place,' said Middleton, 'when he objected to your proposal to plant trees in the kirkyard. Thirty of them, too. Cumming's face was a study.'

But the Principal sounded preoccupied. The lines of worry were habitual now and deeply ingrained. He felt his position in the town daily less secure, yet could not bring himself to compromise where his personal beliefs were concerned. He had attended Communion in Dr Garden's house only last Sunday and would do so again, but he found the secrecy wearying and shameful. Moreover, since the death of Queen Mary the question of who was to succeed the childless William, now in failing health, had given new impetus to the secret sympathizers of the exiled James. But stronger than both religious and political anxieties was the ever-increasing anxiety over the Darien venture. Ugly rumours of failure and disease had begun to filter through by way of pedlars and travellers from the ports.

'Is there any news?' asked the Principal now. His daughter Margrat had been married in the summer to an advocate from Edinburgh, and the settlement agreed was more than Middleton could comfortably afford. The groom's family had insisted on provision being made for any daughters of the union, a provision which Middleton could not reasonably refuse, knowing as he did how such a provision in his own marriage contract would have helped. Isobel was twenty-six now and likely to remain unmarried.

Her care and support would eventually devolve on her brother George, or on young James. But James was a mere student and unreliable, and George had chosen the church. He was at present a tutor with the Earl of Mar and would never make much money. At least little Elspeth would not suffer hardship in her old age. He felt the familiar sadness at her memory. But there was still his wife to be provided for and Isobel.

'I heard a sailor in the New Town had tidings from the settlement.'

'Nothing definite,' said Urquhart carefully. He, too, was worried. He had pledged more than he could afford as it was, and with the succession of poor harvests and the soaring costs of feeding his extensive household, he knew he could not meet his pledge without selling his property, or borrowing at extortionate interest. And he, like Middleton, had other things on his mind. His wife's health was failing and his son Adam made no improvement. He had coughing fits regularly now, and though Adam denied it, the Mediciner suspected that he often coughed blood. Even a summer at the goat's milk had not helped the boy, and Dr Urquhart had no faith in the elaborate concoctions of horse dung and hyssop and the like which had been suggested by other eminent doctors. So he watched his son grow daily weaker and knew there was nothing he could do. Thank God he had opposed the boy's wish to sail to Darien. At least when he died it would be here, at home.

'What did the fellow say?' Middleton's question interrupted his reverie.

'He is reputed to have met someone from one of the ships that sailed in the first expedition. This emigrant had tales of swamp fever and torrential rains. William Paterson's wife died, he said, within a week of landing.'

Middleton was quiet. If true, this was sombre news. It was an ill omen indeed when the leader of the expedition was bereaved so soon after setting foot in the new land.

'Of course we must wait until we hear something official,' went on Urquhart, 'but I fear the worst.'

'At least all we lose is money,' said Middleton. 'Think of all those who will lose sons or husbands. They say in the town that the Cumming boy sailed to Darien with the second expedition.'

'So I have heard. But as far as I know it is mere rumour. The boy has not been seen since that day in the kirkyard two years ago.'

'And may not be seen again,' said Middleton sadly, remembering

Elspeth and her childhood friend. The lad had always been restless. Middleton remembered him as a boy in his own kitchen on a day more than twelve years ago, the day the Highlandmen passed through the town and the Great Tower fell. George had talked of joining Claverhouse then. Claverhouse, too, was dead. So many people, young and old, had died in recent years . . . Determinedly Middleton shook off his melancholy. He was not dead yet and until he was, he had work to do. The College still functioned. The new Session had begun and he was still the Principal.

'Come in and take a dram?' he offered the Mediciner. 'And tell me more about the trees. I think it a commendable plan to plant timber for our children's children. There is not a mature tree left standing in the Old Town. I believe a new approach to gardening is springing up in many parts of the country, though it will be years before you will persuade someone like Cumming that it is not all a plot to rob him of his livelihood and spoil his ground.'

'I was mildly surprised to hear the Minister speak in favour of planting,' said Urquhart. 'I had expected opposition.'

'In some things he seems a forward-thinking and enlightened man,' agreed Middleton. 'But I cannot agree with him about the Bartlat case. The oath of purgation should not be used lightly, and in a case so long forgotten it seems at best inappropriate.'

'Agreed. But it is many years since the oath was taken in public. It will be a solemn occasion and one which might prove a salutary warning to many. I suspect it is that, rather than personal punishment for the hapless pair, which forms our Minister's motive.'

And if it was as the Mediciner suggested, the Minister must have been entirely satisfied. For Bartlat took the solemn oath of purgation, on bended knees before the congregation and in the presence of the woman who accused him, at the close of the morning service on November 29, 1700. Margery Montgomery was there, with the other indwellers, to hear it and the solemn words sent a shiver through her soul.

'I, Andrew Bartlat being charged by the kirk Session of Old Machar and Presbytery of Aberdeen . . . knowing that I am bound to Glorify God by a humble confession of the said sin if I were guilty . . . do therefore in the presence of the Great and Dreadful Majesty of the Eternal Everliving and Everblessed God the searcher of hearts, in the presence of his holy angels and of you his people assembled in his Sanctuary humbly upon my knees with my hand uplifted to heaven protest and swear by the holy and dreadful name of the Lord Jehovah the only true God and as I shall be answerable unto his Majesty in that great and terrible day wherein he shall judge the world . . . that I never committed the said abominable sin . . .'

Margery felt the skin at the back of her neck prickle with fear and knew that she could never go through such an ordeal herself. God himself was there, the searcher of hearts, and must know already which of the two was forsworn. At any moment one of them must be struck dead before them all.

'. . . I take God to record upon my soul my truth and sincerity herein . . . to pursue me with the everlasting fire of his wrath here and hereafter if I be not free and innocent in this matter . . .'

But at the end of the oath the man still knelt, untouched. He must have told the truth and the woman lied. Margery looked at her closed and frightened face. How could the woman bear it?

'Are you all right?' whispered Christian. 'You look very pale. You are not going to faint, are you?'

Margery shook her head.

'Then cheer up. It's not you out there on the block.'

But in some strange, confused way Margery knew that it was.

In December the news came. The Darien Venture had failed, catastrophically and utterly and beyond all hope of rescue. There were horrifying tales of disease and famine far worse than Scotland had ever inflicted on her people, of pitiless rains and steaming, fever-ridden jungles, of Spanish attacks on the crumbling ramparts which surrounded the pitiful palmetto huts of the settlement, and of worse enemies within: drunkenness, blasphemy, quarrelling, greed . . . The tales grew in the telling till the vision was of a vast and howling Hell . . . But beyond the hysterical exaggerations and the horror, the facts stood tall and stark and unequivocal. All the money invested was lost and the Company had called in three-quarters of the amount pledged, the Company's nine ships were either sunk or abandoned, and two thousand settlers had perished.

It was a bitter blow to Scotland and in spite of the King's offers of help to repair the country's financial ruin, many laid the blame squarely on their English neighbours. The English had opposed the venture from the start. They had done all they could to ensure its failure. English treachery had killed the settlers and stolen Scotland's money.

'Perhaps,' said Urquhart wearily. 'But casting blame will not repair our losses or bring back our dead. Besides, I cannot help thinking that Darien was not the healthiest location to choose for the venture, nor even the most appropriate for trade.'

'So you said at the time,' said Middleton. 'I do not like these tales of civil disorders either. It sounds to me as if there was a lack of the right kind of leadership as well as of foresight.'

'I wonder what became of the Cumming boy?' said the Mediciner. 'If ever he finds his way back to the Burgh he should have tales enough to tell to keep himself in free ale for the rest of his life.'

'If he returns. They say that of all the seamen, soldiers and settlers a mere three hundred survived. He may of course be one of them, but he may be no more than an unmarked grave in a Darien swamp.' As might his nephews, he thought sadly. So far the family had heard no news.

'There will be trouble,' said Urquhart, sipping his brandy thoughtfully. 'There is talk of giving the crown to the Electress Sophia of Hanover. William has not long to go now, and even supposing Anne succeeds him, she is childless.'

'And that will make several people's minds stray across the ocean. Was that your implication?' asked Middleton carefully. The Mediciner was his friend, yet it was well known that he supported the new order and held no sympathy with those 'sentimentalists' as he called them who yearned after the old.

'Aye. James Stuart has his supporters yet. And it will be many a year before they see sense and accept the inevitable.'

'Union?'

'Of course. Economically, socially, politically, intellectually, it is the obvious way. Can you not see it, man? It is our only hope of prosperity, and at the moment England is certainly the only hope we have of pulling ourselves up from bankruptcy.'

Middleton was silent. It would be a long time before any of them would be solvent again, but at least the harvest had been good. There would be meal enough for the winter months and good seed for the spring planting. There would need to be economies, but somehow they would survive.

'There's not the money there was,' grumbled Christian. 'And when the College closes for the summer, we'll lose a lot of custom. We must be sure and find a place for you, Margery, then at least one of us will be secure. But it must be a good place, with prospects. I'll not let you go just anywhere, so you leave it to me.'

At the Whitsun hiring fair many girls offered themselves for hire. Margery was shy and young and she limped, but under the Minister's observing eye several offers were made for her too. Christian, however, drove a hard bargain. She would not let her stepdaughter go here for one reason, there for another, until in the late afternoon Mrs Middleton arrived. Mrs Middleton was seeking a replacement kitchen-maid, the previous girl having left to better herself. Christian snapped up the offer.

'The Middletons' is a good house, Margery. You'll be comfortable there and it's not too far away. Do as you're told and they'll be kind to you. The master is a good man. The mistress is a wee bit strict, perhaps, but kindly at heart. You'll come to no harm. And you'll learn something, too, which will stand you in good stead when you want to look around again next year. She trains her maids well.'

So Margery moved out of Christian's ale-house and into the Middletons' kitchen, where she slept under the dresser at a wage of £5 a year and a pair of shoes so that she might go decently clad to the kirk. She found one other servant in the kitchen, Jean Catto the cook.

'She's a proper tartar, the mistress,' Jean Catto informed the girl. 'But you do as you're told and you'll do right enough. The thing to remember is this – never let her see you idle. If you hear her coming, pick up the besom and sweep the hearth, or grab at the spindle. Anything that looks busy. Remember that and you'll do fine.'

'Thank you,' said Margery nervously. She was a little overawed by her new position and even more so by the huge figure of the cook with her beefy forearms and her black moustache. Jean Catto was fifty.

'Twenty years I've been here,' she told Margery cheerfully, 'and I'll not find another place now. I'll drop dead in the broze one morning and that'll be the end of big Jeannie, but I'll have a good run for my money. Have a sup?'

She offered the luggie to Margery, who took it politely and drank.

'Nay, lass, drink deep while you can. It's little enough they pay us so we're entitled to our ale. Sup up, and I'll find you a wee bittie raspberry conserve to take with your piece. I have it put by, you know.' She winked largely. 'For emergencies!'

She pulled out a peat from the elaborately constructed stack, reached into the cavity and drew out a small jar.

'There you are. Jeannie's reinforcements!' She spooned two generous heaps on to the trencher and replaced the jar in its hiding-place. 'Say nothing, mind,' she warned the girl, 'and eat up quick before the mistress comes. The old harridan will be down presently to make sure we're not idling. Yon's a rare tartar,' she added a few minutes later, licking thick lips reminiscently. 'But she's nay a bad wee body, when you get to know her.'

To Margery, such a comment on her new mistress was close to blasphemy. Dutifully she ate the conserve but she expected to be struck by an avenging thunderbolt at any minute, or at the least to hear the door open behind her and the mistress's voice damn her to perdition for theft, duplicity and fraud.

'Margery!' The girl jumped so that her teeth jarred against the rim of the mug. She scrambled hastily to her feet, trembling.

'Can you sew?'

'A little, madam.'

'Here is linen and thread. Stitch me a seam. And do not worry, child, if it is not perfect. I will teach you myself when I see your proficiency. I chose you, Margery, in spite of your lameness, because I believe you to be an honest, hard-working girl and because I knew your mother.'

'Yes, madam,' said Margery in surprise. Her mother had died when she was born and she had rarely heard her mentioned. She would have liked to ask Mrs Middleton more, but she dared not. Instead she took the square of white linen, folded it as her mistress directed and began carefully to sew her seam.

Mrs Middleton was pleased. 'Good,' she said approvingly. 'Now I will show you how I want it to be done and you will watch. Then I shall expect you to do it *exactly* as I do.'

'Yes, madam.' Behind Mrs Middleton's back Jeannie pulled a wry face, but Margery was unperturbed. If nothing more difficult was to be required of her, she need not fear. She watched intently while her mistress stitched a neat, small seam of tiny stitches, repeated the process exactly, and was rewarded with warm commendation, and the request to accompany her mistress upstairs to assist in the mending of the household linen.

In the months that followed Margery learned everything her mistress taught her, and was such a quick and willing pupil that Mrs Middleton was delighted.

'I knew you were a good girl,' she said on one occasion, 'but I really had no idea you were such an intelligent one. See, Isobel, how beautifully Margery has mended James' shirt for me. One can hardly see the stitches, and her currant wine is every bit as good as yours, my dear.'

Isobel looked up from her book, a treatise on the New Testament, and smiled with gentle kindness. She wore small gold-rimmed glasses now, like her father's. 'I am glad,' she said. 'Now that Margrat has left us, we need a pair of good young eyes. Mine, as you know, are fit for nothing but the largest print.'

'I wonder . . .' Mrs Middleton looked speculatively at Margery. 'Can you read?'

'A little, madam.'

'You are a good girl. You work quickly and well. When your spinning is done, Isobel shall teach you for an hour each day until you can read fluently. Would you like that?'

'Oh yes, madam!'

So when Margery had finished her work of scrubbing and sweeping, baking and brewing, mending and spinning and polishing, she sat for an hour with Isobel Middleton and proved an able pupil.

By the end of the year she was writing the accounts at Isobel's dictation and fulfilling many similar tasks.

'She is such a help to me,' explained Isobel to her mother, 'and it saves my poor eyes. Besides, I never ask her unless I know her work for you is done.'

By the end of her first year at the Middletons Margery could bake, brew better ale than Christian, make soap and candles, produce several different conserves and even concoct simple medicines from herbs. She could salt down fish and beef, make cheeses, syllabubs and bread. In fact any dish that Jeannie made, Margery made better. But big Jeannie showed no jealousy.

'You learn what you can, lass,' she said, 'and at the next hiring fair you can state your own price. I reckon you could ask £10 a year and get it, no bother. I'm too old to learn new tricks now. I'm content to jog along to the mistress's tune and I'll stay here till I die – if she'll have me – but you could get a kitchen of your own and servants under you. You might even get one of the big houses

– Invercauld or Mar. The Master is a good man. He'll put in a good word for you.'

'But I don't want to go, Jeannie. I like it here. Besides, there is Christian . . .'

Christian was increasingly a worry. Now that Margery had lived so long apart from her stepmother, in the quiet, clean efficiency of the Middleton household, she saw Christian with new eyes on the days when Jeannie sent her for an hour or two to visit the house in the Close. At first, Christian had kept the place as clean as Margery could wish. She paid one of the Crystal girls to help her out, and worked cheerfully and hard. But as the ale-house became established, Christian began to let things slip. The flagstones were stained and greasy, the ale-cups unwashed. The Crystal girl no longer came. Christian said she had got rid of the idle baggage to save her money and her temper.

'Always slacking, she was, and stealing the ale. I'm better off without her.'

But Margery had heard it whispered that the girl's father had removed her and refused to let her go back to 'yon drunken midden'. Certainly on several occasions when Margery arrived in the evening she found the nightsoil still unemptied from the previous day. Increasingly a sour smell hung about the place, a pungent odour compounded of old ale, urine and vomit, and the midden at the door mounted higher and stood unswept for days on end. When Margery ventured to suggest that cleanliness might be better for trade, Christian laughed aloud.

'They come for the ale and the company, lass, not for the colour of the floor. And there's stink enough in the town already. Why bother about a bit more?'

'The town officers will fine you if you let the midden grow too rank.'

'Then I'll find someone to shift it before they do. What's wrong with a bit of muck anyway?'

Margery did not answer, but busied herself quietly with putting things to rights as best she could in the short time she had to spare from the Middletons' kitchen. Christian did not even thank her.

'Leave it, lass,' she would say. 'We don't need your lady's manners here. Do as I do and enjoy yourself while you can.' She laughed and flung her arms wide. 'What's life for if you can't laugh?'

Christian certainly seemed more reckless and wild these days.

She drank too much, for one thing, and she was growing careless. Once she appeared before the Session on a charge of scandalous converse. She was not only drunk to excess, they said, which is most scandalous in women, but she had been seen to mount the forestair to her bedroom with a man and to close the door. She was fined and censured and remained unrepentant.

'Let them fine me,' she told Margery when the girl ventured to suggest a little discretion. 'I'm making good money now and I can afford it. It's worth £4 to have a good time once in a while.'

'Can you not persuade her, Adam?' asked Margery later as they left the ale-house together, she to return to the Middleton kitchen and he to go home. 'I am worried that if she continues in this openly reckless way she will do herself harm.'

Adam agreed. 'Christian always had a wild streak and a disrespect for authority. I will do my best, but I am not always there.' He stopped until the coughing passed. 'Some days I am weak and have not the spirits for the ale-house jollity. Besides, John Garden is a wild one, too, and he eggs her on. Last week they were dancing on the tables together while James played the penny whistle. It was harmless enough then, but you know what such things can lead to.'

'Watch her for me, Adam,' said Margery, laying a hand on his arm. 'Please?'

'I will do what I can.' They were at the Middletons' house now and Adam waited with her while Jeannie fumbled with the lock to let her in. 'When will I see you again?'

'I do not know. It is not always easy to get away.'

'Please try, Margery, very soon.'

She blushed at the warmth in his voice, but before she could answer Jeannie pulled her inside and closed the door.

'What did that loon want with you, then?' she demanded, arms akimbo. 'And don't tell me he was asking you the time.'

'He was saying goodnight, that is all.'

'When a lad says goodnight in a voice like that, it's time to watch out. Now you mark me, Margery my girl, you're young and you're pretty and with that leg of yours you can't get away as fast as some. Take care. And don't say I didn't warn you.'

Margery smiled affectionately at her fellow-servant. 'It's kind of you to think of me, Jeannie, but there's really no need to worry. I am not interested in any of them.'

'Don't you believe it. Every girl's interested, though there's some pretend they're not. They're usually the ones in no danger, but you're not one of them. You're old enough and pretty enough and ready. I've seen the way young master James looks at you, and I've sent him packing more than once with a flea in his lug for good measure.'

Indeed, when Margery first joined the household James had been an embarrassment to her. His eyes had followed her everywhere, but he never spoke, and on the few occasions when it was necessary for her to speak to him, he blushed scarlet and stammered. He was brave only in the company of friends and when fortified by ale. On more than one occasion at Christian's he had embarrassed her by clumsy attempts at flirtation, but at home he had not the courage to speak a word to her. Jeannie had noticed.

'Master James is meek enough,' she said now, 'but there's others bolder and I'll not always be around to see them off. So you mind what I say and take care.'

'I will, Jeannie.'

'Now get to bed or you'll not have time to shut your eyes before the mistress'll be bawling at you to open them again.'

'It is true though,' thought Margery sleepily. 'I am not interested, even in Adam though he is kind and true. There will be no one for me until I know for certain if George will come back.'

'Have you had any news of that boy of yours, Cumming?' asked Middleton at the meeting of the Council.

'None.' Cumming had not forgiven George for defying him in the kirkyard that December day three years ago. When the boy did come back, there would be matters to settle privately between them.

'They say a number of the lustier lads were captured by the Spaniards and sold for slaves,' said Urquhart. 'At least those have a chance of coming home one day.'

'And many of the settlers made their way safely to our shores,' said Baillie Baxter. 'Though not all immediately to their homes. The Principal's own nephew returned only last week, is that not so?'

Middleton nodded, but his face was grave. Two of his sister's sons had sailed for Darien.

'Your George may well be sampling the life of London,' went on Baxter, 'or some foreign port, before returning home. It is not often a young man gets the chance to see such places.'

'Or an old one either,' snapped Cumming. 'But that's no reason for staying away.'

'You'll hear something of him one day, Cumming,' said Middleton. 'He is not the sort of lad to give in lightly and he is a good tradesman. He can earn a living wherever he goes.'

'Aye,' said Kenneth Fraser. 'Not like some who do nothing but drink and shout and disturb honest folk in their beds.'

'If you are referring to my students,' said the Principal, 'I can assure you that they are all safely locked inside the College by nine o'clock.'

'That's as may be. But they make enough noise on the way there. That Grant woman's place is a scandal and a disgrace. We all know it's not a year past that public sessions and penny bridals were prohibited, yet I'll swear that woman has let her house to scores at a time for the very purpose. She should be made to pay for it.'

'Aye,' agreed Cumming, 'and be banished before she corrupts every youth in the place.'

'Take care, Cumming. That is a serious charge and were we not protected by the four walls of the Council chamber, you might be required to pay the penalty for slander.'

'Oddsfish!' roared Cumming, slamming his fist on the table. 'You make me sick with your "might be's" and your "take cares". Sin is sin whether there is evidence or not. And if you can't see it you're a blind hypocrite.'

The Principal looked at him coldly over gold-rimmed spectacles. 'May I remind you that we are not here to discuss sin, but the question of a new tolbooth?'

'And we'll need it, too, to house the drunkards and the whores from that Grant woman's place.'

'And you too, Cumming, if you don't keep your mouth shut,' snapped George Fraser. Before the blacksmith could reply, Middleton said quickly, 'If you cannot control yourself, George Cumming, the Council requires you to leave.'

'And let you settle the tolbooth business behind my back? When it's practically in my own kale-yard?'

'Then kindly control your temper and your tongue.'

The blacksmith subsided into angry silence. There had been enough argument already about the siting of the new tolbooth and he did not want to miss anything.

'Three rooms should be sufficient,' went on Middleton. 'The lowest for thieves, the next for other prisoners and the third for the bell and clock. Kenneth Fraser will consult with his masons about design and cost, and we will hear his report at the next meeting.'

'There are still loose stones aplenty in the kirkyard,' said George Fraser. 'The stones of the great tower have found their way into many a building in the town and will supply many more before they are done.'

'I will draw up a formal request to the Session,' said William Christie, making a note in his careful script.

'There will have to be a subscription, I suppose?' said Urquhart wearily. It was yet another call upon resources already sorely strained. Six months ago they had sent a petition to the Lords of Committee about the heavy tax roll imposed on the town, but to no apparent effect. The tax still had to be paid and Urquhart's share could ill be spared.

'I will give thirty pounds,' announced Baillie Baxter, who had signed the petition to the Lords of Committee too but who seemed unaffected by their lack of response. Baxter's resources, it was well known, were multifarious and healthy. Now he smiled benignly upon his less fortunate fellows. 'I trust you will all follow my example?'

There was a moment's wary silence. Everyone knew that Baxter could well afford ten times thirty pounds, but there were many present who would be hard put to it to find a quarter that amount.

'I'll give the same,' said George Fraser with obvious reluctance.

'And I.' 'And I.' 'And I.' The response was halting and cautious, but it came.

'On my humble salary I cannot venture to pledge more than a mere twelve pounds,' said William Christie, 'which sum, however, I gladly give.'

'Sanctimonious hypocrite,' said Middleton to the Mediciner as they walked home together. 'He'll choke himself one day on his own virtue.'

'He is a conscientious teacher, nevertheless. When we inspected the school in the summer you will remember his pupils performed most creditably.'

'Talking of pupils, my wife tells me young Margery Montgomery has a remarkably quick understanding. Isobel has taught her to read and to keep simple household accounts.'

'Really? I have always had an interest in that child – purely scientific, I assure you, but she and her father were so obviously unusual. He had creative brilliance and she . . . It is too early to tell of course, but she seems to have a natural if untaught intelligence.'

'Yes.' The Principal hesitated. 'Tell me, do you think it morally right to give a person tastes and appetites for which her life can promise no fulfilment?'

'You mean is it wrong to teach her when she is destined to a life of domestic service, either paid, with you, or unpaid with a husband?'

'Exactly. I can see no other future for her. And will the husband she is likely to find approve of learning in a wife? My own wife laughs at my fears as nonsense, and declares she is only training the girl to be a good housekeeper, yet I am uneasy.'

'It is an interesting point. But if the girl has the capabilities, one could argue it is your moral duty to tend and encourage them as you would a precious plant.'

'And if that plant is destined one day to be put out into the winter cold?'

'One should so strengthen the plant before that time that it may stand alone and survive.'

'The moral duty to improve my own potential, I accept. The moral duty to interfere with another's, I dispute.'

'To interfere, perhaps, but you cannnot dispute the moral duty to help those in need of help and to guide those in need of guidance.'

'But if guidance is imposed unasked for and help given when unrequested, surely that becomes interference?'

They had reached the door of the Principal's house now and stopped.

'Come inside,' said Middleton, 'and we will continue the discussion over a dram.'

'With the greatest pleasure. I shall be interested to hear you develop the theme of interference in my own area of medicine.'

The two men passed inside, still deep in a discussion the original subject of which was already forgotten.

Margery sat at the kitchen table, reading by the light of a single tallow candle. Jeannie was already asleep, on the truckle bed she pulled out at nights from under the table. Margery's own blanket was waiting for her, warming at the fireside, though there was little enough heat now that the peats had been turned and the fire banked for the night. The water in the washing pail had a thin skin of ice and her breath clung in a fine mist about her face. Her fingers as she turned the pages were numb, but she hardly noticed. She was reading a book which Isobel Middleton had lent her *The Principal Navigations, Voyages, Traffiques and Discoveries of the English Nation, made by sea or over land to the remote and farthest distant quarters of the Earth* and searching for any mention of the Americas or the Darien coast. Once she rose to take the blanket and wrap it around her shoulders. It was raining now and cold, but she did not close the book until the candle was quite burnt out and there was no more light.

The rain had been falling steadily for weeks. In the daytime the ground steamed with the heat, and at night the raindrops beat on the leaves of the rain trees with a noise like many drums. George Cumming had never seen such rain – or such trees. They towered thick and high for mile after mile after mile. From the hammock in Hugh Baird's hut the glistening, shield-like leaves seemed to close around him on every side, and the stems of the creepers which festooned the branches swayed like imprisoning ropes. Or like the fishing nets hung to dry on the Links at home.

Home . . . tears of weakness stung his eyes. He tried to raise a hand to brush them away, but had not the strength. His arm was no more than bone and skin.

'How are you now?' Hugh Baird raised George's head and held a mug to his lips. 'Drink this, Andreas's wife made it for you. It will do you good.' He turned his head and said to someone, 'Fetch more.'

In the shadows at the back of the hut a small figure moved on silent, obedient feet. The leaf-fronds, which hung across the doorway to discourage the flies, stirred and were still.

'The Spaniards . . .' said George weakly.

'The Spaniards are gone,' said Hugh patiently, as he had said many times in the months that George had been ill. 'They made a truce with our people and allowed them to leave unmolested. They let them take food and weapons for their journey and they let them go free. You should have sailed with the others,' he added gently. 'Only you were too obstinate to admit defeat, my friend. And too ill to see it when it met you face to face.'

'But my building . . . my houses . . .'

'Are no longer needed. The settlers are gone. And you should have gone with them. This land is not for you. When you are well, you too must go.'

'How?' George had not the strength even to think for himself any more.

'It will not be easy. If the Spaniards find you they will take you for a slave. But we will find a way.'

George lay back wearily, closed his eyes and waited for the girl to appear. She was always the same girl, dark-eyed and strong, and she held out her arms to him, calling, but he could not hear the words.

'Please God,' he prayed, 'if I do not die, let me go home.'

It was two years now since the Mediciner's wife had died. She was buried in the Cheyne aisle and the bells were rung. The bells were rung again that year for the death of the King and the accession of Queen Anne. But Queen Anne was childless and everyone knew her reign was no more than a stopgap. A confrontation between the English Parliament and the Scottish Estates seemed inevitable.

Two years later the Estates formally declared their determination to choose their own sovereign – and it did not take much imagination to know who that sovereign would be – unless England guaranteed them the security and privileges they required. The idea of political Union was brought out and examined afresh, and the wrangling went on, with neither side prepared to make the concessions the other required.

'Political Union is inevitable,' said the Mediciner wearily. 'Why don't they accept the fact and save their breath?'

'Because,' said Middleton carefully, 'there are still men whose loyalties lie first and foremost with their rightful Stuart king.'

'Blind loyalty,' said the Mediciner, 'based on sentiment, not sense. If those men were honest, they would recognize their feelings as nothing more than over-emotional patriotism for a country that needs alliance with its neighbour to survive. You saw how the famine years decimated the population and sucked the land dry. You saw how the Darien venture finished the work the famine began and emptied the country's coffers of every last bawbee. You must see that we need alliance with England before we can even begin to put our domestic accounts in order.'

Middleton forbore to argue. He recognized the value of prudence even in the company of a friend and colleague such as Urquhart. The subject of the exiled Stuart king was not one to be broached lightly in these uncertain times, and certainly not in the ingrown community of the Burgh with its enmities and its feuds and its petty jealousies. Those who felt as he did held their discussions and expressed their hopes in private. So in answer to Urquhart's argument, Middleton merely said, 'Talking of accounts,

I hear that Cumming is spreading some scurrilous rumour about the financing of the new tolbooth.'

'Aye. He demands that the town and trades be allowed to inspect the records of all subscriptions, expenses and disbursements relating to the building.'

'A fair enough request. If there is any unfair profit-making – and we all remember the Cathedral tower scandal – then it ought to be made public. If all is well it will do nobody any harm to put the accounts on display, and it might at least still wagging tongues. The tolbooth is a fine building and one the town can be proud of. Will you take another dram?'

'Thank you.' The two men were in the Principal's room in the College, a pleasant panelled room with an air of quiet scholarship, given as much by the tranquil view of the quadrangle and library which his window afforded, as by the many leather-bound volumes which filled the shelves and lay open on the desk.

'I hear the call to Mr Corse to be assistant Minister is to go through after all,' said Urquhart when his host had replenished the glass.

'Yes. We must avoid a repetition of those lawless years with no one in charge, and Mr Thomson is grown increasingly infirm, and since his wife died, sadly spiritless.'

The Mediciner nodded. 'It is a sad thing to lose a wife after so many years together. One cannot help but feel spiritless. Believe me, George, I know.'

Patrick Urquhart was still stricken by his wife's loss, but his son Adam, now as then, was strangely calm.

'She has gone before me,' he told Margery quietly. 'But it will not be long before I see her again.'

'Don't talk like that, Adam,' said the girl anxiously. 'You know you have been better lately and if you go to the country as you did last year and take the goat's milk again, you will come back in the autumn whole and refreshed.'

'No, Margery, not whole. I can never be whole. I know that now.' He finished on a cough. The spasm lasted so long that Margery was concerned.

'Let me take the basket, Adam. Please.'

It was the Middletons' spring washing week and Margery had spread the linen on the grass at the back of the College to dry. The trees in the College grounds were still leafless and a fresh wind blew from the sea, but though it held the smell of seaweed and wet sand and fish, there was no trace of the haar which so often smothered the town in dank vapour in the winter months. The sky was ice-cold but clear, and the air dry.

Margery was sixteen now and as Christian had predicted, she was beautiful, with the quiet, self-contained beauty of a madonna in a painting. Even when she moved, her limp did not detract from the image but in some strange way added to it. Adam Urquhart had loved her now, hopelessly, for what seemed eternity. She had been moving across the grass, collecting the crisp sheets and petticoats and shifts, folding them neatly and placing them in her basket, when Adam had found her and insisted on carrying her load.

'I saw you from the College window,' he confessed. 'I should be working, but . . .' He stopped and said quickly. 'I have so little time. Why waste it on the dry dust of learning when I can be outside with you?'

'I do not find learning "dry",' said Margery. 'When I read I move into another, pictured world.'

'This world is all I ask for,' said Adam earnestly. 'I have it for so short a time. My mother had a long life, with time for love and many children. She was forty-six and ready to die. But I . . .'

'Don't talk like that, Adam. You will live for many years yet!' But when she looked at his cadaverous face and dark, unnaturally brilliant eyes she felt a painful compassion.

'Give me the basket, Adam,' she repeated gently. 'I am strong enough and it will only make you cough.'

'Yes, you are strong, Margery. Sweet and gentle and strong. It is odd, isn't it?' he went on, moving at her side as she went from patch to patch. 'You are so much younger than I am and have been lame all your life, and yet when I am with you I feel safe.'

When Margery did not answer, he went on, 'Do you ever think of death, Margery?'

'No.' It was not strictly true, for she often thought of the hundred deaths that might have overtaken George, but never of her own. 'Death is inevitable. Why think of it? You did not think about your birth before it happened.'

'Perhaps I did and have forgotten? But there is so much to lose by death.'

'And so much to gain. Or do you not believe in heaven?'

'I suppose so, but . . . what I want is here, in this place, in this town, *now*. Will you walk with me tonight, Margery?' he added urgently, as she packed the last garment into her basket and moved towards the path which led by the College dyke to the High Street.

'No, Adam. It will be dark before my work is done. I will have to press all this linen and then there will be more. If the weather holds fine, Mrs Middleton means to wash the blankets and there will be extra soap to make.'

'Then let me help you gather the heather for the ley,' said Adam eagerly.

'It is already gathered and the ashes made.'

'Then will you be at Christian's soon? I must see you somehow and I dare not come to your kitchen and beard that dreadful Jeannie.'

Margery laughed. 'She is a dear, kind-hearted soul and means no harm.'

'Perhaps. But the sight of that scarlet forearm brandishing her ladle, and that bristling black moustache, would rout a band of the toughest Highlandmen, let alone a timid, godfearing student such as I.'

'And she is right. As a timid, godfearing student, you have no business to come after your Principal's maid.'

'That is nonsense, Margery, and you know it. You and I are equals in the eyes of God. And in my eyes, too. I must see you soon, Margery. Please?'

'The town is small,' said Margery lightly, 'and I am sure to see you before long – if only at the kirk on Sunday – or at Christian's,' she added swiftly as she saw how his expression saddened at the mention of the kirk. 'There will be a party as usual for the end of term and Mrs Middleton has said that I might help.'

In fact, her mistress had said she would not dream of letting Margery go to an ale-house full of drunken students, but Margery knew she would win permission in the end. She was beginning at last to have an idea of her own worth, and Christian after all was her stepmother.

'Then if I am to wait till then, I will,' said Adam. They were almost at the High Street now, where there would be people and animals and all the humdrum bustle of a normal day. But here, beside the College dyke, there were only the two of them on the grassy path. The grass was pale and sparse after the winter cold and the ground soft with mud. Above them a blackbird sang on a leafless tree. He took her hand and said quickly, 'But you must give me something to make the waiting bearable.'

'Must?' she repeated. 'Where is the obligation?'

'Here,' he said and kissed her on the lips. Before she could move away he kissed her again, more slowly and deeply, till she broke away, breathless. From the street nearby came the sound of voices and a woman's laughter. To Margery they were sounds from another world. Her heart was pounding in her breast and her pulse racing and the ache, deep in her body, was sweet . . .

'No, Adam, you mustn't!'

'Why not, when I love you? Please, Margery, do not make me wait too long. Too long may be too . . . late.'

'That is not fair, Adam,' said Margery quietly. He was instantly contrite.

'You are right. Why should you or any girl take a lover who will die within the year?' He turned his back on her and walked away.

'That is not what I meant,' cried Margery. 'Please!' She dropped the basket and ran after him, pleading. 'I only meant,' she cried, clinging to his arm, 'that it is not fair to buy my love by threatening your death.'

'Buy? Then you do not love me?' His voice was very quiet.

'I . . . do not know.' She turned away in confusion. If only the image of George did not always rise between them. George was gone. If he was not already dead, he must be married by now. Either way he was lost to her for ever. Adam raised her chin and looked into her eyes.

'If you do not know,' he said softly, 'I will wait until you do. Give me your hand. Walk with me as far as the street.'

Gladly Margery placed the basket on one hip and walked with Adam, hand in hand, past the College dyke to the corner. Happiness trilled inside her like the song of the blackbird overhead. One day, she knew now, she would go to Adam. One day. . . .

'There's that Montgomery girl again,' said one of the women at the market cross. 'Chasing after the Urquhart boy as usual.'

'Good luck to her,' said the Sledder woman. 'She'll find no other man to take her.'

'She's pretty though.'

'Aye. On the outside. You didn't know her father. She's the devil's spawn, that one.'

The other woman lowered her voice and looked quickly over her shoulder. 'Will you be at Christian's tomorrow? Upstairs?'

'Aye. And you?'

'Are you sure she can do it?'

'She can do it. But let no one see you go. Mind, now!'

'I'll mind. And I'll be there.'

'Drink up, everyone!' called Christian. 'Out you go. The curfew sounded long ago.'

'You wouldn't turn us out into the cold, Christian, would you?' wheedled John Garden. 'On the last day of the Session?'

'It's as good a day as any.' But of course, it wasn't. Many of the students would be going back to their homes in the country, others would be leaving the College for good, and her ale-house gatherings would be sadly depleted. 'Go on with you, you great gowk!' she added, laughing, as he seized her hand and kissed it passionately, moving from hand to wrist and upwards. 'I'll not be rid of you, John Garden, for many a month. Get on home with you while you can still stand.'

'Who says I can?' He raised his ale-cup and drank it dry. 'Or want to? Fill up, lass, and let's make a night of it. Give us a tune, Jamie! The party's just begun.'

Someone thrust a whistle into James Middleton's hands and he began to play, unsteadily at first, but more strongly as the familiar notes took over. There was singing and laughter and the stamping of many feet. Christian had to shout to make herself heard.

'The curfew bell has rung! You'll go now or I'll have the baillies after me! And after you too.'

Margery paused in her passage through the crowded room and waited, her hands laden. She was collecting what luggies she could prise from their owners' hands and stacking them in a dripping heap on the pot-shelf. But already some had disappeared again and she more than half suspected someone had helped himself at the barrel. It would be hard work shifting them tonight. When Christian gave the word, she would have to go for the Baillie. Perhaps she ought to go now? Someone put an arm around her waist with the boldness of drink. When she protested and pulled away, he thrust a hand up her skirt and clumsily fondled her bare thigh. The whistling had stopped now, but the singing continued, and the shouting. James Middleton laughed. She pulled away and flung the slops from the mugs at her tormentor's head. Then someone punched him full in the face. It was hard to see what happened next, except that Adam Urquhart was somewhere in the centre of it while John Garden stood on a bench, a luggie in each hand, alternately roaring encouragement and singing snatches of an obscene song to which he had added the chorus of 'Lovely hopping Maggie'. Everyone else seemed to be fighting.

Christian was slumped on a bench against the wall, her legs spread and her head flung back, laughing till the tears ran down her scarlet cheeks.

Margery forced her way to the door through plucking, thrusting hands. Behind her, above the noise, a voice called after her to come back. She opened the door enough to squeeze through and slammed it behind her. The Close was black and silent. There was no moon and the haar, which had rolled into the town from the sea, masked both outline and sound. A dank and misted blur hung motionless over mud already glinting with frost.

Margery looped her skirts in one hand and hurried for the High Street. She must fetch the Baillie, quick, before Christian got herself into real trouble. Behind her in the Close the door opened again. Light slashed the mist and was as quickly cut off. Stumbling footsteps sounded behind her, their dull echo muffled by the mist and narrow walls. Margery dropped her skirts and hurried faster, skimming the soft ground with light, quick steps in spite of her limp. The footsteps quickened behind her, drawing closer. A voice called, 'Come back, Maggie lass. I didn't mean it.'

At the place where the wynd met the High Street she turned right and ran for the cross and Baillie Knight's house. The High Street was in darkness, her follower close behind her now. A hand caught at her dress, her sleeve. 'Maggie . . . please . . .'

She turned and faced him firmly. 'It is no good. I must fetch the Baillie or Christian will be in trouble.'

'Please, Maggie. Don't spoil everything. It's our last night and . . . you are . . . so lovely.' He lurched against her and she pulled quickly away.

'Go home, Master James, before you get into trouble.'

'You're cold, Margery Montgomery. You always were cold. Cold and scornful. But you're no better than anyone else. You're no better than Christian and she . . . she is kind to me. Always.' He grabbed at her hand. 'I want you to be kind to me now.'

Margery tried to pull her hand away. 'Go on home,' she said again, 'and bathe that swollen eye. I'll come in a minute.'

'Don't want to go home.' He fell against her, breathing heavily now. 'Want to stay with you.'

Margery was beginning to be frightened. The street was black and empty, the mist masking even the faint chink of candlelight from shutters, or the lantern near the ale-house at the cross. She put out a hand behind her and felt the stone cold with freezing fog.

'Just a little way further,' she said carefully. 'Then we will go home together.' She moved away, her hand on the wall, the darkness closing all around her and his bemused and anxious face the only patch of light.

'Gi's a wee kissie first, Maggie, and be friends?'

She ignored him, quickening her step as he stumbled, pleading beside her.

'You've never been my friend, have you? It's always Adam, never me. And I love you too, Maggie. I do.'

Again she tried to shake him off, but she was panting now and breathless, her bare feet slipping and stumbling on the slimy cobbles of the street. His fingers found a grip and he was pulling at her, mumbling, 'I said give me a kiss.' He was growing angry now. 'Damn you, woman, as your master I order you!'

They were at the corner of a wynd now, but Margery had lost all sense of place in the darkness and could not remember which it was. But she had come a long way. It must be Baillie Knight's. She turned down between the high, blank walls and in a moment knew her mistake. For the walls were only the width of a house and after that was space and grass and mud thick underfoot. There were noises in the High Street now, shouting and people running, and close behind her, him. Even then she did not believe it and opened her mouth to scream, too late.

For a hand came from behind to close her mouth before she could cry out.

'I told you, Maggie,' he grunted in her ear. 'I want that kiss.'

He was mauling her bodice now, fumbling at her skirt. She twisted and pushed and fought, but his arms tightened till the breath was crushed from her body. Then her feet slipped from under her and she fell. She managed to scream, once, then the mud and the mist closed over her and his face blacked out the night.

Shutters opened up and down the street. Men came from doorways running. Baillie Knight appeared, correct and neat in black frock coat and periwig, as the noise swelled from Widow Irvine's Close.

The Baillie scanned the faces of the crowd, selected half a dozen men to help him and marched purposefully towards the heart of the commotion. The two bands met where the wynd joined the High Street and no one afterwards could say how the fray began, but students and indwellers fell upon each other with open glee and the hastily assembled baillies were powerless to stop them. Old scores were settled in the slipping dirt of cobblestones and middens, in the dim light of the haar and the lantern. When it was over, a dozen students and as many townsmen filled the new tolbooth, and every baillie in the town was there to see it and to take note.

No one remembered Christian Grant until much later. When Baillie Baxter took it upon himself to visit her and make the town's displeasure known, he found her sitting at the fire, meekly knitting. The room was neat and fresh, the hearthstone swept, the benches and tables in their places and their tops washed clean.

'Come in, Baillie,' said Christian as he stooped his head to enter the room. 'I sent Margery straightaway to fetch help. I knew you would come – sooner or later.'

His eyes darted suspiciously over the room. 'It was Baillie Knight she fetched, not me.'

'She did not like to trouble you with such a trivial affair,' said Christian solemnly. 'But now that you are come, I am honoured. Will you take a drink of my ale? I know it is not the half as good as yours, but it is all I have.'

'Thank you, no,' snapped Baillie Baxter. 'Where is the Montgomery girl?'

'At home, of course.'

'Then I take my leave. I merely wished to check that all is as it should be.'

'Interfering old fool!' said Christian the moment the door closed behind him. 'Pompous spavinned devil! May he rot in hell!'

There was a fumbling sound at the door and Adam Urquhart staggered in, coughing and clutching his chest. He was bleeding from a cut at the temple and his breeches were torn and filthy.

'Adam!' cried Christian, running to help him to a seat. 'What have they done to you?'

But he brushed aside her questions and demanded, 'Where is Margery?'

'Is she not gone home?'

'She was to meet me, here, after curfew.'

'Then she has changed her mind.' Christian soaked a rag in

warm water from the kettle and mopped at Adam's forehead. 'Keep still, will you, or you'll start the bleeding again.'

'She would not go back on her word. I know it! If they have caught her . .'

'Oddsfish, man! Hold still till I've done. You'll be no good to anyone with a bleeding pate.' But Christian had caught Adam's fear, and her fingers were impatient and clumsy as she scrubbed at the blood.

'Drink this!' she ordered, thrusting a mug of ale into his hand. 'I'll go and speak to Jeannie and make sure. Wait here.'

She was back in five minutes, her face grey and drawn. Adam did not need to ask. He pushed past her and out of the house, running.

Margery lay motionless, her eyes unblinking as she stared into the empty night. No stars. No moon. Only trailing mist across the void. And on her breast a man, asleep. His head was turned sideways now, lips slack and parted over a gentle snore which rose and fell like the distant sea. There was no other sound. She felt no fear now, nor anger. Only an aching pity, for herself, and for him and an overwhelming sense of the sadness of the world. She lifted a hand and touched his hair, lightly.

He grunted, stirred, rolled sideways on to the grass and slept again. Gently she disengaged her legs, pulled down her skirts and gently, very gently so as not to wake him, stood up. Then, deliberately, she turned her back on the town and walked due east, towards the sea.

It was Adam who found her. She was standing in the shallows, skirts looped in her hands while the waves endlessly sluiced her legs and thighs. Her face was calm, washed clean of all emotion. She had heard no sound for a long time but the soothing rhythm of the sea, endlessly cleansing, and the brushing of sand on the shore. Her whole body was numb: the cold had spread upwards till she felt green-cool from head to toe and clear as the icicles at the kitchen window. To the east the first faint light lay across the spine of the sea: a gull called lazily and rose upwards, drifting.

'Margery!' She turned her head at the sound of his voice.

'Margery, are you all right?' Then he saw her face. 'Oh my God!'

She walked slowly out of the water then, and came towards him.

'Who was it?' he demanded. His face was white and his whole body trembled.

She shook her head, helplessly. Then she flung her arms around his neck and buried her face in his chest. 'Oh Adam, I wish it had been you.'

But he forced her away, holding her at arm's length with a grip which hurt. '*Who was it?*'

'Please don't ask me, Adam,' she begged. 'But you're hurt!'

He brushed aside her sympathy and demanded again, 'Tell me who?'

'I cannot say.'

'Cannot? Or will not?'

She hesitated, then said quietly, '*May* not. Please, Adam. It was none of my choice and I believe, in spite of everything, that it was none of his. His father is a good man and a gentleman. He would be shamed.'

'And have not you been shamed?'

Margery did not answer. He would not understand, but she knew the real shame was yet to come. She hoped she would have the strength to bear whatever torments the town might inflict.

'Help me, Adam,' she said. 'I love you and I have no one else.' She stood straight and bleak and dry-eyed and more beautiful than ever, but there was a new containment about her which repelled him. He still loved her, with a yearning which tore at his heart, but when he looked at her now he no longer saw his own sweet lass in her simple drugget gown. He saw another man's woman.

As they walked back across the links towards the town, the tears stood in his eyes and he did not take her hand.

'I'll give you something,' said Christian. 'I can mix you a dose that never fails. Ask Isobel Sledder. Ask Alexander Crystal's silly wife. She bought some from me only last month and it worked like a charm. You'll lose the bairn, I guarantee it, and that'll be an end to the wagging, slanderous tongues.'

'Thank you, Christian, but I cannot do it.'

'There is no need to be afraid, Margery. You'll feel a little pain and you'll be sick enough, but it is only for a day or two. Then it will all be over. No one need know.'

'I can't.'

'Then you are more of a fool than I took you for,' snapped Christian. 'If you let that bastard child grow inside you, do you know what will happen to you? They'll hound you till you tell them who the father is and then they'll hound the pair of you. They'll make him marry you and he'll make your life hell on earth, and if he's married already, they'll make life hell for both of you, here at the kirk on the Sabbath, week after week after week. Think, lass! And do as I tell you.'

Margery stood up and moved restlessly about the room. They were in the upstairs chamber above the ale-house. Margery should have been in the Middletons' kitchen, shelling peas, but she had slipped away for half an hour, telling Jeannie that Christian was ailing and she was anxious about her.

Jeannie herself was anxious about Margery, who was increasingly pale and withdrawn. On the night of the rabble between the students and the townsfolk, the girl had not returned till the morning drum, saying she had spent the night at Christian's house because she was afraid to come home in the dark. Jeannie had not quite believed her, especially as Christian herself had been at the Middleton kitchen asking for Margery soon after curfew. But in spite of her probing questions, she had found out nothing. She was puzzled and hurt by Margery's reserve, and watched the girl constantly from sharp black eyes. Now she was beginning to suspect the cause. Another month and she would be sure – and so would madam, whose eyes were sharp as anyone's in detecting such matters. Jeannie resolved to speak to Margery outright when she returned. If it was as she suspected, then someone had wronged the girl and must be made to put things right.

'I can't do it, Christian,' said Margery. 'I know I can't. Whether by my choice or not, the child is mine and trusts me. How can I take his life away from him? That is God's province, not mine.'

'As like as not the child will die anyway. Mine did.'

'I know, Christian, I'm sorry.' Margery put an arm around her shoulders. 'But it was God's will. And if my child is born dead, that will be God's will, too. But I cannot meddle in His affairs. Believe me, Christian, I am terrified of what they might do to me, but the child must be born all the same. I must face the consequences as best I can. If only . . .'

'If only what?' sighed Christian in exasperation. She had been trying for weeks to persuade the girl, ever since that first night when Adam had brought her home, but now as then she made no headway. If only she would say who it was! Christian had a shrewd idea. She had seen who it was who had followed the girl from the ale-house that night, but when she had asked Margery outright the girl said only, 'Name no names. I shall never tell. I want only to forget.'

Christian knew she was beaten.

'If only what?' she snapped now, as Margery made no answer.

'If only Adam had not deserted me.' Her voice was expressionless and her face empty of emotion, but Christian heard the pain behind the simple statement.

'All men are pigs,' she said vehemently. 'You're well rid of him. Selfish, cowardly pigs the lot of them. They take what they want and at the first sign of trouble, they run.'

'Oh no!' cried Margery. 'It is not like that at all.'

'Then what is it like? You tell me. As far as I see it, he took what he wanted and left you.'

'You know it was not Adam, so why do you pretend it was? Or is it to trap me into saying the name?'

'But why not say it, lass? Tell the whole town the name of the evil devil and let him take his punishment. No matter if his father is a gentleman. The gentry have no divine right to do as they like and leave us to take the blame. Tell, lass, and I'll spit on the bastard myself. And as for that peely Urquhart boy, he's jealous someone got there before him and he's sulking.'

Without a word Margery walked out of the room and closed the door. Christian was crude and coarse and prejudiced, but in a cruelly hurtful way she was right. Though Adam was not sulking: he was mourning, as he told her, the lost innocence of their love.

'Are you pregnant?' demanded Jeannie as Margery came into the kitchen.

At the bluntness of the question, the girl's control shattered and the tears came. Jeannie held out her arms and Margery wept on her massive bosom till she could weep no more, while Jeannie held her like a child, rocking gently and murmuring, 'There, lass, there.'

At last Margery sat up, brushed her eyes with the back of her hands and smiled.

'Thank you, Jeannie. Now I shall be all right.'

'But you must tell me, Margery. It is for your own and everybody's good. Tell us who the man was, so that he may be punished and so that you both may be purified by confession and forgiven.' The Minister looked at her over his glasses with stern kindness. 'Come now, child, if you do not tell us, we will begin to think that you were a party to it after all, and a willing victim.'

Margery Montgomery stood in the centre of the Consistory chamber before the assembled Elders of the Session. She wore a plain blue gown, neat and clean, and the plaid which had covered her head had slipped back to reveal thick dark hair and the soft skin of her neck and shoulders. There was a new roundness about her cheeks and breasts which made more than one man in the room think guiltily that whoever the culprit was, he was a lucky fellow.

'I am sorry, sir,' she said with quiet dignity. 'I cannot tell you.'

Middleton sighed audibly. He had heard the line so many times before. First his wife had questioned the girl, then he himself, then both of them together, with always the same result. Isobel, too, had tried with no success. At least James was well out of the way of the whole unsavoury business. It had long been arranged that when term ended he was to visit Edinburgh and his sister Margrat. John Garden, too, was gone and the Urquhart boy had left for the country to try if goat's milk could cure the cough or halt the wasting disease, and the rest of the students had dispersed to their various homes up and down the coast. If the Montgomery girl did tell, they would have to send to find the culprit, or wait until he returned to the Burgh for the autumn term. It was mid-August now and hot.

'And why can you not obey your Minister and bring a sinner to justice?'

Margery looked at him calmly, without answering.

'Come now, girl! You know as well as I do the laws of the church. You, like everyone else, must obey them. Who is the man?'

'I am sorry to offend you, sir, but I cannot tell you. It would do no good.'

'I am the judge of that,' said the Minister sternly.

'Excuse me, sir, but you cannot judge correctly if you do not know the facts. I know them and I tell you they are best forgotten.'

'Impertinent young woman! Who are you to tell your betters what is to be forgotten?'

Margery lowered her eyes and made no answer. But something

237

in the set of her head and shoulders told the assembled company that they would not break this girl easily.

'You realize, Margery, that if you persist in this deliberate disobedience to all orders, even to your master, I shall have no alternative but to dismiss you?'

'Oh no, please!' It was a point that she had not considered. To lose the calm serenity of a life which gave her whole being such satisfaction, in exchange for an ill-ordered, ill-smelling, ignorant ale-house was an idea which appalled her, yet even as she began the plea she realized that her mistress was right.

'I am sorry, madam,' she said. 'You have been good to me and I have been happier than I deserve. I have always obeyed you willingly and would do so now if I were able. I shall be sorry to go.'

'And I to lose you. Please, Margery, can you not change your mind? Could you not tell me, in confidence, if I promise not to divulge your secret? At least then I could judge for myself whether you are misguided.'

'I am sorry, madam, but I cannot tell anyone, least of all you.'

Mrs Middleton misread the girl's loyalty as fear, and sighed with a mixture of sadness, irritation and defeat. She would never find a girl half the worth of Margery Montgomery, who had grown to be as useful as a daughter to her. What other kitchen-maid would read to Isobel when her eyes grew too weak to focus; what other girl could be trusted to check the daily household accounts to the last farthing and never make a mistake? What other girl could possibly do half the things that Margery did, or do them half as well? For five pounds a year, or for twice that amount.

But the Principal himself had formally ordered Margery to tell him the name of the man who had fathered her child and she had refused. Not defiantly, but with a quiet conviction of inner rectitude which baffled and defeated him. After such an open flouting of his authority, there was no other course left to him but dismissal. Besides, he was a member of the kirk Session. The Elders would not be satisfied with the girl's repeated refusals and would not allow him to be so.

So Margery took her minimal possessions and moved out of the Middletons' house to set up house again with her stepmother, Christian Grant. Jeannie Catto wept when she left.

'It's not fair, lassie,' she sobbed. 'Life's wicked and cruel when it gets a lass like you in its filthy clutches. If there's anything you need, Margery, you tell Jeannie and I'll get it for you, if I have to steal to do it.'

'No, Jeannie, you must not think such things! I'll manage. But come and see me if you can. I would like that. You have been kind to me and I'll not forget.'

'And I'll not forget you neither. And when the babe is born, I'll drink the wee thing's health with a glad heart and damn all slanderous, evil tongues to the devil!' She sobbed afresh.

Margery put her arms around her. 'Good-bye Jeannie, and thank you.'

The upper room in Widow Irvine's Close was bleak and cheerless after Jeannie's kitchen. But Margery did what she could to improve matters. She kept the hearth swept and the floor scrubbed clean, the slop-pails emptied and the bowls and platters scoured, but she missed the books which Isobel Middleton had let her read, and though she had brought away with her the small stock of writing materials, ink and paper and several unused quills which the Middletons had given her, she had no accounts worth keeping and no letters to write. So she helped Christian with the stockings which she knitted for merchant Sledder and spun yarn for cloth and tried not to think of the life she had left.

And yet again she was called before the Session.

'And you refuse absolutely to tell us?' said the Minister sadly.

'I am sorry, sir, but I cannot.' Margery was close to tears now. The strain had been long and wearing, and she had nothing to support her in what she did but her own conviction and her own determination not to be swayed.

'We could of course require her to take the solemn oath,' put in Cumming, 'as we did in Bartlat's case.' Margery's heart leapt in her breast with fear. If they made her take the solemn oath she would have to tell, or be damned to eternal fire.

The Minister looked at the blacksmith with distaste. 'And what would she swear?'

Cumming opened and closed his mouth helplessly for a moment before saying, 'She could swear it was *not* so and so. We could go through the names of everyone in the ale-house that night and . . .'

'Don't be ridiculous!' snapped the Minister. 'Even supposing it was someone who was at the ale-house, the process would last till the end of next year! It would turn the kirk into a comic theatre.'

'You know, of course, that a certain name is being mentioned in the town?' Baillie Baxter kept his eyes carefully on the table in front of him.

Margery swallowed, paled, and said in a low voice. 'If you wish me to do so, Minister, I will take my solemn oath that it was not ... Mr Adam Urquhart.'

The Minister looked at her sharply. 'Why him and not others?'

'Because he is dying and should not be wrongfully accused.'

'You know the remedy for all such wrongful accusations,' reminded the Minister. 'Expose the culprit and allow the innocent to shine.'

'I would gladly do so if I could,' she said meekly, 'but I cannot. Please forgive me.'

'Wait outside,' said the Minister, but kindly enough. He was old and tired and close to death, and had no wish to persecute her.

'The girl ought to be excommunicated,' said Cumming when the door of the Session room closed.

'That is a serious punishment,' said the Minister, 'and must be reserved for serious offences. Fornication is dealt with by a fine, public rebuke, and a sojourn on the stool of repentance.'

'But the Montgomery girl has defied the authority of the kirk,' put in Baillie Baxter. 'Is that not an offence of the gravest kind?'

'The girl has comported herself throughout the affair with meekness and humility,' said Middleton quickly. 'She is in no way a vicious or hard-hearted girl and has always obeyed the church most dutifully until now. I believe she was overpowered against her will and that, mistakenly, she withholds the name of her attacker from the best of motives. Suppose,' he added, looking round the assembled company, 'he was the son of someone present?'

'Then he ought to be corrected as severely as anyone else,' snapped Cumming. 'If it was a son of mine, I'd beat him cheerfully and then hand him over to the Minister for spiritual correction.'

The Minister sighed. He agreed with Middleton's assessment of the Montgomery girl. In truth, her bearing had impressed him greatly and, had the nature of the case not prevented it, he would have been tempted merely to fine her and let her go. As it was, she was with child and the whole town knew it.

'I think,' he said slowly, 'that the case has gone on long enough. *If* she knows the identity of the father, I am afraid it is fruitless to try to compel her to tell us. It is, after all, possible that she does not know, or not without some element of doubt. It was a black and misty night, as you recall. We will suggest for the benefit of the indwellers that the identity is doubtful – a stranger, if you like – and the girl must make public penance on the stool.'

'For how long?' demanded Cumming. 'Till the child is born?'

'For six weeks,' said the Minister. 'That will be enough.'

'He is growing soft in the head,' growled Cumming to his neighbour, but found no response. They all knew the Minister had not many weeks left to lead them. In fact, before Margery's six weeks were completed, he was to die. He himself had a premonition of this and he did not wish to leave his charge with the memory of an over-harsh judgement on an innocent girl.

'Now if you please, gentlemen,' he said wearily, 'we will move on to the next item. Alexander Crystal has put in his account for the workmanship and ironwork for the three new stiles in the kirk-yard. With the masons' work, it totals £35 6s 6d.'

'The stiles are well enough made,' said Middleton. 'Crystal is a good, if temperamental, workman.'

'I hear he's talking of going into the country again, seeking work.'

'Aye,' said Cumming. 'It's that new wife of his – a silly, hysterical woman by all accounts, and still childless. No wonder he wants to get away for a spell. But if he stays away too long, he'll find no work when he comes back. The trades won't stand for it.'

'Kindly keep the trades' affairs for their proper place,' said the Minister severely. 'We have more serious matters to consider. I have a formal request from Baillie Gordon for the loan of the Communion Cup for King's College Church.'

'I oppose it,' said Cumming quickly. 'Who is to say it would not be an *Episcopalian* who officiated?'

'I am inclined to agree,' said the Minister. 'Such an act would encourage the schism in the church and in the circumstances I think it wise to reserve the Communion Cup for the use of our own parish kirk. The kirk's authority must at all costs be preserved.'

And on the following Sunday the indwellers saw that authority in action.

241

Margery Montgomery knelt on the stool of repentance in the centre of the church the following Sabbath, in full view of the entire congregation. To Margery, the church seemed crammed to the painted ceiling with inquisitive, prurient eyes. She saw William Walker leering. The Sledder woman whispered behind her hand to her neighbour and the pair of them snorted with laughter. The Cumming boys were sniggering. But she would not lower her eyes. She straightened her back, raised her head and looked straight ahead of her, focusing her eyes on the distant shape of Bishop Scougal's monument and all that remained to her of her father's strength. His hands had cut that stone, she reminded herself as the Minister's words boomed out, '. . . This miserable sinner . . . answerable to the Lord Jehovah on the great and terrible day . . . the searcher of hearts who sees all hidden wickedness . . .' Her father had defied them and remained un-cowed. He would have supported her if he had been here. He would have held her hand in his, as he had done so many years ago when they stood together against the world in the days before Christian came.

Christian . . . Margery's heart ached at the memory of her words.

'You obstinate little fool! Losing the best job you're ever likely to get! If you couldn't think of yourself, you might at least have thought of me. What do you suppose will happen to my ale-house with you about the place as a constant reminder of disgrace?'

'I will stay upstairs,' said Margery quietly. 'I am sorry if I have upset you, but I cannot do otherwise.'

'Please yourself – only don't say I didn't warn you.'

In truth Christian's irritation sprang more from concern for Margery, whom she loved, than from any for herself. The ale-house would not suffer. But Christian suspected that Margery might.

Now as she stood at the back of the kirk and saw the girl's white-faced dignity of bearing, unwavering from first to last, her heart ached with pity and admiration.

'You were splendid, lass,' she told her afterwards. 'I was proud of you. My own Ma couldn't have done better.' Though Isobel Grant, her daughter admitted, would not have brought the same ladylike dignity to the ordeal as Margery had.

'Please take me home,' said Margery. 'I am so weary.'

She wept that first night and on many that followed. For herself and her loneliness and for her pitiful unborn child. But she wept silently and Christian did not hear.

At the beginning of November the students returned: several of the old faces and many new. John Garden and James Middleton remained in Edinburgh, one in an advocate's office, the other as Regent in the university; but Adam Urquhart came back to his father's house, though not to the university. Margery heard of his return through Christian, who complained bitterly that some folk didn't know what friendship meant.

'He can go to the devil for all I care,' she said, slapping the ladle so hard into the cooking-pot that the porridge splashed out on to the hearth, where it sputtered in black, pungent fumes before charring to ash. 'But I mind for your sake, Margery. He's no business to walk out on you because of something that's not your fault. The least he could do is come and ask how you are.'

Margery could find no answer.

'He's looking ill, too,' went on Christian, slamming the lid on the pot and resuming her knitting. 'It'll be a miracle if he lasts the winter.'

That evening, while Christian was downstairs in the ale-house, Margery sat a long time in the candlelight, a quill in her hand and a blank sheet of paper on her knee. But the words would not come and in the end she wrote nothing.

It was the beginning of January before she saw him. Margery was walking along the High Street on her way back from the Sledder house where she had been collecting yarn for the next batch of stockings, when she came face to face with him at the corner of Baillie Knight's Wynd. He looked haggard, his eyes deep sunken and his skin opaque. In contrast Margery looked the personification of health.

'Life meets death,' said Adam quietly and made to move aside.

'No, please don't go.' She laid a hand on his arm. 'I am glad I met you, Adam. Are we not even to part friends?'

'It is not your fault, Margery, but I loved you once.'

The tears sprang to her eyes. 'And I you ...'

The tense lines of his face relaxed. 'Margery, I am sorry. My pride has hurt us both for too long. Forgive me. I have not many days left and you are right. We must part as friends.' He took her hand and held it in both his.

Margery tried to smile through the tears. 'Thank you, Adam. Good-bye and may God bless you.'

'Good-bye, Margery. And pray for me.' He stood aside to let her pass. She walked on down the High Street, stumbling because of the tears which flowed freely now and which she made no attempt to check. Five days later Adam Urquhart died.

That same night, when the ale-house customers had left and Christian at last came upstairs, she found Margery crouched on the stool at the fire, her face white and her eyes huge.

'Christian,' she said quietly. 'My time has come.' At six the following morning, Margery's son was born.

'He's a fine lad, bless him,' crooned Christian, rocking the infant at the fire as she had rocked Margery so many years ago. 'What name shall we give the wee darling? If he's to be allowed anything so fine as a name.'

'William,' said Margery drowsily. She was already drifting into the deep languor of fulfilment. 'William Montgomery. Father would like that. It is a pity he will never know.'

'The devil take the fool who tells him,' muttered Christian as she cradled the infant close.

Two months later, on a morning at the beginning of March, Margery sat at the fireside contentedly suckling her child, while Christian handed meal into the pot for their morning kale. The room was cold, for the fire was not burning well. It was a damp, dark morning, windless and thick with the haar from the sea. Neither of them heard the step on the forestair, and when the door opened on a rush of chill air, both women started.

A man stood in the doorway, his frame so big he blotted out what light there was in that early March morning.

'You!' gasped Christian, starting to her feet and clutching the ladle like some futile weapon of defence. 'You've no business here! Get out! You're banished the town!'

The man stepped inside and shut the door behind him. He deposited his small bundle of tools in a corner and stood, strangely meek, his great hands endlessly twisting and folding.

'I've come to see the babe,' he said.

Margery stood up then and walked towards him, her baby cradled against her breast.

'See, Father,' she said gently. 'He is a strong child. I have named him William as you wanted me to do, and he was baptized in the kirk.'

The stonemason stood silent, looking down at the baby in his daughter's arms. There were tears in his eyes, but his scarred, half-blinded face was radiant.

'My son,' he whispered. 'Give him to me, Margery.'

Christian started forward in alarm, but Margery motioned her back. 'Here, Father. Hold him carefully.' She placed the baby in his arms and he stood, foolishly weeping and crooning and rocking the infant to and fro while he murmured, 'My little son, my dear little son.' Over and over again.

But at last Margery persuaded him to hand back the child and to take a seat at the fireside and a mug of ale.

'How did you hear about the baby?' she asked.

'Alexander Crystal told me. He told me the father was not known, but the child was a boy and strong. I told him the child needed no father but me and I came home.'

Christian and Margery exchanged glances.

'That was good of you, Father,' said Margery carefully. 'But you must not come here again. Tell me where you are living and I will bring William to see you.'

He did not seem to hear her.

'I will teach him the mason's trade,' he said. 'As soon as he can walk he shall come with me and learn the feel of the stone and how it talks to a man through his hands. He shall hold the hammer and feel the weight of his tools. I will teach him to build a monument like no one has seen before, to stand for generations to come. I will teach him . . .'

'You'll go back where you came from,' interrupted Christian, 'before they catch you and brand you and send you packing. You're banished, remember?'

Montgomery looked at Margery questioningly as if to ask, 'Who is she?'

'Drink your ale, Father,' she said gently. 'Then you must go. I will come to you if you tell me where you live. Is it in the New Town?'

But Montgomery was not listening. His eyes were on the baby, where it lay sleeping in the wooden cradle Jeannie Catto had ordered secretly from Alexander Crystal and presented to a delighted Margery the day the baby was born.

'My son,' he said in a voice of wonder. 'My own son.' He stood beside the cradle, rocking it gently with one huge hand.

'He's not your son,' said Christian. 'He's Margery's, and the sooner you get out and leave us in peace the better for everyone. Now drink your ale and go, before someone finds you.'

'But I cannot go,' said Montgomery, smiling. 'There is something I must do first. I cannot leave my son in this place until it has been done. That was why I came.'

'You came to see William,' reminded Margery.

'Yes. And to guard him against evil. She must not harm him as she harmed the others.'

'No one will harm him,' began Margery, but at that moment there was a low knock at the door and, before anyone could move, it opened and the Sledder woman came in.

'I've come for the draught you promised me, Christian,' she began. Then she saw Montgomery and her face went ashen. She took a step backward and clutched at the doorpost, but before she could run, Montgomery had seized her by the arm and pulled her inside the room.

'You have come to harm my son,' he said in a strangely matter-of-fact voice. 'I knew you would. You are a witch and cannot help it. But you must not touch him. I will not let you.' He held the terrified woman in his left hand and now his right emerged from a fold of his shirt and the three women saw the flash of firelight on steel.

At the sight of the knife, Christian pushed past them for the door, flung it open and screamed at the top of her voice for help. Inside the room, the Sledder woman was screaming, too. Mesmerized and powerless to intervene, Margery crouched protectively over the cradle while her father drew the knife blade twice across the woman's forehead, slashing the sign of the cross. Then he loosed his hold, wiped the blade on his breeches and replaced the knife in his belt. He turned to Margery and smiled.

'The witch is scored,' he said. 'The power of Satan is broken. Now my son will be safe.'

Isobel Sledder stumbled blindly out of the room, her face streaming blood. She was hysterical with pain and terror, and the hastily assembled citizens had more difficulty with her than with Montgomery himself.

For the stonemason put up no resistance. He walked willingly to the tolbooth, smiling at everyone and repeating over and over, 'I have done what I came to do. The witch is scored and my son will not be harmed.'

'He's mad,' gasped Christian. 'He is possessed!'

Margery was silent. She knew Christian was right, yet there had been a simple nobility about him even in his madness. He had come to do a service for her son and he had done it. That he would be banished afresh was inevitable, and next time the punishment for re-appearance would be certain branding and scourging by the common hangman. On March 5, 1705, the formal order was made.

When Montgomery was brought out of the tolbooth he was still smiling.

'The witch is scored,' he said to the crowd. 'She will do no more harm. You can sleep safely in your beds.'

He walked on between the silent ranks, nodding and smiling to either side. The scar on his face had faded to the colour of a leather thong and his blind eye was milk-white in the weather-scored face. He walked with the same sideways motion they remembered from the old days, but now it held no threat. He was harmless and happy as a child.

The assembled indwellers watched with closed and wary faces as he passed down the High Street to the College and the Powis Bridge, and onwards again to the south. No one spoke. No one called after him. But when he had passed, a ripple flowed over them and the life of the town resumed on a murmur of relief.

'May he rot in hell,' thought Christian. 'But he'll not live long. The day I hear of his death I'll drink myself stupid with joy. I'm still young and I need to be free . . . Then if ever George comes back . . .' She indulged in her most secret dream. If George Cumming came back, and there had been rumours that he might, she vowed she would not let him escape. No scheming bitch was going to take him from her this time. As the huge bulk of her husband vanished beyond the Powis Bridge, Christian turned her back on the High Street and made for home. As she reached Widow Irvine's Close she was singing.

With her infant son in her arms, Margery walked to the top of the Spital to see her father go. At the boundary he turned.

'Good-bye, lass. Take care of William Montgomery. I have left him the tools of my trade. See that he grows to be a fine mason.'

'I will, Father. I promise.' She knew she would not see him again.

There were tears in her eyes as she watched him out of sight. Then she turned and limped slowly back down the Spital and into the town.

'It is you and me together now, William,' she whispered to the sleeping infant in her arms. 'We have no one else. Unless George comes back.'

At the thought of George she felt the familiar warmth. After all, he had not been reported dead. And until he was, there was always hope. Besides, had he not promised her he would return?

But if George did come back, what would he think of her baby? For the first time she felt doubt. As far as she was concerned, her baby had no father and never had had. He was hers alone, a blessed, beloved accident, already paid for by weeks of public penance, accepted by baptism and now no more than an innocent, fatherless and infinitely precious babe.

Yet Adam had not thought of it like that.

The memory of Adam, as always, brought her pain. Suppose George were to take the same attitude? Determinedly, Margery pushed the fear aside. If George came back, he would forgive her. If George came back, she would make him understand.

The trees at the College were silver lace against a silver sky. At the burn the women were already treading their linen, resuming the work they had left to see the stonemason go. One of them, far away, was singing. One of the little Crystal boys ran past her, laughing, while two more pursued him with shrieks of glee. Through the door of the change-house she could see Baillie Baxter with the Treasurer and other members of the Council who had already returned to their business discussions and the endless consumption of ale.

From the direction of the school came the chant of boys' voices, high as twittering bats and, clearer than them all, the blackbird's song.

As Margery turned the corner into Widow Irvine's Close and saw the familiar mud-trampled square, the draw-well with its little parapet, the turf-roofed buildings with their middens at the door and the sweet smell of peat smoke in the air, her heart swelled till she thought it would burst her breast.

'William,' she murmured, kissing his soft neck and nuzzling the silken hair. 'My own sweet darling love.'

She had lost her father and her lover, but she had her baby son. And one day, perhaps, her man would come home.

William Montgomery died a month later, drowned in the harbour at the New Town. It was three months before his body was washed ashore below Stonehaven, and when it was, it was unidentifiable but for the leather mason's apron which still clung to the scraps of flesh around the pelvis, and the unusual size of his frame.

George Cumming, passing on his way northward, did not recognize the body of the stonemason whom he had once helped in the tower of the Cathedral on the night of the great storm, when they had rescued the bells together. Michael Burgerhuyes' bell and the smaller one of George Kilgour. But George Cumming had walked a long way and his mind was on other things.

Christian saw him first, through the door of the ale-house where she and Margery were clearing up after the day's trade. It was past the curfew hour but on that northern summer evening it was still light.

'George!' she shrieked in incredulous joy. She looped up her skirts and ran to him across the Close. From the doorway Margery saw her throw her arms around his neck and kiss him on the lips. Then, laughing, she drew him towards the house.

'See, Margery! George has come back. Would you have believed it?'

Margery could not speak. She stood looking into George's face and her own was transfigured.

'Well, come on in, George. Don't stand there staring so. It's only Margery. Surely you remember Margery, Montgomery's child? Oh, I know she's grown, she's a woman now and a mother. Some bastard took her in his cups and she won't tell who, but he's a fine bairn nonetheless and healthy, and the only man we have between us. Or had!' She laughed jubilantly. 'Oh George, but it's good to have you back!' She pulled his face down and kissed him again, but George's eyes were on Margery and the child asleep in the fold of her plaid. The baby stirred.

'There now, we've wakened him,' declared Christian. 'Why don't you take him upstairs to feed him, Margery? You'll be quieter there, and George and I have things to talk about.'

Her arm was still round his waist and now she rubbed her cheek against his shoulder, murmuring, 'Remember the Chaplains' Brae and the long summer nights, George?' She laughed, a low laugh of remembered pleasure. 'Well, go on, Margery! What are you waiting for?'

'No,' said George, quickly. 'Please stay. There is no need to leave your hearth on my account. I have travelled a long way and I am weary. Let me sit quietly at your fire, Christian, while you tell me everything that has happened since I have been away.'

Christian shrugged, but her happiness was too strong to be checked for long. She hummed bubbling scraps of song as she drew him fresh ale and stirred the flagging fire into flame. George sat at the hearth with Christian beside him, and drank her ale while she told him the news of the Old Town and on the far side of the hearth Margery suckled her child. The firelight danced over the pale dome of her breast, and when she lifted her face and found George's eyes upon her, her cheeks were pink.

'But enough of the Old Town,' said Christian impatiently. 'It's your adventures I want to hear.'

'Adventures?' George sighed. 'I would not know where to begin. I have been a long time coming home and sometimes I feared I would never get here. Or only after everyone I loved was dead.'

Christian looked startled. This was a new George, quieter and strangely mature, not the light-hearted youth who had slammed out of the Burgh on a wave of rage after that fight with his father. Nor yet the confident lover with the wary heart. Christian studied his face with an interest in which there was puzzlement and a touch of dismay.

'What is the matter, Christian? Have I changed so much?'

'No . . .' she said hesitantly, 'at least, you look thin and weary and . . .' She almost added 'defeated' but instead said, '. . . old'. 'Older, I meant,' she hurried on. 'As we all are. But I haven't changed, have I, George?' There was pleading in her voice and George smiled as he gave her the reassurance she required.

'No, Christian. You are just as I remembered you, strong and healthy and cheerful, and as indomitable as your mother was. But I have travelled far and seen many things. Did you really think I would come back as green and irresponsible and as callous-hearted as I was when I left? I have seen too many men die, in agony and in the loneliness of exile. I have suffered illness and captivity and met death face to face a dozen times.'

'Tell us!' demanded Christian eagerly. 'I want to hear it *all*. What happened in Darien after the settlers left?'

'I was ill for a long time. Then I took a ship to Jamaica. Another northwards to New York. Then to Spain. There were pirates and once we were driven on to the rocks off Finisterre. Then it was Holland. But at last I found a ship to London and I came home.'

'On foot?' asked Margery incredulously. They were the first words she had spoken. Her voice had grown deeper with motherhood and there was a maturity about her which was new to George. He remembered her as self-sufficient always, but at the same time innocent and trusting as a child. Now she had a serene strength which he guessed the world could not shake. Both women were strong in their different ways, and both loved him, but as he looked from one to the other he knew which one he needed and which one he loved.

'Well, did you walk all that way?' prompted Christian impatiently.

'Aye, but it was nothing after the journeys of the past five years. Believe me, Christian, I have seen all of the world I want to see. Now I want only my own woman at my own fireside.'

'Oh George, do you really mean it?' Christian sprang to refill his mug and then stood behind him, her arms twined about his neck and her cheek resting against his hair. 'Montgomery came back, did I tell you? But he was banished again and this time I know the bastard's dead. There's been no word of him for months, but I'll find out somehow, and then I will be free.'

George looked across the hearth to where Margery sat, bare-breasted in the firelight, her little son in her arms. He did not speak. After a moment Christian moved round to sit on the floor at his feet. She laid her head contentedly in his lap. 'Oh George, I'm so happy . . .'

It was beautiful in the birch woods. The leaves were emerald against the clear sky and in the grass the bracken fronds uncurled, soft and cool and rich with sap. The blackbirds and thrushes and finches were all singing, and even the crows' busy call seemed melodious. The river ran full and clear over sparkling stones and where it met the sea, gulls drifted lazily over lapping sands.

George looked at the baby in Margery's looped plaid. She had tied the woollen material over her shoulder and round her waist to form a sling and George was reminded of Hugh Baird's Indian woman with his papoose on her back. Hugh was a good man. He had been right to stay in Darien with his Indian friends. George looked at the baby again. Margery had not told him of the father and he had not asked. It was of no importance. The child was Margery's alone.

'He's a fine bairn,' he said now. 'But he needs a father. And his mother needs a man.'

'I know.' She untied the plaid and laid her son on the grass. Then she turned and held out her arms, and he knew why in all those fevered visions he had heard no words. There was no place for words when what he needed to know was there already, in her eyes.

'Christian will not like it,' said George quietly as he watched Margery gather up the child from the grass. The heat had gone from the sun now and she wrapped the child tight.

Margery stood up with the baby cradled in her arms. 'I know. And I am sorry to hurt her. But I must tell her all the same, now, before she hears it from someone else.'

'I will come with you.' George put an arm around her waist as they moved out of the trees towards the town. 'We will tell her together and then perhaps she will understand and forgive us.' Margery laid her head gratefully against his shoulder, but at the Cluny's Port she drew away.

'No, George. It will only make it worse if you come. I must tell her myself. Take William and wait for me at the forge.'

'But Margery, you can't go alone. It's not safe. Christian can be wild and violent. She might . . .'

'Please, George?' Margery thrust the bundled infant into his arms. 'You can give him his first lesson as a hammerman, and I would rather face Christian alone. Don't worry. I am not afraid.' Then she was gone.

George stood with the unfamiliar bundle held awkwardly in his arms and watched her limping figure hurry round the corner of the new tolbooth, past the market cross and on down the High Street towards Widow Irvine's Close.

'Margery!' he called after her. 'Take care!' But she did not turn her head and after a moment George moved reluctantly towards the forge.

Christian was singing when Margery reached the house, but she stopped abruptly when she saw the girl standing on the threshold. There was something in Margery's face which told her even before the words were spoken.

'George and I are to be married. I hope you will give us your blessing.'

For a moment she thought Christian would faint. She was death-white and swayed as if she would fall. Margery moved towards her in quick concern.

'I am sorry, Christian. I know it is a shock for you, but . . .'

'Bitch!' gasped Christian. 'Scheming, dung-faced bitch! And after all I've done for you. I've loved you, brought you up as my own bairn, and you repay me by stealing my man! I should have strangled you at birth!'

'I am sorry, but . . .'

'Sorry? Don't make me laugh! You've had your eye on him for years!' She was recovering her strength already and her voice rose in screaming fury. 'Two-faced little harlot! You've had him in the woods, haven't you? I can see it in your poxy face. You've trapped him like you trapped that other poor devil, only that one got away. Rape indeed! If anyone was raped, it was him! But if you think you'll keep George that way you're mistaken. He's had every girl in the town, did you know? He's had me, too, and he'd take me again if I let him! And I'd give him twice the pleasure you ever could, you stink-arsed cripple! How much did you pay him to bed you?'

Margery's face was colourless now and her whole body trembled with the effort of control. 'George loves me . . .'

'Loves you?' Christian laughed derisively. 'Even your own father couldn't love you, you spineless, whey-faced freak!'

Margery felt the anger swell inside her till she thought her breast would burst, but still she spoke quietly enough.

'Father loved me more than he ever loved you. But then I gave him love, which is more than you ever did.'

'Love that great gowk?' Christian threw back her head in a harsh roar of scorn.

'You married him. You owed him love. And if not love, at least you owed him kindness and loyalty. But you gave him nothing. You never give anything unless it suits you. You're a selfish, hard-hearted, degenerate woman and you deliberately wrecked my father's life.'

'It was your fault,' retorted Christian. 'I only married him because you wanted it, and now I see why. You wanted me out of the way so you could catch George.'

'You married my father because you were pregnant and because you were frightened of the Session. You used him, as you use everyone, to suit your own ends. You only slept with him in the first place to spite George, because George wouldn't have you. It was a wicked, selfish thing to do. My father was a simple man and would have loved you. Instead you made his life a living hell.'

'Your father was a fool. And you're a bigger one if you think I'll let you have my George.'

'*Your* George? He's not a chattel to be possessed! He's a man with a heart and a mind and a will of his own. And he's asked me to be his wife!'

Christian stood squarely in the centre of the room, hands on hips and head high in the old battle stance which Margery remembered from long ago. Her whole body seemed to swell and grow till it filled the room with power.

'If you so much as look at him again I'll break your neck, you ungrateful little whore. Now get out before I take you in my own two hands and throw you in the midden where you belong.'

Margery could take no more. The rage which had been building up inside her burst into flaming fury.

'Try it! If you dare! I owe you nothing. You took me because it suited you and you kept me because I was useful to you. I've paid my debt to you a hundred times, and if there's a whore in this house, it's you! Lay one finger on me and I'll tear your evil face to shreds!'

With a howl of fury Christian whipped a knife from the table and lunged at the girl, but Margery stood her ground and when the knife blade flashed and her blood sprayed the flagstones, she flung herself at Christian with the clawing passion of a wild thing fighting for survival. She had no awareness of what she did, but let the primitive, blood-red frenzy guide her nails and teeth and feet. She tangled one hand in Christian's hair, tugging a thick swath of it over her eyes so the elder woman was half-blind. The other hand struggled with Christian's wrist, nails digging deep into the flesh while the blood-streaked metal trembled closer and closer and her bare feet kicked and her knees rammed into any part of Christian she could reach. But it was the first time she had fought anyone and Christian was an adept. Besides, Christian was the

254

heavier and by far the stronger. In another moment she would have wrenched herself out of Margery's grip and plunged the knife again, had not the girl as suddenly realized her danger, loosed her hold and bounded backwards out of reach, only to fetch up hard against the ale table.

For a second she stood panting and at bay, mouth open, eyes wild, and her escape blocked by the table behind her. But the table was heaped with the usual clutter of dirty mugs, and as Christian came lunging after her she snatched up the nearest tankard and hurled it full in Christian's face. The mug struck Christian on the side of the head. Ale drenched her hair and face and splashed on the flagstones. Christian hardly felt the blow and the shock of it only incensed her the more. With a roar she leapt for Margery, but the girl had had time to see her escape.

As Christian's feet slipped in the mud of the puddled ale, Margery thrust the table aside and scrambled for the hearth and the fire-irons. Before she could reach them she felt Christian clawing at her clothes to drag her back. She heard the rip of cloth and the triumphant oath, and snatched up the only weapon within her reach – the fireside stool which had been hers for as long as she could remember – and when Christian came at her with knife raised, Margery whipped round and rammed the three legs forward with all her strength.

There was a choked scream, the knife clattered on the hearth-stone and Christian fell in a writhing heap to the dirt-crusted floor. She retched and rolled and clutched her stomach in gasping agony, while Margery stood motionless above her, the stool still clasped like a shield across her breast.

Slowly Margery put down the stool, arranging it carefully in its accustomed place. Slowly she retrieved the knife, wiped it clean and laid it on the pot-shelf. Then she began to disentangle the long strands of Christian's hair from her fingers. Her hands were shaking and there was blood on her cheek and forearm, but she stood exultantly erect.

'I'll get you, Margery Montgomery,' gasped Christian. 'I'll make you wish you'd never been born.'

Margery made no reply. Instead she lifted trembling arms and pushed her dishevelled hair into some sort of order. Her eyes were bright and hard with victory.

'I'll make you pay one day. You see if I don't.' Christian clutched at a bench and tried to pull herself to her feet, but fell back defeated. She was still winded and gasping and her lips were flecked with blood. 'I'll rot that other leg for you,' she managed, 'till you go on all fours like the bitch you are.'

Margery stood impervious and unafraid. As she moved towards the threshold, Christian's voice strengthened to a futile scream. 'I'll damn your marriage bed. I'll blight your hearth. I'll curse your child and wither the seed in your womb! I'll make your life one burning hell!'

Margery was at the door now. She paused to collect the torn shreds of her skirt and tie them firmly at her waist, then stepped out into the Close. Christian's curses clawed after her all the way to the High Street, but she walked steadily on, unheeding. Her face was streaked with dirt and blood, her clothes torn and her limp more pronounced, but there was something about her bearing which made people turn their heads as she passed.

At the market cross there were children playing, and the sun struck gold from the tolbooth weathervane. In Baillie Knight's kale-yard a blackbird sang. She turned left into Cumming's Wynd, and the scent of thyme and honeysuckle wafted thick over Cluny's dyke. The blood was already caking the slash on her arm and netting the clawed furrows on her cheek and breast, but her eyes still held their triumph, and when she saw the fire-glow and the flashing starlight of the forge, she looped her skirts higher and ran...